W9-BZW-145

Effigies

Also by Mary Anna Evans
Artifacts
Relics

Effigies

Mary Anna Evans

Poisoned Pen Press

Copyright © 2006 by Mary Anna Evans

First Edition 2006

10 9 8 7 6 5 4 3 2 1

Library of Congress Catalog Card Number: 2006929246

ISBN 10: 1-59058-342-6/ISBN 13: 978-1-59058-342-5 Hardcover

Poisoned Pen Press
6962 E. First Ave., Ste. 103
Scottsdale, AZ 85251
www.poisonedpenpress.com
info@poisonedpenpress.com

Printed in the United States of America

For the Americans who were here first...

Acknowledgments

I'd like to thank everyone who reviewed *Effigies* in manuscript form: Michael Garmon, Erin Hinnant, Rachel Garmon, David Evans, Deborah Boykin, Rae Vaughn, Lillian Sellers, Robert Connolly, David Reiser, Suzanne Quin, Carl Quin, Leonard Beeghley, Mary Anna Hovey, Kelly Bergdoll, Bruce Bergdoll, Diane Howard, and Jerry Steinberg.

I'd also like to thank these folks for their expertise in an impressive variety of subjects, including archaeology, Choctaw folklore and history, Neshoba County geology, library research, and the mounds and cave of Nanih Waiya: Elizabeth Slater, Robert Connolly, Sam Brookes, Kenneth Carleton, James House, Tom Mould, the faculty and staff of Brentwood School, Maurice Calistro, Greg Cheatham, and Cheryl Breckenridge.

And, as always, my agent Anne Hawkins, and the hard-working crew at Poisoned Pen Press: Barbara Peters, Rob Rosenwald, Marilyn Pizzo, Jessica Tribble, Monty Montee, Nan Beams, and Geetha Perera.

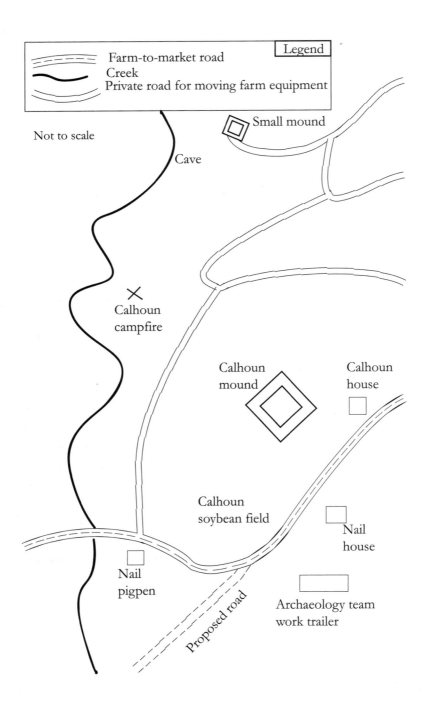

Legend

Farm-to-market road
Creek
Private road for moving farm equipment

Not to scale

Small mound

Cave

Calhoun campfire

Calhoun mound

Calhoun house

Calhoun soybean field

Nail house

Nail pigpen

Proposed road

Archaeology team work trailer

Prologue

Nanih Waiya, the great mother mound of the Choctaw people, has guarded the source of the Pearl River for millennia. The Muskogee people were birthed from her earthen body first, but they left her. The Cherokee and the Chickasaw are her children, too. They lagged behind for a time, drying themselves on their mother's flanks, but the day of leaving came for them. Neither the Cherokee nor the Chickasaw ever caught up with the Muskogee, who were so careless with fire that they obliterated their own trail. Brothers and sisters were parted, and they never met again.

The Choctaw, like most lastborn children, are bound tightly at the heart to their mother. They live in the shadow of Nanih Waiya still. Invaders have tried to rip them away. Disease has stalked them. The mighty Army of the United States of America has hauled them bodily to places they did not want to go. But the trees grow thick around Nanih Waiya, and a remnant of the Choctaw has always found a place to hide there.

How have they outwitted forces so implacable and strong?

They have survived by remembering something that their enemies have forgotten: It is no weakness to love your mother.

Chapter One

Thursday
The eve of the Neshoba County Fair,
Mississippi's Giant House Party

Faye Longchamp had work to do, but it could wait. A tremendous backlog of unfinished tasks seemed to be her lot in life. Taking a weekday afternoon to immerse herself in history and religion simultaneously seemed like an efficient way to use her time. Granted, it was someone else's religion, but Faye had never been too finicky about that kind of thing.

Joe, on the other hand, had a direct connection to the silent mound of dirt beneath their feet. His Creek ancestors believed that their history began here at Nanih Waiya, the Mother Mound. Or maybe in a cave under a natural hill somewhere across the creek. The issue was murky, as spiritual issues tend to be.

Faye considered Nanih Waiya, constructed at about the time Christ walked the earth, to be a most impressive perch. She and Joe sat atop it, forty feet above the natural ground level, surveying Nanih Waiya Creek and a lush forest and a very ordinary pasture full of cattle grazing just outside the fence surrounding the great mound. She had noticed a sour, familiar smell as she climbed the stairs sunk into the old mound, but couldn't quite put her finger on its source. The creek's banks were brimming, so she thought perhaps she was sniffing the musty, peaty smell of a swamp at high water. Either that, or somebody needed to empty the garbage bins at the state park across the road.

Only when her head cleared the top of the mound and she could see the grassy open area beyond did she put a name to the odor. Cow manure.

Did it bother Joe to see this sacred place shorn of its trees and planted in pasture grass? He didn't look perturbed. Faye thought about cows for awhile. They fed their calves out of their own bodies, then fed the land with their manure. Eventually, they fed the land with themselves. Maybe the Mother Mound liked having cows around.

Not being nearly as spiritual as Joe, she figured her revelation about the holiness of cows was the deepest thought she was likely to have that afternoon.

"Let's go, Joe. If we hustle, we can get a look at our work site this afternoon. Dr. Mailer said he'd be there to meet everybody as they rolled into town."

Joe Wolf Mantooth raked a farewell glance over a landscape that had been held holy for centuries. Millennia, in fact. He could see a far distance from up here on top of Nanih Waiya, and he was glad to get the chance to visit the Mother Mound. The afternoon light was already a little softer than it had been at noon, and he knew the quiet summer air would be even quieter soon, as sunset approached.

Perhaps Joe's senses were sharper than most men's. Or perhaps Nature revealed herself more fully to him simply because he paid attention.

As he followed Faye down the mound's flank, he gave one last look at the grassy field and the fecund swamp and the broad sky and, behind him, the towering mound. Was this spot more sacred than the glass-clear Gulf waters around the island home he shared with Faye? More God-touched than the cool, green Appalachians, or the familiar expanses of his native Oklahoma? All those places seemed holy to him. He saw no difference.

It never occurred to Joe that perhaps the holiness lay in a man's appreciation of Nature's gifts. Perhaps those places were more sacred simply because he'd been there.

The route from Nanih Waiya to their worksite had led Faye and Joe through a landscape of farmland and pastures and piney woods, without the necessity of passing through Philadelphia, the only town of any size in Neshoba County, Mississippi. Or in most of the surrounding counties, for that matter. Not being a fan of city living, Faye didn't mind.

She liked the warm and fertile look of the place. She would have preferred to be at home in Florida, but she wanted an education and she needed to earn a living. Joyeuse Island, with its booming population of precisely two, didn't offer much in the way of opportunity on either count, so she was happy enough for the opportunity to spend her summer here while earning graduate credit and money, too.

The map in Joe's hands took them directly to a neat brick farmhouse that looked exactly as Faye's boss had described it. A cluster of people milling around in the field out back looked a great deal like archaeologists. Their worn clothing had the requisite ground-in dirt in all the right places, and their faces were tan beneath hats that provided some solar protection, but not enough. It seemed that Faye had found her co-workers.

As she and Joe approached, she caught snatches of a conversation that sounded a lot more animated and cordial than it looked. An outsider would have interpreted the scientists' lack of eye contact as unfriendliness, but Faye knew better. These people, out of long habit, rarely lifted their glance from the ground—not when they were standing in a known occupation site, where the soil was peppered with fascinating stuff. The young archaeologist who had found the site thought it might date to the Middle Woodland period, which could make it as old as Nanih Waiya herself.

Faye recognized a few faces from school. Dr. Sid Mailer, the principal investigator and her former lithics professor, stood, as he always did, in the center of a knot of his graduate students. Not for the first time, she missed her mentor, Dr. Magda Stockard, who might have directed this project if she hadn't been recovering from the difficult delivery of her first child. Faye liked Dr. Mailer, but she wished she could work for Magda again.

A tall, sunburnt man in his late forties, Dr. Mailer's prematurely white hair made him stand out in any crowd. Bodie Steele, a freckle-faced country boy who might someday take Dr. Mailer's place as a leading expert on Middle Woodland lithics, hung back until Faye flashed him a quick smile. He responded with a nod and a small smile of his own. Toneisha MacGill, who was as good at ceramics as Bodie was at lithics, belted out a "Hey, Faye!" that could be heard across three counties.

A man Faye didn't know stood at Dr. Mailer's elbow. Another stranger crouched near the professor's foot, poking at something embedded in the soil. Dr. Mailer stepped over him, extending a hand to squeeze Faye's elbow.

"Welcome, Faye. You, too, Joe." He reached around her to grasp Joe's hand warmly. "Oke and Chuck, meet our last two team members."

The crouching archaeologist rose to his full height, which wasn't all that much. Barrel-chested and stocky, he was a few inches taller than Faye, but she herself hardly cleared five feet. A smile lit his dark rugged face. "I understand Faye and I have a lot in common. We were both lucky enough to grow up surrounded by our ancestors' junk. Welcome to my playground."

So this was Dr. Oka Hofobi Nail, who grew up pulling stone tools and potsherds out of his family's vegetable garden. His first act as a Ph.D. had been to secure funding to excavate in his own back yard.

A sad truth of archaeology was that sites were not excavated merely because they were interesting, or because they held the potential to explain something important about humanity's past. Archaeology is labor-intensive. Earth doesn't turn itself over. Artifacts don't leap out of the ground unassisted, then clean and catalog themselves. Those artifacts don't explain themselves, and they don't document that explanation in a publishable report, either.

Dr. Nail had found a fascinating site, no question, but he would still be working it himself if the state of Mississippi hadn't wanted to do some road construction. In the course of straightening a bad curve, those road crews would wipe out this occupation site. Faye and her colleagues had been contracted to document it before it was destroyed, which she found depressing when she allowed herself to think about it too much. So she tried not to.

When she set those mixed feelings aside, Faye actually had very high hopes for this project. Oka Hofobi had been politically and financially savvy enough to team with Dr. Mailer, whose reputation was sufficient to secure the client's trust and whose horde of graduate students was sufficient to get the work done cheaply.

Even better, the makeup of this project team represented a real chance to begin healing the long-standing rift between Native Americans and the archaeological profession. Oka Hofobi, a Choctaw, would have the insight to keep them from stubbing their toe when dealing with the Mississippi Band of the Choctaw Indians, who were a powerful force in this neck of the woods.

Joe, who was mostly Creek, should add to their credibility in the Choctaws' eyes. Toneisha, an African-American from Memphis, and Faye, whose ancestry was best described as "all-of-the-above," would do their part to dispel the white-bread atmosphere that typically clings to archaeological crews. Given what she knew about the relaxed personalities of her co-workers, there was even some danger that this job might be fun.

Faye had chosen to spend several years of her life virtually alone on the island passed down to her by her family. Naturally introspective, she had thrived on the work of restoring her ancestral home, so much so that she hadn't minded her isolation much, but she'd been lonely until Joe came to live with her. Going back to school to earn the education she craved had thrown her into contact with a whole world of youthful, vital, energetic people. She loved her work, and she enjoyed her colleagues, even though she was invariably the quietest member of any team.

"I don't think either of you have met Chuck Horowitz." Dr. Mailer gestured to the blond man beside him, whose craggy features matched his angular body. "I expect he'll be working very closely with you, Joe, since I hear you're the best flintknapper around. Chuck's a crackerjack lithics analyst. He can take a pile of flint flakes and reassemble them into the rock somebody used two thousand years ago to make a projectile point. Well, minus the projectile point. But if we dig that point up, Chuck could match it to the flakes of the original rock and rebuild it, no problem."

Chuck looked at Joe without speaking, then turned his attention to Faye. His gaze started somewhere near her nose, then wandered downward while Dr. Mailer continued speaking. "Faye's lithics skills aren't too shabby, either. She was the top student in my class last semester."

Chuck's eyes had reached her chest, where they lingered a few thoughtful seconds before heading south again. In her peripheral vision, Faye caught a flicker of motion as Joe's relaxed hand became a fist. He was leaning forward, prepared to get in Chuck's face, but she put out a hand to stop him.

Dr. Mailer wasn't blind. He demonstrated his superior management skills by smoothly putting himself between Joe and Chuck, who was never remotely aware of his peril. "Chuck, I left my cell phone in the truck. Would you go get it for me?"

"Sure." Chuck shifted his eyes toward the driveway where the truck sat, displaying almost as much interest in the blue pickup as he had in Faye's shapelier parts. His stride was so long that he was out of earshot within thirty seconds.

"It takes an, er, 'special' kind of brain to do the kind of detail work Chuck does every day," Dr. Mailer offered awkwardly. "Social graces aren't a big part of his skill set."

Joe was not mollified. Faye noticed that Toneisha and Bodie sported clenched fists and jaws themselves. Having dealt with problem employees, she felt for Dr. Mailer.

"It's okay," she said. "He's clearly not stupid. Just explain to him that he's got to keep his eyes to himself." Toneisha's firm nod said that Faye wasn't Chuck's first victim.

"I wish I could see these things coming," the professor said. "Then I could just sit Chuck down and spell things out for him all at once. But he just keeps finding new ways to be inappropriate. Maybe it would help if I bought him an etiquette book." There was a moment of silence while the group pondered the ineffectiveness of that approach. "Well, no time like the present." He crossed the distance between him and Chuck at a slow trot.

Eager to distract her colleagues from a problem that centered on her breasts, Faye dropped to a squat to get a better look at the soil that Oka Hofobi had been examining when she walked up. "What did you find here?"

"Just a potsherd," he said, bending down to show her a thumbnail-sized object that would have looked like a chunk of raw clay to most people. Faye's friends gathered around it like kids goggling over a new video game. "I've been finding stuff here since I was five years old. Want to see?" Four open grins said that his colleagues most assuredly did.

He led them through the back door of the farmhouse, through a kitchen where a stout middle-aged woman with Oka Hofobi's broad face hovered over a frying pan. Covering her gray business suit, she wore a blue gingham apron trimmed with chicken-scratch embroidery. A pair of black pumps had been kicked into a corner.

"Ma, I didn't know you were home from work. Meet my friends. Toneisha, Bodie, Faye, Joe—meet my mom. And her cooking." He dodged her spatula, snagging crispy yellow rounds of fried squash off the serving platter at her elbow and handing them around for everybody to taste. "This is why I live at home in my old age."

"You live at home because you can step out the door and dig up a career's worth of my ancestors' house goods before breakfast. Then, because I don't have good sense, I scramble your eggs before I go to work." She shoved the platter in the general direction of her guests and handed them all forks. "Invite your friends to stay for dinner. Right now, I need to get out of this skirt." She picked up her dress shoes and headed down the hall.

"Stay for dinner?" he asked the group. "I don't know what she's cooking, but most of it will be fried. And it'll taste really great."

"Sounds like your cooking," Faye muttered to Joe, but no one else heard her because they were all accepting the offer with the enthusiasm of poor, hungry students.

A screen door slammed, and a tall Choctaw man with stooped shoulders and a lined face walked in. Mrs. Nail's kitchen was spacious, in the old-timey farmhouse style, but it was crowded with chattering young people. Faye was struck by Mr. Nail's economy of movement as he navigated through the crowd without brushing up against anyone, without making eye contact, and without speaking. Loosening his tie as he walked, the older man disappeared down the hall.

Faye looked uncertainly at Oka Hofobi, wondering what to make of his father's behavior. The young archaeologist seemed determined to give her no clue.

"Come see my treasures," he said, jerking his head toward a door that led into the farmhouse's front room.

"I dug those up when I was a little kid," he said, gesturing toward a stupendous collection of spear points and scrapers, "and I mistreated them royally. One of my favorite things was to strap the points to sticks and spear roly-poly bugs with them. I feel pretty bad about the bugs, these days. Good thing most of them were too fast for me." Opening a glass-fronted display case, he pulled out some exquisitely incised potsherds. "Then I grew up a little, and I started reading about the right way to do archaeology. And I developed some taste."

Each artifact was numbered, just as it would be in a museum. The stack of field notebooks stored with them gave Faye a weird pang of familiarity, as if she'd run into her best friend while traveling in a foreign land. She had display cases just like Oka Hofobi's, filled with artifacts dug from her own family's property. He even used the same brand of field notebook that she did. Except he'd spent his childhood digging up relics from the dawn of his own civilization, and she'd spent hers unearthing the slave cabins where her ancestors had been held captive.

Oka Hofobi's mother showed Dr. Mailer and Chuck into the room, and the newly formed team enjoyed a good half-hour fondling the goods in anticipation of finding some treasures of their own.

When Faye noticed Joe moving toward the window, she wasn't sure whether he'd reached the end of his attention span, or whether he was feeling crowded in a room with so many people, or whether the outdoors was simply calling him. Since she was the one who kept coming up with reasons for Joe to leave their Florida home on Joyeuse Island and be with strangers, she sidled over to make sure he was okay.

It turned out that Joe had been called to the window by a sunset made more splendid by a blue-black thunderhead that roiled bigger by the minute. But it wasn't the colorful sky that held him there. Pointing with his chin, he silently called Faye's attention to the flat-topped mound that rose from the property across the road from Oka Hofobi's house. It stood on the far side of a soybean field at the edge of a heavily wooded area. Unlike Nanih Waiya, it had not been cleared of the trees that rose through its flanks. The underbrush covering the mound served as camouflage, so that it could hide in plain sight. It stood in full view of the rural highway that wound through this area, where many people surely saw this large and ancient structure every day without paying it much attention.

Oka Hofobi saw them peering out the window. "One day, I'd love to excavate that. My neighbor, Mr. Calhoun, caught me sneaking around over there when I was fifteen and he told me to get the hell off his land. It was a good thing he didn't think to ask me to empty my pockets. Check these out. I found them in the rootball of a downed tree."

He opened another case and pulled out two nondescript clay balls. They weren't molded into a complex shape or thrown on a wheel. They weren't incised with intricate patterns. They weren't even pretty, but Faye took in a sharp breath while everyone around her erupted with exclamations like, "Hey!" and "Look at that!" and "No shit!"

The two brown lumps were cooking balls typical of the Poverty Point culture, which meant that they could be fifteen hundred years older than the Middle Woodland site that Oka Hofobi had mined for the other artifacts in the room. The cooking balls were so ubiquitous at Poverty Point sites that archaeologists called them PPOs, short for Poverty Point Objects.

Oka Hofobi handed one of the balls to Faye. It felt warm and comfortable in her hand. Perhaps three and a half millennia had passed since someone leaned down and scooped up a lump of clay, squeezed it into a ball, then threw it in the fire. She could feel the contours left by that long-decayed hand. Narrow depressions where slender fingers had squeezed the earth were divided by ridges formed where the clay had squished up between those fingers. This was the soul of archaeology for Faye—forging a human connection with the past.

"Now I can't say for sure Mr. Calhoun's mound is as old as we're all thinking it is. All I've got is these two cooking balls. Maybe they came from somewhere else..."

"You're thinking maybe they flew?" Toneisha asked.

"I don't know. Maybe Mr. Calhoun's great-grandfather traveled all over the state, building a collection of arrowheads and artifacts. Maybe when he died, his kids spread them over the mound in his memory."

Every eyebrow in the room was raised in skepticism.

"Okay. Maybe they're cooking balls and they were made right here, but they're more recent than we're thinking. My point is that out-of-context artifacts aren't likely to tell us what we want to know. We just can't know how old that mound is."

Bodie spoke for them all when he lunged for the window, looked out at the mound, and said, "To hell with this site. Let's go dig over *there*."

Oka Hofobi was shaking his head. "Mr. Calhoun wouldn't—"

"It wouldn't hurt to ask," Toneisha pointed out, reaching for the cooking ball in Faye's hand.

Someone was out walking in the soybean field. Dr. Mailer's face lit up when he saw the man who owned the coveted mound.

"No, it can't hurt to ask. And there's no time like the present." He grabbed his hat and was out the front door.

Oka Hofobi trailed him, explaining why this expedition was a poor idea. "He's watching birds. That's what he likes to do every afternoon, and we shouldn't disturb him. He doesn't take well to strangers, either, and…"

Faye could see that the poor guy might as well be talking to Mr. Calhoun's birds. The professor was on a mission.

Faye, like Oka Hofobi, knew how to behave in a rural setting. Dr. Mailer needed to strike up a casual acquaintance with Mr. Calhoun, and he needed to do it when the farmer wasn't enjoying time alone with his feathered friends. He needed to ask him to recommend a good catfish house, then he needed to go there with him and put away a nice little stack of fried filets, with creamy cole slaw on the side. Before he asked a favor this big, Mr. Calhoun's dog should wag his tail when he saw the archaeologist coming. Dr. Mailer should know the name of the man's dog. His wife's name, too. As things stood, he didn't even know Mr. Calhoun's first name, but he was planning to introduce himself and then, in the same breath, ask for a major incursion into the man's property rights.

Dr. Mailer was an intelligent and educated man, but he was born and raised in Houston. When it came to the traditional ways of rural Southerners, he didn't have a clue. Toneisha, who was urging him on in his headlong quest to alienate the whole countryside, was a city girl from Memphis, so she was just as naïve. Chuck had already proved himself lacking in the most basic people skills, but the rest of them knew an impending train wreck when they saw one. They trailed after their supervisor, unable to stop him and unable to look away.

They crossed the road amid the flutter of multi-colored wings. Mr. Calhoun rose from a lawn chair carefully placed at the boundary between field and forest. Sliding his binoculars into the case hanging by its strap from the chair's arm, he started walking toward them. A good-sized man in height and breadth, he still carried a lot of muscle mass for a man who looked to be seventy or more. He wasn't smiling.

"Oka Hofobi," he said, "you're a smart boy. I didn't think I needed to run you off my land but once."

"No, sir, I learned that lesson a long time ago. I just thought you might want to get acquainted with my colleagues. They'll be working with me across the road. On my family's land."

"It's your daddy's business what happens on his land. Though I don't imagine the Choctaws will be any too happy to have these people mucking around in their ancestors' bones."

"I've never found a burial in all my years on that land. If I ever do, I know the law and I know my people's ways. I went to school a long time so I'd know how to do things right." He didn't ask for permission to dig on Calhoun's land, which Faye knew was the right decision. She hoped Dr. Mailer would recognize the wisdom of earning trust slowly.

Her hopes were dashed. The professor stepped forward and grasped the old farmer's hand enthusiastically. "Sid Mailer here. You've got a beautiful place here, and that mound behind you is absolutely stupendous. Is there a chance in the world that we could talk about my crew excavating over there?"

"No." The monosyllable hung in the damp summer air. The thundercloud overhead rumbled without dropping any rain.

Dr. Mailer rubbed his palms together and cocked his head to an angle that signaled how off-balance he felt. Faye wanted to warn him not to tip his hand, but he was an honest man. Nothing was going to stop him from laying his cards on the table and asking for what he wanted. This was the problem with being forthright. Once a man has forced his adversary to say, "No," it becomes very difficult to find a face-saving way to get to "Yes."

Dr. Mailer plunged ahead anyway. "Perhaps you wouldn't mind if we just walked over the mound? We wouldn't dig. We wouldn't take anything. We just want to look at it."

Calhoun shook his head, as if he couldn't believe such a smart man had painted himself into such a tight corner. Faye could hardly believe it herself. Surely the professor could see that the answer to this question had to be "No." But that wasn't the answer that came out of Calhoun's mouth. Instead he said only, "If that mound wasn't standing over there, we wouldn't be having this conversation, now, would we?"

Then he slung his binoculars around his neck, folded his lawn chair, and walked away.

The archaeologists exchanged uncertain looks before turning to go back to the Nail house. As they skirted Mr. Calhoun's soybean field, dusk spread through air that was oppressive with humidity. Spreading oak trees threw shadows over the Nail house, and Faye could see something flickering in those shadows. It was a lit cigarette, arcing through the air as Oka Hofobi's father raised it to his mouth, took a deep drag, and lowered it to his side, again and again. He stood watching until his son led the archaeological crew across the road, then he disappeared into the house. He was nowhere to be seen when they trooped through the front door, and he never reappeared, not for dinner, and not during the high-spirited conversation that filled the dining room afterward. From time to time during that conversation, Faye noticed Oka Hofobi's eyes stray toward the darkened hallway that must lead to the house's bedrooms.

Chapter Two

Faye's hopes that Mrs. Nail would cook some traditional Choctaw foods were quickly dashed. She'd had hominy once, cooked outdoors with pork and chicken, and she'd enjoyed its soul-satisfying taste. The very notion of *banaha* fascinated her. She'd been told that Choctaw cooks made *banaha* by mixing field peas and corn meal together, then wrapping the resulting mush into corn husks and boiling them. It was as if Mexican tamales had been transported to the Deep South, then adapted to available ingredients—and perhaps they had. The trade routes of America's indigenous cultures had snaked far and wide. Why wouldn't a tasty, nutritious recipe make its way across a continent?

But there was no *banaha* on the Nails' table. Only a tremendous platter of fried chicken and a wealth of vegetables fresh out of the garden. Several chickens had given their all for this spread. And quite a few cobs had been scraped clean to fill the bucket-sized bowl of cut-off corn. Not to mention the bushel of squash that had been sliced, rolled in corn meal, and fried.

The table had been set for eight, but when Oka Hofobi's older brother appeared, Mrs. Nail had hurriedly squeezed a ninth chair into place. The long, broad farmhouse table easily accommodated the crowd. Breathless, Mrs. Nail had said, "Davis, introduce yourself," then disappeared into the kitchen.

Davis seemed taken aback to find a crowd of strangers at his mother's table. He looked a great deal like Mr. Nail, minus the stooped shoulders and wrinkles. Tall and lean, the muscles in his shoulders and chest showed clearly through a tee-shirt that read *Choctaw Fire Department.*

Davis wasn't a big talker. Mrs. Nail, who seemed to be the only big talker in her family, was busy in the kitchen, so Faye took it upon herself to break the awkward silence. "I'm Faye. Are you a firefighter?" she asked.

"Yes," was his succinct answer, but Mrs. Nail's voice wafted out of the kitchen. "And a paramedic, too."

Academia was Dr. Mailer's natural habitat, so he knew how to pick up this conversational ball. "Where do you train for that kind of career?"

"The Mississippi Fire Academy gives the introductory course. And you can take specialized courses like emergency medical care, if you want to move up."

Mrs. Nail bustled in, plunked a gallon pitcher of iced tea on the table, and gave a meaningful nod toward several framed Fire Academy certificates hanging on the dining room wall. They were almost lost among several dozen framed family photos, mostly of round-cheeked, smiling children.

"Then he went to the community college to be a paramedic," she added, taking her seat at the table. The comment was unnecessary, since Davis' community college degree was prominently displayed. Faye also spotted Oka Hofobi's Ph.D., and five high school diplomas. She felt like she knew Mrs. Nail very well, considering that they'd just met, because her own mother never saw a picture of Faye that she didn't want to share with the world.

Faye poured herself a glass of tea and took a sip. There was so much sugar dissolved in it that a spoon could have stood upright, unaided, in the brew. And it was so strong that the tannins would have dissolved said spoon. Just the way Faye's mama had taught her to make it. Maybe her mother and Mrs. Nail were twins, separated at birth.

She squinted at the high school diploma with Davis' name on it. It had been issued by the Cherokee school in North Carolina. Another one with a similar design, but obviously older, hung on the far wall of the dining room. "I see you went to North Carolina for high school. What took you there? Did they have a program for kids who wanted to be firefighters?"

Davis glanced at his mother. "No. Ma wanted one of us to go to her alma mater. I was the lucky one."

"I'm from Hickory. That's not so far from Cherokee," Bodie said, "but it's a long way from here. What took you so far from home?"

"In my day, there wasn't any other way to finish school," Mrs. Nail explained. "The reservation school just went through the eighth grade. We weren't allowed to go to local schools, either black or white, only to schools run by the Bureau of Indian Affairs, and they're all far away. My folks sent me to Cherokee. It changed my life."

"It changed Davis' life, too," Oka Hofobi said. His tone wasn't brotherly.

Within five minutes, Davis had cleaned his plate and taken it into the kitchen. Like his father, he managed to pass back through the crowded dining room without making eye contact and without brushing against his brother or his mother or any of their guests. Without a sound, he disappeared down the same hallway where his father had staged his own retreat.

The dinner table conversation had stumbled after Davis left, but Mrs. Nail and Dr. Mailer were heroic talkers. They'd wrestled the conversation into submission.

Dr. Mailer had launched the first successful strike by admiring the colorful basket that had held a few dozen biscuits before Bodie and Joe got their hands on them.

"Ma made it," Oka Hofobi volunteered, helping himself to two more biscuits and dousing them with sorghum syrup.

"Did she make all those?" Dr. Mailer asked, gesturing at the row of baskets displayed on a shelf that extended the entire length of one wall.

"Oh, no." Mrs. Nail shook her head hard to emphasize her denial. "My daughters made those. My baskets are just—well, I use them. Jane and Sarah make baskets that are way too nice for that."

"That's because you carted them out to Bogue Chitto about a million times, so that the old women there could show them how it's done." Oka Hofobi was clearly enjoying his biscuit-and-syrup dessert.

"Could I see one?" asked Dr. Mailer, ever the scholar. "Do they use traditional methods?"

Mrs. Nail handed him a large basket with a lid, woven in a diamond design. The colors—red, black, yellow, brown, and blue—lit up the room. Toneisha leaned over his shoulder, running her fingers over its tight weave.

"Yes, they use the same methods our people have always used. They cut the swamp cane and split it into lots of thin strips. Then they have to dye the cane before they weave it. It's getting hard to find swamp cane, but the university's doing a study on how to plant it. The old women say the planted cane isn't flexible enough. It won't split right. I figure the scientists will keep trying."

"Now, Ma. You left out one thing that's not traditional, not any more."

Mrs. Nail eyeballed Oka Hofobi. "You try dyeing cane with berries and bark and ashes."

"I wouldn't dream of it." Oka Hofobi grinned at Toneisha, who was still studying the basket and how it was put together. "When Rit Dye showed up in the grocery stores here, our women knew a good thing when they saw it. That was a few generations back, so I guess commercial coloring *is* a traditional method by now. It must be, because Jane and Sarah are all about Rit Dye."

Chuck, who hadn't spoken since they arrived, replenished the syrup on his plate of biscuits.

Oka Hofobi smiled at his mother. "Ma isn't a basket artist like my sisters, but she knows the old stories. Do you want to hear some? You won't have to ask her but once."

They actually asked her two or three times, as Mrs. Nail tried to beg off, saying that she needed to clear the table and start on the dishes.

"Don't be silly," Toneisha butted in. "After you cooked this big meal? We'll do the dishes. You've got to spread your stories around. It's a shame to keep them to yourself."

So Mrs. Nail gathered herself, folding her hands in her lap to lend a ceremonious air to the occasion. She was as gifted at storytelling as she was at cooking, so the hour grew late before her guests made good on their promise to wash the dishes.

The Girl and the Devil

As told by Mrs. Frances Nail

Once, a young girl was walking alone in the woods outside her village. Now, maybe she was gathering cane. Or maybe she was gathering berries to dye that cane. I don't know. But she was alone.

A young man she didn't know asked her to come home with him. Now, maybe he was handsome and she was easily swayed. Or maybe he bewitched her. Or maybe she wasn't very smart. I don't know. But she went with him.

He led her up and down hills, and through woods so dense she could hardly walk. You've seen the woods around here, along the creek bottoms? Yeah? Well, it was like that.

But all of a sudden the woods opened up, and they walked into the yard surrounding his house. It was full of birds and animals, all tied up to the trees. When they were hungry, they were given food, but even an innocent young girl knows when she's looking at something that's not natural.

When he saw that the girl was awakened to her danger, the young man came into his true form, and she knew that she was with the Devil. She tried to run, but he caught her and locked her in a small cave. And a girl locked in a cave is just as unnatural as a tied-up animal. Who ever heard of a robin with a rope tied around its leg? Who ever heard of a bobcat in hobbles?

A frog in the cave had pity on her. He hopped over and said, "Do you know what that noise is?" It was a grinding noise that repeated over and over. Grrrsh. Grrrsh. Grrrsh.

She knew the noise, but she didn't want to know it. "What is it?"

"The Devil is sharpening his knife."

She tried to sit down and just scream, but the frog said no. "If you do as I say, you will escape with your life. When I open the door, flee down the wide road. You will pass a road on the left. Do not take it. Keep to the wide road. When you come to a place where you must decide between three roads, you must take the middle one. Remember. Take the middle one. Near there, you will find a boat on the shore of a broad creek. There is safety there."

The frog hopped up to a rafter over the door and tripped the lock. The girl, who may have been foolish in following the Devil home, redeemed her error. She did everything her friend the frog told her to do. When she reached the boat, she wanted to drop to her knees and kiss its wooden side, but she had better sense. She hopped into the boat, grabbed the paddle, and used it to push out from shore.

Right away, she heard a voice calling her and there stood the Devil, right where she'd left the shore. He called to her and his voice must have been magic, because she stuck her paddle down in the bottom of the creek and started pushing the boat back. Toward the Devil! Can you imagine?

"Come closer," he said. "Let me climb in your boat."

She said, "No," but her hands didn't listen to her mouth. She rested one end of the paddle on the boat and the other on the shore, saying, "Sir, you can walk right out on this bridge. See?"

He stepped out, trusting the power of his Devil's voice, but when he got to the middle, the girl yanked the paddle out from under him. The water closed over his head and he never came up.

The Devil's body broke into pieces on the creek bottom, and the power of the water rolling over it is still breaking the Devil up, even to this day. The old people say that the sharp, hard gravel on the bottom of the creeks around here ain't nothing but his body, broken up by a scared girl with enough brains and heart to take on the Devil.

This is what I've been told.

Chapter Three

Faye and her buddies were sweating before they turned over the first spade of dirt. It was July and it was Mississippi, so the early morning air was not cool. The only good thing that could be said about Mississippi mornings was that they were cooler than Mississippi afternoons.

There were no trees overhanging their work site. In a sense, this was a good thing, since there would be no tree roots garbling the near-surface stratigraphy. Sad to say, the lack of trees meant that there would also be no natural shade. Dr. Mailer planned to hang some awnings, but Faye was taking no chances. She could hardly be seen under the broad brim of her sun hat.

Chuck's workspace was out of the sun. It was even air-conditioned, though Faye would rather work out in the elements than be locked up with him. The project had paid to move a rented trailer to the site, so that their tools and their finds could be secured. It was divided into five rooms, a storage area, three offices for the project's three Ph.D.s—Dr. Mailer, Oka Hofobi, and Chuck—and a communal workspace for everybody else. A table piled with flint flakes, magnifiers, and a powerful lamp marked Chuck's domain. Since he would be working in the trailer day in and day out, Dr. Mailer had put him in charge of keeping the storage space organized, too.

This assignment was probably a good use of personnel; Chuck was renowned for his attention to detail. There would be no time wasted looking for tools that had been piled in the corner of the storeroom, unwashed. Unfortunately, it meant that Faye, along with everybody else, was forced into daily contact with Chuck. She dreaded the day somebody failed to clean every speck of dirt off a trowel.

Faye was happy to let Chuck have his cozy lair. She might be out in the sun's full glare, but she'd enjoy the breezes. As soon as there were some.

The roar of heavy equipment pierced the quiet morning again. When Faye had first arrived, Mr. Calhoun had been out early, as farmers tend to be. He'd seemed to be cutting down the overgrown vegetation between the soybean field and the great mound.

"Cool," Bodie had said. "Now we can get a better look, even if we never actually set a foot on it." He informed his co-workers that the correct word for what Mr. Calhoun was doing was "bush-hogging," which Faye found to be a poetic term.

All bush-hogging activity had ceased shortly after Faye arrived, and there had been little noise beyond the morning birdsong and the voices of her colleagues since, but it had been unreasonable for Faye to hope that the pastoral silence would never be broken. The narrow pavement running in front of Oka Hofobi's house was classed as a farm-to-market road, which meant exactly what it sounded like. It was a critical artery for trucks rushing produce to market. Since larger farm operations were more likely than small ones to beat the law of averages and prove successful, most local farmers owned as many separate parcels of land as they could afford, and many of them were strung out along this roadway. Their equipment—tractors, bush-hogs, harrows, harvesters—was forever being driven from one plot to the next.

Faye rose from her work and cocked an ear toward Calhoun's property. She couldn't see the mound any more—the Nails' house was in the way—but he seemed to have started bush-hogging again. The motor was much louder than it had been that morning, murderously so, and it didn't seem to be getting anywhere fast. Maybe he was trying to clear some land that was more heavily vegetated. She needed to stretch anyway, so she walked around the corner of the house, just to see what in the world was going on.

It took her ten seconds to find her voice.

"Oh, God—y'all come see, this man has lost his mind!" she hollered as she sprinted toward the road. Her co-workers, who may have thought she'd lost her own mind, came running.

The tractor, a tremendous beast with an enclosed cabin, was powered by tracks big enough to crush an economy car. Fitted with a broad blade, its engine roared and screamed as it forced down a tree.

Then it backed up and began an assault on the mound that Dr. Mailer had tried so hard to get a look at the night before. The blade bit into the mound's sloping flank, and hundreds of pounds of earth were peeled away.

She presumed Mr. Calhoun was locked inside the air-conditioned cabin. His words echoed in her ears: "If that mound wasn't standing over there, we wouldn't be having this conversation, now, would we?" He might as well have paid Western Union to telegraph what he intended to do.

"Call 911!" Faye cried as she ran across the road, with her colleagues trailing after her. "Call the National Guard, call anybody that can stop him. He can't do this!" But she wasn't actually sure what he could or couldn't do. How did cultural protection laws apply to sites on private property? All she could do was try to stop the destruction until someone figured it out. Cell phones beeped out a chorus of cries for help.

The engine whined as it forced the behemoth against a tree that didn't want to go down. When it yielded—and it had no choice but to yield—its rootball surfaced, dragging any artifacts tangled in those roots up to the surface to be crushed.

They reached the far boundary of Mr. Calhoun's soybean field, then paused, uncertain of what to do. What could seven puny humans do to stop a man armed with a machine the size of dinosaur?

Did Dr. Mailer realize that this was his fault? Farmers like Mr. Calhoun could be excused for feeling besieged by the government. They owed taxes every year on their land, whether it made them any money or not. Pesticides that they believed might make the difference between a good crop and a disaster were heavily controlled or outlawed. If the government decreed that a road needed building, a strip of fertile land could be condemned and taken, whether the farmer felt he could do without it or not. Mailer should have known that this man might not respond well to even a faint possibility that some arcane historical protection law might hamper his ability to use his own land.

Calhoun's tractor took another bite out of history, and Faye felt it in the pit of her stomach. Another wad of soil, still wet from the night's thunderstorm, slumped to the ground without Calhoun's help. How could Faye and her friends stand up against that many horsepower?

Calhoun backed up for another assault, and Faye ran forward, taking the opportunity to place herself between him and the mound. Within seconds, she felt Joe at her elbow and Chuck at her back. The rest of the project team filled in around her. They surely provided a formidable barrier in the sense that few humans would be willing to bulldoze that many lives. Mass-wise, however, they represented far less of an obstacle than even the smallest tree lying uprooted at their feet.

"Mr. Calhoun!" Dr. Mailer cried. Faye reflected again that this relationship would be more effective if someone had asked the man his first name. "Your property is yours. Your property rights are yours. There's no need to destroy anything. We're on your side."

The cabin door opened and Calhoun's head poked out. "Bullshit. I've seen it happen, more than once. Somebody finds a few arrowheads or an endangered worm. Then the law comes in and tells the person paying the taxes on the land that they can't farm a little spot. 'Just to protect the arrowheads or the worm,' they say. Then they bring in a bunch of experts who basically tear things up and get in the way. And then they write their report that says there's endangered worms or arrowheads all over the damn place, and the farmer's left paying the mortgage and the taxes on land that can't be farmed, ever again. I figure I'd better tear this thing down before you experts tell me it's so special that I need to go bankrupt to save it."

"It's not just special. It's irreplaceable," Oka Hofobi called out.

"You wouldn't know that if you hadn't sneaked onto my land when you were a delinquent kid, now, would you?" He revved the engine. "I got work to do. Step away." He slammed the door shut, closing himself again into the cabin.

The seven archaeologists stood firm.

The tractor started rolling. Its progress was slow, perhaps to show that he didn't want to mow them down, but it was inexorable. Soon, everyone involved would have to make a decision.

Bodie blinked first, taking a step out of the tractor's path. It took a moment for Toneisha to follow him. Faye wasn't sure how long she could hold out, but she wasn't ready to cave in yet.

Out of the corner of her eye, she saw Dr. Mailer stoop down and put a shoulder into Oka Hofobi's chest, knocking him off his feet and out of harm's way with the residual skill of an aging halfback. He tried the same move on Chuck, without success. The two men were well-matched in size, and Chuck was twenty years younger.

Faye was distracted from her own peril. Chuck had already shown himself to be passionate about his work and eccentric to the point of abnormality. He might be capable of letting himself be crushed to save this mound. Faye was not. But she couldn't save herself and just watch Chuck die, either. She weighed all of a hundred pounds, but maybe she was big enough to help Dr. Mailer save Chuck.

One step and one millisecond into her rescue plan, something hit her left side with the force of a brickbat. Joe, who she knew had never played football, had stiff-armed her with a move that would have merited a twenty-yard penalty, at least. Airborne, she flew out of the tractor's path and landed hard on the exposed roots of a downed tree.

With every cubic centimeter of air knocked out of her lungs, all Faye could do was fight for breath and watch three big men try to knock each other down. Did being large all your life completely destroy your instinct for self-protection? Chuck was staring down the tractor as if he thought it incapable of crushing a man his size. And Dr. Mailer and Joe were pummeling him into submission with more deliberation than she thought the situation merited. They were certainly big enough to overpower him, but could they do it before all three were mashed to jelly? The tractor continued to roll.

Then the air was split with racing engines and honking horns and excited voices. Brakes squealed as cars and trucks were driven off the road and their transmissions were thrown into park. A throng formed as bodies boiled out of the vehicles. They arrayed themselves in front of Calhoun's tractor and, though he didn't cut the engine, he did cease his forward motion. Yes, he could crush a few of these people but, given their sheer numbers, he'd sooner or later find himself pulled out of the tractor's cabin and yanked limb from limb. The cavalry had topped the hill, and the day was saved.

Still lying flat on her butt, Faye studied the crowd. Dressed in businesswear and overalls and blue jeans and well-worn housedresses, these people had obviously dropped everything and come running. Their distinctive dark faces were calm and full of resolve, and the sun shone hot on their glossy black hair. Faye reminded herself never to trifle with the Mississippi Band of Choctaw Indians.

In the forefront of the fast-moving crowd was Davis Nail, urging them onward. If Faye had to choose a leader out of that mass of humanity, it would be him. Sometimes, one person can move a crowd into doing something that, without him, would have simply remained undone.

She wished Mr. Calhoun would open the tractor's cabin door. Constructive negotiations begin when you put a human face on your adversary. You can't reason with a tractor.

A second flush of vehicles disgorged a second throng of people. Apparently, Faye was going to meet every Choctaw left in Mississippi. The newcomers gathered behind Calhoun, and Faye felt a shiver of apprehension. Animal instincts surface when human beings are surrounded. It might not be wise to make Calhoun feel cornered.

Then Faye searched the faces of the people gathering behind Calhoun and her own animal instincts bubbled up. These were not Choctaws. They were white people and black people but, on this day, their races were unimportant. Their way of life was everything. Judging by their clothes, she'd guess that these folks had been called away from their field work to stand up for the rights of the small farmer. And, in her heart of hearts, she couldn't blame them any more than she could blame the Choctaws for defending their own heritage. This situation had the potential to get ugly fast.

She struggled to her feet. Squarely between the two factions, she and her friends stood a good chance of being trampled if a riot broke out.

Joe helped her up. "You okay?"

"Oxygen would be good."

A voice from deep in the crowd shouted, "Calhoun's got every right to do what he wants to do on his own land. You people want to stop him, you need to pay him a fair price for his property. Even then, it's his call whether he sells it to you. It's his land."

Half the crowd rumbled in agreement. Through the buzz of all the voices, Faye could make out, time and again, the two critical words: "His land."

"Yes, it's his land," Dr. Mailer called out. "Nobody wants to harm Mr. Calhoun or his livelihood. But history belongs to everybody. I think we can work this thing out."

The crowd didn't agree. When the words "history belongs to everybody" passed the professor's lips, the farmers' hot button was firmly pushed. If they were so unlucky as to own a piece of land that harbored "history"—and, in the end, who wasn't?—then they might lose the ability to plant that land in soybeans. And, with prices being what they were, the loss of a single field might well mean the loss of an entire farm. Calhoun's supporters surged forward.

There were too many people. Faye was shoulder-to-shoulder with people. Her chest was pressed against someone else's back, and her back was being crowded by the chest of someone behind her. Actually, the belly of someone behind her. She was shorter than everyone in her vicinity, which meant that she could see absolutely nothing. Panic whispered in her ear.

The crowd moved forward again and Faye had no choice but to go with it. Then she found herself hanging horizontal in the air.

Joe had tucked her under his arm like a football, and he was making for high ground. Gently pushing people aside, he hauled Faye to the nearest safe place, which was behind the archaeologists and the Choctaws, atop the mound that had caused all these problems.

The raked sunlight of early morning cast shadows that wouldn't be there at noon. The surface of the land around the mound looked odd, unnatural, beneath the blanket of grass, brambles, and vines shorn off by Mr. Calhoun's bush-hogger. Faye could have sworn the morning shadows revealed that the land on either side of the mound was raised ever-so-slightly above the natural ground surface. The raised areas swept out and back like wings. She twisted in Joe's arms to get a look behind her. It was possible that a third berm stretched behind the mound like a vestigial tail. If she squinted, she could make out a low rise ahead of her, where the head of this winged beast should be.

Could this be an effigy mound, constructed in the image of a bird? Such monumental, animal-shaped earthworks were well-known in the Midwest, but there were no undisputed effigy mounds in the Southeast. Many thought that the largest mound at Poverty Point was made in the image of a bird. Oka Hofobi had thought this mound might date to the same period. A bird-shaped mound constructed by the Poverty Point culture would be a dream find. It was probably a good thing that Joe had Faye immobilized. Otherwise, she might have rushed Calhoun and dismantled his tractor single-handedly.

But what were the odds that an effigy mound was sitting, unnoticed, right here by the road? Faye guessed they were low, but maybe…

If the newly bush-hogged area on the flanks of the mound had been overgrown for many years, then an effigy wouldn't have been visible on aerial photographs. If the berms that formed the wings and tail were low enough—and she'd guess that they were—then they wouldn't show up on the geological survey's topographic maps, which were usually plotted at five to ten feet of resolution. And if Mr. Calhoun's ancestors had been as touchy about trespassers as he himself was, then Faye might be the first person outside his family to see this bird in many years.

From Faye's odd vantage point, she could peer out from under Joe's armpit down at the crowd. Across the road, she could see Mr. Nail. The bright morning sun left him no place to hide as he smoked his cigarette and watched the hullabaloo. The fact that he was staying out of this conflict was telling. Which side did he belong on? He was a farmer, born of a long line of farmers. Surely he wouldn't want to see a man's property rights abused. But he was a Choctaw, born of an even longer line of Choctaws. He couldn't possibly feel comfortable about watching a monumental piece of Native American heritage destroyed.

A siren sounded. All motion stopped, momentarily keeping everyone safe from being trampled, and every head turned in the direction of three approaching cars, each of which was topped with flashing lights.

Two officers emerged from each car, five muscle-bound men and one slightly built woman. With their hands resting lightly on their sidearms, they moved as a unit toward the idling tractor.

The woman rapped on the cabin door. "This is nuts, Carroll. Come out and talk to me."

There was no response from the man inside. The engine revved. The five deputies drew their weapons, but the woman merely twitched hers in its holster.

"I don't think you paid extra to have bullet-proof glass installed in this thing. I'm telling you to come out and talk to me."

The door opened, but Calhoun didn't get out. "Your daddy's farm is just down the road, Neely. This could happen to him, you know. Somebody could decide that a few arrowheads are worth bankrupting him."

A murmur of voices rose behind Calhoun. There was fear in the sound. The woman raised a bullhorn. "Nobody's getting bankrupted. Nobody's taking Carroll's land. Look at this thing," she said, gesturing at the mound behind her. "He's never even plowed it. There's no harm in leaving it alone."

A black man stepped forward. "I don't care if he plows it or knocks it down or leaves it alone. It's his business, not the government's. Which means it's not your business, Sheriff."

She lowered her bullhorn to speak directly to him. "I don't know that, Wade, and neither do you. I'm not real clear on whether Carroll's free to knock this thing down, just because it's on his property. This is not a point of law I deal with every day, but I've already got some lawyers looking into it. If Carroll will park his tractor and talk to me, we can work this thing out."

Without closing the door, Calhoun let the tractor start moving forward again. "By the time your lawyers get this figured out, there won't be nothing here but a flat piece of ground."

The bullhorn hit the ground and the woman's sidearm finally left its holster.

Calhoun blinked. "Neely! You would shoot me over this thing? When you don't even know what the law says?"

"You may or may not be breaking any cultural protection laws, but you're sure as hell disturbing the peace, and I know how to deal with that. You, sir, will come down out of that tractor. Right now."

When Carroll Calhoun descended from the tractor of his own free will, Faye went weak with relief. It seemed that no one would die today. The restive crowd behind Calhoun looked eager to prove her wrong.

"We won't stand for it," somebody yelled. "We'll tear this thing down ourselves."

An older Choctaw woman stepped out of the crowd and cried, "You'll have to come through us first." Faye feared for her. The colorfully appliquéd dress she was wearing would make her an easy target.

The sheriff snatched her bullhorn off the ground and charged the mound. Standing firm, legs apart, high above the crowd, she told them, "We're not doing this, folks. If the law says Carroll can tear this thing down, then more power to him. If the law says he has to preserve it, then that's what he's going to do. But we're not going to kill each other over it."

An elderly white man called up to her, "Neely Rutland. When we elected you sheriff, we expected you to look after your own people."

"That's what I'm doing, John. Except maybe my list of 'my own people' is a little bit longer than your list."

Faye noticed that John did not look pleased by this observation.

The bullhorn sounded again. "I was elected to look after all the people in this county. You know what? I was born here in Neshoba County in 1970—years after evil and stupid people killed those civil rights workers and buried them in a dam. But when I tell people from outside the county where I come from, I feel like I've got a tattoo on my forehead that says 'Racist.' I refuse to wake up tomorrow and find out that every headline in the country reads RACIAL CONFLICT IN NESHOBA COUNTY LEAVES FIVE PEOPLE DEAD." Pointing to the damaged mound at her feet, she said, "I'll do everything I can to protect this thing, including sitting in a chair up here all night long. But my first priority is to keep the peace. If I decide there's no other way to keep everybody alive, I'll crank that bulldozer and tear the damned mound down myself. Why don't you people go home?"

And they did.

Chapter Four

"My, Chuck, you were quite the hero out there," Faye said, digging around in the shed until she found a first-aid kit.

Chuck gave a sheepish grunt and fished a bottle of ibuprofen out of the box. "I'm fine, except my head hurts. I think I hurt our fearless leader, though."

"Damn near twisted my hand off. Give me some of that." Dr. Mailer grabbed the ibuprofen out of Chuck's hand. "You could at least pretend to be hurt," he groused in Joe's general direction. "It would make an old man feel better."

"I'm pretty sure one of you bruised me a little bit. Somewhere." He didn't reach for the ibuprofen, so Faye figured he was lying. She noticed that he was holding his right arm at an odd angle, though he wasn't palpating the muscles and the joints like someone who was injured. He just held it out there, studying it now and then, occasionally brushing his fingers lightly over the skin.

Their work day was interminable, even for those workers not nursing cuts and bruises. As they measured and marked the area to be excavated, they were aware of the law enforcement presence just across the road. It was obvious every time a car roared up, then slowed to a crawl as it passed within sight of the mound. Were those cars full of rubberneckers hoping to see what the fuss was all about? Were they driven by Choctaws cruising past to make sure no one had desecrated their heritage? Some of the drivers honked as they passed, so maybe they were Calhoun's friends wanting to let the man know he had their support.

"Why aren't these people at work on a Friday?"

Joe, who had a tendency to answer Faye's rhetorical grumbles, said, "Well, the ones that are farmers work their own hours."

Oka Hofobi, who seemed an awful lot like Joe considering that he had a Ph.D. and Joe was hoping to earn his high school equivalency diploma any day now, chimed in to help him answer the question Faye hadn't really asked. "The casinos are open whenever people have time to throw their money away, so plenty of Choctaws work at night. Besides, lots of people around here took vacation time this week for the Fair."

"Wasn't that a couple of weeks ago?" Bodie asked. "I was wishing I'd gotten here early enough to go. They say nobody dances like the Choctaws. And I'd love to see a modern-day stickball game. Any chance they would let us play?"

"You're talking about the Choctaw Indian Fair, and it's too bad you missed it," Oka Hofobi said. "It's usually a week or two before the Neshoba County Fair. We've got sense enough not to compete with Mississippi's Giant House Party."

"Why do they call it a house party? I thought it was a fair. You know…Ferris wheels. Bumper cars. Deep-fried ice cream. Cotton candy." Toneisha's voice took on a dreamy quality. Faye, who had a deep affinity for fair food, recognized a kindred spirit.

"In Neshoba County, the fairgrounds are full of cabins. Whole neighborhoods of them. I think there's maybe six hundred or so. And there's a family reunion going on in every one of them, all week long," Oka Hofobi explained. "People who are lucky enough to own them—and they're insanely expensive, if you can even find one to buy—just move in for the week. Whole branches of families don't speak to each other because they're unhappy about who inherited Mama's cabin. They're not much to look at, but people are willing to put up with anything just to be where the action is."

"What kind of action? Roller coasters?" Toneisha sounded like she really wanted to know.

"It depends on what you're into. If you're into socializing, you've got fifty thousand people walking right past your front door. The population of Neshoba County practically doubles during the Fair. If you're into politics, you can stroll over to the Pavilion and hear your senator or the governor or, in an election year, maybe even a presidential candidate. If you like music, you can hear any big-name act you like, as long as it's country and western. Plus all the usual rides and livestock exhibits. And the Miss Neshoba County pageant. There's something for pretty much everybody."

Everybody agreed that they'd enjoy a visit to the fair, maybe that very evening, but their enthusiasm had fizzled by the time Chuck locked the shed for the day. Surviving a hostile confrontation before noon will do that to a person.

Faye couldn't wait to get back to the hotel room she shared with Toneisha. They had unusually posh accommodations for a field assignment, thanks to the fact that their Choctaw-owned casino hotel had made Dr. Mailer an extended-stay discount that he couldn't refuse. Faye wished she had enough energy to enjoy the sauna, which was weird because she'd spent the day outdoors where the temperature and the relative humidity were both well in the nineties. Somehow, though she couldn't explain why, sitting in a quiet room that smelled like cedar and letting the dry heat penetrate into her aching bones sounded really good. It was just too bad that her bones were too achy and tired to carry her all the way downstairs to the sauna.

She was in bed before her roommate finished the first step of her four-part nightly skin care regimen. Being a soap-and-water kind of girl offered its own rewards, but being in bed early didn't ensure sleep.

Faye lay under the sheets and thought of what she'd seen as she hurried to the car that took her here to this comfortable bed. The setting sun had thrown harsh shadows across the disputed mound, and Sheriff Rutland's deputies were arrayed around it, their sidearms holstered but ready. The sheriff herself sat alone in a lawn chair high atop the mound. There would be no trouble tonight, not if Neely Rutland could help it.

Joe had refused a ride back to the hotel, setting off on foot instead. Faye had watched him vanish into the trees surrounding Mr. Calhoun's mound. Even a half-dozen armed law enforcement officers wouldn't see or hear Joe hiding out there. Not unless he wanted to be seen or heard.

Faye figured Joe was armed with something ancient and sharp and made of rock. Sheriff Rutland might not know he was out there, but she would be measurably safer tonight with Joe watching over her.

The Story of Nanih Waiya Cave

As told by Mrs. Frances Nail

Everybody around here knows about Nanih Waiya. They know that she is the Mother Mound and that we were born there. Trouble is, when people tell that story, they're not real sure *which* Nanih Waiya is our true mother. There are two of them. One of them stands, big and flat-topped, right beside the road. Some people call it the "temple mound." The other one hides deep in the woods. Inside it, there hides a cave, so most people just call it the "cave mound." I think it is a place of secrets, and the cave is only one of them.

I was always told that there used to be a big hole in the top of the temple mound. That hole was like a navel. It was a place of birth. It was customary to leave a portion of fresh-killed meat in that hole as an offering to our mother. That's what they taught us in school, anyway.

There's another story floating around that says we came out of the cave mound. And maybe we did. I don't know. I do know this: When I was a young woman, I went into the cave, and it did not feel like home to me. It was cold and hard and dark like death.

Atop the temple mound, I feel close to heaven. Beneath the cave mound, I felt death plucking at my sleeve.

My grandmother used to say that the Devil lived in Nanih Waiya Cave. She said that, in the old times, he became angry with the Choctaws. Now, when you think about it, it's a good thing to make the Devil mad at you. It means that you're living right, and that you're teaching your family to live right, so that the good ways will survive.

The Devil knew just the right way to strike the Choctaws directly in the heart. He lured their children into the woods, promising them sweets made out of berries and honey, and he trapped them in his cave. He walled up the entrance so that they couldn't get out and their parents couldn't find them.

Maybe he didn't mean for them to die. Maybe he meant to scare their parents into seeing things his way. Who knows? But children need to breathe, even if Devils don't. My grandmother said that their bones are still sealed in an airless chamber deep under the mound. I have been there and I have smelled the fear in the cave's stale air. I believe her.

Chapter Five

The hotel's breakfast buffet was generously stocked, and Faye was thrilled to see that the spread included biscuits and gravy. She never ceased to be amazed by the wonders that country cooks wrought every morning, using ingredients no more sophisticated than flour and grease.

Bodie and Toneisha and Chuck and Joe apparently were also breakfast fans. They had all piled their plates high. They were up early, considering that it was Saturday and they were all under thirty, but no one seemed to mind that Dr. Mailer had asked them to work on a weekend. Dealing with Carroll Calhoun and his mound-scalping tractor had taken a big bite out of the previous work day and they were anxious to make it up, particularly since the project was paying them to do it.

Dr. Mailer and Oka Hofobi exited the buffet line. Setting down their trays, they dragged a couple of tables together and motioned for everybody to join them. When they'd all sat down, Dr. Mailer began. "I asked Oke to meet us here at the hotel, instead of waiting for us at his house, because I'm rethinking my work plan for this project." Spearing a big chunk of scrambled egg, he explained himself. "I may be older than you guys, but I'm not so set in my habits that I never look for a better way of doing things. Maybe I've been too dead-set on doing work that's easy to measure, like seeing how much dirt we can move in a day. I think I've overlooked the value of getting to know the locals."

No joke, Faye thought. If he'd taken one minute to put himself in Carroll Calhoun's shoes, they might already be making some progress at the site they were hired to investigate. Instead, he'd triggered a near-riot that had left three key personnel, including himself, fairly banged up. No, make that two personnel. It would take a powerful man to hurt Joe, and neither Mailer nor Chuck had managed it.

"In keeping with my new policy, I'm thinking we should wait until tomorrow to catch up on the work we lost yesterday. Today, I think we should all go to the Fair. On company time."

Faye entertained thoughts of funnel cakes and chili dogs. She had never been paid for self-destructive recreational eating before.

"I can't think of a better way to get to know the people of Neshoba County," Mailer said. "Presuming any of them will speak to us after what just happened."

"I know some people who have a cabin. I can get us invited to their party," Oka Hofobi said.

"What time does the party start? And will they let us in the door, after what happened yesterday morning?"

The young Choctaw cleared his throat. "This isn't one of those cabins owned by a whole family of Baptist deacons. We'll be rubbing shoulders with a pretty hard-drinking group."

Bodie pumped his fist in the air, crowing, "Sounds like my kind of folks!"

Oka Hofobi continued answering Dr. Mailer's question, as if he'd never been interrupted. "Will they be friendly? Well, the party started yesterday morning when the Fair opened. It will last until the Fair shuts its doors next Friday evening. By the time we get to the fairgrounds, it'll be after breakfast, so everybody will have a good start on today's drinking. They'll be friendly enough."

The crunch of sawdust underfoot and the sound of lowing cattle gave the fairgrounds a festive agricultural feel. Across Founder's Square, which seemed to be the Fair's nerve center, Faye spotted Miss Neshoba County, who looked more comfortable wearing a tiara before noon than one might suspect. Whole neighborhoods of colorfully painted party cabins clustered around the Square and extended along all the boundaries of the extensive fairgrounds, just as Oka Hofobi had described them. Many of them had porches and all of those porches were full of revelers, who were spilling out into the congested walkways. Oka Hofobi had described the festivities as "a whole bunch of family reunions, all being held in the same place at the same time." Faye didn't think her own family had ever been this skilled at having a good time.

As she worked her way down the street, partiers called out to offer her, in quick succession, lemonade, sweet iced tea, and a Bloody Mary. Recorded music spilled out of many cabin windows, while the luckier hosts had guitar-playing guests lounging on their porches.

Oka Hofobi gestured at a lemon-yellow tin-roofed structure with pink trim. "Ready for this?"

Chuck responded by pushing past him and heading for a huge cooler on the side porch.

"Don't hold back, Chuck," Bodie muttered. "Manners are for wimps."

Faye looked over Chuck's shoulder and noticed that the cooler was full of soft drinks, but she had a good view through the cabin's living room window, and nobody inside was drinking soda pop. "I thought this was a dry county," Faye said. "What's with all the liquor?"

Oka Hofobi's grin showed white teeth made whiter by the contrast with his dark skin. "You can't buy alcohol here. And you can't sell it. But nobody ever said you couldn't drink it. And there ain't no law against giving it away. I don't think."

He took the others on a tour of the house in a vain search for the hosts. It was furnished with a motley mix of cast-off but comfortable furniture, and each room featured at least one large ice chest.

"Our hosts have gone to the Flea Market, Oka Hofobi. Every year, they collect a few more glamorous furnishings for this place." It was Sheriff Rutland's voice. She was in street clothes, which gave Faye a chance to look at her as a person, without the individuality-obscuring cloak of her uniform. Her facial skin was weathered yet resilient, like a young person who has spent all her years in the sun. Faye knew they were about the same age, since Neely had broadcast her birthdate to the countryside at large during the confrontation over Calhoun's mound, and she wondered whether her sun hat was doing a good enough job of protecting her own skin. *More sunscreen,* she vowed to herself.

An ashy brown ponytail hung down Neely's back, and her small, alert eyes were pale blue. Her attention was focused on an old man sitting in a wheelchair with his arms curled awkwardly around his body. Although he was so obese that his thighs hardly fit between the arms of the chair, something about him seemed withered. His unfocused eyes were the same blue as the sheriff's.

"What do you want to do today, Daddy?" she murmured. "There's a big political speech happening at the Pavilion in a few minutes. Would that be fun? It'll be a few more hours before the races start, but we could go out for a walk. Maybe get some ice cream."

Had the woman slept? Faye knew that she'd spent the entire night standing guard atop Calhoun's mound. Remembering Oka Hofobi's description of the Fair and its customs, Faye thought maybe the sheriff had slept in this cabin, coming here after sunrise and crashing for a few hours before assuming her second role as her father's caretaker. Calhoun had spoken to her as if he'd known her all her life. The odds were good that she was insider enough to have snagged a bed here at Ground Zero of the Neshoba County Fair.

Other insiders lurked in the kitchen. Carroll Calhoun and a group of jocular men were pouring drinks far stronger than the cheap beer stocked in the coolers that seemed to be open to anyone thirsty. None of Calhoun's drinking buddies were young; Faye would guess that the youngest was pushing sixty. The smallest of them, a slight man who had lost any muscle bulk he'd once had to age, reminded Faye of a porch lizard. He moved in spurts, separated by long pauses when nothing moved but his eyes. She pulled away from the kitchen door, not anxious to let those reptilian eyes rest on her.

Nudging Joe, who was head-down in the ice chest trying to comparison-shop about eight brands of cheap beer, Faye said, "Let's go. I want to hear this politician speak."

"What kind of beer you want?" The clicking and grinding of ice on aluminum competed with Joe's soft voice.

"The coldest one you can find."

Faye held the can to her face, sacrificing a few degrees of beer chill for the pleasure. Oka Hofobi handed her a blue plastic cup. "Put the beer in this before you go outside. This is still a dry county, and there's no use asking for trouble." Faye reflected that it sure was nice to know an insider when you were visiting such alien terrain.

She and Joe stepped out of the cabin, joining the flow of people heading toward the pavilion. Faye proceeded slowly on purpose, to give the others a chance to get ahead of them. She wanted to talk to Joe. Alone with him for the first time that morning, she finally could ask the question that had been bugging her for hours. "Why'd you dress so funny today?"

"What's so funny? I'm dressed just like you." And he was. He wore olive drab work pants, a button-front cotton shirt, and heavy boots, an ensemble that was astonishingly like her work-a-day clothes, only several sizes larger. Many, many sizes larger, actually. With an artist's innate sense of style, he had wisely chosen a baseball cap that advertised a trucking company, rather than emulating her rather feminine floppy hat.

Why on earth wasn't he wearing his usual garb—traditional Creek-style clothing and hand-made moccasins?

Faye stopped in her tracks to give Joe a good look-over, something she rarely did. When a woman's closest, most intimate friend is a jaw-droppingly handsome man, her best policy is to try not to look at him without squinting. She succeeded in ignoring Joe's finer points most of the time, except when some dazzled woman persisted in enumerating them.

Faye had spent most of the summer wrestling with the question of Joe, and she'd decided that a one-of-a-kind friendship wasn't worth risking—not to pursue a relationship that would have two strikes against it. A nine-year age gap, with her being the older, and an even bigger gap in educational level, just seemed too big a chasm to make love work. Faye had decided to settle for true, pure friendship.

Still, it wasn't smart to look at Joe too closely.

She did it anyway. Just this once.

His cotton shirt hung nicely over massive shoulders. Its casual drape highlighted his trim waist. Joe did not require buckskin trousers to look good in his clothes. Why did she find his new look unsettling?

A Choctaw woman passed them on the sidewalk. She stood out in the crowd, and Faye realized for the first time that nearly everyone around her was white. Ordinarily, long experience would have prompted her to take a racial headcount, a habit she thought was probably second-nature for anyone born non-white in America. Having spent the morning surrounded by Joe and Oka Hofobi and Toneisha, she'd let her defenses fall, and it had felt good.

Joe's flustered glance flicked from the Choctaw woman's face to the back of his right hand. The gimme cap hid his hair, except for the long ponytail down his back, but Faye knew its color, and the woman's hair lacked the chestnut highlights that kept Joe's hair from being completely black. His skin, with its unmistakable bronze tint, was still several shades lighter than hers, but Joe's eyes betrayed him most. They were a clear sea-green. Thrown into contact with people whose Native American blood had flowed unadulterated since before Columbus threw their world into a tailspin, Joe could no longer deny his murky racial status.

The world seemed less safe when Joe, the most centered individual she'd ever met, didn't know who he was. Faye was shaken, but she slipped an arm around his waist and guided him through the crowd, saying only, "Nice shirt."

As Faye and Joe straggled behind, she watched their colleagues break up into companionable pairs. Oka Hofobi and Dr. Mailer looked to be deep in some kind of scholarly conversation. Bodie and Toneisha, like most 23-year-olds, were as high-spirited and gangly as yearling colts. By now, they were far ahead of their older friends, hurrying from one novel sight to the next. Chuck, too, was drawing away from his slower-moving colleagues with his long, economical stride. As far as Faye could tell, he had been successful at avoiding eye contact with anyone in the teeming crowd.

Dr. Mailer, on the other hand, was making good on his plan to charm the natives. He nodded at anyone he could get to look at him. His manner was naturally so appealing that a couple of people stopped in their tracks to shake hands and introduce themselves, but he was oblivious to the miniature dramas staging themselves just a few feet away. Oka Hofobi, a lifelong resident who by rights should have found many acquaintances to greet, walked quietly with his head slightly bowed. Twice, Faye saw him crowded and jostled by people she thought she recognized from the confrontation at Mr. Calhoun's mound.

It occurred to her that the rest of them could pack up and go home when their summer's work was done, but Oka Hofobi would have to live here, among farmers who saw his work as a threat to their way of life. While she was pondering that uncomfortable possibility, she saw the young Choctaw take a staggering step to the right as he was jostled again, hard.

This had to stop.

A distinctive figure appeared in the distance, walking toward them. Unless Faye missed her guess, it was Davis, and she was glad. He must have seen Oka Hofobi's discomfort. Older brothers weren't known for tolerating mistreatment of their younger siblings, even when those siblings were past thirty.

Davis wore the traditional Choctaw broad-brimmed black hat with a beaded band, and so did the shorter man walking next to him. As they passed Oka Hofobi, the two men kept their eyes straight ahead, never acknowledging Davis' own brother. If Faye wasn't mistaken, the shorter man spit on the ground as they walked past.

She looked up at Joe, who said, "He's okay, but I'm watching. I can get to him if he needs me, but I think he'd rather deal with this his own self."

Oka Hofobi turned his head toward Davis and spoke a couple of words, but he kept moving. There would be no confrontation this morning.

The two men didn't pause when they brushed past Faye and Joe, either. As they passed, Faye was almost sure she heard Davis say, "Graverobbers." Then, as if he wanted to show off for someone he looked up to, the shorter man echoed him. As if afraid they hadn't heard him, he raised his voice a little more and said, "Ghouls." Then the two men were gone.

So the farmers saw Oka Hofobi as a threat to their property rights and the Choctaws—or two of them, at least—saw him as someone who'd be willing to desecrate their ancestors' bones.

Poor guy. He was taking grief from everybody.

The Pavilion was crowded with people waiting for a look at one of Neshoba County's most famous natives. Never mind that he hadn't set foot in the county—no, in the state—since he graduated from high school forty years before. When a local boy does good, people like to bask in the reflected glory.

After a fawning and flowery introduction, Lawrence Johnson Judd, former U.S. Representative from the state of Michigan and high-ranking official in the Democratic Party, rose to address the excited crowd.

"My friends," he began, "when you reach my advanced age, you develop mental clarity. Or," he said as he chuckled and shook his head, "you try to do so."

He pulled a pen out of his breast pocket and fumbled with it to avoid looking at his audience. Its gleaming gold metal contrasted with the cocoa-dark skin of his hands. Faye was intrigued. This was not the mannerism of a man who had spent his life in politics. It was as if coming home had transported him back in time and returned a shy boy to life.

"I guess I'll come out and say this: I'm not here to talk politics. I'm more than sixty years old, and I'm looking old age in the face. My blood pressure and my cholesterol are high and heading higher, and I'm going gray. It is time to exorcise my past. When I was nineteen years old, I nearly died. Because I was a black man."

It was as if everyone seated in the Pavilion expelled their breath simultaneously, stirring a breeze that had been absent from this sweltering day. Faye heard more than one person whisper, "Not again."

"I was kidnapped from my own front yard by a man who threw a hood over my head and held a knife to my throat. He drove me so far into the woods that I thought my corpse might never be found. I was tied to a tree. Beaten. As the blows fell, I did my damndest to figure out what I'd done. Had I been so intoxicated by the speed of my souped-up car that I passed a white man who was driving a little too slow? Had I said hello to a white girl with the wrong light in my eye? I could hear my daddy's voice telling me I needed to get right with God, just like he did every Sunday from the pulpit, God rest his soul, but I couldn't concentrate on my salvation. I just desperately wanted to know what I'd done to earn an early death."

Faye looked around and was gratified to see tears on cheeks of every color. Sheriff Rutland had clapped her hands over her father's ears, as if he were a child who shouldn't hear such things.

The man sitting beside her grasped the wheelchair's handles to help her, and the crowd parted to let the three of them escape. Faye's heart went out to the young sheriff. She had shown such courage in the face of yesterday's racial conflict. Somebody had taught her right from wrong, and Neely's solicitude toward her father made Faye think it had been him. He deserved peace in his declining years.

"As the violence escalated," Judd continued, "I heard footsteps approaching, fast and hard. If it was a lynching party, I dearly hoped they would do their work quickly. Then the voice of my rescuer rose up like the terrible and beautiful voice of Jehovah, and he shouted, 'Are you out of your mind? Stop that right now!'" Faye could hear the ministerial tones of the Congressman's father echoing in the man's words. "As the two men struggled, like Jacob and the mighty angel who gave him a new name and a new life, I took the opportunity to yank myself free."

Standing in silence before a crowd listening rapt to his story, he raised an arm clad in an impeccably tailored shirt and rolled back the cuff to display the scars where he had flayed his own skin with the confining ropes. "I ran away, still ripping at the hood tied to my head, running headlong into trees, just getting away any way I could. I didn't get a look at my attacker or my rescuer. I hid in a cave for a night and a day, like a beaten animal afraid to raise its head. There was a spring in the cave and I might have stayed there a week before I got hungry enough to crawl out into the light, but something in my gut told me it was time to be a man again. I found my way out of the woods and to my Mama. She gave me all the money she had, enough to get me on a bus to Detroit. I haven't been home since."

He rolled down his sleeve and fastened the cufflink. "Here's what I know. My attacker took me far into the country, down miles of dirt road. Then he walked me deep into the woods. My savior came from even deeper in the woods, in the opposite direction from the way we came. I have no idea how he knew what was going on. There was a creek nearby, and a cave. I never knew about any caves around here, except for the one in the mound by Nanih Waiya Creek, and this wasn't it. Maybe somebody here knows where it is. Maybe they know who tried to kill me and why. Or maybe they can find out. And, while they're at it, I hope they find out who saved me, so I can thank him."

He spread his hands and shrugged. "Or maybe they're both dead. Even so, two people besides me knew what happened that day. I cannot believe that neither of them ever opened their mouths. Or that nobody ever noticed two white men coming home beaten and bloody on April 3, 1965. My guess is that they are both at least in their sixties. I've spent my career seeking justice for others. Help me find it for myself."

Out of the corner of her eye, Faye saw Carroll Calhoun and his cronies step out of the thunderstruck crowd and disappear into the distance.

Chapter Six

The house party was still rocking when Faye and Joe dragged themselves out of the crowd fighting to shake Congressman Judd's hand. The partygoers who had taken time from their drinking to go hear his speech were readily identifiable. Their faces were blank with shell shock, which is quite a different look from simple intoxication.

Sheriff Rutland emerged from a bedroom, backing through the door and hauling her father's wheelchair over a high threshold. Parking him next to a bright window right beside Faye and Joe, she sank into an armchair vacated by a woman smart enough to recognize total fatigue when she saw it. Neely turned her face to the window long enough to rake the heel of her hand across her eyes and Faye looked away. It wasn't seemly to watch a sheriff cry.

"The man that did the beating would have to be someone at least as old as Mr. Judd," said a man in a Molly Hatchet tee-shirt. "Late fifties at the youngest."

Several people nodded. An underage boy holding a root beer said, "He could be a lot older, too. Could've been middle-aged at the time. Older, even."

"Judd himself already said it," said a woman with bottle-blonde curls. "The man who beat him could be dead. Probably *is* dead."

"Well, if he's not, let's put him up for a medal." The barest quaver in his voice gave a hint of the speaker's age. It was Calhoun's friend, the one whose lizard eyes gave Faye the willies.

A queasy silence fell. Most everyone in the room developed a consuming interest in their toes, but Faye kept her eyes focused on their faces. They didn't all agree with this man's racist poison. She knew it. All the way back from the Pavilion, they had talked about Judd's ordeal and she'd heard the revulsion in their voices. How did this dried-up little old man turn them into cowards?

"Preston Silver…" began the least lily-livered man in the room, but a quick glance silenced him. Faye watched Silver's lizard eyes rake the room, lingering on her own dark face longer than she liked.

Sheriff Rutland, the only person in the room that Faye was sure had the gumption to stand up to him, hid her face by bending over the bag hanging on the back of her father's wheelchair. Pulling out a spoon and a jar of puréed peas, she asserted her authority only far enough to say, "Stop stirring things up, Preston. It's not constructive." She opened the baby food jar. Faye was close enough to smell the sick-sweet, green odor of the peas.

Watching Neely's father's visible enjoyment of his jar of green paste and noticing a bulge in his trousers in the shape of an adult diaper, Faye was inclined to forgive the woman for her temporary cowardice. She wasn't clear how far she herself wanted to go in stirring up a confrontation, but it wasn't in Faye's nature to slink away and let a bigot dominate an important conversation.

"Speaking of medals," she piped up, "I hear that Congressman Judd's up for the Congressional Medal of Freedom—the highest honor our country can give a civilian. If his speech today doesn't make the national news, you know it will if that medal comes through. It will look a lot better for Neshoba County if Judd's attacker is behind bars, and you're throwing a parade for the man who rescued him."

Silver's gaze swiveled her way, then everybody else in the room lifted their eyes from their toes and focused them on her. Dr. Mailer had brought the team to the Fair to get acquainted with the locals. Well, she may not have strictly made their acquaintance, but she surely had their attention.

Thinking of Dr. Mailer, she realized that she'd barely seen him since they'd arrived at the Pavilion. Oka Hofobi, Toneisha, Chuck, and Bodie—they'd all faded away after Judd's speech. She and Joe should probably ease out of this party, too, but she couldn't bring herself to slink away and let Silver think he'd intimidated her. She decided to have one more beer and leave when it was empty. Joe, who knew her well, leaned far to the left and accessed the nearest cooler with his long, rangy arm. He grabbed the can on top, without checking to see whether it was the tastiest cheap brand, and opened it for her. Faye drank slowly, trying to calculate how long she should make her twelve-fluid-ounce stalling tactic last.

Silver rose from his chair with a grunt and disappeared into the kitchen. Calhoun and their friends followed him. Faye took a long sip.

The blonde woman handed Faye a bag of chips. "I didn't know that Congressman Judd was up for the Medal of Freedom. That is so cool. And he's from right here in Neshoba County."

"Too bad we didn't treat him better when we had him," said the Molly Hatchet fan, passing Faye the French onion dip. "I'm Todd and this is my wife, Jennifer." He gestured to the blonde. "What's your name, anyway? You're not from around here, are you?"

"I'm Faye and this is my friend, Joe. We're with the archaeological team working out at the Nail place."

"You folks ran into a little trouble yesterday, didn't you?" Jennifer said. "Is everybody okay?"

"Everybody's fine," Sheriff Rutland said, still spooning mashed peas. "I gotta say that I never thought a bunch of scholars would have such guts. You two in particular. I believe you could chew the heads off nails."

"Faye eats nails for breakfast." Joe popped open a beer of his own.

"That's how I get my minimum daily requirement of iron." Faye quaffed about half the beer. She was gratified to hear laughter come from all corners of the room. If Silver felt like lynching her, he wouldn't be able to count on these people to help him.

Faye leaned close to Neely's ear, so that she couldn't be heard by Calhoun in the next room. Or by any spies remaining behind. "You know, Sheriff, Mr. Calhoun's mound is really important. I spent just a minute on top of it yesterday, and I got a new perspective on the lay of the land all around it."

"I know what you mean. I spent last night up there, you know."

"I do know, and I want to shake your hand for what you did yesterday." Neely stuck out a hand and Faye pumped it once. "As I was saying, you get a good feel for the topography of the land when you're standing up on that mound, and I saw some decent evidence that Calhoun's mound is both bigger and more important than it looks at first sight."

"What does your professor think about that?"

"I didn't get a chance to tell him yet. But he'll agree. So do you think you can get me permission just to go up there once? All I'll do is stand still and look around. Truly."

"No way." The authority of an enforcer of the law had crept back into Neely's tired voice.

"Mr. Calhoun's got a right to be mad, but he knows you, and—"

"To hell with Carroll Calhoun. I don't care about his property rights. I don't care about your historical preservation. I just care about keeping the peace. Neshoba County is chock-full of good people, and they come in all colors, but there are a few Neanderthals who would shoot you right off the top of that mound. Nobody goes up there but me."

An odor like incense wafted out of the kitchen, along with laughter and the voices of a covey of old men. Could they possibly be smoking pot in there? With the sheriff in the next room?

The cabin's windows were open. They looked out on another cabin so close that Faye could have reached out her window and snagged a piece of coconut cake off the kitchen table. Smoking pot in such close quarters was nuts.

Everybody got interested in their toes again. Faye couldn't get a good look at Neely's face. After a few minutes, the sheriff closed the empty jar and wiped off the spoon. Sliding them into the bag, she pulled out a wet wipe and cleaned her father's mouth. "There, Daddy. Did that taste good?" She wheeled the old man's wheelchair out into the night.

Fragrant smoke continued to fill the room.

It was dark and she couldn't see his face, but Faye could tell that Joe was perturbed. His disapproval filled the still evening air.

What made him so special that nobody else could play his little lookout game with him? Anyone with eyes could see that Neely Rutland would not be spending tonight perched atop Calhoun's mound. Nobody was superhuman, though Neely would like to be. She was probably even now lying face-down and dreamless on a cot at the Neshoba County Fairgrounds.

While Neely's deputies would surely be arriving any minute now for another night's watch, there could be no substitute for having a sentry on the high ground. Yet she had plainly said that nobody would be climbing the mound but her. Her deputies would need help. Joe was more than happy to provide it, but he had proved notably resistant to the idea that Faye might be able to help. Too bad. She was crouched beside him beneath a tree made invisible by the moonless night. He'd just have to learn to live with it.

Her supper roiled in her stomach. The plateful of roast beef, gravy, rice, macaroni salad, and green beans, while undeniably delicious, was not sitting well atop the afternoon's beers. Or the afternoon's interpersonal nastiness. She and Joe had escaped the Fair as quickly as they could manage it, without showing weakness in the face of Silver and his cronies.

Stopping at a diner where they could linger over tasty food loaded with grease and salt had seemed comforting at the time. For dessert, she and Joe had enjoyed a tremendous argument over whether he needed her to help him in his self-appointed role of Chief Mound Protector. She had won, since Joe wasn't in the habit of telling her No, so now she sat beside him, suffering from indigestion and his festering disapproval.

A tremendous grind and roar split the night. Beams from twin headlights jiggled frantically as the tractor behind them raced across the uneven terrain between Calhoun's house and the mound.

"He's doing it again," Faye said out loud, knowing that Calhoun wouldn't hear her over the tractor's din. "He's stoned, and he knows Neely's half-dead with fatigue, and he thinks he can get away with it." She yanked her phone out of her pocket and dialed 911. "We've got an emergency. I don't know the address, but we're in a field right across the road from the Nail house. We're on Carroll Calhoun's land. He's, um...he's threatening people with his tractor." That seemed close enough to the truth, and it should bring a prompt response. She listened a moment. "Yeah, you can send an ambulance, just in case, but what we really need are some armed deputies. And Sheriff Rutland."

The tractor's gears shrieked, and it took an abrupt right turn. When Faye saw where it was now headed, she hurled the phone to the ground and started running. She needed to stop this.

How could she stop it? The destructive edge of the tractor's blade was headed for the faint remnant of one of the berms she thought she'd seen from atop the mound. A wing. He was going to scrape up one of the eagle's wings.

Faye put her head down and ran harder. She could hear Joe behind her, but now, just this once, she might be able to outrun him, because she was on the side of the angels. Come hell or high water, she was going to save this magnificent bird built out of earth. Presuming it was really there. But how would she ever know if this man destroyed it before she got a chance to see?

"Faye, it's not worth getting killed over." Joe's voice came closer. "He's mad, and he's high. He might be sorry later, but you'd still be dead." She kept running. When she felt Joe's arms wrap around her chest and slam her to the ground, she was mightily perturbed that he could overtake her and tackle her, with enough wind left over to talk to her while he was doing it.

The tractor ground to a halt a few feet from the mound's wing, and Faye was jubilant. He'd seen them and he didn't want witnesses to the destruction. Then the headlights swung around and the beast started rolling in their direction.

"Get up, get up, get off me!" she chanted, shoving at Joe. "He's coming this way."

The tractor was moving at four times the speed Calhoun had used to intimidate the archaeologists only a day before. This was not simple intimidation. He was announcing his intention to roll right over them.

Jumping up in one motion, Joe grabbed Faye by the hand and yanked her onto her feet. By stumbling and sliding and taking impossibly long strides, she managed to keep up with him, but where would they go? Oka Hofobi's house lay across the road, hidden in the dark. Its cozy safety beckoned her, but Joe had other ideas. A dense forest was his notion of safety, not a homey brick house. If she could have gotten a breath, she would have reminded him that Calhoun's tractor could eat trees for breakfast, but Joe was in no state to listen to reason. They plunged into a forest so dense and dark that only Joe's sharp eyes kept them from slamming headfirst into a waiting tree.

A tree crashed to the ground behind them. Still, Faye was beginning to feel some hope. They were moving a lot faster than the tractor now, since it took a considerable amount of time for Calhoun to pause and batter down the trees in his way.

Joe kept dragging her deeper into a sheltering thicket that she couldn't see. When he stopped, she crashed hard into his back. Only then did she realize why their flight had ended so abruptly. The tractor had stopped moving.

A flashlight beam wavered in the air, swinging back and forth in a search pattern that said Calhoun didn't know where they were. Joe firmly pushed her behind a tree, but he did it slowly, so that she wouldn't put a foot down on a twig and give them away with a dry, wooden snap. Then he vanished behind a tree located precisely between her and danger, because that was simply who he was.

Don't breathe so hard, she told herself, as if she believed that her mind could control her body's autonomic nervous system. When her breathing quieted, she wondered what other powers her mind possessed that she didn't know about.

Her vision and hearing and sense of smell sharpened in response to danger, obeying prehistoric instructions buried in her DNA. Things that she would never ordinarily have noticed assaulted her now, sometimes painfully. This must be how Joe, with his woodsman's gifts, felt all the time.

She could hear the creak of the fabric in Calhoun's pants every time he bent a knee and took a step. She couldn't smell him—only Joe had senses that refined—but she could smell something acrid. What was it?

Smoke. It was smoke. Was she smelling the remnants of the pot that Calhoun had been enjoying a few hours before, still clinging to his clothes? No, it was simple wood smoke.

Calhoun's boots continued to crunch through the underbrush.

How long he looked for them Faye couldn't say, though she did know that the flashlight's beam played more than once over the bark of the tree that hid her. Only the sound of sirens in the distance saved them. Calhoun fled deeper into the woods.

Minutes passed while they listened to their rescuers' sirens approach. When Calhoun was out of earshot, Faye risked a peek behind her. Much deeper into the woods was a prickle of orange light so faint that she would never have seen it without her adrenaline-enhanced vision.

Faye and Joe knew the law had arrived when the sirens stopped growing closer. So far from the road that they couldn't even see the law officer's flashing lights, Faye and Joe let the screaming sirens atop the now-stationary cars lead them to their rescuers. When they emerged from their hiding place, they found only an empty house, an idling tractor, and a silent pickup truck.

One officer stated the obvious. "He's on foot."

Oka Hofobi, Davis, and their father rushed up, hauling hunting rifles. "We heard the racket," Oka Hofobi started, but he was interrupted by a six-and-a-half-foot-tall deputy who said only, "We've got no need for armed civilians." The three Choctaws hung their rifles on their pickup's gun rack, but they didn't leave until they were told to go.

"Sheriff Rutland—" Faye wheezed, surprised to feel her breath leave her again.

"She's on her way."

Neely Rutland would probably be gratified to know how safe that made Faye feel. She made a mental note to tell her.

"Look, there may be someone else out here tonight," she told the big deputy who seemed to be in charge. "I saw a campfire way out in the woods."

"Can you get us there?"

Faye looked up at the stars as if they could give her directional guidance, but in the end, she would have had to say "No," if Joe hadn't interrupted.

"I can take you."

Well, of course he could. Joe could probably tell them what kind of wood had been used to build the campfire, just by the smell. Or by the color of the glowing embers.

Faye realized how hard she and Joe had run during their escape when she saw how long it took to reach the campfire. They found its dying embers at the edge of a sizeable clearing planted in rows of lush, healthy marijuana plants.

The man who had built the fire was no longer seated on the well-worn stump beside it. He was sprawled on the ground nearby. Faye recognized him, even with his face half-obscured by blood, by his clothes and his size and his iron-gray hair. The ragged wound across his neck and the blood soaking into the ground around his head told Faye everything she needed to know about what had happened here. His throat had been slit, and the implement lying on the ground beside him was surely sharp enough to do it. The sleek stone knife looked like it would do a very efficient job of cutting a man's trachea open. Its single cutting edge was bloody.

The tall deputy nodded to the other lawman, before whipping out his radio to alert Sheriff Rutland. The smaller deputy started resuscitation, but Carroll Calhoun was surely dead.

Faye tried to make sense of the crime scene. Had Mr. Calhoun built the fire, then left it long enough to chase her and Joe with a tractor? Had someone been waiting for him when he returned? Or was this someone else's campfire? Had he surprised someone who killed him rather than let him report the illegal crop?

One thing was certain. His killer hadn't had much time to flee. As if reading her mind, the tall deputy and his colleague began a routine search pattern, shining bright lights at their feet to illuminate any tracks the killer had left.

Who wanted Calhoun dead? Well, maybe Faye had, a little bit, if she were to be perfectly honest. And the rest of the archaeological team. And the entire Mississippi Band of Choctaw Indians. The man hadn't done much to attract friends lately.

She wondered if she would be considered a suspect in the killing. Sheriff Rutland would be a fool if she didn't investigate a woman who was nearby when the crime occurred. Especially one who'd had two, maybe three run-ins with the victim. Faye wasn't overly concerned. She had the utmost respect for the truth, and the truth was that she'd had nothing to do with Calhoun's death.

She could handle being under suspicion. She was innocent and she believed in the integrity of the law. Still, there was one thing that bothered her. No one other than Faye and Joe and Sheriff Mike McKenzie, back home in Florida, knew that Joe had once killed a man with a stone implement, but if she ever breathed a word of that truth to anyone, Joe would be in serious trouble now.

Sweet Jesus. Joe probably had his pockets full, right this minute, of deadly sharpened rocks that he'd made himself. Flintknapping was simply what he did, and he carried his treasures with him everywhere. If he were searched, then Joe would be headed for questions and accusations and maybe even jail. If he escaped arrest tonight, but Sheriff Rutland learned later about his special skills, he would again be in jeopardy.

She was Joe's alibi for this killing, just as he was hers. If she were sheriff, she wouldn't believe either of them, not for a minute. Faye knew she could take care of herself. If it came down to it, she could hire a lawyer who would help her say the right things to law enforcement and in court. Joe, on the other hand, didn't know how to tell anything but the truth. A crafty prosecutor could trick him into hanging himself.

Faye would be damned before she'd let that happen.

Chapter Seven

Sheriff Rutland marshaled her resources with aplomb. Neshoba County couldn't have much more than a dozen sworn officers but, in Faye's inexpert opinion, Neely Rutland knew how to make good use of what she had. She had quickly found a well-traveled dirt track through the woods that was just barely wide enough for the SUV carrying the county's spanking-new mobile crime lab, then she'd told an investigator to note the track's presence in the site sketch. Perhaps Calhoun had used it to bring in a tractor to cultivate the field of contraband where he was found dead.

Armed with powerful lights, Neely had searched for footprints herself along the track before allowing the mobile lab's tires to obliterate any evidence. No prints were found, but Joe wasn't surprised.

"Mr. Calhoun wouldn't have wanted people to see him walking out to his own private field of pot. That wide-open trail is almost as big as a road. I bet he only used it when he had to move something big, and I bet he didn't do that any more than he had to."

Joe's theory sounded good to Faye, but it led naturally to a disappointing situation. The rest of the wooded area was heavily carpeted with leaves and pine straw. Maybe, if Neely and her staff were damn good, they could find where the killer had walked, but they'd have to be damn lucky to find a spot of bare ground big enough to retain any prints. Then, they'd have to distinguish those prints from the ones Faye and Joe and the deputies had left on their way to discovering the murder site. Not to mention the ones Calhoun left while he was hunting Faye and Joe. Plus the ones he'd made on his last trip out to the marijuana field where he'd died.

Faye and Joe sat together in matching lawn chairs that had been thoughtfully provided by the Neshoba County Sheriff's Department. There had been a nervous heartbeat's worth of hesitation on Neely's face while she decided what to do with the two of them. They were witnesses, and she might need them. They were also potential sources of contamination that she didn't dare allow near her crime scene. And her crime scene had no obvious boundaries. It could theoretically extend all the way to town and beyond, getting bigger every second that the killer was able to flee.

Even worse, the moonless night was surely obscuring critical clues. Neely was working against time. While she waited for the sun to rise, blood was soaking into the soil and drying. Footprints were being obscured by falling leaves and by the feet of nocturnal animals. The killer was receding into the darkness, footfall by footfall, until reaching a car that could travel hundreds of miles before dawn.

Instead of drawing lines around her crime scene prematurely, Neely had taken a logical approach to dealing with Faye and Joe. She'd had a technician thoroughly search a few square yards of ground for footprints and blood spatters and fibers and other stuff Faye couldn't even imagine. Then, having found nothing, the technician had strung crime scene tape around the area and plunked two lawn chairs inside for the comfort of their star witnesses.

At least they were calling them witnesses and not suspects. Faye was working hard at looking relaxed and…well, innocent. Because if somebody got the bright idea of searching Joe, the walking arsenal of stone weapons, then they were in serious trouble. Fortunately, Joe was so good-hearted that he didn't even know how to look guilty.

Neither do sociopaths, said the pitiless and logical voice inside Faye's head.

It was intellectually interesting to watch a crime scene investigation up close. The body was lit by floodlights, and a photographer was recording its condition and its surroundings. A technician searched the soil around the body, while Neely and the rest of her staff took their systematic search of the surrounding woods farther away every minute. Fatigue and disappointment were apparent in the technician's voice when he said, "The bastard swept his prints away. The brushmarks are obvious."

Then he looked at Faye and Joe, and her mouth went dry. Approaching the yellow tape that enclosed them, he said, "We'll want casts of both your prints."

Faye wanted to ask why, but figured that the question would make her sound guilty. She hoped Joe didn't ask it. Fortunately, the technician delivered the answer without hearing the question.

"If we find he missed brushing away any prints here in the clearing—or if we find any in the woods, which I guess is a long shot—then we'll need to make sure they don't belong to people that we know were here."

So they both dutifully stepped in some soft soil and waited for the tech to place a form around each of their prints. Watching him mix something gloppy in a plastic bag, Faye had asked, "Plaster of Paris?" only to see him shake his head.

"Dental stone works better."

They went back to watching the photographer work, which was only slightly more interesting than watching dental stone dry.

A flashlight beam emerged from the dark woods. Its light played briefly across Faye's eyes, waking her from a vivid dream. She had slept, her torso leaning awkwardly against the plastic arm of the lawn chair. Joe, whose uncanny control of his physical body seemed to include the ability to be awake or asleep at will, sat alert and relaxed beside her.

Reality was echoing Faye's dream. She had seen herself sitting in the spot where Calhoun now lay dead, but she hadn't been in utter darkness. The clearing had been lit by a roaring fire, as it was now being lit by the first light of dawn. In the dream, a flashlight beam just like this one had emerged from the trees surrounding the small patch of light. Such a beam must have been one of the last things Calhoun had seen, only there had been a killer holding that flashlight. Empathy for the dead man shivered through her.

Neely flipped off the light in her hand and let it drop to her side. She didn't look like a woman who had successfully tracked down a killer, so Faye knew that the night-long search had been unsuccessful.

"Maybe the forensics folks will turn up something useful." She smoothed back the frizzy brown hair that had escaped from her ponytail and looked at Faye and Joe. "Tell me again what you saw last night. And I swear I've forgotten why you said you were out here in the first place."

"We were planning to sit out here and watch the mound, like you did the night before. We didn't know whether you were planning to do that again—"

"Actually, I was. I just hadn't gotten out here yet. It looks like I would have found Calhoun tearing the thing down when I did eventually arrive."

"Yep," Joe said, with his usual economy of words.

"Why, exactly, did you decide it was your job to help me do *my* job?"

Joe's answer was as quick as it was politically incorrect. "I don't like to see a lady be a target."

Faye cringed at Joe's suggestion that the sheriff might be a damsel in need of protection.

"I wasn't out here alone, you know. I had backup. And I would have had backup when I got here last night, too."

"Sure. I just figured there wasn't any harm in having one more person keeping an eye out for you. I was out here the first night you were standing guard, too."

"I know. I saw you."

Faye had seen Joe stalk a flock of wild turkeys without catching their attention. Her admiration for Neely Rutland jumped up another notch. Admiration for the woman aside, she needed to derail this conversation. Her next obvious question for Joe would be, "Were you armed?" and Joe couldn't afford to answer it. Not with his pockets full of stone weapons.

Faye had always had the scientist's love-hate relationship with intuition. She didn't trust a conclusion that couldn't be proved through step-by-step logic, yet she knew that she had been led to that critical first step through flashes of insight. Now, standing half-asleep in the rosy light of dawn, she knew instinctively what she needed to do.

She needed to help Neely find the real killer, whether the sheriff wanted her help or not. She had done it before when she helped Fire Marshal Adam Strahan find the arsonist who killed her friend Carmen, but this time the stakes were higher. The sooner Neely found out who killed Calhoun, the less time she would have to realize that Joe made an exceptionally fine suspect.

What expertise could she offer that would speed this investigation along? It occurred to her that she knew a lot more about stone tools than any run-of-the-mill crime lab employee would.

"Your lab probably hasn't dealt with stone weapons all that much," she blurted out, thinking as she talked. "It seems like it'd be important to know whether the murder weapon was ancient, or whether it was recently made."

"I didn't think you could get that information out of a chunk of rock. I thought you could only use carbon-dating on something that has been alive—like wood or bone."

Nobody ever said the sheriff was dumb.

"That's true, but there are other ways to date artifacts," Faye said. "If I had a stone tool that I suspected was prehistoric, the first thing I'd do is look for some evidence of use-wear, so I could see if it matched known prehistoric uses. Use-wear specialists can tell whether a tool has been attached to a haft so it could be used as a knife. They can tell by impact fractures whether it was attached to an arrow and shot with a bow. They can tell if the edge has been reshaped because it got dull. Most of that stuff you have to measure in a lab, because it's microscopic. But some of it you can see with the naked eye. Sickle sheen is one of those things."

"I can't let you do any of those things with my evidence right now, but I'm listening. What's 'sickle sheen'?"

"The edge of a tool that was used to cut grassy plants—which would include early domesticated crops—looks almost like it's been polished. The silica in the plants is abrasive and, over time, it polishes the tool's edge into a sheen that's easy to see, when you know what to look for. Why don't you stop by our work site tomorrow? We can talk about use-wear, and I can show you what sickle sheen looks like. I can show you some tools without any sheen at all, too, just for comparison. If the murder weapon has sickle sheen, then it's pretty safe to say that the killer found an old tool and used it."

"Which will tell us just about nothing. There's hardly a house around here without an arrowhead collection."

"Some information is better than none," Faye pointed out.

Neely nodded to concede her point. "I'll stop by the site, but it might not be tomorrow. I need to walk these woods in the daylight and see if any important clues were hiding in the dark. I don't see that a little bit of sickle sheen will help me find a killer, but information is always a good thing."

"You can have any information that Joe and I have got. But do you need us any more? We might be able to get a little sleep before work if we head back to the hotel right now."

Neely dismissed them with a nod, and told them that the technician who'd taken the footprint impressions would show them back to their car. Faye walked directly in his footsteps, to avoid introducing still more prints to Neely's list of problems. She walked casually, trying to look like an innocent woman who was in no hurry to get out of the sheriff's sight. She willed Joe to do the same, though her biggest concern was that no one should hear the stone weapons in his pockets clicking together as he walked.

Faye went directly from the murder scene to the work trailer parked beside the Nails' house. She wanted to separate Joe from any incriminating evidence and she wanted to do it immediately.

Unlocking the trailer door, she flipped on the air conditioner. The resulting blast stirred the dust coating every horizontal surface in the archaeologists' workspace. Well, except for Chuck's work table. Faye knew from personal observation that he wiped it down six times a day.

"Empty your pockets."

Joe did as he was told. When he was finished, a fearsome collection of multicolored stone was arrayed on the table. A palm-sized spear point that looked like it was from the Middle Woodland period, except Joe had made it himself. Two tiny projectile points. A single-edged tool uncomfortably like the one that had sliced Calhoun's neck. A sharpened piece of deer antler. An unchipped piece of rock that was probably destined to become something deadly.

Faye couldn't decide whether Joe was the least dangerous man on Earth or the most dangerous man on Earth.

"We need to hide these things in plain sight," she said. "If Sheriff Rutland asks to see them, we'll show them to her, but we don't want to call her attention to your special skills."

"Why would she...you don't think she thinks I killed Mr. Calhoun, do you, Faye?"

"I don't know what she thinks, but you and I both know you've got the skills." She swiped her hand across the table, raking Joe's treasures into an empty storage box, then she set it on a shelf alongside dozens of identical boxes. After labeling the box and writing the identifying number in her field notebook, she tossed the notebook into a desk drawer and said. "Remember, Joe. Leave the deadly weapons at work."

Joe looked bereft.

"Okay, how's this: Leave the deadly weapons at work, for the time being."

"I'm not the only one that carries this stuff around."

Faye scanned the surface of Chuck's work table, which was covered with neat piles of ancient weapons and the razor-sharp flakes that were the by-product of their manufacture. If she had to pick the most dangerous person she'd met in Neshoba County, she'd have to name Chuck. He was the kind of scientist who chose to study inanimate objects precisely because they weren't people. She didn't think Chuck liked people and their inexplicable ways all that much. She wondered where he'd been when Calhoun was killed.

Picturing the detachment in Chuck's eyes, she remembered someone else whose glance had chilled her. Preston Silver. He knew Calhoun, to be sure, but Faye had the feeling that a man with those eyes wouldn't hesitate to kill someone who crossed him.

The Gift of Kowi Anukasha

As told by Mrs. Frances Nail

To us Choctaws, the Mississippi forests are alive with magical beings. We know of shapechanging spirits who can read men's thoughts. Some of us have heard the womanish cry of Kashehotapalo, half-deer and half-man. If you should ever hear him, remember this: Kashehotapalo will not hurt you, but he delights in the frightening power of his own voice.

Kowi Anukasha, an old, old spirit with the tiny body of a child, can give the greatest gift—the gift of choice. He watches for lost children, stealing them away to his own house where three ancient spirits wait with gifts.

The first spirit always offers the child a knife. If he takes it, he will grow into a bad man. Perhaps he will even kill his friends.

The second spirit extends a handful of herbs. This looks like a good gift to most folks, because everybody knows that herbs can heal. But it is dangerous to forget that herbs can also kill. Most times, the child reaches out a hand and takes the poisonous herbs, forever losing the power to help or heal others.

The third spirit holds out healing herbs, and the child who waits for this good gift will become a great doctor, trusted by his entire tribe.

Wise Choctaws know that few children have the wisdom to wait for a good gift, so few will grow into the leaders their people need. But Kowi Anukasha will always be looking for wisdom and patience, so that he can reward them with knowledge.

This is true.

Chapter Eight

Sunday
Day 3 of the Neshoba County Fair

It had seemed so reasonable when she agreed to work on a Sunday. Faye's workweek had begun late on Thursday afternoon. She and her colleagues had lost half of Friday to their confrontation with Mr. Calhoun. They'd happily accepted Dr. Mailer's offer to let them frolic at the Fair on company time. Ordinarily, Faye would feel fresh as a daisy after such light service. Of course, she'd been willing to pay her boss back by working today.

But that was before she'd been chased by a tractor, and it was before she stumbled onto a brutally murdered man. It was before she'd sat up all night, wondering whether she and Joe were prime suspects. Faye didn't want to work today. She wanted to sleep like she'd been drugged.

As she brushed her teeth over the bathroom sink, elbow-to-elbow with Toneisha, a knock sounded at their door. Sheriff Rutland was standing there, looking far less bleary-eyed and rumpled than Faye felt after only an hour of sleep.

"Since the murder occurred right across the street from you archaeologists' work site, and since there was no love lost between you people and the murder victim, I'm trying to establish alibis. Just to be complete. I know where you were, Faye. Why don't you have some breakfast downstairs while I talk to your roommate?"

Faye found her colleagues downstairs eating sweet rolls and comparing notes. The sheriff had already questioned them all, and she'd found that their alibis were uniformly frail. Mailer was alone in his hotel room. So was Chuck. Oka Hofobi was home with his parents, which wasn't actually much of an alibi, since the odds that his parents would allow him to remain alibi-free were nil. Toneisha and Bodie had been drinking in the room Bodie shared with Joe.

Toneisha and the sheriff entered the room. Both women stopped for a cup of coffee before settling down at the table next to Faye.

"I have never in my life heard such a flimsy set of alibis. Couldn't just one of you manage to be in a public place so that someone you never met could be a witness?" Neely asked.

"Wouldn't guilty people have great alibis, since they can plan ahead?" Bodie asked.

"Usually. Except for the stupid ones. But you people aren't stupid, so let's move on. Anybody got any ideas they want to share?"

"Did Calhoun do much damage to the mound before he died?" Chuck asked, cementing Faye's opinion of where his priorities lay.

"Not that I could tell," Neely said, "although I did have more pressing worries." Chuck didn't respond, since she didn't provide him with the information he needed. Instead, he went back to the buffet for seconds.

Dr. Mailer's cell phone trilled, and he retreated to a corner to take the call. Neely lowered her voice and continued. "I know that Chuck isn't the only person in these parts that cared more about that mound than he did about Carroll Calhoun. If any of you wants to talk to me in private about that, I'm all ears."

Dr. Mailer approached their table, handing the phone to the sheriff. As she took it, he cocked an eyebrow at his crew. "It seems that we have been summoned by the Mississippi Band of Choctaw Indians."

"What for?" Toneisha asked.

"The Tribal Council would like to hear more about Carroll Calhoun's mound. They've heard what their lawyers have to say, but their cultural committee wants to hear what we archaeologists know. And they're asking Sheriff Rutland to come, because they're exceedingly interested in her take on the law and how it pertains to that mound. I wouldn't be surprised if the Chief himself was there."

The group was quiet for a moment, remembering what they'd learned about his forty-year tenure in tribal government. During his tenure as elected Chief, the Choctaws had built casinos and resorts. They had attracted manufacturing interests that ranged from plastics to automotive components to greeting cards. They weren't just the largest employer in Neshoba County. They were among the largest employers in the state of Mississippi. Yet when the Chief entered tribal politics, a third of the homes on the reservation had been without electricity and only a tenth had indoor plumbing. It was a safe bet that they all had those things now.

"I'd like to meet the Chief," Bodie offered.

"I don't know how much 'meeting' we're going to get to do," Dr. Mailer said. "I expect they just want to pick our brains. Now why don't we go try to get a little work done?"

Faye wanted to crawl into the shady spot underneath the trailer and get a little sleep, but her pride wouldn't let her, so she just kept her eyes on her work. Sometimes she had trouble getting those eyes to focus, but she stayed upright and mostly awake.

Toneisha and Bodie, who hadn't suffered through the same difficult night as Faye and Joe, were energetic and chatty half the time. Now and then, as if they suddenly remembered that a man had been murdered not far from where they stood, they fell silent. The absence of their youthful banter only served to highlight the poignance of the silent Calhoun house across the street.

Under other circumstances, it might have been a glorious day at work. They'd found a soil stratum that was peppered with varicolored flakes of stone. It didn't take much imagination to picture long-ago flintknappers, lots of them, gathered here to make stone tools. Dr. Mailer had expected to find activity centers like this—separate areas for sleeping and toolmaking and pottery manufacture. Judging by this single snapshot in time, he just might be right. He was buzzing around, happy and nervous, rubbing his hands together like a man trying to erase his anxiety. Faye was happy for him.

Chuck, on the other hand, was absolutely getting on her nerves. He, too, could hardly be happier. They were digging up the stuff of his dreams, the physical evidence of ancient toolmakers. He had chastised everyone present at least once for violating his notion of proper field technique, and he was starting in on Oka Hofobi for the second time when the young Choctaw cracked.

"Chuck. I know what I'm doing, just as well as you do. Maybe better. Would you get out of my face?"

Then, instead of waiting for Chuck to back off, Oka Hofobi had brushed the red dust off his pants legs and stalked off to the trailer. More than an hour passed before he emerged. In the meantime, Chuck ruled over the team with obsessive care, and Dr. Mailer let him.

Oka Hofobi was taking a little too long to clean his gear and put it away for the night. Faye walked over intending to help, but when she saw his face, she realized that the man had simply wanted a little privacy. It was too late to back away gracefully, so she just said, "Did you have a hard day? I thought I was going to have a heat stroke, and I'm from Florida."

"My day started out fine, but it took a turn for the worse about lunchtime. Ma called. She and my father heard about the council meeting tonight. Word sure gets around fast in these parts, but I should be used to that by now. They want to come, and I reckon they will. The Council's not big on closed meetings."

"You're worried about what your parents will say?"

"No. They probably won't talk at all. They'll probably just...*sit* there."

Faye hefted a box of cleaned equipment and walked alongside Oka Hofobi toward the shed, saving him a trip. "I remember when my mother could embarrass me just by the way she sat. You've got a Ph.D. now. I think you can move past that."

"It's not that I'm ashamed. It's more that I don't want to make them ashamed. I'm sure you know that indigenous people and archaeologists have never gotten along all that well. Things have eased up since the Native American Graves Protection and Repatriation Act passed. At least we've got some legal assurance that human burials will be treated with respect. Unfortunately, that's not enough for people like my brother."

"Davis?"

"Yeah. When Ma went away to school, she came back proud. She wanted to learn as much about her culture as she could. Then, when the time came, she wanted that for Davis. Instead, he came back mad. These days, he's especially mad at me."

"Because you chose to be a 'graverobber'?"

Oka Hofobi's eyes flicked toward the ground at the insulting sound of the word. "It's more than that. Historically, there's been a lot of racism sort of built into archaeology. Take the wheel. None of America's indigenous peoples invented the wheel. For a long time, that meant they were considered to be less technologically sophisticated than the rest of the world. Then somebody said, 'Hey! They didn't have horses, or any other animal big enough to haul a cart. And a lot of those civilizations were built in muddy or hilly places where wheels just wouldn't roll. They didn't invent the wheel because it didn't work *for them.*' I became an archaeologist to correct those mistakes. Davis just got mad. And I think he's going to stay that way."

"Maybe I'm biased, but your way seems to be more constructive. You could open so many doors." Faye knew she sounded as optimistic and naïve as Dr. Mailer, but she wanted her words to be true.

"Yeah, well, when the Tribal Council is staring me down tonight, I'll try to remember that."

"Sounds to me like your mom and dad will be staring right back. Is that why they want to go? To make sure the Council knows you have their support?"

"That's why my mother's coming. She listens to me when I talk, and I'm starting to make her see my vision of archaeology. It's a way for me to pay respect to my ancestors by getting to know how they lived."

"Your father doesn't agree."

He set the box he was carrying on a shelf and pulled out a bandanna out of his back pocket to wipe the sweat off his neck. "My father—well, that explanation doesn't fly with him. He says he knows all he needs to know about his ancestors, because his father explained it to him with the ancient stories he learned from his own father. Now, bear in mind that our family's been Baptist for just about ever. My folks have found a way to reconcile their ancestors' stories with the Christian Bible, which I think is pretty cool. I'm looking for a way to reconcile all those things with science, but that's just a little too much for my dad. Digging up his ancestors' possessions is disrespectful, he tells me. It shows that I doubt the old stories that are so precious to him. And to my mother, too."

"You've really been able to sway your mother's opinions that much?"

"Not so much. She just wants me to be happy, so she goes along with my foul modern notions. Just because my parents have got fancy executive jobs, it doesn't mean that they aren't very traditional people. I mean, just look at my name."

"I've noticed that most Choctaws have plain old English-sounding names like Sam and Martha." Faye set her box down on top of Oka Hofobi's. Everyone else had stored their tools and hurried away, so she pulled out her keys and locked the door as they left.

"Yeah," he said, wiping his dusty hands on the seat of his khakis, "my brother and sisters have names like Sarah and Jane and Davis, but I came last. Not that they don't have Choctaw names, too. We all do. It's just that their birth certificates show names that the rest of America can understand. My parents got serious about their heritage just in time to give me a legal name that screamed 'Choctaw!' every time I wrote it on a high school term paper."

"So you don't like it?"

"No, I do. Quite a lot, actually. I just feel like I'll spend a whole lifetime growing into it."

"What does it mean?"

"Uh…it means 'Deep Water,'" Oka Hofobi said, wrinkling his brow as if he felt pretentious even saying such a thing.

Faye pictured a small boy playing alone outdoors, digging up arrowheads, rinsing them in the clear creek waters, turning them over and over in his hands to admire the wet stone. She remembered her mother saying that she, Faye, had been born with the fierce and thoughtful personality that still marked her. *You were your own self from the minute you opened your eyes,* her mother had said. Maybe Oka Hofobi's parents had seen the depth in their baby's eyes and chosen just the right name for him.

"Dr. Mailer calls you Oke. Do you like that? Or do you prefer to go by your whole name?"

"Oke doesn't really mean anything. If I'm going to be hung with a name worth living up to, then I'd rather use it all instead of chopping it up. Ma and Pa wouldn't dream of calling me anything else."

"Aren't they proud of their son the doctor?"

"Ma does look for reasons to mention that Ph.D., but she does worry about the people I have to associate with. Both my parents are pretty sure most archaeologists are graverobbers. Besides me, of course. That's why she invited you all to dinner. She wanted to check you out." When Oka Hofobi smiled, his dark hooded eyes looked very much like Joe's.

"Now I'm afraid to look your mother in the face."

"Then don't look behind you. She's walking this way. But don't worry about Ma. She likes you. In fact, she told me to ask you out to a movie."

Faye sneaked a glance over her shoulder. Mrs. Nail was a hundred feet away, but moving fast for a woman of her bulk. Oka Hofobi kept talking. "Unfortunately, there's nothing worth seeing at the theater in Philadelphia, but why don't I beat my mother to the question she's hustling over here to ask? Would you like to stay for dinner?"

Thirty seconds later, Mrs. Nail asked her the same question.

Dinner was very tasty. Oka Hofobi had exaggerated when he said that his mother fried everything. She also stewed vegetables thoroughly and well. Sitting, once again, in the cozy, wood-paneled dining room, Faye had been made to feel welcome by the friendly woman, who had quizzed her politely about her work in a friendly, parental way.

About every five minutes, Oka Hofobi interrupted, urging his mother to share some more of her grandfather's tales. Maybe he was just trying to steer the conversation away from the personal questions his mother liked to ask—"You live alone with young Mr. Mantooth? But you're not dating?"—or maybe he knew just how much Faye enjoyed the woman's old stories.

"Later," Mrs. Nail kept saying. "I'll tell the tales, and I'm so glad you want to hear them, but they're better told when the sun gets low."

"Ma would be happier if we'd just go outside and light a campfire. That way, her ghost stories would be much more effective."

Mrs. Nail swatted a hand in the air, as if to smack her lastborn on the shoulder, but the blow connected with nothing but air. Faye didn't think she was capable of swatting a fly.

"You used to run screaming to your room when I told the story of 'The Girl and The Devil.' And let's not even talk about 'The White People of the Water'..." She turned a wide, warm smile on Faye.

Her hospitality made Mr. Nail's silence all the more glaring. Faye guessed that he would prefer not to eat with someone he regarded as a graverobber, and she could see his point.

Mrs. Nail had been so thrilled to hear that Faye's great-great-great-great-grandmother was half-Creek that she'd felt like a long-lost cousin—but a very distant cousin who still might be a suitable match for a son who should have gotten married long before the clock tolled midnight on his thirtieth birthday. Mrs. Nail didn't have to speak that concern out loud. The photos of children and grandchildren and nieces and nephews that papered the walls delivered her message quite well.

If Faye had been a trifle uncomfortable with the way the dinner table conversation constantly veered back to matters of marriage and children—she'd been told more than once that two more Nail grandchildren would arrive before the end of the year, and the eldest grandson planned to marry immediately after his college graduation—she quickly learned that there were far worse topics of discussion. For example, any mention of Oka Hofobi's work was a distinctly terrible idea.

When Mrs. Nail asked, "Did you two have a nice day at work?", Faye made the ghastly mistake of actually answering her. Later, when she had time to think about the question, she realized that it was just the conversational tactic of a meddling mother strategically highlighting their similar interests. Faye, in her straightforward way, presumed that the woman was actually interested.

"We found evidence today that your property was the site of a toolmaking center a couple of thousand years ago. Pretty cool, don't you think? Of course, Oka Hofobi had been telling us that all along, so this just makes him look like a genius."

"I can't see any reason to dig up my ancestors' goods, just to prove something you already know," Mr. Nail rumbled. "And I don't think people should keep telling my son he's a genius, either. Look where it's gotten him."

Faye wanted to point out that they had disturbed nothing more than a little bit of trash, in the form of stone chips, but it wouldn't have helped. Mr. Nail knew as well as she did that they could find personal treasures tomorrow—jewelry, art, religious objects. Certainly, they could find bones. Faye knew that Dr. Mailer would rigidly adhere to the laws governing the discovery of human burials, but it would be too late, from Mr. Nail's point of view. His ancestors' rest would have already been disturbed.

Oka Hofobi pushed his chair back. "What would you like me to do? Wander in the woods until I meet a magic spirit that'll tell me what to do with my life? Well, maybe I did. Did you ever ask me *why* I do what I do?"

Oka Hofobi was rising to his feet, ready to stalk out of the room, but his father beat him to it. The older man slammed the hall door behind him, leaving his son half-crouched at the table. Oka Hofobi awkwardly lowered himself back into his chair, saying, "Well, that was fun. Maybe we can consider it a dress rehearsal for the Tribal Council meeting. I'm betting they pretty much agree with Pa. Only there are twelve of them. We'll be taking flak from all sides."

Faye got out of the back seat of the Nails' minivan at the Tribal Council Hall and slid the door shut behind her. She'd enjoyed their drive through the reservation, probably because Mr. Nail had decided to drive separately, in his own truck. Time spent with Mrs. Nail and Oka Hofobi alone felt like time spent among newfound friends.

The reservation, with its material trappings of the modern Choctaws, had been an effective setting for Mrs. Nail's stories. The old tales simply flowed out of the woman, and the language they were told in varied from story to story. It was as if she were channeling the spirit of the person who had originally told the tale to her. Or maybe this was just what a gifted storyteller did—let the story tell itself the in the best language possible.

Faye would have felt crass taking notes, but she'd once known a very talented oral historian named Carmen Martinez. When Faye got back to the hotel, she was going to write down every scrap of every story that she could recall. It was the least she could do for Carmen's memory.

Outside the van's windows, Faye saw that evidence of the Choctaws' growing prosperity was everywhere. Mrs. Nail and Oka Hofobi had proudly driven her past the neon-lit casinos and the brand-spanking-new fire hall where Davis worked. Choctaw-owned businesses were poised along the highway to sell gasoline and groceries and souvenirs to the legions of tourists drawn by the resorts.

Turning off the main highway, they drove through the industrial park that housed the tribe's manufacturing interests. Entering the portion of the reservation devoted to tribal government, Faye saw one building after another that advertised the efforts being made at social and economic change. These buildings housed agencies dedicated to public transportation, housing, employment, and health. Near the Choctaw Justice Complex, also brand-spanking-new, Oka Hofobi took a detour so that Faye could see new housing developments filled with spacious houses on large lots.

"They just can't build housing fast enough," Mrs. Nail said, "and it's hard on the young people. A lot of single people live with their parents while they wait their turn. Families have priority, so you just about can't get reservation housing until you get married. Davis has been waiting a long time since his divorce."

"And you, Oka Hofobi?" Faye asked.

"If I can keep getting contracts to do work around here, I may just buy a place near Ma and Pa. I like it out there."

Near the governmental center, some of the reservation's buildings were older, showing that the tribe's economic progress had come in waves. The Tribal Council Hall was one of them. Smaller and less grand than the tribal offices that stood right next door, the Council Hall had a more intimate feel, but Faye was intimidated, nonetheless. Seeing Mr. Nail park his truck and walk alone into the hall troubled her even more. He couldn't abide even being in the van with her? Or, even worse, maybe he couldn't stand the company of his own son.

She and Oka Hofobi and his mother joined the rest of the archaeological crew in the Council Hall, a room that would have held a much bigger crowd. Sheriff Rutland walked in a moment later. Mr. Nail had chosen a chair in the far back corner of the room. If anybody was going to sit beside him, Faye judged that it would be because they walked across the room and sat there on purpose.

Twenty seconds after Faye made that judgment, Davis sauntered in and did that very thing. He nodded at Mrs. Nail, but never even glanced at his brother.

The array of chairs reserved for council members was a trifle intimidating. At precisely seven-thirty, the members filed in and the Chief called the meeting to order.

"The extraordinary events of the past few days give us cause for concern. The mound that Carroll Calhoun tried to destroy is not on tribal land. Neither is the site being excavated by Dr. Mailer's team. Carroll Calhoun was not killed on Choctaw land. We have no jurisdiction over these issues, but I think it is obvious that they concern us. If we can assist in your murder investigation in any way, Sheriff, please ask."

"Thank you, sir."

"Now. Our Council has a committee on tribal culture that is best suited to discuss our concerns related to archaeological activities. I'll let their chair speak."

A handsome woman in her mid-forties took the floor. "Sheriff, can you clarify the law related to the mound on the Calhoun property? We consider it an important part of our heritage. What are our rights if his widow decides to finish what he started?"

"I've had some lawyers checking out that very question, and you won't like the answer." As the sheriff rose and spoke, she looked at each council member in turn. "When human remains are found, some extremely restrictive laws kick in to protect the burial and the artifacts found with it. This is not the case here. There is no evidence that this is a burial mound, so your rights are quite limited, and so is my jurisdiction. No," she said, looking back at the Chief. "That's not exactly true. Our rights are not limited in the case. The truth is that we have no rights. If the new owner of that property, Mr. Calhoun's widow, decides to bulldoze that mound, then she can do it."

The councilwoman leaned to her right and conferred with a younger man, before turning her attention back to the sheriff. "That's what our lawyers tell us, too, but it doesn't seem right," she said.

The sheriff nodded to acknowledge her point. "Here's how it was explained to me. If I owned an original copy of the Declaration of Independence, it would be mine to do with as I pleased. I could put an ad in the paper, stating my intention to stand in my driveway tomorrow and set it on fire, and nobody could stop me. Now, people could try. They could get some historical society to offer to buy it from me. The newspaper could run a scathing editorial trying to shame me out of the idea. Nevertheless, I am free to destroy my property if I see fit. Short of having the mound declared a Mississippi Landmark, or proving that there are human remains buried there, or ramming a last-minute law through the legislature—which might or might not even be possible—the Calhoun mound is his to destroy. Well, now, it's his widow's mound to destroy. It may not be right, but it's the law."

"We are not without political power," the woman reminded the sheriff.

"Then use it. I don't want to see that mound destroyed any more than you do."

Turning her attention to Dr. Mailer, the councilwoman continued. "I understand that you're in the county because you were contracted to do an archaeological survey for a proposed road construction project."

"Yes. The highway department would like to straighten a dangerous curve, but there might be cultural materials in their way. My co-investigator, Dr. Nail, has documented some pretty good evidence that your ancestors used that spot as a lithics manufacturing site. Our preliminary work appears to confirm his suspicions."

Another council member, an elderly man, laughed. "Sounds like we Choctaws have been big into manufacturing for a long, long time."

Faye saw the tension in Mailer's shoulders ease a bit. He laughed, too. "You could say that. We're just sifting through the trash they left behind—flint chips left over from knapping stone tools—but my flintknapping specialists tell me that your ancestors were very good at what they did." He nodded at Joe and Chuck, as if to acknowledge their expertise.

Faye noticed Neely's eyes follow Mailer's gaze. She didn't like him calling the sheriff's attention to Joe's special skills.

The elderly man chuckled again. "If they weren't, then they didn't eat." He grew more serious. "Oka Hofobi. You realize that you must be our representative in this."

The younger man nodded in assent.

"It always concerns us when our ancestors' possessions are uncovered and studied. It has not been so long since their bones were treated the same way. How do you think your colleagues would like it if their grandmothers' bones were on display in museums?"

Faye cast a glance over her shoulder. Davis was leaning forward in his chair, intense and focused. His father's eyes were glued to him.

"It's my job to ask my colleagues that very question. I ask it often."

Toneisha and Bodie nodded vigorously to confirm Oka Hofobi's words.

"I'm deeply interested in my culture," the young Choctaw continued. "I love it. That's why I chose to do what I do."

"We aren't against archaeology, only its misapplication," the Chief interjected. "In 1981, this Council drafted a resolution asking the Corps of Engineers and others planning to develop our historic lands to hire archaeologists to survey land before development destroyed our people's historical record. We urged everyone involved, the government included, to apply pressure to make sure this was done. I would like to think we made a difference. You, Oka Hofobi, are young. You are in a unique position to make a difference for a very long time. Do not throw away this opportunity. Do not shame us."

Oka Hofobi, his mother, his father, his brother—all of them kept their eyes fastened on the Chief's face. Perhaps it was out of respect for him. Or perhaps it was a convenient way to keep from looking at each other.

Faye had come straight to the council meeting in her work clothes. Given a chance, she would have changed, but staying for dinner with the Nails had forced her to make do with cleaning up at their bathroom sink.

She hadn't been especially dirty. It had been a week since Neshoba County had had much rain, so the dry red dust had mostly brushed off her clothes. Still, she hadn't dressed to be on television.

Why was she surprised to find that the council had called a press conference? A business entity that, like the Mississippi Band of Choctaw Indians, had 9,000 employees would be well-versed in handling the media. And, when summoned by the Choctaws, the media had turned out in their honor.

Or that's what Faye had assumed until she saw the shock on the faces of the Council. This was not a pre-rehearsed press conference. Someone had alerted the media to this informal meeting and caught the Council members flat-footed.

Who would have done it? As always, the answer to that question was buried in another one. *Who stood to gain from this publicity?*

Not the archaeologists, whose client would prefer they kept a low profile. And not the Council, who were muttering among themselves, trying to regroup. Perhaps one of the farmers who had shown up at the mound to defend Mr. Calhoun's property rights wanted some public attention to that cause.

Or maybe one of the Choctaws wanted more attention paid to the tribe's grievance. Faye sneaked a glance at Davis. His expression was remote, shielded. He seemed like a man who would become impatient with the Council's deliberate approach to an issue that, in his view, should arouse action and passion. Faye would bet money that it was Davis who called in the reporters.

Television stations from as far away as Jackson had sent camera crews. Someone was there from the state public radio network. Newspaper reporters shuffled forward, hoping for a quote. Gathered on the sidewalk outside the Council Hall, they converged on the Chief, who hadn't lived his life in politics without acquiring some media management skills. Thinking on his feet, he spread his arms to encompass them and said warmly, "Thank you all for coming out tonight. We've had a most productive meeting."

A sandy-haired young man thrust a microphone in the Chief's direction and asked, "Is this about the murder of Carroll Calhoun? The tribe can't be happy with his attempt to bulldoze that mound."

A young woman, either the chief's press secretary or just someone with good instincts, stepped forward to take the question, standing between her boss and controversy. "Mr. Calhoun was found in a place where…well, where illegal activity was going on. The fact that he was killed just after he threatened to destroy an important piece of history may have been just a coincidence. We grieve with Mrs. Calhoun for her husband's untimely death."

The microphone holder lunged even closer. Sheriff Rutland moved forward to a spot where she could insert herself between the reporter and his prey with a single step.

"They say that Calhoun was killed by a Choctaw arrowhead," the reporter continued.

Chuck caught everyone concerned off-guard by reaching over the reporter's shoulder and grabbing the microphone right out of his hand. "Could you try not to display your ignorance? An arrow is a projectile. The man's throat was cut, so if the killer had any sense, he would have used a single-edged blade to keep from cutting his own hand off with the other edge. And I'm guessing a crime lab doesn't have anybody qualified to assess whether it was made by Choctaws, so why don't you leave that line of questioning alone, too?"

The expressions on the faces around Faye were comical. Every last one of the council members seemed to be wondering who in the heck this guy was. The reporters looked overjoyed, because anything unexpected is news. Besides, Chuck had all the earmarks of somebody who might say absolutely anything.

Faye could almost hear the gears in the sheriff's head turning. She was asking herself, *Who is this guy who knows so much about a murder weapon he hasn't seen?*

And Mailer had the terrified expression of a man whose client was not going to like reading the morning papers. His client, a huge firm contracted by the highway department to conduct pre-construction tasks, expected subcontractors to get to the site, do the job, deliver a bill—preferably a small one—then leave, so that nothing got in the way of getting the road built. Publicity was a bad thing. Publicity could stop a road construction project dead.

"Can you tell me who you are, sir?" the reporter asked.

"My name is Chuck Horowitz, and I'm a lithics analyst with the highway project west of town. We're working for SGM&T."

Faye's heart sank. He'd just mentioned their client on TV. In the context of a murder investigation. Poor Dr. Mailer.

Chuck plunged deeper into ticklish political territory. "We're just trying to do our work, but the Choctaws here don't think we should. They think human history should just stay buried, so that their tender sensibilities can be protected. Why? So that, eventually, some idiot like Carroll Calhoun can destroy it?"

Great. Now he'd spoken ill of the dead. And the entire Mississippi Band of Choctaw Indians.

"There's so much history here. So much. Every flake of stone, every chip, tells a story. I could sit all day every day, and let those chips talk to me. In a big pile of flakes like this," Chuck held out his two cupped hands, "there might be two that fit together, but it's worth spending a week to find them, because it's *history*.

Somebody broke that stone apart hundreds of years ago, and I'm putting it back together. I don't have time for people who want to stop me."

Even better. Now he sounded crazy. Their client would be thrilled.

Was Chuck crazy? Could he have killed Calhoun because of his threat to the history that Chuck found so sacred? Faye wavered. She barely knew the man, but she didn't want to think so. It was as if some primitive instinct wanted her to believe that no one in her personal circle of acquaintances could ever pick up a sharpened stone and slice a man's throat with it.

If asked to practice psychology without a license, Faye would have said that Chuck wasn't crazy, but that he reminded her of the articles she'd read about autism and Asperger's syndrome. She understood that empathy was difficult for people with those disorders. Chuck hadn't seemed to understand that his leering made her uncomfortable and, right now, he seemed oblivious to the fact that he should pay some bit of respect to the recently dead. And to the elected leadership of a sovereign nation.

As she thought of it, Chuck's chosen profession, fitting stone flakes together in a three-dimensional jigsaw puzzle with an unknown number of missing pieces, required a near-autistic attention to detail. Compassion stirred, and she wished someone would protect Chuck from himself.

Neely Rutland stepped up to the task. She took the microphone from Chuck's hand so deftly that he didn't have time to fight her for it, then she said, "The murder is under investigation, and discussing its details would jeopardize that investigation. There are no suspects as yet, and there is no reason to believe that the killer is Choctaw. Or white. Or black. Or anything else. We just don't know. Thank you folks for coming out, but we're going home now."

The White People of the Water

As told by Mrs. Frances Nail

You ever walk out in the woods around here? Walk down one of our creeks? Well, if you get a chance, you should. There aren't many places so pretty left in this world. Maybe in Heaven, but not here.

Most times, you'll see brown creek water, clear brown water. It looks like tea. You can see right through it, down to the gravel on the bottom. That gravel is what's left of the Devil's body, but I already told you that story. This is safe water.

In some places, you'll see thick, muddy water, and that's okay, too. Not as pretty as the clear water, maybe, but it's safe.

You need to watch out for the clear pools, deep and cold. Everybody wants to swim in those...until the day they meet up with one of the *okwa nahollo*.

Okwa nahollo means "white people of the water." They look a lot more like white people than they do Choctaws. My grandmother saw one once, and she said its skin looked like the skin of a trout. So I guess it's shimmery and smooth.

If you were to be so foolish as to swim in a pool where the *okwa nahollo* live, then they would swim up from the depths and grab you. They would pull you down to their home, where you would become one of them. It takes three days—only three days!—for your skin to go shimmery and white, like a trout. Before long, you would know how to swim and live just like a fish, but you could never leave the water and live in the air, never again.

Later, your friends might come to visit you. If they sat on the creek bank near your pool and sang, you could rise to the surface and talk to them. Maybe even sing with them. But you couldn't step out of the water and sit on the dirt beside them, or you would die.

This almost happened to my grandmother. She was such a swimmer, good Lord. She could lay on top of the water like it was a bed and float right down the creek.

She wanted to swim in one of those clear pools pretty bad, and she probably thought she could get away with it, because the water was like a home to her. But a shimmery white arm shot up from the deep depths and grabbed her.

She was sinking beneath the water. The *okwa nahollo* were dragging her down, down. At the very last second, when she had opened her mouth to breathe in water, because there wasn't nothing else to breathe, her friends grabbed her by the hair and brought her back into her own world.

You can go where you like and do what you like, but I wouldn't go swimming in a clear, deep pool. Not around here. No, I sure wouldn't.

Chapter Nine

Monday
Day 4 of the Neshoba County Fair

Faye was still hauling the day's equipment out of the trailer when the sheriff's car pulled up. Would the whole summer pass before she got a solid hour's worth of work done?

Dr. Mailer turned to Chuck and said, "You know, I forgot to stock up on bottled water. Would you drive to the convenience store and get a few cases? If one of you had a heat stroke, it wouldn't look good for me."

Chuck nodded, striking out for his truck at top speed. It didn't seem to occur to him to say, "Hey! Why don't you send somebody without a Ph.D.?" And it certainly didn't occur to him to dawdle. It seemed to Faye that Chuck was cooperative when asked to do something for a reason that made sense to him. She suspected he would balk if, for instance, Mailer insisted that Chuck use a filing system that he didn't like, just because he was the boss.

"Smooth," she said to Mailer. "You didn't want Chuck and the sheriff in the same place at the same time?"

"If I'd been really smooth, you'd never have noticed that I was getting rid of Chuck. I wonder what the sheriff wants."

It seemed that the sheriff wanted Faye. "You were going to show me some…was it 'sickle shine'?"

"Close. It was 'sickle sheen.' Let's go look at some rocks."

Faye ushered the sheriff into Chuck's domain, grateful that he wasn't around to see them fingering his prized possessions. She shuffled through the storage boxes on the shelves that ringed his office, carefully avoiding the box full of Joe's homemade weapons. It only took a moment to put her hands on some good examples.

She laid them out on Chuck's desk. "Now, understand that we're talking seat-of-the-pants work. To get real answers that'll be defensible in court, you're going to need analyses that your forensics lab probably can't do. They should send the blade out to experts—"

The look on Neely's face said that her murder weapon wasn't going anywhere. "—or maybe you can bring some experts in. There are people who are wizards with a microscope. Judging by the patterns of use-wear, they could tell you whether a tool had been used to scrape hides or carve antler."

"What about that sickle sheen you were going to show me?"

"Here's some." Faye held out a blade very similar in shape to the one that had killed Carroll Calhoun. "When you see sickle sheen, then there's a good chance that your tool is old, and that it was used in a prehistoric agricultural society."

"And that would help me how?"

"If it's new, then your suspect probably either made it or bought it from somebody who did. There might be a bill of sale and a flintknapper who could identify the buyer. If it's old, then, again, the killer could have bought it, which would give you a receipt to look for. Or you could be dealing with a collector. A farmer, for instance, can build up quite a collection of stone tools during a lifetime of walking a plowed field."

"No kidding. My father framed a bunch of his best pieces. He laid them out on brown velvet and built a shadow box frame to hold them. He had a bowl full of run-of-the-mill arrowheads just sitting out on the table next to his recliner where he could look at them whenever he wanted to. Somebody stole one during a football party one time, years ago. Can you believe it? Everybody around here's got a bowl of arrowheads, and somebody stole one of Daddy's. He didn't speak to Preston Silver for a week, thinking he was the thief, but he and Preston patched things up. Then he suspected Carroll Calhoun. Never did get it back." Neely picked up a spear point and turned it over in her hand, running a finger along its still-sharp edge.

"How'd he know it was missing?"

"They were like his babies. He knew their color and shape. He liked the way they felt in his hand. He still likes me to put that bowl in his lap so he can pick them up and look them over, one by one."

"Would your father know who the collectors are around here? Maybe somebody would recognize the murder weapon."

"My father doesn't even know who I am any more."

Faye could have bitten her tongue out for making Neely admit that.

The sheriff recovered quickly. "An old tool wouldn't necessarily point to a collector. It could implicate a Choctaw. Or one of your archaeologists. And a new tool could point to a collector, too. Like you said, people buy brand-new arrowheads from flintknappers all the time. It's an art form, just like painting or sculpture. And I understand that some people don't just like to make stone tools. They like to practice shooting their homemade arrows."

Faye thought fast. Bodie just happened to be the Florida state atlatl champion, a competition that required him to fit a homemade spear to a spear thrower of ancient design. If Calhoun had been felled by a spear through the heart, Bodie would have been Faye's first suspect. Except he was so soft-hearted, she wasn't sure he could stomp a cockroach.

Should she say something about Bodie's accomplishment? Since anyone with an Internet connection had immediate access to the information, it seemed unwise not to mention it to the sheriff. The sheriff would find out eventually, and then she'd wonder what else Faye wasn't telling her. Which could lead to some uncomfortable questions like *Do you know anybody else with that kind of primitive skill?*

"You do know that Bodie, Dr. Mailer's assistant, is one of the best spear throwers around? Not that I think that makes him a suspect. If he'd wanted to kill Calhoun, he could have done it from fifty paces."

So could Joe. What was more, Joe had actually put a spear through a man's throat once, but there was no need for Neely to know that. Joe was a practical man, who couldn't conceive of why he'd want to enter a contest to prove himself, so there was no official record of his skill. Joe saw no value in aiming at a target, not when he couldn't eat it. Faye had enjoyed many a dinner featuring rabbits that Joe had felled with stone projectiles.

"Besides, there's not much overlap in skill between throwing a spear at a target and holding a blade in your hand and slicing someone's throat with it," Faye pointed out, hoping that Neely would leave Bodie alone. "Anyway, back to the question of sickle sheen, anybody who works with lithics could take a look at your murder weapon and give you a fairly good idea of its age—even if it's a modern fake, and somebody purposely tried to simulate edge wear. You could use that knowledge to guide your investigation, but in the end, you'll need a lab to confirm it."

"The murder weapon looks a lot like this one," Neely said, pointing to the tool Faye had selected as a prime example of sickle sheen. "So you can tell any flintknapping friends you've got to rest easy."

Faye nearly lost her poker face.

A knock on the door saved her from blurting out something stupid. Dr. Mailer stuck his head in and beckoned to Faye. Someone stood close behind him.

"Chuck is back." Mailer's tone of voice was pleasant and even, but his clenched jaw said that he wished Chuck had stayed gone just a little longer. "Joe told him that the sheriff was interested in learning how to distinguish ancient tools from modern reproductions. Chuck would just love to spend some time showing her his reference collection."

It couldn't have been more obvious that Mailer didn't want Chuck left alone with the sheriff. Faye squeezed through the doorway and crowded herself onto the entry stairs where the two men waited. She closed the door behind her, and she could tell that Mailer was glad she did. "I don't think that's necessary, Chuck. I've shown the sheriff a good example of sickle sheen, which is really all she's interested in today. She knows that she'll eventually have to have the murder weapon examined by an expert. I'll tell her that you have some recommendations when she's ready to select a lab."

Chuck's response was quick and eager. "I could examine the weapon for her."

His face was flushed at the thought of using his esoteric knowledge for something concrete and useful. Faye doubted very much that the sheriff would consider using someone who'd been in direct conflict with the victim barely a day before he died, but she said, "Thanks, Chuck. I'll tell her."

She backed through the door and shut it behind her, hoping Chuck didn't follow. It was, after all, his office. The door stayed shut.

The sheriff, whose poker face was better than Faye's, was waiting quietly. "This is his office?" She gestured toward the door.

"Chuck's? Or Dr. Mailer's?"

"The...unusual...one."

"That would be Chuck."

Neely shoved the points around on Chuck's desk, shuffling them like dominos.

"Whoever sits in this office has access to all this stuff and more. So, I guess, do all the rest of you. But this guy...you said his name was Chuck? He's the one that worries me."

Faye couldn't argue with her.

Before the sheriff had even reached her car, another car pulled into the makeshift parking lot in the Nails' side yard. When a slender black man emerged from the car, Faye realized that they were being graced with the presence of a retired congressman. And that he wasn't happy.

Judd strode directly toward the sheriff. "Your receptionist said you were out here, and I needed to talk to you right away, so I just drove out." His voice was high-pitched and agitated.

Faye didn't like the tremor in his hands, not when she'd heard him tell everybody at the Neshoba County Fair that his health problems included high blood pressure and God-knew-what-else. She stepped forward, putting a hand on his elbow to steady him, and turned to Bodie. "We need a chair."

Bodie got to the trailer and back with a chair in seconds. He helped the older man ease himself into the desk chair.

"Wouldn't you like to talk privately?" the sheriff asked. "These folks—"

Judd started talking, blurting his story out quickly, as if he couldn't bother to wait and listen to what she had to say.

"I don't know how many times I've read the newspaper article about Mr. Calhoun's death. Well, not the part about his death. I just couldn't stop reading the part that described where he was found. He was in a marijuana field, wasn't he? Well, that got me to thinking about something that happened not too long before I was beaten. Before someone tried to kill me." He took a ragged breath.

"Chuck," Mailer said quietly. "The man needs a drink of water."

As if relieved to be given something useful to do, Chuck ripped the shrinkwrap off one of the cases that he'd just bought, and plucked out a water bottle. Removing the cap, he held out the open bottle with a gesture that was almost tender. His manner made Faye feel a little tender towards him, too.

"One day not long before the beating, I'd gotten up early to go fishing. My favorite spot was very near here, close to where the creek goes under the road. It had been a dry summer and the creek was low. There wasn't much water in my regular fishing hole, so I followed the creek further into the woods than I'd ever been before, looking for a better spot. I walked quite a ways, and I remember passing an open field that was planted with a crop I didn't recognize."

He paused and drew a long sip from the bottle. "I know now that it must have been a marijuana field that I saw, but I was a preacher's kid and it was a simpler time. I don't think I even knew what marijuana was. Anyway, right after I passed that field, I remember walking past an overgrown cemetery that was on top of a little hill."

Oka Hofobi said, "You must have been way out in the woods. I've walked over most of the land around here, time and again. I don't know of any cemeteries near here."

"You spend a lot of time trespassing?" the sheriff asked tartly.

"Not since I learned better."

Judd lowered his face into his hands. Faye thought for a second that he was going to faint, but he pulled himself together and looked up at Dr. Mailer. "There are some pills in the glove box of my car, and there's one or two that I could use right about now. I've got too darn many meds to carry them in my pockets."

Mailer nodded to Chuck, who hurried to the car.

Oka Hofobi pulled a cell phone out of his pocket. "I'll call my doctor."

Judd waved a hand at him and shook his head. "Lord, no. This happens a lot. More often than I'd like, that's for certain. If I keel over, go ahead and call. Otherwise, just let me sit here and breathe for a minute."

Chuck had crossed the yard quickly, at an easy lope. He brought with him a prescription bottle and a case with multiple compartments, one for each day of the week. "I didn't know which you needed."

Judd took the bottle. "My wife keeps that big one filled with all the stuff I have to take every day. This one's for angina. When the chest pain comes, I'm supposed to take one of these." He put a pill under his tongue and closed his eyes.

Faye stepped away from the crowd of archaeologists hovering around Judd and beckoned to the sheriff. "Maybe he wasn't being lynched that day. Maybe somebody knew he saw their field of pot and wanted to shut him up before he called in the law."

Neely looked over her shoulder at the sick man. "I don't know, Faye. Mr. Judd is smart and well-spoken, and Lord knows teenage boys are cocky beasts. He was probably a lynching waiting to happen. Maybe it just comes from growing up around here and hearing the stories about what things were like in the sixties, but my gut tells me that his attack was racially motivated. I'll give your theory some thought, but I've got my hopes set on an interview I'm doing this afternoon. The guy's a former Klansman and he's got cancer. I think he's willing to talk before he dies."

An image of white sheets and hoods flashed through Faye's head, and her skin crawled. "They say confession is good for the soul. Sounds like this guy has some atonement to do. Maybe he'll tell you what you need to know."

"Let's hope so. And I might get lucky and learn something about Calhoun's killing, too. There have always been rumors that his buddy Preston Silver was big in the local Klan. The KKK is a shadow of its old self now, and thank God for that, but Preston's getting up there in years. He could have been part of some nasty things, back in the day. And maybe Calhoun was, too."

"Nailing a Klansman or two is a good use of a sheriff's time."

"Well, I like to think so."

They returned to Judd's side. His color was improving, and the pain-generated tension around his closed eyes had eased.

"Can I take you back to your hotel?" Neely asked gently. "I'm going back to town, anyway."

"I can drive," he insisted, though his trembling hands said otherwise. "I can't just leave my car out here."

"I'll bring it," Faye offered.

"You'll need to get back out here to work, and the sheriff has other places to be," Joe pointed out quickly. "I'll drive Mr. Judd, Faye, and you can follow in your car." Having just earned his driver's license, after several frustrating efforts to pass the written test, he was always eager to exercise his new independence. Plus, Joe was, by nature, happiest when he was helping someone else.

But the sheriff was shaking her head. "I want to drive the congressman myself. I'll just feel better if I can keep an eye on him till he's feeling better."

Faye didn't really think Neely needed to add another older man in ill health to her list of burdens, but she could see that there would be no arguing with the sheriff. She herself had nursed both her mother and her grandmother through their last illnesses, and she recognized a born caretaker when she saw one. If she got a chance, she wanted to tell Neely that it was no crime to take care of herself now and then.

Joe had ciphered through the vehicle situation and come up with a second-best scenario. "Okay. We take three cars. The sheriff drives Mr. Judd in her car. Faye follows in his car. And I bring up the rear in Faye's car, so I can take her back to work."

"Good plan," Faye said. Within minutes, their convoy was pulling out of the Nails' driveway. The road into Philadelphia was deserted—probably because everyone with a pulse was at the Fair—so they made good time.

Faye knew that Judd was staying at the same hotel as the archaeologists. Owned by the Choctaws, it boasted a wide range of amenities, including a casino. Ex-congressmen might be accustomed to such luxury, but archaeologists weren't. Faye had unkinked her muscles nearly every night since they arrived in the nice, toasty sauna.

She was looking forward to more of the same, and not paying very much attention to the road, when Neely swung a hard right into a parking lot. By taking the turn at a higher rate of speed than was wise (all the while hoping that the sheriff didn't write her up for reckless driving) she managed to follow. Joe, whose reflexes were perfect, as were his powers of observation, made the turn effortlessly. And to think that the state of Florida hadn't wanted to let him drive. Faye was still irate on his behalf over that snub.

As Faye put the car in park, Neely tapped on her window and Faye lowered it. "Would you hand me Mr. Judd's pills out of the glove box? He needs to refill one of his prescriptions. I'll go in and do it for him. Would you and Joe like to sit with him while I'm gone?"

"No problem," Faye said, rounding up Joe and walking over to the sheriff's car. She gestured for Joe to join Judd in the front seat, while she sat in the back behind the divider that protected the sheriff from hardened criminals. From the look of him, Joe enjoyed the sight of her back there entirely too much.

Judd nodded at Neely's back as she disappeared into the pharmacy. "She's worse than my wife."

Faye raised an eyebrow. "How so?"

"I told Neely I wanted to get a look at that old cemetery, just to see if I could find the spot where I saw that marijuana field all those years ago. Maybe it's the same place where Mr. Calhoun was killed. She said 'No,' and gave me a long list of reasons why I shouldn't go. First, she said that the idea that I was attacked to keep me from telling somebody about the pot field is far-fetched. She said, 'Mr. Judd, you grew up here. You knew that your attack was racially motivated while it was happening, and you know it now.'"

"That's what she told me," Faye said. "Just because she believes it doesn't make it true."

"My point, exactly. Then, she pointed out that Calhoun's widow owns all that land now, and Neely says she's more preju-diced than her husband ever was. Neely declared that she'd never allow me to set foot on it. Actually, what the sheriff really said was, 'That woman would shoot you dead before she'd let you traipse over her property looking for evidence that her husband's been growing pot for forty years.'"

"Well, the sheriff knows her jurisdiction," Faye pointed out. "She might be right about Mrs. Calhoun."

Judd shrugged. "I don't know the woman, so I can't say. She doesn't sound like a real reasonable person, for sure. The sheriff says that even now, with him being found dead in the middle of his own field full of contraband, his wife's insisting that he didn't plant it. She claims that somebody else must have planted it, then, when he stumbled onto it on his own property, he got killed by the real drug dealer."

"People generally believe what they want to be true," Joe said.

"Yes," said Judd, "but that doesn't help me any. The sheriff told me to give it up, that she wouldn't help me look for the truth."

"I will," said Faye.

Chapter Ten

Neely plopped down in the driver's seat. Faye tried to look like she hadn't just been discussing the possibility of doing an end run around her authority as a sheriff. She willed Joe and Mr. Judd to do the same thing.

Neely pulled the pill case that held Judd's routine medications out of her purse. Opening the bottle, she put one pill in each slot, then dropped the empty bottle into a wastebasket on the car's floorboard. She did it methodically, talking all the while, like someone who sorted other people's medications all the time. Which, of course, she did. Remembering Neely's father's condition, Faye understood her solicitous care of Mr. Judd a little better.

"I just got you a week's worth of this pill, to tide you over until you get home to your own pharmacy." Gesturing with the pill box toward the sign reading *Silver's Pharmacy and Sundries*, she said, "I don't know why I still come here. Probably because my folks shopped here and their folks before them. Daddy gets all upset whenever I do something different from what he's used to. When Walgreens opened a store near our house, I tried to transfer all his prescriptions there. I thought it would make life a little easier if I used a store closer to home. That was a joke. Daddy wouldn't get out of the car, then he wouldn't take the pills. I guess I'm stuck with Preston Silver as my pharmacist for the rest of my natural life."

Faye reflected that this wasn't strictly true. Neely was only stuck with Silver for the rest of her *father's* natural life, but it wouldn't be kind to split hairs and point that out.

Neely handed the pill case, filled and up-to-date, to Mr. Judd. "Every time I come here, Preston Silver stands there and looks at me with those nasty lizard eyes while he counts my pills. Gives me the creeps."

"I'd say he's more dragon than lizard," Judd said quietly. "Everybody knew he was big in the Klan, even back when I lived here. He's bound to be some kind of Grand Dragon by now."

"I infiltrated the Ku Klux Klan once. Well, I guess it would be more accurate to say I did some informal spying," Neely said.

"I'm not sure I'd be talking about that," Judd said. "They're not completely toothless, even now."

"Um…Being the only white person in the car, I guess it's okay for me to say that none of you look like folks who are likely to be card-carrying members," she pointed out. "Besides, it was years ago, when I was young and stupid. Eighteen, maybe. I was dating a guy who was a member, and he sneaked me in. There's an upside and a downside to wearing hoods. I couldn't tell who else was there, but they didn't know who I was, either. All they knew was that I was there because a member had vouched for me. But you know what? A hood can't cover your voice."

Judd put a hand over his eyes, and Faye remembered that his attacker had pulled a hood over his face before beating him. Neely didn't seem to notice his discomfort. She kept talking.

"I heard an impassioned speech introducing a particularly high-ranking bigot, and there was no mistaking the voice. Preston Silver was there that night, and he was not a casual attendee. He wasn't there just because he hoped his membership would help him professionally, like some kind of perverted Rotary Club. He was a true believer. The things he said turned my stomach. Actually, they changed my life. Even looking back at myself with the harshest eye possible, I wouldn't say I was ever a racist. I wasn't taught it at home." Her right hand wandered upward to her badge and gave it a little stroke. "Little girls were shielded from that ugliness in a lot of ways. But I just never gave a second thought to the fact that white people and black people lived their own separate lives, and that some people thought it was okay for us white people to make their lives miserable. I left the meeting before Preston finished spewing garbage, and I broke up with my idiot boyfriend, the Klansman, that very night."

Judd had dropped his hand from his eyes. Those eyes were fastened on her face.

"It took me four years of college to decide to come back home," she went on. "Here's what I figured. It's true that there were a lot of people at that meeting—I counted them—but there's a whole lot more people living in this county that *weren't* there. It's not right to let a few evil people run things. The Klan has lost a lot of power since then, and it's because of people like me who didn't leave. We stayed and made our home a better place."

"Do you think Silver might have been the man who attacked me?" Judd asked quietly.

"He would be at the top of my list, but he wouldn't be the only one," Neely said. She cranked the engine, signaling to Faye and Joe that it was time to get out of the car. "We need to get you back to the hotel, so you can get some rest."

"Thank you," Judd said. "It's nice to know that somebody like you is taking care of things."

Faye was glad to see Mr. Judd looking a lot stronger as she, Joe, and Neely escorted him back to his room. There was a survivor's swing to his walk that said a little angina and high blood pressure couldn't get him down.

It was slow going, making their way through the slot machine obstacle course in the hotel lobby. The narrow aisles between the one-armed bandits were thronged with people who wanted to wish the former Congressman well. Though no one knew how ill he had been barely an hour before, everyone knew by now what had happened to him in 1965.

Several hotel employees left their posts and rushed to shake his hand. Many of them were Choctaws and, thus, not just employees but co-owners of the sprawling casino/hotel complex. Their guests joined them in crowding around the sick man, each of them saying that they personally had no idea who had attacked him, but surely someone else would know.

Sheriff Rutland finally barked, "Back off! The man needs to breathe." At her signal, Joe gently fended off the worst offenders by sheer physical intimidation. Faye just stood close to Mr. Judd and let him lean on her arm. The three of them formed a protective bubble around Judd and rushed him across the lobby. Ever the politician, Judd smiled, waved, and shook hands, even as he was being hustled away from his fawning constituency.

Only one person had the tenacity to stay with them until they reached the elevator. Faye guessed that Neely had better sense than to let anyone know where Judd's room was, and Faye was right. When Joe reached out to press the button, Neely stayed his hand and turned to face their follower.

"Can I help you, sir?"

"I have an urgent request for Congressman Judd."

Faye was in the mood to tell him to write a letter to his own congressman. That mood passed when she looked up into the man's face. He had the strong, proud, ebony-dark features of west Africa, the homeland of virtually all Americans of African descent, and he had the rangy, powerful body a face like that demanded. He was also the most handsome man Faye had ever seen. Excepting, of course, Joe.

His face and form seemed to have the same effect on Neely as it had on Faye, because the sheriff did nothing to stop him from making his pitch. Judd, himself, did nothing to stop him. In fact, he encouraged him, reaching out a hand and responding like a man who truly believes in his party and what it stands for. "Nice to meet you, son. May I presume that you, too, are a Democrat?"

"I will support any political party who gives my people their due. I haven't seen one of those yet."

"I'm listening. But why don't you tell me your name, first?"

"My name is Ross Donnelly." Spreading well-muscled arms sheathed in a well-fitting business suit, Donnelly flung his hands outward and said, "Look around you, sir, at this fine hotel. It makes money for the Choctaws, every day. What does black America have that can compare with this?"

Judd's brow grew a bit more furrowed. "You think we should build some casinos?"

The outstretched hands clenched into fists, and Donnelly's low voice boomed as strongly as if he were the one who was a politician. "No. I think we deserve compensation for historic wrongs. Native Americans were surely mistreated. They were herded onto reservations, and even the income due them from the use of those lands was misused by the Bureau of Indian Affairs. Stolen. But they at least had some land, and they had their sovereignty. Some of them were lucky enough to find oil or minerals on that land. Some of them have built casinos, where the rest of America lines up for the chance to hand over money, every day and every night. Some of them, like the Choctaw, have built an empire on the scrap of land that nobody else wanted. That land was a form of capital. I just think my people deserve the capital they need to build a better life."

Judd nodded, as if it had taken him a moment to gather the gist of Donnelly's argument. "You're talking about reparations. That's a hot topic, Ross."

"Why shouldn't we be compensated for the wealth we left behind in Africa? Why shouldn't we inherit the payment our enslaved ancestors didn't receive for their labor? Why shouldn't we have the chance to claw our way up society's ladder, like the Choctaws have? Don't you think we're due something, sir?"

He gazed into Judd's eyes, which were unreadable. Then he turned his attention to Faye. "Don't you?"

Faye, who had relentlessly pursued regaining the lands stolen from her African-American ancestors during the Jim Crow years, wasn't sure she agreed with Ross, but she couldn't bring herself to say no. She broke the festering silence by introducing herself, instead. Extending a hand, she said, "My name's Faye Longchamp. You make an interesting argument."

Donnelly reached into his breast pocket and retrieved a sleek case full of business cards. His dark eyes communicated something different each time he handed out a card. When fastened on Faye, their expression suggested that he had more than business on his mind. When directed at Joe and Sheriff Rutland, his expression was more perfunctory, as if he'd rather not give personal information to law enforcement, nor to a man whose allegiance might be elsewhere. If Joe were wearing his customary Native American garb, instead of continuing his odd campaign to look like a white man, Donnelly might have guarded his words still more carefully.

Turning his attention to Judd last, he looked at him like a man approaching an equal for help with a cause that concerned them both. As Ross extended the card in the older man's direction, Judd turned and pressed the elevator button, saying, "I'd like to hear more of your thoughts, Ross. I'm feeling a little tired right now, but there's no reason you can't come up and talk to me while I relax a little."

Would it take a coronary to make Mr. Judd rest? Faye thought Neely was going to roll her eyes in frustration. She wanted to tell her to just let it go. Some people simply can't be protected from themselves.

Waving good-bye to Neely after they'd left Mr. Judd and Ross in Judd's suite, Faye led Joe toward the grill where the hotel's cheaper lunches were to be had. "Let's grab a bite here. I want to talk to Mr. Judd, and I don't want to do it in front of his new friend Ross."

"You mean *your* new friend Ross."

Faye smirked instead of answering him.

"I've been thinking," Joe said, nodding his thanks to the waitress for his burger and fries. "I noticed that you've been fretting over the sheriff suspecting that somebody on Dr. Mailer's team might have killed Mr. Calhoun."

"Well, I don't like to think about somebody who's innocent being accused of murder." Faye didn't point out that her biggest fear had been that the sheriff would focus on Joe as a suspect. Looking out for her other friends had always been secondary to protecting Joe. She wasn't sure whether he understood that.

"So you helped the sheriff figure out that the murder weapon was old, which took some focus off any flintknappers. Mostly off of me, I guess."

Okay. So maybe Joe *had* understood how desperate she'd been to keep him off Neely Rutland's suspect list.

Joe was still talking. "You said it bothered you to tell her that Bodie was a champion atlatl thrower. But how well do you know Bodie, anyway?"

"Well, he was the teaching assistant in my lithics lab last semester. A bunch of us went to happy hour a couple of times, and he was in the group. I went to a party at his house, once. And…well, that's about all. But he seems like a nice guy."

"That's what they said about Ted Bundy. You don't know anything else about him?"

A dim memory surfaced of harsh words between Bodie and another classmate that mushroomed into the kind of barroom argument where the arguers are told to take it outside. And the more she thought about it, the more sure she was that Bodie was passed out on the couch before she left his party.

"He drinks. And when he drinks, he has a temper."

"Plus, he has a lot of skill with a deadly weapon," Joe pointed out. "Just like I do. What about Toneisha?"

"She was in a couple of my classes last semester. We had lunch once after class. That's about all. But I like her."

"Me, too. Not that it makes much of a difference. I wouldn't know a killer if they bit me."

"Toneisha, on the other hand, likes Bodie. A whole lot. He has no idea." An unwelcome thought entered Faye's mind. "Didn't Toneisha and Bodie give each other alibis for the night Mr. Calhoun died?"

Joe nodded. "I was waiting for you to notice that."

Now and then, Faye still found herself surprised by the logic of Joe's thought processes. Then she found herself surprised by her own prejudices. If anyone should see past his lack of a formal education, it should be her. Joe possessed the equivalent of a Ph.D. in ancient weapons, but he worked as a lowly technician because learning disabilities and school don't mix. After six months of intensive tutoring, he was nearly ready to take his high school equivalency test, except for that pesky math requirement. Every time Joe shot an arrow at a moving squirrel, he did sophisticated calculus in his head. But instead of getting a good grade, he got dinner.

"Since Toneisha and Bodie provided alibis for each other," she said, "I don't think we can say for sure where either of them were that night. Toneisha would do anything for Bodie."

"And then there's Chuck and Dr. Mailer and Oka Hofobi," Joe continued relentlessly.

"Oh, Oka Hofobi is so quiet. He's like you, in some ways. Dr. Mailer is such a gentle man, and Chuck is weird and all, but I just don't think..."

Joe's green eyes glinted in amusement. "But they're all dead serious about archaeology. You're really so sure none of them killed Mr. Calhoun to save that mound? Think back. You knew some people who killed other folks. Did you see it coming?"

The answer was no. She'd looked two cold-blooded murderers in the face and never suspected a thing. Her obliviousness had nearly gotten her killed, twice. Joe had saved her both times...but both times he'd had to kill somebody to do it. Granted, both of those somebodies had needed killing. Still, if asked beforehand whether Joe had it in him to kill, even in self-defense, her answer would have been no. Clearly, she was a rotten judge of character.

She admitted defeat. "When will I stop needing you to protect me from myself?"

"Probably never, which is okay by me."

They chewed on their lunches in silence for awhile, but Joe wasn't through with her yet.

"You sure have been worried about Mr. Judd today."

"He was really sick. What's your point?"

"How well do you know him?"

Faye beckoned the waitress for their check. "Now don't tell me you think *he* killed Mr. Calhoun. He looks a little frail to overpower a man that size."

"So he does. I'm just pointing out how dead-set you were on making sure he was okay."

"This is wrong?"

"No. It's just that you take care of everybody but Faye. You made sure that Neely doesn't suspect me of killing Mr. Calhoun. Any fool could see what you were up to. I did, and Neely probably did, too."

"Why wouldn't I want her to know you're innocent? You are. We were together the whole day and night that Mr. Calhoun was killed." Faye charged their meals to her room and rose to leave. "Isn't it okay for me to presume you're innocent?"

"Sure. Since I am, and you know it. But there's no point in running interference for the whole crew, when you don't know they're innocent and nobody's asked you to."

Faye glared at him and stalked toward the elevator. Joe, with his long easy strides, kept up with her easily.

"I think I finally figured out why you try to take care of everybody, Faye. I think it's because you need a baby."

It crossed Faye's mind to snap back at him by asking, "You offering to help with that?", but there was no telling what honest Joe might say.

Instead she retorted, "I've got time," in a tone of voice that didn't invite further conversation.

Chapter Eleven

Congressman Judd answered their knock promptly, saying, "I thought you'd be back."

"I heard the sheriff discouraging you from trying to find that old cemetery," Faye said as she and Joe entered the suite. She looked around for Ross Donnelly, but he'd had the social finesse not to overstay his welcome. She wasn't surprised. "The sheriff may be right. It may be dangerous for us to go trekking through the woods, and there may be nothing to learn there about your attack, even if you do find the cemetery. But I know a way to get to it without trespassing on anybody's property."

"I'm listening." Judd backed away from the door and gestured at two chairs, settling himself on the sofa. Faye wished he would cast good manners aside and rest on the bed. For a moment she wondered whether Joe would think she was being overly solicitous if he knew what she was thinking. She decided she didn't care. Much.

"Are you familiar with the concept of 'Waters of the State'?" she asked the congressman.

"I understand that it means that nobody can own a body of water, so nobody can keep you out of it. One time, my friend took me for a boat ride on the Silver River in Florida. We rode that river right up to the headwaters at Silver Springs, and just sat there for a while, looking at all the people who paid to get into the theme park. The glass-bottomed boats floated around us, doing their tourist thing, and I'm sure they wished we'd go away, but there wasn't a damn thing anybody could do to make us leave. Waters of the State. The phrase has a populist ring to it. I like that. But how does it get me where I want to go?"

"Yeah, I love to run my john boat up and down the coastline and look at all those million-dollar houses," Joe said. "Me and my old boat don't do much for their million-dollar view, but it's as much mine as it is theirs."

Faye reflected that Joe could never be anything but an enhancement to any seascape she'd ever seen. She turned to Judd. "You said you walked along the creek a long way, and at some point you saw a marijuana field. Then, not much further down the creek, you saw a hill with a cemetery on top of it. Could you see these things if you were standing in the creek?"

"Yes...so you're saying that we can walk almost the same route I did all those years ago, only we'll never leave the creek."

"You can't be trespassing when you're standing in a Water of the State."

Joe cleared his throat. "Faye, I understand about the law. It's not against the law to take this walk you're talking about. I get that. But do you think Mrs. Calhoun is going to wait while we explain it to her? Or do you think she's just going to shoot our heads off?"

"The man's got a point," Judd said. "We won't be trespassing, but that still doesn't make this expedition safe."

"Everybody around here goes to prayer meeting. When's that?" Faye asked.

"Prayer meeting is on Wednesday nights, halfway between Sundays. That way, people get reminded not to sin every three or four days," said Judd, the grown-up preacher's kid. "It's only Monday. I don't want to wait till Wednesday. Reckon she might go to the Fair sometime tomorrow?"

"The woman's husband died day before yesterday," Faye pointed out. "I don't think she'll be heading out for a concert and some cotton candy tonight."

Joe picked up a newspaper from the floor beside his chair and flipped through it while Faye and Judd pondered the problem.

"We could get Mrs. Nail to invite her to dinner," she suggested. "It would be neighborly of her."

Mr. Judd shook his head. "Then we'd be dragging innocent folks into this."

"Besides," Joe interjected, "they live right across the road from where we want to go. If Mrs. Calhoun sees us, she'll just walk across the highway to her own house, grab her shotgun, and come out shooting."

"Good point," Faye said, "but not the answer I was looking for."

Joe was squinting at the newspaper, running his finger along a tiny line of type. He looked up and said, "I say we just go, and we don't worry about Mrs. Calhoun and her shotgun."

"I'm surprised to hear you say that, son, being as how you're bigger than me and your lady friend put together. You'd make an excellent target."

Joe pointed to a two-column-inch article buried in the middle of the Local News section. "It says here that there will be an open casket viewing of Mr. Carroll Calhoun tonight at seven-thirty. The funeral is tomorrow night at the same time. So we get to pick which night we ain't trespassing on his wife's property. You weren't feeling so good this morning. You want to rest up before we do this? We could wait till tomorrow or Wednesday."

"I don't like to waste time," Judd said. "I'll meet you two tonight at the Nails' when you get off work at five. Then we can watch Mrs. Calhoun's house until we see her car leave."

"If you bring a big bouquet of flowers," Faye said, "I bet Mrs. Nail will feed us something while we wait."

Chapter Twelve

Finally, Faye was getting some work done. She had never understood people who goofed off on the job. She certainly understood the concept of disliking your job, since her own resumé included several stints of hamburger flipping. But slacking off didn't give a girl her personal time back. It just meant that she was standing in a smelly fast food kitchen, doing nothing. Faye would rather have something to show for her time, even if it was just a steaming pile of cheeseburgers.

Faye had traded those cheeseburgers for a big pile of backdirt, but she was so thrilled to be back in school that she attacked the monotonous work with vigor. So did everybody else on the archaeology team, although some of them managed to talk an awful lot while they were doing it. Faye couldn't work and talk at the same time, so she just listened.

Toneisha lifted her eyes from her own steadily growing pile of backdirt and studied the Calhoun mound with greedy eyes. "I'd love a chance to look that thing over. I'm fascinated with the Poverty Point culture."

"Ever been there?" Bodie asked.

"Poverty Point? Not yet."

"Mighty impressive. And not just the mounds. I mean, I wouldn't want to tote a million basketloads of dirt, but building a mound isn't necessarily such a big engineering achievement. Not compared to the geometry at Poverty Point. You've seen pictures of the ridges? Those people built a set of concentric ridges, shaped like a perfectly symmetrical rainbow that's 4,000 feet across at the base. Almost a mile! Then they built their houses on those ridges, lifting them up out of the muck and trash that goes along with big-city life. And I can't imagine how they oriented the mounds west of the ridges on such a straight line. I'd say it was a more sophisticated design than anything built in North America for a long, long time. Europe, too."

"Probably more comfortable than a European city of that time period, too." Toneisha was head-down in her pit, looking around. Her disembodied voice emerged, loud and clear. The woman had a powerful set of lungs.

Oka Hofobi dropped his trowel, like a man who had heard enough. "Would you listen to yourselves? You can't go around comparing cultures that way. It's racist."

Toneisha's lifted her head out of the hole.

Bodie's mouth gaped open like a kid who couldn't figure out what he did to get in trouble. "What'd I say that was racist? I think I said that North American builders were *better* than European builders."

"You just pronounced Poverty Point as more sophisticated than hundreds of other cultures, because its geometry is pleasing to your eye. That's a European construct. A tiny settlement built of wattle-and-daub houses could have been perfectly designed for its landscape, but we wouldn't know about it, because it wouldn't have left much behind for us to dig up. But if its people were comfortable and happy, then its design was just as sophisticated as Poverty Point. Or Stonehenge. Or the pyramids at Giza. We're too hung up on monumental architecture. Bigger isn't always better." He picked up his trowel and dug into the soil as if it had offended him personally.

Bodie walked over to Oka Hofobi and stuck out a hand. "Oke. I'm sorry, man. Thanks for yanking my chain on that one. If you hear me do something like that again, yank it again."

Oka Hofobi took a while to get around to shaking Bodie's proffered hand. Faye saw that he covered his hesitation by yanking his bandanna out of his pocket to wipe the dirt off his hands, but he did hesitate. Eventually, he shook Bodie's hand and Toneisha's, too, saying, "I know you didn't mean anything. But maybe you could just try not to talk around my father. Or my brother. Or the Tribal Council. It's all I can do to defend myself against them. I can't look out for you, too."

A late afternoon phone call ended Faye's workday on an ebullient note. All her friend Mike McKenzie had needed to say was, "Faye!" and she knew all she needed to know. His wife—and her dear friend—Magda had earned a clean bill of health from her doctor, and so had the new baby.

She cried out "How's fatherhood treating you, now that everybody's out of the hospital?" and the entire work crew gathered around her. Everybody in the department liked Magda. (Except for a few professors who disagreed with her on purely professional grounds, which meant that they felt obliged to dislike her personally, too.)

Oka Hofobi said, "Wait till I tell Ma. She loves babies, and she doesn't much care whose they are. She just likes to know there's another one in the world."

The students on Dr. Mailer's team were surely aware that Magda's pregnancy hadn't run smoothly. Her near-total absence from the department had been hard to miss. But only Faye knew about the bed rest and the anti-labor drugs and the nine months of worry. She'd even been Mike's stand-in on those nights when his sheriff's duties kept him away from their Lamaze classes. Faye now knew things about the female anatomy that no one who'd never given birth had any right to know.

After Faye's phone got passed around so that everybody could give Magda and Mike their good wishes, the workday was effectively over.

"Oh, go have a beer in honor of Little Miss McKenzie," Dr. Mailer said, and everyone had happily complied—everyone except Faye and Joe, who had an appointment to meet Lawrence Judd on that very spot and thus couldn't afford to leave.

Waving good-bye, they sat in the trailer and settled in to wait for Mr. Judd, who was a very long time in coming.

Faye paced back and forth across the Nails' back yard, poking numbers into her cell phone and getting no answer. Over the past hour, she had established a frustrating, monotonous two-part sequence.

First, she punched in Mr. Judd's cell phone number and waited until his voice mail picked up. Having already left six messages, she had taken to hanging up on the voice mail recording, which would have been more satisfying if she could have generated some noise by slamming an old-style receiver onto a solid handset. Pressing a button and getting a polite beep didn't do much for her state of mind.

Next, she dialed the hotel and talked to the front desk staff, who continued to assure her that they hadn't seen Mr. Judd, but that they were happy to buzz his room. Again. Since he never answered, they were also happy to put her through to his voice mail, which was already full of her messages. Faye had to admit that the Choctaws trained their hotel staff well. Nobody had told her yet that she needed to put down the phone and get a life, which Faye would have probably done by now, if she'd been in their shoes.

"It's way past six, Joe. I'm worried. Maybe we shouldn't have left him alone, but he looked like he was feeling so much better."

"Did you try Dr. Mailer? Maybe he's back at the hotel by now. He could just go upstairs and knock on Mr. Judd's door."

"Yeah, I called him. He's not there. He took everybody else back out to the Fair after work. By the time they took a bus to the parking lot and drove all the way back to the hotel, we could just get in our car and be there."

"Then let's do that."

As they walked to the car, Joe's sharp eyes caught a glimmer of motion through the trees that blanketed the property across the road. He pointed in that direction with his chin in the silent, subtle motion of a hunter. Faye, long accustomed to Joe's ways, immediately saw what he wanted her to see. Mrs. Calhoun had left her house and was walking—no, running—in their direction.

Still rattled by Judd's failure to show up, Faye nearly panicked at the woman's appearance. She even went so far as to check to see whether Mrs. Calhoun was carrying a gun, before she realized that her guilty conscience was working on her. She and Joe were not trespassing on the Calhoun property, and Mrs. Calhoun had no reason to know that they were planning to do so. She had no reason to shoot them. She actually had no reason to even give them the time of day. But why was she running and where was she going?

As Mrs. Calhoun grew nearer, Faye saw that she was wearing a black dress, well-cut but sober. Her shoes, also black, had the sturdy heel and cushioned sole of dress shoes designed for a woman old enough to care more about comfort than style. Instead of a purse, she clutched a plastic-wrapped bundle under one arm. When Faye recognized the bundle as a loaf of bread, she understood.

The older woman burst out of the trees into the open field where Faye had met Mr. Calhoun just four days before, then she came to an abrupt stop. Panting, she ripped open the plastic bag and dug her hand deep into it, pinching off bits of bread and throwing them onto the ground around her. The birds came, as they had for years, expecting crumbs and a quiet visit with an old friend. They found only a frantic woman, pulling bigger and bigger chunks out of the bread bag until she was reduced to grabbing whole slices of bread and hurling them at the gathered flock.

Even half-tame birds like these can only take such a pelting for a short time. Hopping and flapping their varicolored wings, they scattered, but not quickly enough to suit the new widow. She ran screaming through the thick of them, and they rose like a billowing fog around her, then vanished.

Alone again, Mrs. Calhoun wiped the back of her hand across her eyes and trudged back to her empty home. A few minutes later, Faye and Joe watched as a car stopped to pick her up and drive her to the place where her husband's body waited.

Faye was so rattled that she let Joe, who was never rattled, do the driving. Their plan to outsmart Mrs. Calhoun and get access to her property had distracted Faye from the fact that the woman was preparing for her husband's funeral. A man was dead, and one of that man's last actions had been to terrorize Faye and Joe.

The violence that had been done to Mr. Judd was forty years old, but Faye was only now realizing how hard his story had shaken her, too. Deep down, she needed to know who had attacked him, and she needed for that person to see justice. Even after all these years, the law still had the power to make things right. It could not repair the damage done to a young man's life, but it could say to the world, "We the people recognize that a wrong has been done, and we will not tolerate it." Mr. Judd's attacker was surely quite old by now, so he had only a few years left to pay for his crime. Nevertheless, it was important that society recognize that crime and repudiate it.

Faye hadn't realized how much this exploratory trip along the creek had meant to her. She wanted the man who had beaten a teenaged boy to see justice, and she wanted Judd to see it happen. Even more, she wanted to know who had saved him all those years ago, because she wanted to shake his hand.

Her nerves weren't soothed by the quiet ride. She and Joe hurried through the hotel parking lot and lobby, not wanting to attract attention, but when the elevator doors opened onto Mr. Judd's floor, Faye gave in to her fears and pelted down the hall at a dead run. There was no answer to her knock.

Faye pressed her cheek to the door and called the older man's name. A smooth sliding noise sounded, followed by a metallic clunk and the muted sound of glass breaking, as if a lamp had been pushed across a table onto a carpeted floor. The next sound she heard was a groan.

"Go downstairs and get a key!"

Joe was already halfway down the hall before the words were out of her mouth.

"Mr. Judd. Can you hear me? Can you get to the door?"

The door handle shivered.

"Just pull down on the handle and push. If you can get the door open a crack, I can get in and help you."

Another groan sounded, but Faye could hear the latch moving. She grabbed the handle and pulled, ready to yank the door open as soon as he got it unlatched, before it could close and lock again. "You can do it, sir. I'm right here on the other side of the door."

Another wordless sound, softer this time, came to her, but the door moved a fraction of a degree. She yanked hard and Judd's body slumped through the open door.

A Choctaw woman rolled a housecleaning cart out of a room down the hall. Seeing them, she let out a small scream and ran for help.

Faye snatched up his limp wrist and pressed her fingers hard against it, hoping for a pulse. She found one, but she didn't need a clock with a second hand to tell her that the beats were way too far apart.

Was he breathing? She promised God she'd take a CPR course if only this man would breathe. Faye rolled him over onto his back, tried to make sure his airway was open, then she held her own breath. After an inordinately long time, Judd's chest rose and fell. Good.

Grabbing her phone out of her pocket, she dialed 911 and called in the cavalry, in the form of an ambulance team. Joe came running a minute later with a hotel employee bearing a key. When he saw Judd, he sank to the floor next to him and asked, "What happened?"

Faye could only say, "I don't know."

She and Joe sat together on the floor beside their new friend and held his hands until the ambulance arrived.

Lawrence Judd thought the pretty girl holding his hand was remarkably young to be so self-assured in a crisis. Maybe that meant that she'd seen more than her share of crises in her short life. Or maybe she wasn't all that young. The strangest part of turning sixty had been the fact that he saw most everybody as young, these days. A person could be a high-powered executive or a mother of three, it didn't matter, Judd still considered them young if their wrinkles were sparse and their hair wasn't very gray.

How odd that he was thinking so clearly, yet he couldn't even focus his eyes on the pretty girl's face. The thoughts in his head were so much more clear than anything in the outside world. The feel of the carpet against his back. The smell of disinfectant that emanated from the hotel room's toilet. The sound of footsteps approaching, footsteps that might be bringing help. All these things were growing less real by the second.

Perhaps this was what it was like to die.

Chapter Thirteen

The paramedic checking Mr. Judd's vital signs seem capable and levelheaded, considering that she was a child. Faye wondered how old you had to be to go around saving lives. Watching the young thing work, Faye decided that she was old enough.

The serious young woman threaded an IV into Judd's arm, while a man with a familiar face poked an oxygen cannula in his nose. Davis Nail didn't talk much when he was working, just as he didn't talk much in everyday life. But here, doing the work he obviously loved, he didn't radiate anger and resentment. He exuded competence.

"Are you a relative?" the young woman asked Faye.

"No, just a friend. He's from out of town. I think his family's all up north. He was supposed to meet me for...um, for dinner. When he didn't show up, I came looking for him. He was like this when I got here."

"He hasn't been responsive at all?"

"No. He was unconscious, just like he is now, but he's been breathing the whole time."

The woman was taking notes, while keeping a constant eye on the patient. "Do you know if he takes any medications regularly?"

Here was a question Faye could answer. "Yes, he does. He has high blood pressure, for sure. And angina and high cholesterol. Maybe some other stuff. I think he takes pills for all those things." She shuffled through the possessions scattered around the suite, finally locating the pill case that held his daily medications in the bathroom. That day's compartment, marked Monday, was empty, and the rest were full. "There's at least one more bottle that he takes when he feels bad." She found it in the pocket of a pair of pants draped over the desk chair. "There may be more, but these are all I know about."

"This is for angina," Davis said, taking the prescription bottle and reading the label.

"Has he had a heart attack?" Faye asked. "He was feeling pretty weak this morning."

"It's hard to say at this point. These medications look like the typical middle-aged man's cocktail—diuretic, beta-blocker, ibuprofen, cholesterol drug, multi-vitamin—but the prescription drugs are generic, so they all look sorta alike. Little white bullets."

The emergency personnel lifted Judd onto a stretcher and hustled him down toward the elevator. "Meet us at the hospital. We'll take good care of him."

Faye had always considered hospital waiting rooms to be obnoxious places, well-stocked with magazines which assumed that the whole world was interested in the serpentine love lives of Hollywood stars. They were also always well-stocked with people suffering through the worst day of their lives. Whenever the volunteer at the information desk rose and called out a name, the shadowed eyes of the waiters not called sunk deeper into their sockets.

She and Joe had spent three hours in medical purgatory when Ross Donnelly burst into the room. "I'm staying at the same hotel as Mr. Judd, and I heard one of the employees say that he'd been rushed to the hospital. How is he?"

Faye was assembling a jaundiced opinion of Ross Donnelly— why would he care so much about a man he just met, unless it was because he was hoping for a favor?—until she remembered Joe asking her much the same question. Why did she care about

Mr. Judd, whom she didn't know well? Why did she care about Bodie and Toneisha and Chuck and Dr. Mailer and Oka Hofobi? What did it matter? She just did.

She answered his question. "The paramedics were still trying to get him stable when they loaded him on the ambulance. That's all we know."

Ross sank into the chair next to Faye and looked her full in the face. "I heard that you were the one that found him and called 911. Word in the hotel casino is that you're the hero of the day. How are you holding up?" He leaned in so close that she could smell his after-shave, and his eyes never left hers. His fingers brushed lightly across the back of her right hand.

The man had impeccable romantic radar. Most guys gave Faye a wide berth whenever Joe was sitting right beside her. His six-plus feet of well-toned muscle tended to have that effect on men. Ross had obviously intuited that she and Joe were just friends, and he didn't mind making a move on Faye right in front of him.

This made Faye more than a little uncomfortable, so her answer was awkward. "Uh, it wasn't just me. Joe did a lot, too. And the paramedics, of course."

Joe, who was a little smoother than Faye, rose and asked, "Anyone want anything from the vending machines?"

Faye and Ross both shook their heads and Joe ambled down the hall.

Continuing her efforts at scintillating conversation, Faye asked, "You're not from around here, are you? I guess that's obvious, since you're staying at the hotel."

"I'm from Brooklyn, but I came south to go to Emory, and I've never looked back. I wasn't made for ice and snow."

"They get ice in Atlanta now and then."

"Yeah, and you should see those Georgians try to drive in it. It's like amateur night at the demolition derby. I think I need to go further south."

Faye laughed and said, "I'm from Florida. I've never seen snow." Then she caught herself short when she heard how the light-hearted sound of laughter vibrated in the tense atmosphere of the waiting room.

"I've always intended to get to Florida, but I was too busy working. People say I'm a workaholic, but I believe in what I do."

Faye was trying to decide whether to confess to being a workaholic, too, or whether to ask him to tell her more about the work that he believed in so fervently, when the volunteer at the information desk announced, "Friends of Lawrence Judd?"

She and Ross rushed forward. The volunteer held out a phone and said, "Mr. Judd's wife wants to talk to the young woman who helped her husband. Is that you?"

Faye noticed that the woman's statement was carefully phrased to avoid revealing anything about the patient's condition, or even whether he was still alive. She put the phone to her ear and braced herself for a conversation with a woman freshly widowed.

A quavering voice asked, "Are you Faye Longchamp?" and Faye was confused. Mr. Judd had some health problems, but he was barely over sixty. That was hardly elderly, these days. Did this frail, old voice belong to his wife or to his mother?

"Yes, this is Faye Longchamp. I'm so sorry for your husband's trouble." Was that the right thing to say? What if he was dead?

"Oh, my dear, if it weren't for you, I might have lost him."

Faye blew out a sigh of relief.

The tremulous voice continued. "I wonder if I could ask a favor of you. Lawrence is all alone down there, and my multiple sclerosis hasn't let me travel for many years." That explained the shaky voice, and it explained why a wife solicitous enough to load her husband's pill box for him wasn't already on a plane to Mississippi. "Will you talk to the doctor for me? And will you talk to Lawrence, then call me and tell me how he looks? I'm just sick with worry, and the doctor's in such a tearing hurry to get off the phone. I can't be sure I understand everything that's going on."

"Do you think they'll talk to me?" Faye asked. "I'm not family, and they're persnickety about privacy around here."

The voice was no less quavery, but it grew stronger. "I gave the doctor my verbal permission to speak to you, which he resisted, so I faxed a letter to the hospital giving my written permission. I told him that I had not been married to a lawyer for thirty-five years, only to be shunted aside by his arrogance. And I'll tell you that, even in my day, Bennett College had an excellent English program, so I have learned to express myself well on the printed page. I trust that my letter melted his fax machine."

To heck with Joe and his accusation that Faye liked everybody, even ax-murderers. She *really* liked Mrs. Judd. "Yes, ma'am. I will gladly do battle with the medical system, if it will help you and your husband. Count on me."

Ross Donnelly had stepped away to give Faye some privacy for her conversation with Mrs. Judd, so he couldn't hear what she said. It didn't matter. The few steps he'd taken away from Faye only served to give him some perspective on the woman. Looking at her like this, from head to toe, it was impossible to ignore the fact that she was dressed like a manual laborer. There wasn't a woman in Ross' circle of acquaintance who shopped for her work clothes at the army surplus store. Now that he'd met Faye, it occurred to him that he might need to expand his social circle. Because under those shabby clothes was a body that was as slender and shapely as the ones belonging to his debutante friends.

Above that body, under a heavy coat of dust, was a most appealing face. He liked her eyes, not just because of their exotic up-tilt, but because of their unmistakable intelligence. Her sleek cap of black hair didn't require mousse or spray to do its job of framing Faye's delicate features. Her skin, the color of dark honey, was stretched tautly over a most determined jawline. And her full lips were soft, but not weak.

He didn't know what those lips were saying to Mr. Judd's wife, but he sensed that her words offered comfort. He sensed that Faye was a woman you could count on. He'd never sought out that quality in a woman, but now that he'd seen it, he wanted it. A hospital cardiac unit was not a propitious place to ask a woman for a first date, but Ross would be looking for a chance to woo Faye. No, not just looking for a chance. He would make his own chance, because that was the kind of man Ross Donnelly was.

Faye was relieved to see that Mr. Judd was conscious and alert. Even better, he made sense when he talked. But the bilious green, ill-fitting hospital gown made him look like a man at death's door. Cables emerged from beneath the gown, emanating from the general vicinity of his chest. They converged on a fist-sized electronic instrument tucked into a pocket on the front of his gown.

He pointed to the pocket machine, saying, "They say this'll let them watch my heart beat all night long. If it looks good, I'll get out of here tomorrow. Did you talk to Sallie? How's she holding up?"

"Your wife is doing just fine, and you know it, because she's tough. I understand that she told your doctor where to get off."

He adjusted the oxygen cannula resting on his upper lip, which had slipped when he chuckled at the thought of his wife chewing out his doctor. "Sallie's body may not take good care of her, but her mind and her will—well, I've never met a stronger woman. No. Let me rephrase that. I've never met a stronger person. It looks like my body might be turning on me, too, so maybe I'll take a page out of Sallie's book." Thinking about his wife had brought a bit of color back to the sick man's face. Faye would like to mean that much to somebody, someday.

"I'll tell her that you're looking much better, because you are. But first, she wants me to corner your doctor and get the whole truth out of him."

"Good luck with that."

The ER doctor looked like he thought he was way too busy to talk to the friend of a man who was going to pull through.

Despite what Joe said, Faye found that she did not, in fact, like everybody.

"We've got to watch him a few more hours, so he'll be here overnight." He moved toward the door.

"Did he have a heart attack?"

"No." Apparently deciding that, since she insisted on making him talk to her, then he would just whip out as many polysyllabic words as possible, he went on, "His hypotension and bradycardia have resolved. He responded well to atropine, and there's no sign of pulmonary edema. We'll have him on telemetry all night, then send him home tomorrow afternoon if everything checks out. My best guess is that he took an extra beta-blocker or two, since you say he was feeling ill this morning, but it'll be a few days before we get the lab results to confirm that. It's a good thing he's on a fairly low dose, or the extra pill might have killed him. That drug is particularly dosage-sensitive, so taking extra was a bad idea, but it happens more than you'd think. Some people have the notion that if a little is good, then a lot is better."

Having dismissed a powerful and educated man as someone who might have done something so dimwitted as taking an overdose of a dangerous drug, just on a whim, the doctor took his leave of her.

Tales of the Removal

As told by Mrs. Frances Nail

This is not an old tale, but it is a true one. Stories have to be told, or they are forgotten. Almost two hundred years ago, my people lost everything. Most of Mississippi was ours and part of Alabama, but the United States government wanted our land. And they took it, too.

We were the first. Did you know that? We were the first tribe taken away from our home to the Indian Territory. That's Oklahoma, now. You ever been to Oklahoma? Me neither, but I've seen pictures and movies. Does it look anything like Mississippi to you? How did anybody think us Choctaws would know how to farm or hunt or stay warm in such a different place? I'm guessing that they didn't much care.

President Jackson wanted us to go. I think he wanted us dead. They taught us his words in school, and I remember them, because they are important. I taught them to my children. We won't forget. He said:

> *"That those tribes can not exist surrounded...in continual contact with our citizens is certain... Established in the midst of another and a superior race...they must necessarily yield to the force of circumstances and ere long disappear."*

The great chief Pushmataha went to Washington and asked Congress for help, but he got none. I learned his words, too. He said:

> *"I can boast and say, and tell the truth, that none of my fathers, or grandfathers, nor any Choctaw ever drew bows against the United States...We have held*

the hands of the United States so long that our nails
are long like bird's claws; and there is no danger of
their slipping out. I came here when a young man to
see my Father Jefferson. He told me if ever we got in
trouble we must run and tell him. I am come."

The Treaty of Dancing Rabbit Creek was the final straw. It traded all our land here for a scrap of Oklahoma, and it didn't promise much else. Just a trip west led by people who would be "kind and brotherly to them." That's what the treaty said! But do you know what one of the men leading the Removal said? He said:

"Death is hourly among us. The road is lined with
the sick. Fortunately they are a people that will walk to
the last, or I do not know how we would get on."

Thousands of Choctaws died on the Trail of Tears that winter, from cold and thirst and starvation. Some of us stayed behind, and we fared little better, but we still had our home. And we had our mother, Nanih Waiya.

While she stands, there will always be Choctaws here.

Chapter Fourteen

Tuesday
Day 5 of the Neshoba County Fair

"Mr. Judd's wife was not pleased when I told her that the doctor thought he'd taken too much of his beta-blocker," Faye asked Joe as she perused the breakfast buffet and settled, again, on a sumptuous pile of biscuits and gravy. "'My husband is many things,' she said, 'but he is not an idiot.'"

"Doesn't seem like one to me."

"So, let's say Mr. Judd took an extra pill or two. Where did it come from?" Faye speared a chunk of biscuit on her fork and twirled it around in the gravy.

"You didn't find any other bottles in his room? Not even in the trash can?"

"Nope, and you and the paramedics all saw me looking. I tore that suite apart."

Joe dug into a pile of eggs and sausage that would put him in need of beta-blockers of his own in about thirty years. "Maybe he took all the ones he had left in the box, one for every day of the week. That would have been six pills too many."

"No, he couldn't have done that. Davis said he saw beta-blockers in there. And the ER doctor must have seen some, too, because he knew the dosage. If there had been some missing—say, if the Tuesday and Wednesday slots didn't have beta-blockers in them—then I think he would have said something definite like, 'The man took two extra pills.' Doctors are definite people. Since he said something vague like he thinks Mr. Judd took 'an extra pill or two,' then I'd say it's because he doesn't have a clue how many he actually took, and he won't have a clue until the lab tests come back."

"Maybe there's nothing funny at all about the pills left in the box," Joe said. He stopped to chew. "Maybe they're just what Davis said they were—beta blockers and ibuprofen and stuff. One of each for every day of the week."

"So do you think he just got sick for no reason?"

"Well, it's possible. Even the doctor won't be sure without those lab tests. But, no, that's not what I meant." His thought processes were interrupted by more chewing. "I was thinking that maybe those pills are fine, but there was something funny about one of the ones he took yesterday afternoon."

"You think they were defective?" An unattractive thought surfaced. "Or you think somebody poisoned him."

"Well, no, I hadn't gotten that far in thinking this through. I was just crossing the other things off the list. We don't think he took too many pills, because we can't find the bottle they came out of. Also, because none of the pills in his day-of-the-week case was missing."

"Right."

"So that only leaves two things. Either he got sick for some reason besides the pills, something the doctors couldn't find. And it seems to me like they would have looked pretty hard, since he's famous and all. Or else something was wrong about the ones he took."

"Well, let's walk back through the day. I watched Neely put the pills in the box, right out of the prescription bottle...that was filled by Preston Silver. Now that's a man who I wouldn't want handling my drugs."

"Maybe if he was wearing rubber gloves," Joe offered.

"I don't think rubber gloves would be enough to keep the Klansman contamination off. But let's be fair. Chuck had his hands on that pill case, too, earlier in the day. We know Mr. Judd has a habit of leaving it in his glove box, so someone could have tampered with it earlier, and we wouldn't know. And hotel personnel would have had access to his room, if he'd left the case unattended in there."

Joe looked at her expectantly, as if there was one more suspect, but he wanted her to be the one who named him.

"Ross Donnelly," Faye continued slowly. "He was alone in the room with Mr. Judd. He may even have been the last person to see him before his medical crisis."

Joe nodded, with a facial expression that said he was proud of her.

"I'm still not letting Mr. Silver fill any prescriptions for me," he said, heading back for seconds.

"Agreed. But I think we have time to stop by his pharmacy before we go to work."

Silver's Drugs was a throwback to a simpler time, a time before the nation was criss-crossed with big-box pharmacies that all looked alike. The floors were covered with black-and-white linoleum tiles laid in a diamond pattern. The worn tiles were waxed and buffed to a high gloss. Long, low display racks stretched across the room, and a scar on the floor showed where an old-timey lunch counter had once taken up space now devoted to over-the-counter drugs. High, modern shelving would have been a more efficient use of space, but these old racks apparently held enough of a selection to suit Preston Silver's loyal customers. Though the store had just opened, there were already several people milling about, waiting for a chance to fill their prescriptions.

Faye checked her watch. She figured she had twenty minutes to kill before she and Joe were irredeemably late for work, so she busied herself perusing a selection of cut-rate pantyhose on the aisle furthest from the pharmacy counter. Within ten minutes of watching Preston Silver do business, she'd detected a pattern that she didn't like. Eight people had approached the counter, which was staffed by Silver and a silver-haired African-American woman who looked as if her feet already hurt. Five of the customers were white, two were black, and one was Native American, probably Choctaw.

This was a reasonable approximation of the population of Neshoba County which, because of the reservation, had its own unique racial balance. During their project orientation, Dr. Mailer had been careful to call their attention to that balance—roughly 65% white, 20% black, and 15% Native American—which was an inescapable part of the local landscape.

It wasn't the diversity of Preston Silver's clientele that put a cold lump in the center of her chest. It was the way he treated them. As each person reached the front of the line, Silver either took the prescription from an outstretched hand, or he gave a curt nod at his assistant, who reached out a hand to take the slip of paper. It was impossible for Faye, who had been born biracial in the 1960s South, not to notice that Silver waited on all five white customers, handing the people of color over to his assistant.

Faye sat on her anger for five more minutes, watching Silver wait on three more white people, while his assistant deftly intervened to capture the two non-white customers before they had a chance to notice that the boss didn't want to talk to them. She decided to use her last five minutes well.

Approaching the counter, she sidestepped the efforts of Silver's assistant pharmacist to intercept her, presenting herself to the great man himself.

"My associate can take your prescription—" Silver began.

Faye wished she could do this without subjecting herself to the clammy aura that surrounded Silver, but she couldn't, so she spoke up. "I don't have a prescription. I just want to ask a question." She held up a bottle of Pepto-Bismol. "I heard it wasn't safe to take aspirin with this stuff. I took some last night. How long should I wait before I can have an aspirin?"

"My associate is well-versed in drug interactions," he began again. "If you'll just step—"

Joe, whose powers of observation exceeded even Faye's, had seen what was happening and done precisely the right thing. When Silver tried again to shunt Faye aside, he found that Joe was already standing beside her, engaging the assistant in a spirited discussion of the relative merits of several cold remedies.

Faye looked expectantly at the cornered Klansman, brandishing the bottle of pink stuff, but he untied his apron, dumped it on the counter, and stalked away. She wondered if no one had ever challenged him and his ugly approach to business. Or maybe, like Neely Rutland had done just the day before, people simply bustled into the store, conducted their business, and left without noticing who waited on them.

She set the bottle of Pepto-Bismol on the counter, turned to leave, then thought twice. Retrieving the bottle, she handed it to Silver's long-suffering assistant, along with a ten dollar bill. She'd faced down a dragon and won. Something inside her wanted to keep the Pepto as a trophy.

"Did we prove something, Faye?" Joe asked, eying the set of her jaw and the pink bottle in her hand. "I mean, did we prove something besides that he's prejudiced and that we're smarter than he is?"

"Isn't that enough?" Faye liked the contrast between the pink stomach remedy and the light brown skin of her hand. She hoped her impertinence made Preston Silver so sick that he needed a few doses of his own stomach medicine.

"We went in there because we wondered whether Silver poisoned Mr. Judd. Did we learn anything?"

Faye set the bottle aside and cranked the car. "Not exactly. We already had ample evidence that he's a racist. Now we've seen it with our own eyes. But that doesn't mean he's a killer." She pursed her lips while her thoughts raced ahead of her ability to sort through them. "Wait. We did learn something slightly useful. I'd bet fifty dollars that Preston Silver waited on Neely yesterday. She *is* white, after all. Then, when he had to help her track down Mr.

Judd's prescription, he would have known he was counting pills for a black man. A rich famous black man with political views he vehemently opposed. A rich famous black man who just gave a public speech calculated to stir up the past. Would it be tempting for a man like that to slip in a pill that could kill the patient?"

"Poison?"

"It wouldn't have to be something we'd think of as poison, like arsenic or strychnine. There's lots of perfectly ordinary things that can kill you if you take it wrong, or if you take too much. Simple aspirin would do it. Even water. To kill with one of those ordinary things, you just have to convince the victim to poison himself willingly. I suspect it wouldn't be that hard."

She wondered whether Preston Silver had stood behind his pharmacist's counter all these years, refining his plan for the perfect murder, waiting for his chance. Had Neely given it to him?

"I need to call the sheriff," Faye said, thumbing open the address book on her cell phone.

"So Preston tried some of his stupid bigot's tricks on you? I'll bet you made him eat his pharmacist's apron."

"You know about it?" Faye wished she'd asked Joe to drive while she talked on the phone. This country road appeared to have been laid out along an old cow path. Navigating around another abrupt twist, she wondered whether the cows had been drunk. "Neely, his behavior's illegal. You know that. It's a throwback to the days when only whites could eat at lunch counters."

"Why do you think Preston closed his lunch counter?"

"Because he didn't want to be forced to serve the likes of me."

Neely cleared her throat. "Well, I wouldn't have put it quite that way, but yes. The law has pushed Preston and people like him into a corner. They push back in little ways, just to prove they can. He behaves when I'm in the store. He knows everyone on my payroll by name, so he's not likely to screw up in front of them. I don't doubt that he pushes his luck when none of us are in the store."

"You've got my testimony…" Faye paused. "Wait. No, you don't. Joe and I both got waited on. We were made a little uncomfortable in the process, but I'm not sure any laws were broken."

Neely's voice was warm, even after it had been bounced off a few cell towers and filtered through the electronic guts of Faye's phone. "I guess I could get somebody he doesn't know to go in there wearing a recorder, and get some hard evidence but, Faye, I'm a little busy. I'm in the middle of a murder investigation. I wish people would vote with their feet and with their dollars. If people would shop somewhere else, then Preston could be prejudiced all by his lonesome self. Well, I guess he'll always have me, as long as I'm buying Daddy's medicine."

"Do you really think he's harmless enough to ignore? You said yourself that he was a known Klansman. Doesn't it worry you that Lawrence Judd collapsed shortly after taking pills from Silver's Pharmacy?"

The silence on Neely's end of the line was so complete that Faye checked her phone's display to see whether their connection had been broken. After a few long seconds, the sheriff spoke. "I heard Mr. Judd had been sick. I spoke with the doctor about his condition, but not as the sheriff and not because I thought there was a crime involved. I just felt…"

"Sympathetic?"

"Yeah, sympathetic. Because of Daddy. I know how hard it is to be sick. I was going to call his wife this evening, because I have an even better idea of what she's going through. Anyway, the doctor didn't give me even a breath of suspicion that there might be anything criminal about Mr. Judd's collapse."

Feeling sheepish, Faye said, "I guess I'm just the suspicious type."

"Well…" The phone was silent again for awhile, presumably because Neely was thinking. Faye congratulated herself for getting this far. Most law enforcement types would have dismissed her tenuous suspicions out of hand. She was grateful to Neely for taking her seriously.

"Well," Neely said again. "I'm supposed to talk to Preston Silver this afternoon. Nothing dramatic, just a conversation about his friendship with Carroll Calhoun, concluding with a discussion of why Preston thinks the man turned up dead. I had hoped to press him for information on Mr. Judd's attack, since I feel like there's is a decent chance that his attacker was in the Klan. Maybe he bragged to the Klavern about what he'd done. While I'm at it, I'll try to find out what he knows about why Judd collapsed yesterday, but I need something besides, 'I think you slipped him a bad pill because everybody knows you're a racist.' I'll do my best, Faye, but don't get your hopes up. Preston Silver has had more than forty years of practice in keeping his mouth shut."

Chapter Fifteen

Faye and Joe had slinked in late to work. Granted, they were hardly ten minutes late, but there were bosses in the world who would have chewed them up and spit them out for much less serious transgressions. Dr. Mailer was not one of those bosses.

Twenty minutes later, Toneisha and Bodie had arrived. Dr. Mailer had missed their arrival, having been in his office at the time, but Faye knew that he was aware of their tardiness. He said nothing.

Faye caught Joe's eye, then cast a knowing glance in the direction of the two tardy archaeologists. Joe just grinned. Faye hadn't mentioned to him that Toneisha had been out all night, figuring that her roommate's business was her own. Joe had apparently taken the same position regarding Bodie's whereabouts.

Privacy was tough to achieve under their close working conditions, but Bodie and Toneisha might as well have broadcast their budding relationship on the Internet. If they'd just managed to be on time for work (and if they'd been discreet enough to arrive in separate cars), the rest of the crew would still be wondering. Faye harbored naughty thoughts of buying Toneisha a travel alarm.

The morning passed uneventfully. At eleven o'clock, Dr. Mailer looked at his watch and said, "Would you look at that? We've been out here three hours and nobody's threatened anybody with a bulldozer. No law enforcement officers have driven out here to check our alibis for anything. No aging politicians have had any medical crises today. Nobody's been killed with a weapon that looks a lot like the stuff we've got stored in the trailer. And every last one of you has a dirty trowel in your hand. Even Faye."

Faye looked up from her excavation unit. "Hey. It's not my fault that the sheriff came all the way out here to talk to me. Or that Mr. Judd needed a ride."

"Sounds like slacker talk to me," said Toneisha, secure in the knowledge that, though she'd arrived late, she'd made up for it by moving more dirt than anybody on that particular morning.

"Folks that are talking are folks that aren't working," observed Bodie.

Faye tossed a rock in his general direction.

Mailer lifted his head from the potsherd he was measuring, and raised his reading glasses up onto his forehead so that he could focus on the car turning into the Nails' driveway. A spiffy-looking logo on the door proclaimed that it was owned by SGM&T. Their client had arrived.

Mailer muttered, "Well, I'll be John Brown," which was as close to cursing as he ever got. "Looks like my big mouth has conjured up a client visit. I won't be getting much more accomplished today, but if you people keep your heads down, maybe he'll ignore you and let you work." He rose and brushed the dirt from his knees. "Tell you what. If he tries to bother any of you, I'll tally up how much his project is paying, per minute, for this team's time."

"It's not all that much," Oka Hofobi said.

"Yeah," Mailer said as he walked toward the car, "but he's cheap. If you're on the clock, then he'll want you working. I'll deal with him on my own."

Mailer, as good as his word, had kept the contractor as far from his team as possible, but sound travels far and fast, so the team had heard every word of their client's diatribe. He was unquestionably unhappy. His client, the state department of transportation, was unhappy, too, and he was happy to pass that dissatisfaction down to his lowly archaeological subcontractors. To hear him talk, anybody who had ever driven a car on Mississippi highways, not to mention everyone who ever hoped to drive a car on those highways, was extremely unhappy with Dr. Mailer and his management of this project.

His opening salvo went right to the heart of the problem. "Do you know how quickly you people could stop this project if you tell the whole world that there might be Indian artifacts here?"

"Sir," Dr. Mailer began, taking the obsequiously respectful approach, "you hired us to look for cultural artifacts, and that's what we're doing. Not just Native American artifacts, but anything of cultural value that could be destroyed by road construction. That's not a secret."

It's also the law, Faye was tempted to interject, but there was no point in antagonizing the man. Also, he was standing quite some distance away, so she would have had to express her opinion at a significant decibel level. This was not the way to win friends and influence people.

"Of course it's not a secret. It's the law, and I run all my projects according to the law," the man said, redeeming himself a trifle in Faye's eyes, by echoing her thoughts. "But was there any need to go on television and shout it out to the countryside?"

And here was the crux of the problem. Their client was worried about bad PR. It was entirely possible that a road project could be completed within the law, by excavating any cultural materials and removing them, yet still be politically impossible. If the public rose up and protested the destruction of an archaeological site, then a road project through that spot could be dead in the water.

Here, in the Choctaws' literal back yard, winning approval for construction was even more perilous. The Choctaws absolutely possessed the financial and political clout to make themselves heard. Considering past history, Faye found it refreshing on those rare occasions when the government had to tiptoe around the sensibilities of Native Americans.

From their client's point of view, the archaeologists they hired should do their work, turn in their report quietly, then let the engineers decide where the new road should go. Heaven forbid that the public should get any more information than the law required.

"You've got a Ph.D., so I guess you're not stupid," ranted the client, who clearly enjoyed having his subcontractors by the financial scruff of the neck, "but I'll tell you SGM&T's position one more time. You are here because our client, the highway department, needs a permit to build this road. You are not here to make trouble. You are not here to find any reason *not* to build this road. And you are certainly not here to be on television talking about murdered farmers. Not when we'll be coming back next year to work on a much bigger project right across the road."

Dr. Mailer listened, nervously rubbing his palms together with his hands clasped in front of him. Faye wondered whether the client thought Dr. Mailer had killed Carroll Calhoun himself, just to antagonize SGM&T. She also wondered whether the red-faced agent was going to be the second person in two days to have a cardiac event right here in the Nails' driveway.

It seemed to her that Dr. Mailer needed a little moral support. And he needed someone to help him gather his wits so that he could jump on the insider information his client had just handed him. Somebody was going to do the archaeology work next year for that big project across the street. Why not Dr. Mailer and his job-hungry students? More to the point, why not Oka Hofobi? Here was a chance for him to get paid, again, for pursuing the questions he'd asked all his life. What were his ancestors' lives like when they lived here, all those years ago?

She wiped her hands on the seat of her jeans and reached into the cooler that Dr. Mailer kept stocked with bottled water for his team. His team might have preferred beer, but they appreciated the gesture. He was a good boss and he deserved for Faye to go to bat for him.

Wiping the bottle dry, she handed it to the client. "It's pretty hot out here. Would you like a drink?"

He thanked her, cracked the bottle's seal, and took a healthy swig. He even smiled. Offering food to placate an angry enemy was a human custom that went back...how far? Faye would have bet that the Neanderthals and Cro-Magnons did the self-same thing.

"Do you know when the contract for next year's project will go out for bid?" she asked. "The one that you just mentioned?"

"Oh, the contracts people at the highway department will keep fiddling with it until the end of this fiscal year, but then they'll be in a big rush to hire somebody. If we get the job, we'll be looking to hire some archaeologists again. You folks interested?" His fury seemed to have spent itself when he realized that Dr. Mailer wasn't going to respond in kind, and that he wasn't going to cower, either. A soft answer does indeed turn away wrath.

Faye looked at Dr. Mailer, inviting him to take this opportunity and run with it.

"Yes," he said, shoving a white shock of hair off his high forehead, "we definitely are interested, and we'd be the obvious choice. We're gaining more site-specific knowledge every day, which we could use to help you write the proposal. And, of course, we have young Dr. Nail, who lives right here. He's a huge asset to getting the work done cost-effectively."

Good job, Faye thought. *Get him in the pocketbook.* Out loud, she only said, "Can you tell us anything about the proposed location of the road?"

"Right over there," the man said, gesturing across the street to the left of the Calhoun house. He didn't seem to be pointing at Calhoun's mound, which was a relief to Faye. She'd hate to see it standing in the median of a four-lane highway.

Their client pulled a handkerchief out of his pocket and mopped at the sweat on his neck. "The traffic engineers are still running the numbers, but I imagine the road'll go down one side of the creek. If they can avoid crossing the creek, then maybe they can avoid messing up the wetlands. Not to mention avoiding the permitting that would go along with that. Also, staying on one side of the creek will avoid the expense of building a bridge. Of course, that all presumes that you people don't find evidence that Columbus himself camped here in 1492. Then we'd have to map out a road that preserved what's left of his privy."

Mailer wisely let that comment slide. "And the road will go…"

"It'll go right straight through to town. Probably cut the drive time to Philadelphia in half. It's a popular project. I sure hope Columbus and his outhouse don't mess it up."

Peach pie was an excellent chaser for the undistinguished box lunches that the hotel had packed for the archaeology team. They had dragged as many chairs into Dr. Mailer's office as they could manage, so everyone could eat together. All that body heat overwhelmed the air conditioning that had drawn them indoors in the first place, but anything was cooler than a Neshoba County summer noon.

"Is your mom going to cook us dessert every day, Oke?" Bodie asked, licking peach juice off his fork. "Please say yes."

"That's an awful lot of work," Faye said, also hoping Oka Hofobi would say yes.

"Ma cooks the way other people meditate. It calms her mind. But don't worry that we're taking too much advantage of her. Dr. Mailer just had twenty pounds of shrimp delivered to her kitchen door. And he told her that if she tried to serve it to the work team, that he wouldn't let us eat it."

Mailer hid his sheepish face behind a forkful of flaky crust. "Just seemed like the mannerly thing to do."

Five bottles of water were raised in his honor. The sixth bottle was somewhere out of sight, in Chuck's hand. He never ate with the others, so he invariably missed Mrs. Nail's desserts, since his colleagues weren't quite mannerly enough to save him a piece.

"About that project across the street—" Faye began.

"Business, business, business," Toneisha groused. "Is it always business with you?"

"If we get that project, we'll be back here next summer, eating whatever Mrs. Nail decides she wants to cook for us," Faye observed.

Toneisha saw her point.

"So, Dr. Mailer, would you like me to look over the aerial photographs we're using for this site, so that I can start thinking about next year's project? I got the impression that the proposal will have a tight deadline, but we're in a good position to be ahead of the competition. It wouldn't hurt to do some of the legwork now, before the request for proposals hits the streets."

"I think Faye just wants to work in the air conditioning this afternoon," Bodie declared. "I think we should keep her outside until she's moved as much dirt as me and Toneisha."

"That won't take long," Faye said, setting aside her plate and heading for the door.

"Leave Faye alone," Mailer said.

Joe, who didn't take criticism of Faye well at all, visibly relaxed.

"She's a heckuva researcher," Mailer continued. "When Faye compiles the background data, the proposal practically writes itself. We might not be sitting here now, if it hadn't been for the prep work she did for the proposal that got us this work. It's okay with me if she wants to take the afternoon to develop a battle plan for winning us another job like this one, only bigger. But Faye, keep track of how you spend your time. It wouldn't be right to bill the client for hours spent trying to get even more money out of them."

"Oh, don't worry. My time sheet will be accurate."

Within minutes, Dr. Mailer's office wastebasket was full of paper plates and plastic forks, and Faye was alone in an air conditioned room.

The aerial photographs were stored in Chuck's office. They were meticulously organized, as was everything else that Chuck touched. Even better, they were cross-referenced to a file holding topographic maps of the area surrounding the Nails' farm. Faye left Chuck's desk alone and, instead, spread the photos out, one by one, across the bare work table behind it. She studied them, first with a magnifier, then she laid duplicate copies side-by-side so that she could use a stereoscope to get a three-dimensional feel for the lay of the land.

It was true that she was looking for information on how to plan a field survey, and she was keeping an eye out for details that might help this billable project, as well, but she had yet another motive she hadn't shared with Dr. Mailer. Her gut told her that studying these photos might help her find the hilltop cemetery that she and Mr. Judd would be seeking just as soon as he was well enough to walk.

The sheriff seemed too preoccupied with Calhoun's murder to give Mr. Judd's decades-old attack much thought. Faye, however, was nearly obsessed with it. It was a crime that cried out for resolution, before all the participants were dead and their secrets were buried with them. What was more, there was the tantalizing possibility that the two crimes were related. Calhoun was found dead in a marijuana field, and Judd remembered seeing a marijuana field just days before he was kidnapped.

Preston Silver seemed to be another recurring factor in both crimes. He was a friend of the dead man, and they were seen together on the night of the murder. He was reputed to be a Klansman, and Judd's kidnapping seemed racially motivated. Most telling of all, Judd nearly died just hours after Preston Silver handled his medicines.

Locating a hilltop graveyard based on a man's forty-year-old recollections might seem unimportant to the sheriff, but Faye thought differently. She promised herself that she would deliver that cemetery to Lawrence Judd, one way or another.

She squinted hard at the aerial photographs, looking for evidence of a graveyard. Unfortunately—or fortunately, if you were a woodland creature—the land near the creek was heavily treed. If there was a small hill somewhere near the water, she sure couldn't see it.

Faye was always fascinated by the things you could see from the air that were obscured at ground level. Standing in the Nails' front yard, she would have said that the land north of the highway was near-wilderness, except for the few fields and pastures visible from the road, but she'd have been wrong.

It was true that a heavy fringe of trees bordered on the highway, probably because the land spread out in a low bowl on either side of the creek in that area. North of that, though, there was an irregular patchwork of agricultural land that started not too far from Calhoun's unlucky pot field. These fields were bounded by heavy woods that extended along the creek and across scattered wetlands. When standing on the ground in one of those clearings, you got the impression of being surrounded by wilderness, but that impression was misleading.

Even more interesting to Faye was the network of...what would she call them? Paths? Or roads? They looked like the dirt track that ran from the highway to the field where Calhoun was killed, and Faye judged that they were just wide enough and just smooth enough to move farming equipment from one field to another. She imagined it would be a tooth-rattling experience, but tractors moved slow.

Turning her attention from the aerial photos, she pored over the topographic maps, since they could show her how the property would look if somebody shaved off all the trees. They also depicted most cemeteries, though it was dangerous to base a professional decision on them. Small family plots were sometimes omitted from these maps, a fact that had bit a few archaeologists on the butt. Whenever a big, expensive roadbuilding crew was forced to stand idle because somebody failed to tell them that Great-Aunt Nancy's tombstone lay in their path, the archaeologist in question looked very, very bad.

There was no cemetery shown on the most recent topo. Faye only felt confident in inferring that no large, public cemetery had existed in the area at the time of the survey. Could there have been a small, family cemetery, private and overgrown? There certainly could.

Squinting at the little black contour lines that showed her where the land sloped up and where it dipped down, she tried to imagine what Mr. Judd's cemetery hill would have looked like and where it had been. Nothing jumped off the page at her, but there was a texture to the surrounding landscape that was most intriguing to an archaeologist.

Mr. Calhoun's mound stood, large and obvious, near the road. She couldn't make out the sweeping wings that she'd seen extending to either side, but the map's contour intervals were 10 feet apart. The human eye could distinguish contours a fraction of that size.

The creek was easy to follow, and Faye's eyes were drawn to its shape. It looked somehow…artificial. It seemed too straight in some places, and there were other places where it took curves that didn't seem natural. Its banks looked wrong, too. In some places, they were quite steep. They could have been natural bluffs, or they could have been the remnants of ancient earthworks. Small expanses of water trapped by these long curving banks of earth put Faye in mind of the Fort Ancient site in Ohio, where ancient Americans had built sophisticated water control structures as part of a vast mound complex.

An elliptical basin west of the creek also caught Faye's eye. As best she could tell, it was dry. Whether it was natural was anybody's guess, but one thing was clear. If ancient Americans had built mounds and dikes and ceremonial earthworks throughout these woods, they would have had to get the dirt from somewhere. This depression might be the borrow pit where they got that dirt. Or it might be just a big hole in the ground. There was no way to know without going there to look.

Faye admired the creek's elegant, sweeping curves. Modern civil engineers were very proud of their ability to put water where they wanted it. They were even prouder when they were able to keep it there.

The aftermath of Hurricane Katrina showed that they weren't always successful with their water-moving, but the Americas' ancient moundbuilding cultures had built levees that were still doing their job after standing for millennia. And it was just possible that they'd done it right here in Carroll Calhoun's back yard. Maybe the man had been right to worry about losing the use of his property. If Faye was reading these maps right, an important mound complex might cover vast tracts of his farmland. Well, she guessed it was his wife's farmland, now.

Faye followed the path of the creek with her finger. She ran out of map before she ran out of potential earthworks. That meant that there was still hope that she would find Mr. Judd's mysterious hill on a map that showed the area just north of this one.

A theory was tickling at her brain, one that tied two of her goals together. Faye just loved it when that happened. If there truly had been a mound complex here, then it was missing some mounds. Actually, it was missing a lot of mounds. Which didn't surprise Faye in the least.

Many ancient mounds had been lost over time. Some of them were destroyed on purpose, to clear land for farming. Busy farmers sometimes just plowed over the dirt humps that they saw as nuisances. Every year, another layer of dirt was lost to the plow and to erosion, until nothing was left. And some mounds were loved to death, by people who dug into them looking for arrowheads and pottery. Once disturbed, erosion took over and wiped those mounds out, too.

These days, there was usually a reason why a mound was still standing. A number of early settlers had actually built houses atop ancient mounds, destroying anything in the top layers, but preserving the rest. Mr. Calhoun, despite his resentment of Faye and her archaeologist friends, had chosen not to plow his mound. Perhaps, deep down, he had appreciated its value. For whatever reason, it still stood because he had allowed it to stand.

Another common factor that preserved ancient mounds was the fact that their artificial high ground made an idyllic site for cemeteries. Nobody was going to raze a hill that supported a graveyard. *So,* Faye wondered, *what if Mr. Judd's cemetery looked like it was on a hilltop because it had been built on top of an old mound?* The location was logical, if she was right about this being the site of an ancient complex. And the cemetery would have preserved that mound when all the others, except for Mr. Calhoun's, were long gone.

Clearly, she needed to get as much information on these properties as possible. This would mean a call to the Mississippi Department of Archives and History and a trip to the property assessor's, for sure. These government offices were air conditioned, which would generate still more ribbing from her co-workers. Faye was pretty sure she could handle it.

Chuck shuffled in the door, taking great care to wipe the mud off his feet. His knees were muddy, too, and so was the ever-present rag that hung out of his back pocket so that he could wipe his hands clean at any time. It wasn't in his nature to tolerate dirt or disarray.

"I believe this is my office," he said, and he wasn't smiling.

"I believe our boss asked me to do some work in here," Faye said in a most polite tone of voice, but she couldn't resist adding, "and I believe you are very late getting back from lunch."

Chuck didn't speak again, but something in the way that he spread his work over the desktop felt vaguely threatening. Large men had the power to intimidate because they had the ability to simply *loom.* Faye respected men like Joe and Dr. Mailer, who never used their size in that way. She would wager that it never occurred to them that it might be useful to look threatening. And maybe it didn't occur to Chuck, either, but he was doing it, anyway. Faye cleared out as quickly as she could.

Chapter Sixteen

Quitting time had come and gone, but only Bodie and Toneisha had left. They had driven away, laughing so loudly that Faye could still hear them after their car door had swung closed. Before strolling to the car, Bodie had taken a few minutes to show off his atlatl skills for his new girlfriend. The flintknapped head of his spear was well-weighted, and his control of the hinged throwing mechanism multiplied the significant power of his arms. His spear left the thrower with a force that left no doubt in Faye's mind that Bodie would never starve if he were stranded in the wilderness.

She surrendered to an unwelcome vision of a spear very like Bodie's piercing a man's neck from behind with such power that its head protruded through his throat. She had once watched a man die in just that way. Shaking her head to chase away that image, she searched around for something more pleasant to watch.

A few yards away, outside the trailer where she sat, Faye could see Joe getting paid for having fun. He was crouched in the shadow of the project trailer, squatting in the position that all humans used before chairs were invented. His feet rested in the center of a large drop cloth, and he held a rock in one hand and a piece of antler in the other. Chuck hovered just outside the boundary of the drop cloth, watching Joe's every move.

Joe, as relaxed as ever, hung motionless in a squatting position that would have made Faye's entire body shriek. Using the antler tool, he patiently shaped the stone in his hand into something useful. It would have been more useful a few centuries in the past but, for people like Joe, it would still serve its purpose.

Chuck took notes every time the antler pressed out another stone flake. Periodically, he motioned for Joe to stop what he was doing, so that he could take pictures and note each flake's shape and size. Then he marked identifying numbers on the chips that corresponded with numbers he inscribed on the drop cloth.

It was interesting work that they were doing. Preliminary testing at the site—augmented substantially with the records that Oka Hofobi had kept as his life's work—suggested that ancient Americans had used portions of the land under their feet as a factory of sorts. They had manufactured stone tools on this one spot, and they had done little else. They hadn't cooked or made pottery or tanned hides here. Oka Hofobi had found tenuous evidence of those other activities over the years, but not within many yards of the spot where they were now digging. To avoid muddying the waters, Joe and Chuck had picked a spot for their re-enactment where no artifacts had been found, to avoid contaminating an old site with their modern research.

Fully investigating this site would give an overview of how a society organized itself, a topic that was of some interest to current archaeology. Faye knew that the Poverty Point site appeared to have separate activity areas, but the Nails' property was inhabited 1500 years after the glory days at Poverty Point. That was a long time for communities to function in the same way, which suggested that this setup was a useful and practical one.

Chuck clearly didn't care how the community organized itself. If Faye was a generalist at heart, then Chuck was the ultimate specialist. He wanted to know how ancient stone tools were constructed, and that was all he wanted to know. Joe was the answer to his professional dreams. If Chuck had his way, Joe would do nothing all day, every day, but knap flint. Not that Joe would object to that in the least.

Faye watched the two of them interact as she worked quietly next to Oka Hofobi, cleaning the finds of the day. Sherds of

pottery and flakes of stone and bits of bone…the stuff of archaeology could easily be mistaken for trash. They had actually once
been trash, but time had enhanced their value. Faye gloried in the
information that could be gleaned from such unprepossessing
things. This was meditative, quiet work, and having someone
working nearby was a comfortable experience, even when that
someone wasn't talking. Now and then, one of them broke the
silence. This time, it was Faye.

"Wouldn't it be nice if we got the big project our client was
talking about this morning?"

"It'd sure be nice for me. There's nothing like being able to
walk to work."

Faye held a flake of flint up to the light. It was a different
shade of brown than the others she'd uncovered. She'd wager
that Chuck could tell her where it had been dug, down to the
specific quarry, all those centuries ago. Unless it had been collected from a pile of gravel beside a long-ago creekbed. Whatever
its source, Chuck would know.

"If we get next year's project, we might run into one tiny
little problem," Faye mused as she worked. "Remember the
tantrum our client threw this morning? Well, if we excavate
across the road, I think we might find some things that will
make him absolutely nuts. We archaeologists, however, will be
very, very happy."

"I'm listening." Oka Hofobi picked up a tiny scrap of bone
and began brushing it clean.

"It looks to me like Mr. Calhoun's mound is the tip of an
ancient iceberg. You've got to look at the maps, too, and tell me
what you see. I think it's just possible that there are remnants
of a very large mound complex. Right there!" She gestured out
the trailer window. "I think I see traces of earthworks and water
control structures. This could be big."

"A site like that could stop any highway project. Even a
popular one. Our client will be livid. Why do I find that funny?"
Oka Hofobi's smile showed only in the crinkles at the corners
of his eyes.

Faye studied that smile for awhile. "Something's bothering you."

"Ma's got herself in an uproar. She was fussing this morning when she walked out the door, and I could tell by the set of her head when she drove into the garage a minute ago that she's not feeling any happier."

"What about your dad?"

"You ever heard Pa put more than two words together? Ma does the talking. She does the thinking, too, most of the time. It works for them."

Faye saw the Nails' back door open. Mrs. Nail leaned out, looking around. She apparently didn't see what she was looking for, so she pulled her head back in and closed the door. Slammed the door, actually.

"What's she upset about?"

"There's talk on the reservation that the sheriff's been interviewing the Choctaws who were here for the ruckus over Mr. Calhoun's mound."

This was news to Faye. She'd had more than one conversation with Sheriff Rutland over Calhoun's murder. She'd heard Neely mention Preston Silver's name more than once. The sheriff had seemed intrigued by Chuck's knowledge of stone tools and his enigmatic behavior. Actually, she'd seemed interested in the specialized knowledge of everybody on the archaeological team. If she'd now embarked on the task of interviewing everybody who was present when Mr. Calhoun attacked his mound with a tractor, she'd be working that angle for days. It would be like emptying the ocean with a leaky teaspoon.

Then the true reason for Mrs. Nail's indignation dawned. Was Sheriff Rutland truly interviewing everyone who'd been present that day? Or just the Choctaws?

Faye knew what it was like to be singled out for her race, and the Choctaws' history of discrimination in America was as long as African-Americans' was. Maybe longer.

Faye pictured the scene as she had viewed it from atop the disputed mound. She and her archaeologist friends had been defending it, so they were natural suspects in Calhoun's death. The same logic applied to the Choctaws. It had been Faye's impression that everybody else present, black and white, had come to defend Mr. Calhoun and his property rights.

Viewed objectively, the sheriff's choice to focus on the archaeologists and the Choctaws made perfect sense. Faye had no intention of explaining this to Mrs. Nail.

A new thought occurred to her. "Is your family full-blooded Choctaw?"

"As far back as anybody remembers."

"Then why don't you live on the reservation?"

"Like most questions involving the First Americans, you can't understand the answer to that unless you know a lot of history. This answer goes back to 1830, when the Treaty of Dancing Rabbit Creek sent most Choctaws to Oklahoma. We have the distinction of being the first tribe to be sent there, but the treaty had provisions for people who didn't want to go. Adults who registered as Choctaw within six months were allotted land of their own: 640 acres for each adult, plus a smaller amount for each child still living at home. There was no reservation at that time. I don't know it for a fact, but I think our land has come down to us from one of those original grants. We don't have anything like 640 acres any more, probably because land was sold over the years to make ends meet. I'm sure it wasn't easy to hang on to what's left, but it's still ours. It's killing my father to lose the little piece that the highway department's taking for its road. He wanted to fight them—to make them take the land through eminent domain. Ma talked him out of it."

Faye's island had been in her family even longer than that, and her ancestors had had their struggles to keep it. Heck, *she'd* had her struggles to keep it. She knew how Oka Hofobi's father felt when he stood here and looked around at this land that was his, really his.

"I thought he resented the road project because it brought us evil archaeologists into his life."

"Um, I think I did that to him long before you arrived. Don't forget that he lives with an evil archaeologist. Sometimes, I think my father resents…everything."

Faye focused her eyes intently on her work, unwilling to make eye contact that might leave Oka Hofobi too self-conscious to unburden himself. "Has he always been this way?"

"No. He loved farming. There's no man alive that knows more about pigs or cows or soybeans. But you can't make a living doing that any more. Well, some years you can, but you have to eat every year. When I was in high school, my mother got a job in an office at the health center on the reservation, and they just can't quit promoting her. She's very good at everything she does."

"I've noticed."

"So's my father, but you need a high school diploma to get a job like my mother's. Have you seen the reservation high school?"

"Yeah. Big, nice building. Did you go there?"

"Yeah, and both my sisters. Did you notice the date on the older building?"

"I noticed that it says '1963' in big, black numbers. We archaeologists have a good head for dates."

"It says 1963 because there was no high school on the reservation until then. Anybody who wanted to go past eighth grade had to go to boarding school on another reservation. Some people did what Ma's family did and sent their kids to the Cherokee school in North Carolina, but think of what it would be like to split up a family like that. Pa never had that chance. When our family finances got to the point where the farm couldn't support us, he got a job managing a convenience store. It's a good job for someone without a high school education and he's plenty smart enough to run it well, but don't you know he spends every minute at work wishing he was here? On his own land?"

Faye was still trying to figure out one aspect of the Choctaws' tangled history, so she pointed out the obvious. "So the government moved the Choctaws west, except for a few who accepted land here. How come there's a reservation here, now?"

"In the early 1900s, a congressional report called the Choctaws the 'poorest pocket of poverty in the poorest state in the country.' Most of them had been forced to sell their land grants by then...or been swindled out of them. Reform was obviously needed, but reform takes time. The land for the reservation was bought and put in trust in 1939, not so long before my father was born. There was a world war on, so the Choctaw constitution wasn't ratified until 1944. That's when the land was finally set aside for the tribe."

Faye considered the hotel where she was staying, with its casino and all the other trimmings of a big-time resort. "They're doing okay with that land now."

"Finally."

"Did you say the treaty that banished most of the Choctaws to Oklahoma was called the Treaty of Dancing Rabbit Creek?"

"Yeah. Not the United States of America's finest moment, was it?"

"But didn't I see a Dancing Rabbit Golf Course near my hotel?"

"Yeah. And it costs an awful lot to golf there." Oka Hofobi's head was still bowed over his work, but Faye could see the suggestion of a smile lighting his face. "Don't ever let anybody tell you that my people don't have an exquisite sense of irony."

Dr. Mailer's office door opened, and their boss peered through it at Faye and Oka Hofobi. Crossing the room and peering out the window, he stood watching Joe and Chuck, who were still working as the sun sunk behind the treetops. "Are you people workaholics or something? I have done my dead level best to outlast you but, darn it, I'm hungry."

"We can quit whenever the boss says so," Faye said. "Of course, long days mean fewer expense account meals and lower hotel bills..."

"Just because the client thinks you should kill yourself to save him a little money, that doesn't mean he's right. Oke, can you point me in the general direction of a barbecue joint? And I'd be glad for some company if any of you want to come."

As she and Oka Hofobi put their tools away, Faye seized the opportunity to wangle permission for another task that wasn't billable to the client. "Our maps and photos don't cover a big enough area for me to do that proposal justice. Do you mind if I spend tomorrow morning gathering up those documents?"

"Trying to get out of some good, honest back-breaking labor?"

Faye checked his face. He was smiling, so she said, "A minute ago, you called me a workaholic."

"That's because you are. If the governmental agencies that have those maps and photos were open at night, you'd be at their offices after supper. Then you'd go back to your hotel room and take them to bed with you. Fortunately for workaholics like you, government workers go home at night. Come eat some barbecue with us. You've got my permission to do your non-billable research tomorrow. Charge it to my overhead account."

When Faye and Joe, completely stuffed with barbecue, reached the hotel, they found that Mr. Judd had been released from the hospital. He was happily ensconced in his room, enjoying a room service meal that looked a lot better than the box lunches that had been packed for the field crew by the self-same kitchen.

Faye felt a weird pang of guilt at finding out that he'd been released without her knowing about it. Why? She decided it was because Mrs. Judd had charged Faye with keeping her informed on his condition. Since he had just finished talking to his wife with his own lips, Faye figured her duty had been discharged. She hated to think about anybody leaving the hospital in a taxi, but the sight of Ross Donnelly's solicitous figure at the sick man's bedside suggested that maybe he'd been Judd's ride home. This was nice of him, but it wasn't a particularly selfless act when one remembered that Ross wanted the former congressman's support in a major way.

Faye leaned over toward Ross, asking, "So what kind of business brings you here to Philadelphia?" He was as conspicuously well-dressed as he'd been the day before, though his knit polo shirt and khakis were far more casual than the business suit had been.

"I'm here for the Fair."

"So this is a pleasure trip?"

"No, I work as a lobbyist for—well, you heard me tell Mr. Judd what our position is. Politicians hover over the Neshoba County Fair like vultures. It's a good place for me to get the attention of people I need to know."

Faye noticed that, like anyone in politics, he had kept certain key information close to his vest. Like, for instance, the name of the group for whom he lobbied.

"Ross," Judd interjected. "I have some business I need to discuss with Faye. Do you mind?"

"Not a bit. Faye, I'm in Room 710. When you leave, let me know if you think he shouldn't be alone. I'll come back and sit with him." His exit was deft and quick. Nobody would accuse Ross Donnelly of overstaying his welcome.

Now that she had a chance to really look at him without distractions, Faye could see that Congressman Judd looked terrible. Faye would guess that he'd lost five pounds that he couldn't spare in the twenty-four hours since his collapse. His skin was gray, and when he reached out to shake her hand, she could see each finger tremble independently of the others. But he was, by God, ready to go do some cross-country trespassing.

"I think we should wait a day or two," Faye began, but she wasn't allowed to finish.

"If I recall correctly, we knew that Mrs. Calhoun was going to be out of the house on Monday evening because there was to be an open-casket viewing of her husband at the funeral home."

Joe's expression said that he found the idea distasteful, and Faye rather agreed. She much preferred his Creek-style funerary practices, which mostly consisted of washing himself with water and cleansing herbs, then burning stuff that smelled good. After that, Joe just sat and thought good thoughts about the deceased. All in all, Faye thought the process to be quite constructive.

"—and Mr. Calhoun's funeral should be going on about now," Mr. Judd was saying, "so we've missed today's opportunity to go sneaking around on his widow's land. Tomorrow's Wednesday, and I hear that Mrs. Calhoun's a big churchgoer, so she'll be gone for hours. She'll go to prayer meeting, for sure, where they'll remember her husband. Then she'll go to choir practice, because those little country churches can't ever spare a single voice out of the choir. She's probably part of some kind of women's charitable group, and they always meet on Wednesday nights. Faye, tomorrow is our last safe day until she goes back to church on Sunday. I'm not in the mood to wait that long. As I was reminded yesterday, life's short."

Faye's gaze wandered down to the older man's legs, which were trembling as noticeably as his fingers. He noticed. "I've never been strong. This is not new. But no one has a stronger will than mine. Don't you worry, I can haul my puny self down that creek and back. And if I can't, this young man," he pointed to Joe, "is more than big enough to carry me home. Tomorrow evening, I'll meet you at the Nails' house, just like we planned before. Somebody in Neshoba County knows the truth about what happened to me in 1965, but nobody has admitted it yet. Something tells me that you, young lady, have what it takes to get to the bottom of things."

Chapter Seventeen

Faye had often found that fate was a matter of split-second timing. If she had followed through on her plan to walk straight into the shower—possibly while still wearing her nasty clothes— she would never have heard the phone ring. The only thing that stayed her rush to the bathroom was a vision of herself, fresh and clean, wrapped in her bathrobe and reclining on the bed.

This vision was achievable within fifteen minutes, with one tiny problem. In her daydream, Faye was languidly munching on a chocolate bar, and she had no such thing in her possession. Fortunately, she knew the gift shop downstairs to be well-stocked. Figuring that it was better to venture out in public in dirty clothes than to be seen in her pajamas, she grabbed her purse and went on a chocolate-stalking expedition.

The phone beside her bed rang as she stood outside her locked door, juggling her purse, her key, and the chocolate bar. By stuffing the candy into her purse, she was able to answer the phone on its fourth ring. The mellifluous baritone of Ross Donnelly wafted gently out of the receiver and into her ear.

"Hello, Faye. It's Ross. Congressman Judd warned me that you were the kind of woman who didn't quit work at dinnertime, so I'm not surprised that you're so late getting back to your room. I'm guessing you've already eaten, which destroys my plan to ask you out for dinner. The selection of movies in Philadelphia isn't great—"

"So I've been told."

"That doesn't leave us many entertainment options. You don't seem like the gambling type."

Faye reflected that the man was a good judge of character. "I'm too cheap to enjoy gambling. Too many years spent nursing an overloaded bank book will do that to a girl. The joy of winning a few dollars just can't wipe out the fear of losing those dollars and more. I'd be a killjoy in the casino."

"Okay, then gambling's out. I'm not crazy about it, myself. The fact that casinos stay in business is proof-positive that the odds are stacked against you. My meticulous research tells me that we only have a few other entertainment options, this time of the evening. We could go frog-gigging."

Faye made it a policy not to delve too deeply into where her fried frogs' legs came from. "I'm not much into frog-gigging, but if you're set on going, I'll see if Joe's in the mood. I swear the man can talk to frogs. He charms them right out of the water and into his boat."

"I'm more interested in your company than I am in how we spend our time. So let me throw out a couple of other ideas. We could go out to the Fair—"

"It's pretty late. What time does it close?"

"I have no idea. That'll be part of the adventure. How many rides can we ride before they kick us out? We could even bet on it, except you don't like to gamble. I say we can squeeze in the Ferris wheel and a couple of turns on the biggest roller coaster, then close down the evening on that giant pendulum thing. The one that swings back and forth about a dozen times before it works up the energy to flip all the way over."

"Sounds enticing. If you're into terror. But you said you had a couple more ideas. What's the other one?"

"It's not as exciting as the Fair, I'm afraid. I figured that if none of the other options suited you, we could just take a drive."

Faye, who rarely turned down a spin on a Ferris wheel, was surprised at how attractive a simple drive sounded. The intensity of the past few days had left her drained, and she wasn't cut out to live in a casino. The act of walking from her hotel room to her car required her to pass a zillion beeping, flashing, ringing slot machines, and the experience left her disoriented. Nighttime on her island home was black-dark and quiet, and she knew that kind of nurturing stillness waited for her on any number of lonely roads just a few miles from downtown Philadelphia.

When she was at home on Joyeuse Island, she didn't have to tiptoe around egos. Career advancement was a faraway concern. She had no need to impress anyone there, mostly because no one lived there but her and Joe. If there were ever a person who expected nothing more from Faye than that she simply be herself, Joe was that person.

She made her decision. "A drive would be lovely. Give me ten minutes."

Not for the first time, Faye was grateful that her short hair dried exceptionally fast.

The car and Ross were a perfect match. It was sleek and stylish. It was also small, as fabulous sports cars tend to be, yet it still managed to be perfectly proportioned to his substantial frame. It fit him as if it had been manufactured to his measurements, just like his clothes, and it was obvious that neither clothes nor car had come cheap.

Faye was relieved when he opened the passenger door for her, not because she required old-fashioned displays of chivalry, but because she was afraid she might leave a fingerprint on the door's coal-black paint job. He bent over her solicitously as she lowered herself into the low-slung car, and she suffered a last-minute pang of apprehension.

What was she doing? What would she say to a woman friend who was prepared to crawl into a car with a man she hardly knew?

Probably nothing. No matter how many times a woman met a man for lunch, talked to him on the phone, or met him for drinks, there still came a moment when she chose to let herself be alone with him. Alone and vulnerable. It wasn't necessarily a good plan, but the western world had a name for this risk-taking behavior. It was called "dating."

She buckled her seat belt and waited to see where Ross intended to take her.

With a push of a button, he lowered the convertible top, and Faye's animal instincts relaxed just a bit. She wasn't actually going to be sealed up in a car with a man she didn't know. If disaster loomed, she could just hurl herself out of the moving car. (Why did this thought cheer her?) Besides, it was her impression that serial killers rigged their car doors so that victims couldn't open them from the inside. Lowering a convertible top would spoil that plan. It was time to put her paranoid thoughts away and simply enjoy the ride.

Ross drove with speed and control, and his car ate up the miles. Faye had never ridden on a toboggan, but she imagined it felt like this, skidding smoothly just above the surface of the land. When their speed suddenly slowed, Faye glanced over at Ross, who gestured out her car window. The curve of a Ferris wheel rose above the trees, and multicolored lights twinkled through their branches. A teeming hive of humanity milled among the colorful cabins that stood between them and the Midway.

"I thought it might be fun just to pull the car over and have a glass of wine while we watch the big wheel turn. But now I think that's probably a bad idea. We're too close to the Fair and all its traffic. Too many cars. And there's no shoulder on any of these backroads." A pickup truck whooshed past, proving his point. "Somebody might sideswipe us if we stopped here. Besides, we'd have no privacy at all." He took his eyes off the road to look at her sidewise.

"I know just the place," Faye said. "But we'll need a flashlight. Do you have one?"

"Are you kidding? This thing has a trunk the size of a bread-box. The bottle of wine barely fits. But I'm sure we can scare up a flashlight somewhere."

Two convenience stores later, Faye and Ross had acquired the necessary flashlight and she was giving him directions.

"Go slow. I think we're getting close."

"What are we looking for? Cows? I don't see any cows, because this is the darkest road I've ever been on—"

"Hence the flashlight."

"Praise God for the flashlight. And for my halogen headlights. Anyway, the cows may be hiding in the dark, but I recognize pastureland when I see it. Even in the black of night."

"And I recognize a state park when I see it," Faye said. "Pull over into that parking lot. Right there. See it?"

"Barely." He shut off the engine and silent darkness dropped down on them. "I have never in my life seen stars like those."

"Let's see. You said you grew up in Brooklyn. Now you live in Atlanta. I'm surprised you've ever seen stars at all."

"A few of the bright ones poke through the haze. Even in Atlanta."

"The bright ones are usually planets, so we still can't be sure you've ever seen an actual star." Faye reclined her seat a couple of degrees. "Look there. See the three bright stars overhead? That's the summer triangle. Vega. Deneb. Altair. Deneb's part of Cygnus the Swan. See that cross? The long line is the body of a flying bird. The short line crossing it is the bird's wings."

Faye's thoughts strayed to Mr. Calhoun's mound. She had been so sure she saw wings stretching out on either side of it, but the human brain is conditioned to read patterns as familiar forms. Two dots and a line are invariably interpreted by a normal brain as the two eyes and mouth of a human face. Two lines of unequal length, crossing each other at right angles, could be interpreted as a bird or a human torso or a religious symbol, but those lines were rarely perceived as random. What had the builders of that mound intended it to be?

"Do all archaeologists know as much about stars as you do?"

"There's actually a branch of the science called 'archaeoastronomy.' Ancient people often oriented their monumental architecture to the sun and moon and stars."

"Like Stonehenge."

"Right. And like those Mayan pyramids that do funky things on the solstice. Some of them make shadows that look like their snake god is slithering down the pyramids' steps. I'd like to see that someday."

"But I take it that archaeoastronomy isn't your specialty?"

"Um, I'm still trying to choose a specialty. I just can't seem to narrow down my interest in archaeology. All of it fascinates me. But to succeed in academia, I have to pick one thing and learn all I can about it. That won't leave much time to explore all the wonderful questions that fall outside my specialty."

Faye touched her finger to her lips, silencing herself. A first date was a poor time for a woman to parade all her insecurities. She redirected her musings toward something innocuous. "Astronomy, on the other hand, is just a hobby for me. I live on an island, so I'm in charge of all the lights. When I want it dark, I just turn off the generator. Some nights, there's nothing to do but look at the stars. I keep thinking maybe I might get a telescope, but there's always someplace else to spend my money. That's the trouble with owning a two-hundred-year-old house."

"Ouch. I bet my new townhouse is cheap by comparison."

Faye would have bet her ancient Pontiac Bonneville that it wasn't.

"You don't live on that island all alone, do you?"

"No. Joe lives there, too."

She thought of trying to explain her relationship with Joe, but she didn't know how. Was he like a brother to her? No. More like an exceptionally hot first cousin—interesting to look at, but off-limits.

"But he's okay that you're here with me?"

"Oh, yeah. Sure. Actually, he dated someone seriously last winter, and he's still getting over it." Casting about for a less intense subject, she remembered why she'd brought Ross all the way out here. "I bet you're wondering why we needed a flashlight."

"And I bet you were wondering when I was going to haul out that bottle of wine."

Ross retrieved the bottle from a trunk that was indeed about the size of a breadbox. Faye trained the flashlight on the bottle and saw that the writing on the label was in French.

"You seemed like a Bordeaux kind of woman," he said, pouring a generous slosh into a glass and handing it to her.

Faye knew that if "Bordeaux" meant "expensive"—and she reckoned it did—then nary a drop of it had ever crossed her lips. She rolled a sip over her tongue and let it trickle down her throat. It sure tasted expensive.

She remembered something. "Hey! Did you bring this all the way from Atlanta? Neshoba County is dry."

"Which calls into question whether I was lying when I said you looked like a Bordeaux kind of girl. You're thinking maybe I just carry a bottle of the stuff around, then tell random unsuspecting women that they make me think of Bordeaux. Nope. I confess to buying the wine earlier in the evening, before I called you, because I was hoping I could convince you to see me tonight. But I promise I didn't bring it with me all the way from Georgia. And I can prove it."

He pointed the flashlight beam at her wine glass. Engraved on the side were the words *Pearl River Resort*. "Surely you've noticed that they sell liquor at the casino. I found the souvenir glasses in a gift shop, but I couldn't find a liquor store, so I just ordered the wine from room service. The Choctaws are a sovereign nation. The rules are different for them."

"And you resent them for it."

"Not so much. I'm glad they've had their opportunity for success. If anybody should have a shot at the American dream, it should be the Americans who were here first. But what about our people, Faye?"

Faye was strangely stirred by his use of the phrase "our people." With bloodlines that reached back to Europe and Africa and North America and probably other places, too, she'd never felt right about claiming any one people as her own.

"What are you proposing? Should we get to build a few casinos, too?"

"What? You're not inspired by the thought of the South Central Los Angeles Gaming Emporium? You don't think we should build racetracks in Harlem or downtown New Orleans?" He allowed himself a small chuckle at the thought, and Faye liked the sound of it. "No, I'm talking lump-sum cash grants for Americans of African descent. Not a fortune, but enough to boost hardworking people into the middle class. Enough money to put a down payment on a house. Enough money to make an education possible for anyone who wants it. We're the richest nation in the world, Faye. We can afford to make recompense for millions of hours of unpaid labor. And the government will be repaid eventually by the taxes those new middle-class citizens will be paying."

Faye's overly analytical brain usually dismissed such schemes as pipe dreams. Who would decide who got the money? How would they prove themselves to be the descendants of slaves? How many drops of African blood would it take? How much money was fair payment for the loss of an entire lifetime of freedom? More to the point, who would decide the answers to these questions?

Faye was never sure of her political opinions, because she was so good at poking holes in the logic of ideologues from either party. Tonight, though, it was refreshing to be in the company of someone who knew exactly what he thought.

"I pity the politicians who try to argue with you," she said, taking another drag on the wine, which did, indeed, taste more expensive by the sip. "You're such a good talker that I still haven't told you why we're here."

"Or why we needed a flashlight."

She took the flashlight from his hand and led him across the narrow road to a large sign that proclaimed the site to be Nanih Waiya State Park. Then she waved its beam back and forth over the mound of Nanih Waiya itself. It was so massive that she could only illuminate it a piece at a time but, as their eyes adjusted to the darkness, they found that starlight and the flashlight's tiny beam were enough to give them a sense of its presence.

"The Choctaw believe their race was born here. This is their most sacred place," she told him. "In the 1840s, government representatives came to deal with the Choctaws who had refused to go away quietly to the Indian Territories. Elderly Choctaws told them that they were born at Nanih Waiya. Not the tribe, but the individual Choctaws themselves believed that they were born here. They said that she was their mother and that they would not quit this land while she stood. It's a miracle someone didn't call out the troops to raze it."

"Do I read that sign right?" he asked. "If this is a state park, does that mean the state owns it?"

"For the moment. The state's been talking about shutting down this park, among several others. There's no money for maintenance."

"Maintenance of what?" He held out the flashlight and turned in a full circle. "I see a fence around the mound. A couple of small buildings. Some beaten-up picnic tables. A parking lot that nobody's wasted any pavement on in a long time. Maybe never."

"Somebody's got to mow the grass and pick up the trash. And there's another part of the park about a mile away, centered on a mound with a cave running clear through it. I tried to get a look at it but the gate's locked. Closing that part of the park saved them the money that would be spent on cleaning the bathrooms and patching up the picnic pavilion. Maybe the park people want to spend their money on parks that get more use. We are way out in the sticks here."

"No kidding. But if they're going to close this place, why don't they give it back to the Choctaws?" Faye could tell by his tone of voice that Ross' political sensibilities were aflame. Perhaps the Choctaws were about to acquire themselves a new lobbyist. "I bet they'd take care of it. You said this was their most sacred place. How did the government get it away from them in the first place?"

Faye took a deep breath of the Bordeaux's aroma. "Same way the Dutch got Manhattan, I guess. The Chief has said that the state should give Nanih Waiya back to the Choctaws, but I'm not holding my breath. Will New York give Manhattan back?

Will the museums of the world empty themselves of mummies and return them to Egypt? It'll never happen. I don't begrudge the Choctaws a few casinos."

Ross held the wine bottle out by its neck and waggled it at her. "Shall we have another glass and finish this thing off? I'll warn you. I am a strict observer of DUI laws. If I have another drink, I'll have to give my liver an hour to process it before I'm willing to get back behind the wheel."

Faye felt like another glass of Ross' scrumptious Bordeaux would be an excellent idea. "In your car, I have a purse. And in that purse, I have a chocolate bar. We could have a picnic."

While she fetched the candy, Ross set the flashlight on a picnic table with its beam pointing straight up toward the night sky. Viewed with the right attitude, it looked rather like a candle, which gave a nice romantic glow to their picnic. Ross plunked the wine bottle down beside their makeshift candle, then Faye tore the candy wrapper open so that it lay flat under the chocolate bar, like a flimsy plate. They settled themselves in for an hour—more than an hour—of talking about his years in law school and her dream of earning a Ph.D. She told him how Dr. Mailer was urging her to specialize in lithics, so that he could supervise her dissertation.

"Lithics work is intellectually interesting. I enjoy it. I would be employable with that specialization. But my passion isn't there. All my life, I've dug up the bits and pieces my ancestors left behind on my island. I've probed around in the foundations of slave cabins so long that I feel a real connection with the people who lived there. My own house is nothing but a huge artifact of plantation culture. I know so much about how it was built and how its owners lived that I could probably write a dissertation without stepping out my front door. But I couldn't work with Dr. Mailer. And I couldn't work with my dear friend Magda, who really made my education possible. I'd have to step completely into the unknown. Can I find a professor who'll take me on? Will I find a job when I graduate? It's a hard choice."

"I could make more money in private practice—"

Faye cast the sports car a skeptical glance.

Ross laughed. "Really, Faye. I could. But happiness has a real value and you have to factor it into your calculations." He responded to her sheepish expression by saying, "You have to realize how obvious it is that you treat all your decisions like math problems. You weigh the pros and cons, then you force the equation to balance. Don't forget to include the intangibles in your calculations."

"Like sipping wine and stargazing? Are those intangible enough for you?"

She showed him the North Star, and they lingered over their picnic so long that even Ross' unpracticed eyes could see that all the other stars in the sky wheeled around that one.

The Mother Mound rested just a few yards away. Courtship, like the other way stations in the cycle of human life, was familiar to her, intimately so. While she watched, Faye and Ross sat under those spinning stars, eating cheap chocolate and washing it down with fine wine. Between sips, he kissed her, more than once.

The Spectre and the Hunter

As told by Mrs. Frances Nail

On a night lit by bright stars, a hunter named Kowayhoommah kindled a fire. He was proud and satisfied. His bow was well-formed and its aim was true. His dog was a fine hunter and a faithful companion who watched over their camp by night. His stomach was full of jerked venison. Best of all, he had pitched his camp in a spot thick with game. Deer tracks cut into the rich soil. Now and then, a "cluck" gave away the presence of turkeys deep in the thickets. Spreading his deerskin and his blanket, he dreamed of the kills he would make.

Now, sounds travel well under starlight. Surely you've noticed that. As Kowayhoommah laid there, a keen cry rose out of the night. It was human, but it was not. It might have been the cry of a lost hunter, but a true hunter is never lost.

The piercing cry sounded again, and the hunter felt his heart's blood run cool. Before long, footsteps approached. Unable to look away, he watched a tall, gaunt figure shuffle toward him. Its robe was tattered, and its withered hand clutched an unstrung bow and a few broken arrows. Shivering, it stretched its bony hands toward the fire and turned its hollow gaze on Kowayhoommah, who was moved by pity.

He rose and offered his deerskin for the visitor to sit on, but the spectre refused, gathering up an armload of briers instead. He stretched himself on this thorny couch, saying nothing, but always staring at Kowayhoommah.

When its deepset eyes closed, the dog finally spoke. "Arise, and flee for your life. He is sleeping, but if you sleep, you will be lost. Run, while I stay and watch!"

Hunters spend their lives learning to move quietly. Kowayhoommah crept silently from the fireside, advanced a few hundred paces, then paused to listen. He heard nothing, so he began to run.

Hunters spend their lives learning to run quickly. He had traveled several miles before the stars had completed half their night's path. Feeling confident of his escape, he paused on a hilltop beneath the constant stars to thank them for watching over his escape.

Alas! The quiet air carried the distant baying of his faithful dog, growing nearer, nearer, warning him that the spectre was still coming. Again, he ran through the countryside, until he reached a river too deep and swift to cross. He stood, too afraid to jump in and too afraid to stand still, until his dog's voice convinced him to plunge into the water. An instant later, the panting dog joined him.

Behind his dog was something with skeleton hands and glassy eyes. Kowayhoommah had prepared himself for death when his faithful dog seized the bony spectre in its jaws and disappeared with it below the water. Neither hound nor spectre ever surfaced again.

A changed man, Kowayhoommah was never again prideful or boastful. He shunned pleasures like dance and stickball. Some say that he one day set off to make war on a distant enemy and never returned.

I like to think that he was lured into the forest by the baying of a faithful dog, and that they wander there together, still.

Chapter Eighteen

Faye spent a lot of time in property assessors' offices, a fact that made its own poetic sense. History is inextricably bound into the land where it happened and where its relics lie buried. And the land is bound to the people who own it and farm it and pay the taxes on it. The offices of the folks who assess those taxes harbor an amazing amount of information, free for the asking.

Archaeologists might be known for dashing around the countryside digging up exciting artifacts, but a small fraction of their time is actually spent doing just that. Some of Faye's colleagues spent their entire careers deep in the bowels of museums "excavating the collections." Far more artifacts were uncovered during the glorious romantic years of the Victorians and Edwardians than could ever have been properly cataloged and interpreted. Much worthwhile work was being done by scientists who merely studied stuff that was already dug up.

There were some who used the overstuffed collections of the world's museums to say that it was wrong to continue excavating. "If no one ever took the time to properly write up the excavations of the past, then what makes it necessary to dig up more artifacts?" they wanted to know.

It was hard for a thoughtful person to ignore their most persuasive argument: excavation is by its nature an act of destruction. Pulling dirt and artifacts and information out of the ground is like letting a genie out of its bottle. You can't put it back in. If you miss a critical piece of information, it's gone forever.

On the other hand, if you put a worthless piece of information in a governmental file, it's preserved forever. Faye hefted the tax files on the portion of the Calhoun property under consideration for the road construction project. It was going to take her some time to sort out the useful information from the legalese. The aerial photographs, on the other hand, would be immediately useful.

She spread them out on a cramped work table in a corner of the file room, using a reference map to piece each one together in the correct sequence. The creek and the highway served as handy reference points to help her orient herself to the landscape she already understood on a human scale.

Starting at the bottom of the southernmost photo, she could see the roof of Oka Hofobi's house and, across the highway to the right, the roof of the Calhoun home. Directly across from Oka Hofobi's place, the massive presence of the ancient mound was unmistakable, though heavily shrouded in ground-level vegetation that masked the areas where Faye had seen wings and a tail. Noticing that the tree cover seemed lighter than she remembered, she checked the date on the photo. It had been taken within the past five years, so any difference she noticed was probably because the photo was shot in the autumn, as the leaves were starting to fall. This was encouraging. She wanted a good look at the ground.

The creek and its surrounding wetlands were obvious by the texture of the trees and vegetation growing there, even when the water wasn't visible. She winced inwardly at the sight of a small clearing that was surely the spot where Carroll Calhoun had died. And nearby, just out of range of the photos and maps she'd reviewed in the trailer—maybe, maybe that might be a faint rise in the ground surface. And maybe it was more lightly treed than the surrounding area, which would make sense if this was the site of an overgrown old cemetery that had succumbed to neglect.

She poked Dr. Mailer's cell number into her phone. "Hey— I've got most of what we need, but neither the geological survey nor the soil conservation service has a field office here. They have offices in Jackson, and I'll eventually want to go there to talk to the people at Archives and History. In the meantime, I could probably grab some topos someplace where they sell stuff to hunters and hikers, but it might be easier to just pay a little more and download the ones we want. Joe does that for me all the time. I don't know the quadrangle names, but this should get him in the neighborhood."

She reeled off the UTM coordinates that bounded the area in question, and hoped Dr. Mailer would notice that Joe was useful for tasks that required more than a strong back or a preternatural understanding of ancient man's toolmaking abilities. As she waited for him to write the information down, another thought struck her.

"You know, I think I could use some historical topos, too. They're a good source of information on old structures that aren't there anymore. Joe's worked with several companies that can get their hands on old maps that aren't available on the web yet. It takes some time, but they'll go find the maps, scan them, and zap them right back to you in a day or two."

She listened as he groused about the expense of such a thing and about the wisdom of taking yet another worker out of the field. Then, when he agreed—as she'd known he would—she thanked him, saying, "This is the kind of preparation that will make our project work stand out. It'll make that proposal stand out, too, which is the way to win contracts."

And, she neglected to add, *the USGS very considerately marks cemeteries on their topographical maps.*

Having gleaned as much information as she could on her first perusal of the tax assessor's photos, Faye decided which ones she needed and put in an order with the clerk. While she was waiting for them to be duplicated, she pulled the title information out of the files, and adjusted her mind to the numbing process of reading legal documents. She had found important and unexpected information in such files before. Once, she'd even found evidence of criminal activity. If she could just get over the presumption that she was headed for an hour of boring reading, she might learn something.

Within fifteen minutes, she was certain that her presumption had been wrong, which reminded her yet again not to be presumptuous.

Mr. Calhoun's ancestral land wasn't. Ancestral, that is. He had owned the land surrounding his house for many years, it was true. He had inherited it, along with the marijuana field and the peanut field where the mound sat, from his father, who had inherited it from his own father.

At the time of his death, he had owned everything in the immediate vicinity, on both sides of the creek. Acres and acres of land bore his name, extending far north of the roadway that served as its southern border, but he didn't get it from his father. He had bought it, piece by piece, over a period of nearly forty years. The most recent purchase was less than two years old.

Faye, who was a storyteller at heart, constructed a tale of two neighbors, a successful man and, right next door, a man who had reeled from one disaster to another. And each financial setback had cost him a piece of the legacy left him by his parents. This being agricultural country, "next door" was a relative term. The unfortunate neighbor's house was more than a mile down the road. And his name was Kenneth Rutland.

Faye was sad for Neely. In a sense, she'd watched her father decay all her life. Long before his mind and his body failed him, fortune had failed him first. Whatever had caused his financial reversal (poor crops, medical bills, poor business decisions—the possibilities were depressingly endless), he'd had to give up his land, acre by acre. Over time, Neely would have become aware that the creek and woods where she'd played weren't hers any more. No wonder she was so protective of her father.

All Mr. Calhoun had done was buy land that was for sale but, since Faye hadn't liked him all that much, she resented him for it. Probably Neely's family did, too, but property sales that were legal and above-board and necessary didn't seem worth killing someone over. Still, Faye wondered who else the prosperous Mr. Calhoun might have bested in a business deal. She was stuck in this office while the blueline printer disgorged a big pile of the photos she'd ordered. Perhaps she should spend that time looking into the Calhouns' property holdings.

She thumbed through the legal documents that described Mr. Calhoun's business life, but found no other purchases or sales. As she thought about it, she realized that the dead man probably had much more dangerous business associates that would never surface in any governmental file. When you're found dead in a field of marijuana, a field that you yourself own, the presumption would be that you were a criminal, and that you associated with criminals. Drug deals were so much more deadly than real estate transactions.

Chapter Nineteen

Faye returned from a morning spent chasing paper trails, only to find an unsettled work crew. An after-lunch thundercloud had chased them into the cramped quarters of the trailer. They unquestionably had plenty of work to do in there, and after Faye arrived, they passed a chatty hour cleaning and cataloging their finds. A particularly well-shaped stone point had made the rounds, passing from hand to hand so its fine workmanship could be appreciated by people who knew it when they saw it. Faye enjoyed the feel of the finely worked stone.

It had been a productive way to spend the weather-enforced time indoors, but these were not people who enjoyed standing shoulder-to-shoulder and breathing stale air. All six of them cast the occasional glance out the window, but it was Toneisha who noticed that the storm had blown through.

"Would you look at the sun shine?" she said. "All that wind and thunder, and not the first drop of rain ever hit the ground." She looked expectantly at Dr. Mailer, and so did everybody else. He was staring distractedly at the door, probably because he (and all the rest of them) knew that there were supposed to be seven people working in the cramped trailer. Not six. Chuck had now been missing for a protracted period during working hours for the second day in a row. Not late. Missing. Dr. Mailer was going to have to do something.

Belatedly responding to Toneisha's comment, Dr. Mailer looked around the room as if he'd just come back from a faraway place. "Yes. Yes, let's get back outside where we can have some fun."

Faye was still gathering her tools when she saw Chuck walking up the driveway. He was almost completely wet, except for his head and upper trunk, even though it hadn't rained. Thundershowers were spotty propositions. Chuck might have been rained on if he'd been far enough away, and his upper body might have stayed dry if he'd draped a newspaper or something over his head, but Faye didn't think so. The brownish-red tint of the water soaking his socks suggested that he'd been just as dirty as she'd seen him the day before. If he'd waded into the creek in a clumsy attempt to clean off the mud, then he'd look just like he did now.

Where did he go on these mysterious jaunts? He could only get so far on foot, even with his long legs. Judging by what she'd learned from the property assessor's files, he'd been on the Nails' land if he had stayed south of the highway, or he'd been on the Calhouns' land if he'd wandered north of the highway. It was a fifty-fifty shot. Well, she was planning to stray onto the Calhouns' land that very evening, so she couldn't judge Chuck too harshly, but Dr. Mailer could. And he probably should.

Faye and Joe were uncharacteristically swift in leaving work, slipping into their car just as fast as Toneisha hopped into Bodie's passenger seat. Mr. Judd was waiting for them at the hotel.

As she left the trailer, she brushed past Oka Hofobi's desk. She caught his eye, then, feeling a bit flustered, she looked away. He'd mentioned a movie and invited her to dinner with his family, but there had been no more advances on his part. And Faye hadn't made any either.

It was true that Ross was more classically handsome than Oka Hofobi, but Faye found the young archaeologist attractive, too. She liked his quiet calm, which belied the intensity in his black eyes. But was she interested in developing that initial attraction? Apparently not, because she wasn't pursuing it and neither was he.

Perhaps he'd lost interest because his mother liked her. That could be a romantic kiss of death for some men.

She gave him a friendly wave and backed out the door. It was time to fetch Lawrence Judd.

Faye drove out of Philadelphia with Joe riding shotgun and Mr. Judd resting in the back seat. A single sentence kept running through her brain.

This is a really bad idea.

Her mother's and grandmother's childrearing tactics had left her constitutionally incapable of talking back to her elders, though she'd tried to rise above that handicap repeatedly as Mr. Judd herded them toward the car.

"I want to do this," he had insisted repeatedly. "I don't even care if I die doing it. If there's a chance that I can learn something about what happened to me all those years ago, then I'm taking a walk in the woods. Right now."

In the midst of the discussion, Faye's cell phone had rung and, heart sinking, she'd seen the caller's number and its faraway area code.

"Hello, Mrs. Judd."

Mr. Judd had begun a series of frantic gesticulations that appeared to mean, "Whatever you do, don't tell her where we're going!" The man wasn't afraid of death, but he was absolutely afraid of Sallie Judd.

Faye knew that she held his fate in her cell-phone-wielding hand, but she didn't have the heart to press her advantage. If Mr. Judd wanted to take a walk in the woods, she guessed she'd help him. Because if she wouldn't, she suspected Ross Donnelly would. Or he'd try. He didn't look like a man who'd been slogging down any creekbeds lately, so Mr. Judd's chances of survival might be better with Faye and Joe.

"Oh, he's looking just great, Mrs. Judd," she cooed. It was almost true. Anticipation of the afternoon's discoveries had brought the warm color back to his face. What was more, his urgent gestures in her direction showed that he retained quite a lot of agility. Maybe they could get him to Faye's suspected cemetery mound without Joe having to haul his unconscious form back to the car.

At least he had bowed to her insistence that they amend their original plan enough to spare him the drive out to the work site. Faye and Joe had driven into town to fetch him, but the extra few minutes of waiting had made him still more anxious to go wading in a Water of the State.

Faye parked her car by the project trailer, knowing that the Nails wouldn't think twice about seeing it there at any time of the day or night. Oka Hofobi had his workaholic tendencies, too. Of course, if he walked back to the trailer to see what she was up to, only to find her missing, she'd eventually have to explain herself. Knowing that the Nails were as devoted to Wednesday night prayer meeting as Mrs. Calhoun, Faye felt fairly sure that they'd never know she'd been there. She intended to be out of the woods and way up the road before prayer meeting was finished.

The Nail house was deserted. The Calhoun house was deserted. No cars were in sight in either direction. There would be no better time. Faye and Joe stood on either side of Judd, each steadying him with a hand resting lightly on his back, just in case.

Faye took a deep breath and said, "Let's go." The three of them were across the street and concealed in the creekbank foliage within minutes. Faye and Joe each tied their laces together and hung their boots around their necks. Mr. Judd, who hadn't packed his suitcase for an outing like this, just slipped off his loafers and carried them in one hand. A brief tussle ensued when Joe tried to carry them for him. Mr. Judd won.

Rolling their pants legs above their knees, the three of them crossed a broad sand bar and stepped into a creek that was gloriously cool on Faye's bare feet and legs. Fine sand shifted under her feet, and gravel poked into her soles. Remembering Mrs. Nail's story, Faye smiled to think that she was stomping on the Devil's body. She remembered now that she had been looking forward to this jaunt.

"There's a lot more water today than there was on…that day," Mr. Judd said, stepping back into the shallows.

The creek deepened sharply as Faye stepped further from the sandy bank. Within a few steps, the water was lapping at her rolled-up pants legs. The tea-colored murkiness on the far side suggested that the creek was chest-deep or deeper there. Being the shortest, Faye stepped out in front. If she kept her pants dry, then Mr. Judd surely would. Long-legged Joe, whose knees seemed to be roughly level with Faye's hips, would stay practically dry, if he followed in her footsteps.

"I hear they've had a wet summer, so it makes sense that the water's high," Faye observed, picking her way around a small patch of gravel. "What time of year was it when you were attacked?"

"Early spring. I remember running past dogwoods and red-buds. They were blooming so pretty, and it didn't seem right for the natural world to be beautiful, because I was so scared. It had been a dry winter, I'm sure of that. So I guess that's why there's such a difference in the water level. Remember, I told you that I saw the cemetery and the marijuana field because I had to go looking for someplace with enough water where I could fish."

Faye reached out, again, to brush away overhanging vegetation. This place would look very different in the springtime, when most plants hadn't started leafing out yet. She was keeping a close eye on the creek's banks. They rose high, first on one side of the water, then on the other, and years of rushing water had deeply eroded the base of each small bluff. It wouldn't be smart to stand on top of those overhanging banks.

Faye studied the exposed soil of each bank as she passed it. Were any of them—or all of them—altered by humans? Maybe. If so, the soil had been built up in places, one basketload at a time, by an endless procession of workers.

Faye had seen photos of mounds in cross-section, where a slice through the earth revealed the pattern of those basketloads, still distinguishable as a separate "hunk" of dirt after so many years. Try as she might, she couldn't make out anything that obvious.

Grass grew over much of the banks' surfaces. Erosion had washed dirt down from the top, covering the original surface of these bluffs or mounds or fortifications or whatever you wanted to call them. Or maybe they were just natural creek banks. She couldn't be sure without taking a trowel and cutting a slice down through the grass and debris, right into the original pile of dirt.

Mr. Judd seemed to find the creek water invigorating. He was walking along, scuffing his feet now and then to kick up a spray, looking for all the world like the nineteen-year-old boy who had once fled this place in terror. Joe didn't look like he was suffering much, either.

Faye was getting worried that they might walk past an important landmark, so every time the bluffs dipped down to a manageable height, she climbed up and looked around. Technically, she was leaving the Waters of the State when she did that, but neither Joe nor Mr. Judd seemed willing to call her on it.

"Okay," she said, on the fourth or fifth try, "I can see the marijuana field from here. We must be getting close to your cemetery hill. We'll walk a little way further and check again."

The water grew slightly deeper as they progressed. Faye had given up trying to keep her pants dry. A late afternoon ray of sunlight pierced the trees overhead and lit up a silver-sided fish swimming past her ankle. She remembered that Mr. Judd had been holding a fishing pole the last time he walked through these woods as a free man.

It seemed like it was about time to crawl up the bank and look around again, but Faye's attention was caught by a dark spot on the bank ahead.

"Oh, sweet Jesus." Mr. Judd had stopped dead in his tracks, staring dull-eyed at the dark thing that had captured Faye's attention. "It's my cave. The place where I hid from my kidnapper." He slogged through the water to take a closer look. The carefree young man had disappeared, and now he simply looked old.

The three of them gathered around the mouth of the cave, though upon close inspection, Faye wasn't sure that's exactly what she'd call it. It just looked like a hole in the bank, partially obscured by soils that had washed down from above. Using her hands to rake away some of that soil, she could see a smooth-walled corridor that extended far back into the earth.

Was it a natural feature? Caves weren't common in Mississippi, but they existed, and one of the most well-known could be found a few miles away in one of the mounds at Nanih Waiya State Park. Some people thought that Nanih Waiya Cave had been enlarged and extended by prehistoric humans. She wondered whether this cave, too, was a remnant of the moundbuilding culture that she was coming to believe had altered the course of the creek. She knew that there were surviving drains at Ohio's Fort Ancient site, which only made sense when you realized how important water control was to unmechanized agricultural societies. This cave—Hole? Structure?—She hardly knew what to call it—would bear closer inspection.

But not today. She had no interest in wading into a cave filled with waist-deep water, not without a change of clothes. And not when they were already pushing their chances of getting back to the car before dark.

And certainly not when Mr. Judd looked measurably sicker every minute he stood looking at the place where he'd suffered so completely. "The water's up farther than I thought," he muttered. "The floor of that cave was dry. Almost dry. There were a few puddles, and it was mucky everywhere, but..." His voice trailed off, and he turned a pair of eyes on Faye that simply broke her heart.

"Let's find us a cemetery hill," she said briskly, grabbing his elbow and dragging him over to a spot where the bank dipped down almost to the level of the creek. Not looking where she was going, she stepped hard into a spot where the creek grew suddenly deeper. If she hadn't had a good hold on Mr. Judd's arm, she would have toppled right in.

Faye stared down into the hole's cool, clear depths, unable to forget her memory of Mrs. Nail's voice. She'd said that water monsters, White People of the Water, lived in pools just like this one. She twitched her shoulders hard, trying to physically shake off the eerie story. Faye wasn't superstitious, but standing here within spitting distance of the cave where Mr. Judd had suffered gave her the creeps. Thoughts of water monsters only made things worse.

She hauled Mr. Judd right out of the Waters of the State and onto Mrs. Calhoun's land, saying, "Why don't you look around?"

They all three saw it at once.

A small flat-topped hill, like a miniature of Mr. Calhoun's tremendous mound, was clearly visible not far away. They had almost passed it.

Faye saw nothing to make her think that a cemetery had ever graced its top, nothing except a dirt track that curved up its side. Whether they are brought by a modern hearse, or hauled in a wagon, or carried by pallbearers, the dead in their caskets are heavy. It only made sense that some kind of driveway would be associated with a graveyard.

"There was an iron fence on top, draped with running roses," Mr. Judd said, transfixed. "And one of those tall marble monuments that rich people put in their family plots. We'd be able to see them from here, if they were still up there." He turned to Faye. "You realize that this means we were right?"

"You're talking about our theory that you were attacked because you knew too much about Calhoun's marijuana plot?"

"Yeah. If that plot was back there," he pointed behind him, "and not far past it is this mound where the cemetery was. And not far past *it* is the cave where I hid just a week later after somebody tried to kill me right nearby. Well, it just seems like too much of a coincidence. Surely the field and the mound and the cave and the beating would all be connected somehow."

"It's still not proof," Faye said, but, deep down, she agreed with him.

Chapter Twenty

It was obvious that Dr. Mailer hadn't listened to a word that left Faye's mouth. He had stopped casting caustic glances at the damp mud on her pants and shoes. Instead, his eyes kept wandering toward the floor, and his verbal responses had deteriorated to the level of an occasional grunt.

If she could have crossed the hotel lobby without running into her boss, he'd never have known about her semi-legal doings. As it was, she'd been caught hours after her workday ended, and she was far dirtier than she'd been the last time he saw her. She could hardly deny that she'd been up to something. She'd hoped that Mailer's scientific curiosity would save her from his disapproval.

"I thought you'd be excited by what Joe and I found—another mound and maybe some prehistoric water diversion devices. Besides that, I still think that Calhoun's mound might have been a bird effigy. Think of how beautiful it would have been when it was first built!"

"Well, we can't do much besides think about it, now, can we? We've got no permission to even walk over and look at it. And you had no permission to go stomping through Mrs. Calhoun's private property tonight."

Faye opened her mouth to defend herself, but Dr. Mailer had finally started to talk. He wasn't about to quit. "Don't give me that stuff about 'Waters of the State.' You're probably right, if you want to split legal hairs, but that won't help Mrs. Calhoun's feelings, if she finds out what you did. It also won't help the bad publicity we'll get if word gets out."

Faye tried to talk again, but she failed.

"And you took Joe with you. You're supposed to be the smart one."

She blurted out, "Joe's not dumb," even though it wasn't strictly pertinent to the conversation, because it just needed saying.

Dr. Mailer was relentless. "I know he's not dumb, but he's not savvy like you are, either. He depends on you. Why would you want to get that man in trouble?"

Faye was desperately grateful she hadn't told Dr. Mailer that she'd taken Mr. Judd with her on her exploratory jaunt. There seemed nothing for her to say but, "I'm sorry."

Because dressing down a subordinate came about as naturally to Mailer as flying without an airplane, he immediately relented. "I know you're sorry. But Chuck's not, and I have no idea what to do about it."

"You think he's been trespassing on Mrs. Calhoun's property?"

"I don't know what in the heck he's been up to, but he can't keep walking off the job site without saying a word. He can't keep coming back wet and covered in mud, either. Did you see him today? His pants weren't just filthy. They were actually torn."

"Chuck *is* a management challenge…"

"And I'm a management failure."

Faye tried to interrupt with a tactful denial but, in an uncharacteristically forceful tone, Mailer wouldn't let her.

"I don't manage. I encourage and direct people who want to work. I'm not a boss. I wasn't trained to be one, and I don't really want to be one. I'm an archaeologist and a teacher. I'm good at those things. Project management is a necessary evil in my line of work."

Faye, who wasn't a manager either, but who knew how to attack a problem instead of wallowing in it, tried a straightforward tactic. "Have you talked to Chuck?"

"I've tried, but he doesn't say anything that makes any sense. He gets upset and says things like, 'People shouldn't stand in the way of science.' Or 'People aren't important. Knowledge is.' Then he stops talking to me and starts spreading stone tools out on his desk. It's the same pieces, every time. He keeps them in a box under his desk. He sorts them by type—points, unifaces, manufacturing flakes. Next, he sorts them by the type of rock they're made from. Then he sorts them by age. He talks to himself the whole time, like I'm not there. For a while I couldn't figure out what he was saying, but I finally understood him today, and it shook me up."

Mailer paused so long that Faye couldn't stand it any longer. "What did he say?" Mailer was still silent, so she tried again. "What did Chuck say?"

"He just keeps repeating five words: 'One of them is missing.'"

The significance of those words hit Faye like a jab in the stomach. They couldn't be ignored, not when a man had been killed just days before with a razor-sharp stone tool.

"It looks bad for Chuck," he went on, "but let's think about this like scientists. Anybody on our team could have taken a tool from Chuck's box. Every one of us was angry at Mr. Calhoun for what he did with his tractor. I don't see that Chuck's motive is any stronger than anybody else's. If Calhoun was killed over his destruction of the mound, then one of us has a lot bigger reason to be upset about that."

"Oka Hofobi."

"Yep. I don't think he did it, but his alibi is paper-thin. Who's going to believe his mother? Especially a mother like Mrs. Nail, who'll protect her baby until he's eligible for Medicare. If I'm not going to doubt Oka Hofobi's innocence, I don't feel right about doubting Chuck's, just because he's strange."

Faye followed his logic, and she agreed.

"I've been thinking about calling a friend of mine who's a psychologist," Mailer went on. "Just to get some advice on how to handle Chuck."

"He scares you, doesn't he?"

"Yeah, and I'm ashamed of it." Mailer absently rubbed the palms of his hands together. Faye recognized the gesture as something he did when he was nervous or off-balance. When Chuck was anxious, he counted his arrowheads and talked to himself. The two habits served the same purpose, but Mailer's mannerisms were socially acceptable and Chuck's just weren't. And that, she realized, crossed over into the realm of psychology.

"It wouldn't hurt to talk to an expert," she said cautiously, "particularly since we don't know where Chuck was when Mr. Calhoun was killed."

"I know that, and the sheriff knows that, but she hasn't followed up on it. At least, not that I can tell. I've tried to tell myself that Chuck's behavior just looks bad. It doesn't make him guilty. One side of my brain says I should tell the sheriff about his erratic habits. The other side of my brain is afraid of making Chuck a target of her suspicion. Deep down, I think he's innocent. And I think he may be mentally ill. People like Chuck have suffered from witch hunts for all of history. My instinct tells me to protect him. Does that make me weak?"

Faye hardly had the energy to drag herself off the elevator. She hoped she had enough energy to take a shower, because she felt truly filthy. She summoned the courage to step through the sliding metal doors. There in the elevator lobby's small sitting area, wearing clothes that proclaimed that he, too, had not showered, sat Joe.

It had only taken Mailer a quarter-hour to give Faye a solid dressing-down. Joe seemed to have spent that time here in meditation. There could be no other explanation for the fact that he looked serene and rested, while she felt like dog meat.

"I saw Mailer drag you off," he said, "and I figured he was going to give you a good talking-to."

"My mama would have called it a 'come-to-Jesus meeting.' She had more talent in that direction than Mailer, come to think of it. Before he got finished with me, he started ragging on himself."

"So you're okay?" Joe said, standing up with the air of a man who was finally going to get his shower.

"It'd take somebody a lot meaner than Dr. Mailer to get me down. But Joe?"

"Yeah?"

She looked around to see whether anyone was listening. "I think he's really worried about Chuck. I think he's worried that Chuck may have killed Mr. Calhoun. What do you think?"

"Nah. He's too tall."

"Too tall? I can see how somebody could be too small to overpower a big man like Mr. Calhoun, but how could somebody be too tall?"

"You got a good look at Mr. Calhoun's body, same as I did. Couldn't you tell from the cut on his neck that the killer had to be shorter than him? Also, he'd have to be right-handed." He grabbed Faye's shoulders and turned her around so that he was facing her back. "See? If I grabbed your head from behind and pulled it back so's I could cut your throat, the natural way my arm moves would make the cut side-to-side, with maybe a little uptick on the right side." He dropped to his knees. "Now, if I'm shorter than you, I've got to reach up with my left hand to grab your head. I can't pull it straight back, so your neck is stretched back at a cockeyed angle. My right hand, the one that's holding the knife, has the same problem. It's hard for me to slice from side-to-side without dragging the knife down as it moves to the right."

Thoroughly creeped out by having her throat slashed twice, even in pantomime, Faye pulled away. "Well, no, I didn't know those things. I haven't made a science of studying mortal wounds. I guess it's just not part of my skill set."

"Maybe you need to go hunting with me sometime." Joe grinned like a man who was pleased to know something Faye didn't, just this once.

"I figure there are a few things so grisly that I don't even care to know them. Why didn't you tell the sheriff?"

"I figured she knew. She's a sheriff and all. Mortal wounds are everyday business for her. Besides, I wasn't about to do any talking. You kept twitching around and looking at me like you was afraid I'd say something stupid. So I didn't say anything at all."

Faye wondered if she'd been as obvious to anyone else. Like, say, the sheriff.

"Maybe that's why Sheriff Rutland never suspected you like I thought she might. The shape of the wound told her that you couldn't have done it. Did you notice anything else at the murder scene? Like you say, the sheriff probably saw all you did, and maybe more, but I'm not experienced with killing and how it's done. Enlighten me."

"Judging from where the blood was, I'd say Calhoun was killed where he was found, right out in the middle of that open field. I couldn't see any scuff marks on the ground, like he would've made if there'd been a big fight."

"So he knew his killer. Or he thought he had nothing to fear."

"Right. Or else he didn't hear the person sneaking up behind him, but that don't seem real likely, since I get the impression he was a real outdoorsman. I think he would've heard something, or at least he'd have recognized that something wasn't right. The sound of the night animals and bugs would've told him that."

Faye realized that Joe was crediting Mr. Calhoun with his own skills, which could be an overestimate, but she didn't say anything. "So you think he saw the killer, and he wasn't afraid."

Joe nodded once. "Not at first. But you can bet he was afraid after that friend of his twisted his arm behind him and broke it."

The thought of suffering such a violent assault from someone she assumed to be her friend brought the gorge into Faye's throat. She asked, "Did you notice any other gory details?"

Joe shook his head.

They were silent a moment, pondering the unpleasant facts, until a cheery thought occurred to Faye. "Chuck's at least as tall as Mr. Calhoun was, and I'm pretty sure he's left-handed. We should tell Dr. Mailer not to worry so much about him. He's weird, but he's not a killer. I don't think." She tried to remember how tall Calhoun had been. "Can we eliminate anybody else?"

"Mr. Calhoun was pretty tall, almost as tall as me. I'd say the only other person we know who's even close to his height, besides me and Chuck, is Dr. Mailer. I haven't noticed that anybody else is left-handed, so that doesn't help us any."

Faye was willing to take whatever she could get.

The light on Faye's bedside phone was signaling that she had a message waiting for her. She considered ignoring it, but she'd never get any sleep with that red light flashing on and off interminably. Besides, Faye could be antisocial at times, but she wasn't stupid. There was a killer out there somewhere, as much as she hated to think about it. It would be foolish to ignore a message that might say something like, "There's an ax-murderer under your bed!"

Besides, there was a new man in her life. Well, maybe Ross wasn't in her life yet, but he was knocking on the door. Of course, she was going to check that message.

The phone rang before she reached it, and the voice that said, "Hello, Faye," did belong to that new man who was hovering around the corners of her life.

"Hello, Ross."

"How was work today?" he asked in a voice that did not speak of work or of anything practical at all. "Did you dig up any treasures?"

Faye remembered the embankments along the creek and the mysterious hole in its bank and the ancient mound that rose above them. Those were treasures that she hadn't even needed to dig up. They were right out in the world for anyone to see—if they had Mrs. Calhoun's permission. Faye decided that she didn't know Ross well enough yet to admit to him that she'd been trespassing all evening, so she said, "No treasures today. Only tax documents and other boring paperwork."

"Tax documents? That sounds like lawyer stuff. People study archaeology because it's glamorous—"

"—or otherwise they'd never accept such low salaries?"

"Yeah. My theory is that our society pays lawyers well because it's the only way people will agree to spend their lives analyzing tax documents."

Faye sank down on the bed and kicked off her muddy boots. Realizing what her nasty clothes were doing to the comforter, she slid off the bed and sat cross-legged on the floor. "I notice that your work brought you to the Neshoba County Fair. They call it 'America's Giant House Party.' I wouldn't say that you're suffering much over that assignment. What boring and lawyerly thing did you do today to earn your princely salary?"

"It was bad." A low groan came out of the phone to emphasize how bad his day had been. "I don't know if I should even tell you about my day, because it was that bad."

"Don't tell me. You spent all day on the Midway, riding rides and eating snow cones."

"Worse." Another pitiful groan escaped him. "I just left Meridian, so you'll be sound asleep a long time before I roll into Philadelphia and knock off work for the day. I spent today at an economic development conference. Every speech was equally scintillating, so I think my brain may have started to rot. Tomorrow, I'll be around Philadelphia most of the morning—hey, maybe I'll go to the Fair and eat a snow cone in your honor—but tomorrow night will be deadly. I've got to go to Jackson for a charity fundraiser where I'll have a chance at some face-time with a few key legislators. Unfortunately, since I do think brain rot has started to set in, I may not survive."

"Sounds like you'll be pretty late getting back here tomorrow night, too." Faye tried not to sound like she wished he was right down the hall, though she did.

"Yeah. I've got to spend tomorrow afternoon at the Capitol, doing all those things lobbyists do. Then I have to go to that fundraiser. Black tie."

Ross sounded like the thought of a formal evening made him want to groan again, but Faye entertained an extravagantly detailed mental image of Ross in a tux. For about fifty cents, she'd drive all the way to Jackson, just to get a look at that.

"I'll have to get up at the crack of dawn Friday," he continued in the same suffering tone, "so that I can be back here in time to hear Neely Rutland and Lawrence Judd speak at the Fair that morning. I was thinking maybe we might have dinner that evening. Would you like to?"

"That sounds lovely," Faye said, realizing that she sounded as prim as a Grace Kelly character in a 1950s movie. Still, whenever she was afraid she might embarrass herself by saying something like, "Yes, indeed. Anything you want, you handsome thing," she always fell back on her mother's outdated but outstandingly correct version of good manners.

"Shall I pick you up at eight?"

Again, Faye's voice spoke, but her mother's words came out. "That will be just fine." Which was a lot better than what she was thinking, which was *Praise God. I can shop for some decent clothes at lunchtime, then I'll have until eight o'clock to scrub all the dirt off me.*

"I'll call you tomorrow night, if the party gets over at a decent hour. Otherwise, I'll talk to you on Friday. Sleep well, Faye."

"You, too, Ross."

Despite Ross' good-night wish that she sleep well, Faye didn't rest at all comfortably, and not for the first time in the week. The excitement of discovering both the cave and the mound that Mr. Judd remembered from his youth stirred the treasure-hunter in her soul. Archaeologists were not born through the sheer love of science. It was the thrill of the search that lured Faye and others like her into a difficult and poorly paid field.

Half the time—most of the time—she wasn't even sure what she hoped to find when she poked her trowel into the ground. Something old. Something interesting, no, fascinating. Something that would snatch her up out of her pedestrian twenty-first-century life and plunk her down into the past. Scratch the surface of an archaeologist in her practical field clothing and her sensible shoes, and you will find an incurable romantic.

Eventually, after mentally reviewing the glorious relics of history she might find if she were ever allowed to excavate on the Calhoun land, she drifted off and slept soundly for a time. The pre-dawn hours found her awake again, with her thoughts straying to the interesting possibilities that walked around in the form of Ross Donnelly. If she could have sat down and drawn up specifications for God to use when designing her ideal man, the result would have looked a lot like Ross.

Her interest wasn't as shallow as his face and body, as pleasant as those were to behold. She'd always valued intellect in a man, as well as the drive to develop that intellect. Emory Law School wasn't known for accepting and graduating slackers. Ross rose further in her esteem when she considered that he was using his gifts to pursue a cause that he obviously believed in. Faye wasn't sure she cared much what a man's heartfelt cause was—provided it didn't involve lying, cheating, stealing, or killing—as long as he had a real passion for it.

The fact that Ross' cause was intimately associated with his African-American identity was more than a little intriguing to Faye. She'd spent more than thirty years grappling with her own ambiguous ancestry. Was she white? Was she black? After the passage of eight generations, how strongly should she identify with her tenuous connection to the Creek nation?

Ross knew who he was, and he accepted her African descent as sufficient to include her in the phrase, "our people." The child inside her who had never felt part of any group was charmed by that. No, she was more than charmed. She felt affirmed for being herself. Nobody but her mother, her grandmother, Joe, and a select few friends had ever given her that gift.

She rolled over and told herself sternly to sleep. Her job required a lot from her, physically, and she needed her rest.

Again, she slipped away, but this time her sleep was light and troubled. When her alarm sounded, she knew only that she had dreamed, but the details flitted away like vapor. She was mumbling when she awoke, which caused her to glance quickly at Toneisha's bed to see if she'd disturbed her roommate. The bed was empty. Faye was alone.

What had she been saying? It seemed important to remember the words. She could almost hear them. Ross had been in her dream, looking down at her and smiling. Joe had been there, too, though she wasn't so sure that he'd worn such a pleasant expression. It hadn't been a romantic dream, nor a nightmare, but she sensed that there was a decision to be made, a question to be answered.

What had she been trying to say?

She could almost taste the words on her tongue. Blanking out her mind, she tried to slip back under the blanket of sleep. As it engulfed her, she heard the words and realized what had been troubling her.

Who's taller? Ross or Joe?

She tried repeating the words again, with her conscious mind turned on.

"Who's taller? Ross or Joe?"

Or, more to the point: "Who was taller? Ross or Mr. Calhoun?"

And when did Ross Donnelly arrive in Neshoba County?

The Choctaws and the Irish

As told by Mrs. Frances Nail

This is another story I learned in school. It ought to be taught in all the schools, but I don't think it is.

In 1845, the potato crop in Ireland didn't make. Now, I know all you folks grew up on land like this land here. You can drop a pea off your plate onto the ground, and it'll come up. Next year, you'll have a whole crop of peas. The old folks say that's how we got corn. A crow flew far and wide—maybe to Central America, since I hear that's where they invented corn. It snatched up a cob and flew away with it. When it flew over Choctaw country, one little kernel dropped off and hit the ground. The next year, a corn plant grew. And the next year, there were two plants. Now, everybody has corn, the whole world over.

It wasn't that way in Ireland. All the poor people could grow was potatoes, and when the potatoes didn't make, they started to starve. The next year, the potatoes didn't grow again. The next year, there weren't even enough potatoes left for seed. People left their homes, or they died. Millions of them, or so I've been told.

In 1847, our Choctaw brothers and sisters in Oklahoma raised a bunch of money, more than seven hundred dollars, and sent it to Ireland to help the hungry people. Now, I've got no notion how much money that is in today's dollars, and it doesn't much matter. It's beside the point. The thing to remember is that it had only been sixteen years since the Treaty of Dancing Rabbit Creek left those Choctaws starving and homeless and cold. When you look at it from that perspective, that seven hundred dollars was the biggest fortune anybody ever gave away.

I'll say this for the Irish. They didn't forget. In 1997, for the hundred-and-fiftieth anniversary of the Great Potato Famine, a bunch of them flew to Oklahoma to say thank you. Then, they walked five hundred miles until they got here, to Nanih Waiya. After that, they donated a hundred thousand dollars to feed hungry people in Africa, in honor of our brothers and sisters in Oklahoma.

They should teach these things in all the schools. The world would be a better place.

Chapter Twenty-one

Thursday
Day 7 of the Neshoba County Fair

Faye believed that no one should have to listen to a cell phone ringing before breakfast, but hers was singing to her from the pocket of yesterday's muddy jeans. She crawled out of bed and put the foul thing to her ear.

The quavery voice was familiar. Faye got a bad feeling in her stomach.

"Ms. Longchamp—"

"Call me Faye, please," Faye said, partially out of good manners and partially to delay news that she suspected was bad.

"All right, Faye. I wanted to let you know that Lawrence had another weak spell last night. He's back in the hospital."

Faye felt a little weak and sick herself. He had seemed so much better when she last saw him, hardly nine hours before. Had their walk in the creek been too much for him? She berated herself for letting him talk her into taking that risk. Then she berated herself some more for not checking on him during the night. "Have you talked to him, Mrs. Judd?"

"You should call me Sallie, after all you've done for us. No, I haven't talked to him yet. I think he's still unconscious, but I really don't know. The doctor has not been forthcoming with information."

Big surprise, Faye thought. Framing her words more diplomatically for the benefit of the sick man's sick wife, she said, "I'll drive over there and see what I can get out of the doctor on duty. I'll do my best to get in to see your husband. And don't worry. The doctor I met isn't going to win any personality contests, but I have no reason to think he doesn't know his business."

Unless one counts patient and family education as part of his business, she groused to herself as she phoned Joe and told him that they needed to make a little detour on their way to work.

"Okay, here's the plan," Faye said, letting Joe drive so that she could do a couple of last-minute grooming tasks like combing her hair and applying sunscreen. "While I'm getting the doctor's attention, you go to the hospital cafeteria and get us some breakfast to go. We can eat on our way to work. Dr. Mailer's not used to having anybody show up on time, but it would be nice to surprise him, just this once. He's under a lot of stress. We should try not to add to it."

She was worried about leaving Mr. Judd to the tender mercies of the impatient doctor. Pulling her cell phone out of her purse, she called Ross Donnelly. He'd said he would be in town this morning, and she'd understood him to say that his important business would happen later in the day. Maybe he had better things to do than sit in a hospital room, but then again, maybe he didn't.

She had the impression that Ross had driven over from Atlanta primarily to have a chance to meet Lawrence Judd, and that these other political activities were just nice things to do while he was here. The Neshoba County Fair was crammed full of powerful politicos, so he might have had his sights set on more than one mover-and-shaker, but here was a chance for quality time with one of them. It was no surprise when Ross immediately said he'd see her at the hospital.

Joe dropped Faye off at the hospital entrance, then zipped away to park the car. Faye knew her way to the emergency room, a fact that was depressing in itself. It was a fairly small hospital, so she was there within minutes.

The doctor she'd met during Mr. Judd's last hospital visit was standing at the nurse's station reviewing a chart. She could tell that he was not overjoyed to see her.

"How is Mr. Judd?" she asked, hoping that Mrs. Judd's earlier permission for her to speak with medical personnel still held. Or that Mrs. Judd had faxed him another one already, with the sun still hardly up.

"I just spoke with his wife, but I'll repeat what I told her. This time, he was able to call 911 before losing consciousness, but the paramedics found him in the same condition this morning as he was when he was brought in earlier this week. Very low blood pressure. Very slow heart rate. These symptoms may have been even more pronounced than upon his first visit, but they fluctuate from minute to minute, so I don't want to say that for certain."

"How is he now?"

"His blood pressure and heart rate have improved since he was admitted, though we have no idea why his condition deteriorated again. He's been conscious, but he's drifting in and out, and I'm not sure he's completely coherent when he's talking. I've asked his wife again whether he's had this kind of episode before. She denies it. She sounded a little insulted to be asked the same question a second time."

Faye wondered how he'd respond to a question that suggested he might be dangerously careless or forgetful.

The doctor continued. "She says he was prescribed medication for chest pains—angina—a year ago, and that his doctor recently added a beta-blocker for his hypertension, but that he's had no other problems. Certainly no episodes like this."

"I happen to know that he took a long vigorous walk in the country yesterday evening," Faye ventured cautiously. "Could that have caused this kind of problem?"

"He had no difficulty breathing while he was walking? He wasn't dizzy or faint?"

Faye shook her head.

"Walking is one of the best exercises for patients like Mr. Judd. I wouldn't want him to give up aerobic exercise for fear of another attack. Unless we find something structurally wrong that we didn't find two days ago, then I would encourage him to keep taking those walks. But first we have to track down the cause of his problem."

Faye was relieved to hear that she probably didn't instigate this new crisis by caving in to Judd's desire to take a long walk in the creek.

"Can I see him?"

The doctor nodded, and a nurse escorted her to a curtained cubicle that was filled with flashing, beeping medical instruments and a hospital bed. The bed was short and narrow, but Mr. Judd still looked small in it. His skin was gray, as before, and his eyes didn't open when she took his hand and said, "Sallie sent me. Are they treating you okay?"

A little smile twisted his lips, and he gave her hand an imperceptible squeeze. Perhaps he was more responsive than the medical personnel realized. Or perhaps Faye had played a trump card they didn't have, simply by mentioning Sallie's name.

"What happened? Did you just wake up feeling bad?"

No response.

"Sallie says she's going to hop a plane and come get you, even if they have to put you both in an ambulance to get you back to Michigan."

A bare shake of the head said that he wanted Sallie to stay right where she was.

A deep voice outside the curtain asked, "Can I come in?"

Faye said, quietly, "Of course you can," and Ross slid into the narrow space between the foot of the bed and the curtain.

Mr. Judd's lips moved, trying to frame a word. Something unintelligible came out.

Faye and Ross gathered at his elbow. Together, they said, "You're talking!"

"See you...again."

Ross thought for a second, then said, "Good to see you again, too, sir! I wish you were looking better, but I'm glad you're talking."

Faye was glad Mr. Judd was talking, too, but she was preoccupied with trying to figure out what he'd actually said. All she was sure of was that he said something about seeing Ross again. Maybe he meant he was looking forward to seeing him again. Maybe he meant that he'd seen Ross recently and, thus, was seeing him again. If so, then the obvious question was this: How long ago did he see Ross last? If he'd seen him shortly before his mysterious collapse, some uncomfortable questions needed to be asked.

Another deep voice asked permission to enter and, again, she said, "Come in." Joe ducked in carrying two Styrofoam takeout trays from the cafeteria. He stood quietly by Ross. Faye couldn't help looking at the two men and taking their measure. Ross couldn't be as much as an inch shorter than Joe.

Faye was working in air-conditioned luxury again. She'd merely pointed out to Dr. Mailer how useful his exciting new software could be to the project—and their upcoming proposal. "Think how persuasive our presentation will be if we can show the selection committee a computer-generated fly-over of the project site."

"Well, I imagine their engineers will have already created a fly-over when they planned the road," was Dr. Mailer's deflating comment. Fortunately, the man was unnaturally easy to work for. "Still, we could create one that shows where we think we'll find cultural remains. It might help them tweak the proposed right-of-way before we start our work. That would save money, which makes bureaucrats happy. Taxpayers, too."

Faye took that as permission to get started, so she turned to go, but he stopped her. "Before you go too far with that fly-over, why don't you see what Google's got? I've seen satellite images with as much detail as we'll ever need that are out there on the

Web for free. Maybe not out here in the country, but it wouldn't hurt to check."

Well, duh. Faye felt her age, and not for the first time. Which was a little sad, considering that she could still see 35 in her rearview mirror, and 40 was still years away. She scuttled her plans to download topographic coordinates. It would be so much easier to simply center the earth on her screen and dive in.

Faye felt like an astronaut swooping down on the earth from outer space. She centered her screen on North America and watched the continent swell to fill her monitor. Pointing the mouse at the southeastern United States, she made the image larger still. The Mississippi River snaked up the left-hand edge of her screen, disappearing off its upper and lower edges. The Gulf of Mexico took a big blue bite out of the bottom of the image, distracting Faye from her mission. Maybe she needed to take a little trip home...

The coast of Florida's Panhandle, with its white rim of beaches, appeared on the screen. A pearly string of islands hugged that coastline. One of them was Faye's.

Faye centered the image on Joyeuse Island and zoomed in again. It was hugged up so close to the swampy coastline that only Faye's loving eyes could have picked it out from the encroaching wetlands. Her island was the green of live oak treetops, but a narrow stretch of beach was discernible on the ocean side. Amid the soft outlines of nature, the hard straight lines of a man-made artifact were obvious. The walls of her home, also named Joyeuse, traced a perfect square on the computer screen.

The image was so real that Faye felt like she was inspecting the work of the roofers who repaired the great hurricane's damage. She was unlikely to ever get a better look at their work. Now, that wasn't true. Next year, when the technology improved, she'd get a better look at her roof. And the next year, she'd get a better look again. Soon enough, she'd be able to count every shingle.

Homesickness seized her. She shoved it aside every morning. Every night, when she settled in to sleep, she refused to let it sneak into her heart, but she never stopped wishing she were home. If she'd simply commit herself to one field of study, it could happen. Choosing to earn a doctorate in the specialty that most obviously suited her—racial relations in the pre-Civil-War Southeast—would mean that she could go home and look for enlightenment in her own back yard. Which meant she'd have to turn her back on interesting work on other historical periods, like the work she was doing here.

Faye was born to be a generalist. The thought of choosing a specialty scared her to death.

She stroked the screen, saying good-bye to Joyeuse in her own way, then zoomed out again. Centering the image on east-central Mississippi, she dove again toward the surface. Finding Nanih Waiya took her only seconds. She loomed out of the surrounding pasture like an eternal breast. Faye had no reason for visiting her, other than to pay her respects. The nearby cave mound was invisible beneath its sheath of trees.

She moved her cursor southwest and clicked. Now she was looking down at herself. Not really. These satellite photos weren't displayed in real time. Still, the roofs of the Nail and Calhoun houses were recognizable, as was the Calhoun mound.

For fun, she took a "ride" up the creek, just to get an aerial perspective on the trip she'd taken the day before. Mr. Judd's cave was way too small to see at this resolution, but his mound—the one where he'd seen a cemetery all those years ago—was visible through the obscuring trees, if you knew where to look. To Faye's eye, the earthworks along the creek were almost as obvious, but she knew there were those who would argue the point.

She clicked back over to the Calhoun mound. Were its wings a figment of her imagination?

The answer was an unequivocal "Maybe not." She thought she saw a suggestive shadow here and another there, even through the underbrush crowding up the mound's side. Still, she'd never have recognized the shape of a bird without having seen the land shorn of its vegetation.

The fact that Calhoun and his ancestors had avoided plowing a large area around the mound for all these years might have been telling. Land was money, but they'd left a big chunk of it alone. Though Calhoun himself might not have known why, maybe the eagle's wings were obvious when his ancestors settled the land. Perhaps they had been farsighted enough to preserve them.

Faye zoomed out just a tiny bit and laughed out loud. Maybe there was no eagle effigy to be discovered around that mound. But if there was, then its beak was pointed directly toward the lone mound that remained deep in the woods.

Perhaps it had supported a cemetery in Mr. Judd's day. Faye believed there had been a time when a long-dead people had seen it as something else entirely.

Chapter Twenty-two

Faye pondered the missing cemetery. Mr. Judd had seen it, and his memory had not been dimmed by time. He even remembered the cast iron fence and the marble monuments that had replaced the ceremonial temple that would have stood atop the mound in antiquity.

Who besides Mr. Judd would remember that cemetery? Mr. Calhoun, certainly, but he was dead. And Mr. Rutland had once owned it, but his mind was as unreachable now as Mr. Calhoun's. Maybe their wives would remember, but Mrs. Rutland must be dead, or she wouldn't be letting Neely take the full brunt of her father's care. Faye didn't care to toy with a woman of Mrs. Calhoun's trigger-happy reputation. Not when she had another option.

She dug in a desk drawer and found a phone book. The sheriff's number was published with the other emergency contacts inside the front cover. It was a small department, so Faye spent surprisingly little time on hold before Neely's voice came out of the receiver.

"Faye. How's the archaeology going?"

"Just fine, but our work would go faster if we didn't stay upset all the time. First, some crank tries to bulldoze history. Then that crank—God rest his soul—turns up dead. Not to mention Congressman Judd, who shocked everybody at the Fair with his sad tale."

"And I hear he hasn't stopped collapsing."

"Maybe he'd do better if he always had the sheriff around to look after him."

Neely's short laugh came out of the phone. "Faye, I think you do a better job taking care of him than I do. He just picked a bad time to get sick this morning. Neither of us was anywhere around."

"So you know he's back in the hospital. Does the sheriff get notified every time somebody gets sick around here?"

"She does when that someone is a retired congressman. And when he's at the center of a high-profile investigation into an old crime. Also, it doesn't hurt that one of my deputies goes to church with the admissions clerk."

"Well, I just happen to be sitting here with my computer, using a satellite to study your entire jurisdiction," Faye said, patting the computer protectively. She had a question she'd been itching to ask the sheriff, and this machine had just given her a way to do it without admitting to some serious trespassing. "You remember how Mr. Judd mentioned a hill with a cemetery on top of it?"

"I do. And this isn't the first time you've brought it up. I think it's an archaeologist thing to be interested in old stuff. Especially old bones. You people really have a thing about bones."

Faye smiled at the sheriff's companionable banter. She didn't have a lot of time to socialize with women her own age, not when her classmates were ten or more years younger. She wished Philadelphia was a little bit closer to Joyeuse. She and Neely might have been good friends.

"Thanks to the Internet, I have my own personal satellite pointed at Mr. Calhoun's property. Now, it isn't strong enough to see individual bones, especially when they're buried. But I've got a pretty good view of an old mound tucked deep in the woods that might fit Mr. Judd's description. You've lived in the area a long time. Do you know anything about it?"

"Not the first thing. Carroll Calhoun was always touchy about his property."

Faye knew that he hadn't always had this particular piece of land—Neely's father had once owned it—but she neglected to point that out. It just seemed rude. Instead, she said, "There's almost always a real good reason for a mound to survive, rather than getting plowed over. One of those good reasons is because it was used for something so special that people wanted to preserve it. Like maybe as a site for a cemetery. I can't see a cemetery on top of it now, but it's worth checking out."

"Then send me the web link to your own personal satellite. I'll go take a look at the mound."

"After you get a look, do you want to talk about it? Maybe we could go out there and take a look together."

Neely laughed again. "You just want to use my badge as an excuse to get onto Mrs. Calhoun's property. I don't think so, Faye. But we can get together here at my office tomorrow afternoon, if you like. Tomorrow morning won't work. Mr. Judd and I are supposed to talk to a big crowd out at the fairgrounds, if he gets out of the hospital. If he doesn't, I guess I'll have to do it alone. His story's gotten out to the national media, and the Fair people think we should deliver an update. They also love the idea of reminding the world of the Neshoba County Fair's significance as a political forum. It'll close down tomorrow evening, and the partiers and politicians will go home. I'm about ready for my life to get back to normal."

Faye wasn't sure she wanted to wait until Neely's life grew peaceful before she got the information on Mr. Judd's cemetery that she needed. Perhaps she and Joe might take another walk tonight. And perhaps this time they wouldn't be so persnickety about staying within the Waters of the State.

"The man's pretty sick." Ross' voice came out of the phone with none of the flirtatious edge that Faye had enjoyed the night before. "Mr. Judd wants to leave the hospital, but his doctor says no. He threatened to sign himself out against doctor's orders, but I talked him out of it."

"That was good legal advice."

"Yeah, and Mr. Judd's a lawyer, too, so he was smart enough to take it."

"You say he's pretty sick. Can you be more specific?"

In the background, Faye could hear the mechanical sound of a human voice filtered through a hospital intercom. *Housekeeping to the ER,* the intercom announced. Then it repeated itself, in case somebody missed the message: *Housekeeping to ER.*

Ross waited until it was silent, then continued. "They're having a harder time getting him to snap out of this 'weak spell,' as he calls it. His heart rate will stabilize for a while, then it'll drop to nearly nothing. His blood pressure bottoms out with it, then he passes out. No wonder he feels weak whenever he's conscious. If you heart can't pump some oxygen to your brain and your muscles, your body just can't go. His doctor says he's probably not in immediate danger, but his poker face is slipping. I think he's really worried about our friend the congressman."

"Did any of his labwork come back?" Faye liked lab reports. They provided numbers and facts. The information was couched in specific terms. If she didn't understand the medical terms, she could always look them up. She had pored over the laboratory findings of more loved ones than she liked, but hard facts drove the uncertainty away. Faye hated uncertainty.

"Some of the quick-and-dirty tests are back—complete blood count, dip-stick urinalysis, stuff like that, but we're still waiting on the rest."

It sounded to Faye like Ross had pored over the laboratory reports of more loved ones than he cared to count, too. If they ever had another moment alone, maybe she'd ask him.

Instead, she said, "I know you need to get to Jackson."

"I hate to leave, but I really do need to get over there if I can."

Faye sifted through her list of local acquaintances. Dr. Mailer would do an excellent job of advocating for Mr. Judd with his doctors. But he was such a nice guy, he'd probably just urge Faye to take the afternoon off and go to the hospital. That would wreak havoc with her plan to snoop around for Mr. Judd's cemetery.

Toneisha and Bodie were too immature. Chuck was too weird. She needed Joe for her expedition. Maybe Oka Hofobi…

As it turned out, Ross had already solved his own problem. "Are you listening, Faye? What do you think about me leaving Neely Rutland with him? She's offered to stay for a while, and she's here now."

"The sheriff? Doesn't she have better things to do?"

"Think, Faye. An ex-congressman flies into her jurisdiction, drops a political bombshell, then becomes deathly ill. She's supposed to hold a press conference—with the sick man—tomorrow morning. Yes, she's got a murder investigation going on, but she's got a staff. You better bet she'll be making sure the sick ex-congressman gets taken care of."

"Well, if you and Neely already have things worked out, you don't need to check with me. It'd be nice to let his wife know, though. I'll tell you what. Let me call Sallie and give her an update. You go to Jackson and dazzle some power-mongers."

As she turned off her phone, Joe thrust his head through the office door. "Faye—you gotta come out here and see this!"

Faye rushed outside to find her colleagues crouched and kneeling in a circle around a smiling Toneisha. Protruding out of the soil was the refined curve of a clay pot that had been nothing special when it was made. Two thousand years had turned it into something special indeed.

"Look. It's hardly broken at all," Bodie said, beaming proudly at Toneisha. "Maybe three or four big pieces. And look at that cross-hatching at the top."

As Oka Hofobi wielded a camera, Toneisha spent much of the rest of the afternoon uncovering the shapely little pot. Faye took notes and helped label the sherds—just three big chunks, but a host of tiny fragments. As the tedious work progressed, she found herself wondering whether Chuck reconstructed broken pottery with the same passion that he studied chipped stone. Observing how quickly he wandered away from the exciting find and resumed his own work, she thought not.

Faye's own enthusiasm for the pot blurred her ordinarily rational thought processes a bit, just enough to completely drive Sallie Judd from her conscious mind. When Faye eventually remembered that she should have given the woman an update on her husband's condition, she would be chagrined at her own thoughtlessness. Right this minute, she was lost in the work she loved so well.

Oka Hofobi was only asking for a simple favor, and it was quitting time, so Faye knew she could honor his request easily…if she weren't planning to take Joe on an illegal foray into the woods.

"Faye, I need to get my car to the mechanic before he closes shop at six. It's just a five-minute drive up the road. Could you follow me over there, then bring me back home?"

Faye couldn't think of a face-saving way to say no. She looked around for somebody else who could help him. Toneisha and Bodie had evaporated fifteen minutes before, as soon as the clock struck five. Dr. Mailer had left right behind them. Chuck remained, but he was deep into the arcane details of whatever he did with those flint chips. She wouldn't dare suggest that Oka Hofobi bother him.

Faye knew that she and Joe needed all the daylight they could get. The just-discovered mound was way up the creek. They needed time to get there, look for evidence of the former cemetery, and get back before dark. She couldn't think of any way to sidestep Oka Hofobi's request, not when her car was going to be sitting in his back yard all evening. Her best bet was to rush him to the mechanic, rush him back home, then…then what? Go in the trailer and pretend to work until she and Joe could sneak across the street without Oka Hofobi noticing?

On the way back from taking Oka Hofobi to the mechanic, Faye figured out the solution to her problem. Why should she and Joe hide their activities from Oka Hofobi when she knew full well he'd love to go with them?

"How'd you like to get a good look at that mound complex I've been talking about?"

"On the Calhoun land? You feeling brave?"

"Yep. Joe and I are heading over there, whether Mrs. Calhoun likes it or not. Since you're local, maybe you know a way for us to do it without getting caught."

"Well, yeah, I want to go. I can't believe you were thinking about going without me."

"What was all that high-and-mighty talk I heard you telling Mr. Calhoun about how you didn't trespass?"

"I don't. At least, not much any more. But I sure did when I was a little kid. I'd love to see that land along the creek one more time before somebody builds a road through it."

Faye pulled into the Nails' driveway and parked her car outside the project trailer.

"Do you need to go in the trailer, or have you got everything you need?" Oka Hofobi asked.

Faye pointed to a small day pack on her back seat. "I've got a couple of maps and a compass in there, in case we get lost. That'd be hard to do, since we'll be in sight of the creek the whole time. We might want to get a long-range perspective on the earthworks, so I put in a set of binoculars. I never go anywhere without a trowel. There's a couple of flashlights in there, just in case, and a camera. I also packed a couple of bottles of water and some trail mix. Oh, and some apples."

Oka Hofobi looked at the pack as if he couldn't figure out how she crammed so much into such a small space. "How long are you two planning on being gone? Even if you walked all the way from here to Philadelphia without food, you still wouldn't starve to death. It's not like we're setting out to hike the Appalachian Trail."

"I figure we'll be out there a couple of hours. Besides, a man Joe's size needs plenty of fuel."

This was not true. When he was hunting, Joe could crouch for hours, quiet and still, waiting for just the right shot. He didn't waste motion with something so simple as eating. Faye, at five-foot-nothing and a hundred pounds, was the one with the metabolism of a hummingbird. If she missed a meal—or even a snack—she got cold, tired, and cranky. Very cranky.

"Since you packed for a safari, we don't need any food. I would like to get my cell phone, though."

Faye and Joe waited in the car, but the open door gave them an unobstructed view into the trailer. Chuck was at his desk, and Oka Hofobi nodded and spoke as he passed through Chuck's office on the way to his own. Not only did Chuck refuse to acknowledge the greeting, he never even looked up from his work.

While Oka Hofobi was fetching his cell phone, Faye's own phone began to ring. She would have let her voice mail take a message, but habit made her glance at the caller's number. It was Sallie Judd.

Faye wanted to kick herself. She had meant to check on Sallie long before now. She'd planned to call the hospital and check on Mr. Judd by now, too, but she'd been too wrapped up in her fascination with Toneisha's little pot. She answered the phone.

"Faye, dear, I wanted to let you know that Lawrence is feeling better. I can tell that he's feeling better because he's finally starting to make sense."

"Oh, that's good news. What does the doctor say?"

"The doctor on duty today still can't explain why Lawrence can't stay out of the hospital for two days running. He says there's nothing wrong with his heart, which is a blessing."

"It sure is."

"He wants to take a good hard look at his medications, in case there's some kind of drug interaction going on."

Faye remembered the orderly box full of pills. According to Mr. Judd, his wife was meticulous about loading it every week. If anybody could get his medication back on an even keel, it was Sallie Judd.

"He thinks maybe the beta-blocker dosage is too high. I've been trying to sort out the bottles in our medicine cabinet, but my eyes are so weak these days that I can't even tell which one he's talking about. I'm pretty sure the beige one is a beta-blocker. It's actually yellow, but it's a beigey-yellow and that's how I remember which one it is. Beige. Beta. Blocker. All Bs. Except he wants to cut the dose back to 200 milligrams. If I squint, I can almost read that label, and I could swear it says 150 milligrams. That doesn't make a bit of sense. How can he cut that pill back to a dose higher than Lawrence was already taking? I'm waiting for a doctor to call me back. I don't know which one—he's had so many. I know you're busy, but could you call me the next time you're over at the hospital? Maybe if you and his doctor—well, one of his doctors—were in the same room and I could talk to you both..."

"Of course I can do that. I'm working until dark, but I was already planning to go straight to the hospital after that. You should definitely call right now, though, and talk to a doctor or a nurse or somebody, if you've got any question at all about the dosage of his drugs. And you *do*. If he's been taking 150 milligrams of a drug that keeps his blood pressure down, we can't let them start giving him even more. Not when his blood pressure keeps dropping so low that he can't even stand up."

"You're right. I knew that all along, but this is all so confusing. I'll call them right away. I'll let you go now, and I promise not to bother you until you call me from the hospital, so—"

"Mrs. Judd!" Faye cringed as she violated her mother's rule about interrupting people, but she didn't want to let the older woman break the connection. There was something strange about this conversation, and she'd just figured out what it was.

"Yes, dear?"

"What beige pill? All the pills I saw in your husband's pill box were white. They were different shapes and sizes, but they were all white. I'm certain of it."

"Do you think he might have run out of the beta-blocker? Maybe that's what made him sick? Oh, that doesn't make a bit of sense. The doctor wants to decrease that dose, because it's doing too good a job of keeping his pressure down. If he wasn't taking his beige pill, then his pressure would be too high."

Not if Preston Silver gave him the wrong pill, Faye thought. She didn't dare say it out loud to Sallie Judd, who might have a coronary herself if she thought her husband had been poisoned by a licensed pharmacist. But who would be better able to kill someone with a legal drug than a pharmacist?

Why would Silver want to kill Mr. Judd? Out of sheer racial prejudice? It was possible, but far-fetched. He could poison anyone of any color who walked into his store, at any time. This had the feel of a personal crime. Perhaps Silver resented Judd's success or violently disagreed with his political leanings. Or maybe his hatred stretched all the way back to 1965.

The possibility that Preston Silver had been Lawrence Judd's long-ago attacker seemed increasingly likely. Until this week, only three people had known about Judd's beating—his attacker, his rescuer, and Judd himself. Now the whole world knew, and the person who did the crime would be desperate to keep it quiet. If Preston Silver had tried to kill Mr. Judd, then logic said that he was the attacker. Why would the rescuer want to keep his good deed quiet?

The sheriff needed to know about Mr. Judd's beige beta-blockers.

"Mrs. Judd—this is what you need to do. It's important. When you call the hospital, tell them what you've just told me about your husband's pills. If anybody knows what color his pills are supposed to be, it's the doctors and nurses taking care of him. They can start trying to untangle this mess. I promise I'll go over there as soon as I can, so that I can help them any way I can. Everything's going to be fine. Okay?"

Mrs. Judd's voice was as weak as ever, but it sounded firmer because of the decisiveness with which she spoke. "Of course. If anybody can help those doctors make my husband well, it's two hardheaded women like you and me."

Oka Hofobi settled himself in the back seat and closed the car door. Faye waved hello, but didn't speak. She was too busy thumbing through her phone's menu, looking for "Recent Calls." With a touch of a button, she could reach Neely Rutland without looking for a hardcopy phone book. She didn't even have to remember to put a number in her phone's address book. It just remembered any number she'd called lately, on the off chance she might need it again.

Faye loved technology. Owning such a kind and considerate cell phone was almost like having a butler. Except it didn't bring her hot tea in bed every morning.

The sheriff's receptionist gave Faye the sheriff's cell phone number, since she was still at the hospital with Mr. Judd. Having that closely held number made Faye feel very important. Neely had been slow to take Faye's concerns seriously. She hadn't thought that the marijuana field was such an important clue to Mr. Judd's beating, and she hadn't been all that excited over the prospect of taking a look at the cemetery mound. It was Faye's impression that the sheriff had her eye on Preston Silver, either as a suspect in Mr. Calhoun's murder or as Mr. Judd's attacker. Maybe Neely thought he'd done both. If so, she should be happy with the information Faye was about to give her.

"Neely, I think I may have something on Preston Silver."

"You're not calling to tell me more about his discriminatory business practices, are you? Faye, I know he's a racist. Everybody does."

"No. I'm calling to tell you that I think he poisoned Mr. Judd. No, that's not what I mean. I think he's *poisoning* Mr. Judd."

No sound came out of Faye's cell phone. She plowed ahead without waiting for Neely to answer. "Didn't you notice that he got better in the hospital, then got sick again before he'd even been out twenty-four hours?"

"People have relapses…"

"Yes, they do. But Mr. Judd's wife tells me that she's absolutely confused over the dosages of his medicines. His doctor wants to lower the dosage of his beta-blocker, but to a level that's *higher* than what he takes now. And something's wrong about the color of his pills. His beta-blocker's usually beige, but now it's white. I think Preston Silver saw an opportunity when you filled that prescription. My guess is that he wanted to eliminate the last witness to his crime."

"You mean the crime of kidnapping and beating Lawrence Judd? There was another witness—the man who saved him."

"Not if that man was Carroll Calhoun. Didn't you tell me that Preston Silver collected stone tools? That he was obsessed enough with them that he might have stolen one from your father?"

"I'll have him brought in for questioning right this minute." Neely's words were clipped and her voice was rough. Law enforcement was a tough job for a woman, but this woman seemed up to it. "I'll stay here at the hospital until I get to the bottom of Mr. Judd's problems. Can you meet me here?"

"I'm...working," Faye said, feeling like the sheriff could handle this problem without her help. Why did she feel like the whole world was trying to stop her from taking this expedition? Couldn't anybody get along for two hours without her help? "I can't get away before dark. Do you want me to check in with you then?"

"Please do. I hope I have some solid information before then, but you seem very good at ferreting out secrets. I'd like to bounce a few things off you. I can't afford to miss anything that might let a killer go free, and it looks like I might already have. If Preston put poison into my hands and let me pass it to that man...well, I won't have to make him pay. The law is fully capable of doing that. Thanks for your help, Faye."

Chapter Twenty-three

Finally, finally, Faye let herself melt into the dark and overgrown vegetation that covers every square foot of unplowed ground in Mississippi. Ample—way more than ample—rainfall tends to encourage rampant plant life. When those plants have their feet in deep, fertile soil, their growth can hardly be checked. Oka Hofobi, Faye, and Joe were crowded into a single file by lush undergrowth as they plunged deeper into the wilderness. The path where Oka Hofobi led them had been trampled for enough years that nothing grew on its hardpacked surface, but that didn't stop the branches and underbrush from reaching out to impede their progress.

Joe brought up the rear, instinctively putting Faye in the protected position between two men. He didn't look nervous—Joe never looked nervous—but he looked acutely alert. In civilized territory, Joe often seemed overwhelmed with the constant input of human-generated sights and sounds and smells. In nature, he understood every message his senses brought him. Faye had no doubt that his sharp eyes had already located enough game to feed them dinner, if need be. He had also probably cataloged several mortal dangers and shepherded Faye and Oka Hofobi past them without their ever knowing it. Deep, dangerous pits. Poisonous plants. Unfriendly creatures. If they were around, Joe had spotted them.

With every step, it seemed that another vine's corkscrew tendrils wound themselves into Faye's hair. It bothered her to be so dependent on someone else's navigation skills. She liked to take care of herself. "Glad we've got a local guide," she said. "I'd never have known this trail was here. I never could have followed it. And I never would have known that it would get me where I want to go. I'm counting on you to get us out of here."

"Go ahead," Oka Hofobi said. "Tell me how impressed you were with the place we stashed the car."

"Most impressive. What a blessing for us that your family doesn't keep pigs any more."

It had been so easy, with Oka Hofobi's help, to trespass deeply into Mrs. Calhoun's property with almost no risk of detection. A quarter-mile down the road, out of sight of both the Calhoun house and the Nail house, was a gated drive that led to the remnants of the Nails' former pig-raising operation. A pen, a shed, a gate—that's about all there was to see. Faye had parked her car behind the shed, then the three of them had simply walked across the road onto Calhoun land. They hadn't even had to wait until traffic died down. There wasn't a car in sight.

Oka Hofobi assured them that this trail would lead directly to the wider drive that Mr. Calhoun had used to move his farming equipment from field to field. It was the same drive that the sheriff had used to get her forensic equipment to Calhoun's murder scene, but Faye didn't like to think about that. From there, they'd actually have some choices. They could follow the farm road deeper into the property, planning to cut across toward the creek when they thought they were near the cemetery mound. It would be easier walking, but would require some guesswork and maybe some backtracking if they guessed wrong.

Probably a better choice would be to cut across the marijuana field to the creek. They would have a choice of routes from there to their destination, in the creek or on the bank. Faye had already taken the creek route, when she was trying to stay within the law. Now that they were openly flouting Mrs. Calhoun's property rights, she preferred to keep her feet dry. Oka Hofobi and Joe had wholeheartedly agreed.

Faye, with her tendency toward single-mindedness, had not considered how she'd feel upon revisiting the murder site. She wasn't creeped out until they had penetrated deep into the tall marijuana plants, which obviously enjoyed Mississippi's copious sun, ample rain, and fertile soils just as much as the woodland plants did. A quick glance around showed her the campfire where Carroll Calhoun had sat until his killer arrived. His corpse had rested mere steps away. She remembered the color of the blood, vivid even when lit by flashlight. Other details had dimmed, but she would never forget the blood.

Joe had seen the corpse and the blood and the bloody weapon, too, but he seemed completely unperturbed. How did he do it? Had he absorbed a little cannabis juice where the pot plants touched his skin? Nah. Joe didn't need illegal drugs. He probably knew how to manufacture hallucinogens out of woodland flowers, so he didn't have to break any laws. Faye suspected that even tobacco, in Joe's hands, had a mind-altering power. Not to mention the noxious weeds he brewed into his traditional Black Drink.

Faye didn't have access to any calming chemicals, except those her body made for itself. She picked up her pace, eager to reach the creek and hoping for an endorphin rush. The stream's clear liquid sound would wash thoughts of murder from her mind. The bank was shallow here, and someone had clearly walked down to the water's edge many times. Well, of course. Why else would the marijuana be planted in just this spot? Because it had nearby access to water, in case of drought.

Oka Hofobi continued to lead the way, and Joe continued to guard their rear. Oka Hofobi considerately honored her choice to take the dry route down the creek, but there were times when Faye thought it would have been easier to just get wet. Wading had been a direct route to their destination, and no pesky trees and bushes had stood in their way. Traveling atop the creek bluffs was an uncertain proposition. Sometimes the bank rose eight or ten feet above the creek, overhanging the water so far that Faye urged her companions to stay back. She didn't want to see either man go down in a miniature avalanche when the ground beneath him failed.

At other times, the growth on the bank was so rank that the damp creekside below looked far more attractive. Every time that happened, they scrambled down to walk along the sandbars lining the waterway for a while. Just when Faye thought there was no hope of getting any further without wading up to her hips in the creek, the familiar, flat-topped mound rose in front of her.

She was the first one to reach the top.

There were no headstones. No marble or granite monuments. No stone at all. Still, Faye had no doubt that this had been a place of burial. There was no mistaking the four shallow depressions sunken into the top of the mound, or the old garden roses gone wild where their headstones had been. The graves were about six feet long and three feet wide, and they were clustered in a family group, side-by-side and parallel. If they had ever had markers, someone had taken them, but it was possible that they'd left the people—the corpses—behind.

She reached into her day pack and pulled out her trowel. Oka Hofobi, who had recognized the graves as quickly as she had, was aghast, and Joe didn't look much happier.

Oka Hofobi was the first one to speak. "Surely you don't intend to..."

"No, I'm not going to exhume four bodies all by myself. But we're going to need proof, gentlemen. Don't you understand why the grave markers and the fence are gone? Isn't it obvious what's going on here?"

Apparently not, since both men continued to look at her like she was a ghoul.

She enlightened them. "The highway department is planning to build a road through here, and soon. These projects don't just come out of nowhere. Years of planning happen before contracts go out. People know about this road. In fact, our client told us they did. Remember? He called it 'a very popular project.'"

Oka Hofobi was nodding slowly, as if he were catching her drift. Joe still looked baffled, but his inattention to matters of money had always been his most charming quality. Other than his face. And his body.

"I don't know how long that project has been on the drawing table, but Mr. Calhoun just bought the last piece of property—maybe this very parcel—within the past five years. A large sum of money will go to the owner of this property when the road project is built."

"I know," Oka Hofobi interjected. "My father only sold a little piece for the road project where we're excavating now, but the money was good. Mr. Calhoun could have funded his retirement with a land sale this big." He gestured up and down the creek.

"So don't you think he might have been willing to 'hide' a cemetery, if he thought they might reroute the road to avoid it? Think how bad the publicity would be for the highway department, if it got out that they didn't let a little graveyard stand in the way of their roadbuilding. They wouldn't have done it. They would've built the road someplace else. Of course, they wouldn't have built it through this mound, either, but Calhoun might not have recognized it as anything but a little hill."

Joe was poking around in the underbrush covering the far corner of the mound. "Ain't no gravestones here, but there's a mighty lot of wrought iron." Gathering on either side of him, Faye and Oka Hofobi looked down at a pile of twisted metal. It had to be the wrought iron fencing that Mr. Judd had described.

"I reckon you could get a tractor up here," Joe said, nodding toward the driveway that had once carried coffins and mourners to this place. "You saw what Calhoun did with his. He got it all the way back to that pot field. If you had a tractor, it wouldn't be all that hard to shove the fence over here, then drag the headstones—"

"—the *really* incriminating evidence—" Faye interrupted.

"Yep. He would have used the tractor to haul the stones someplace where nobody would find them," Joe finished. "Did he raise cattle? I'm thinking they're at the bottom of a cow pond somewhere on his land."

Faye thought so, too.

"You two stand back," she said. "I've got to do something unpleasant."

Faye looked up into the faces of two men who had completely internalized the Native American proscription against disturbing the dead. She wasn't sure they were going to let her pass.

Oka Hofobi's attitude didn't surprise her much. He had wrestled with this very issue when he made the decision to pursue archaeology, and he'd grappled with it every day since then. He knew exactly where he stood on the subject of this particular taboo. She had expected him to be a problem.

Joe, on the other hand, had never once stood between Faye and something she wanted to do. Judging by the expression on his face, this might be the first time. He spoke first. "Why don't we call the sheriff and tell her what we found? There's no need to go disturbing the dead, not when Sheriff Rutland can just call the highway people. It's not too late for them to change their plans for the road. Then these people can just rest right here."

Oka Hofobi was nodding. He liked this plan.

"We can't risk that. Don't you remember what happened when Mr. Calhoun thought we were a threat to his property rights? Twelve hours later, he was using his tractor to destroy that threat."

"Carroll Calhoun is dead," Oka Hofobi pointed out in a reasonable tone of voice.

"Yeah, I know. I saw his body and it wasn't pretty. You're still missing the point. Mrs. Calhoun probably knows what her husband did here, and she won't want the word to get out. Even more important, she's probably counting on the money from this property sale to take care of her for the rest of her life. Now think through what will happen when Sheriff Rutland calls her and asks permission to take a look at this spot. And she *will* ask. She would never just come barreling in with a warrant. Mrs. Calhoun hasn't committed a crime, and people around here are touchy about property rights. Neely will handle this thing very carefully."

Joe crossed his arms like a man who didn't intend to step away, but he grudgingly nodded his understanding of Faye's argument, saying, "I noticed that you tried more'n once to get the sheriff to take a look at this mound, and she had better things to do. She won't be any hurry to follow up, just because you've got another suspicion."

"Exactly." She waved her trowel for emphasis. "And what happens while Neely takes this thing slow? While she's waiting for permission to come on the property, Mrs. Calhoun gets one of her hired men to hook up a trailer to the back of that tractor. He digs these four people up and hauls them away. Is that ghoulish enough for you two? Is what I'm planning to do anywhere near that disrespectful? This is all presuming they're still here at all. We don't know that yet, and you two won't let me look."

Two expressionless bronze faces looked down on her. If she was getting anywhere with these guys, she sure couldn't tell it. "Think about it this way. You two just let me confirm that there's at least one burial up here, and that somebody tried to hide it. If I can prove that fact to Neely, then I believe she'll get a warrant to search here without notifying Mrs. Calhoun first. Or else we can do it your way. Just don't come running to me when somebody dumps these four people in a cow pond."

Oka Hofobi and Joe reluctantly stepped aside.

Just because Faye had used all her powers of persuasion to get a chance to disturb one of these graves, it didn't mean she liked doing it. She'd picked the grave that looked biggest. It was only a few inches longer than the smallest one, but she hoped it was the least likely to harbor a child.

She was already a couple of feet below the ground surface, but people burying loved ones are serious about putting a lot of dirt between their loved ones and prowling scavengers. Just because she hadn't found a body within seconds didn't mean there wasn't one down there.

She could tell she was working in disturbed soil, so someone had been digging here before. Of course, there is no natural soil atop a human-constructed mound; it's all disturbed soil, by definition. Nevertheless, she could see the straight-edged outline at the edges of the rectangular hole that she hoped was a grave. This soil had been disturbed at least twice.

Oka Hofobi was pacing. Joe was sitting on the ground, eyes closed, probably engaging in some spiritual practice she didn't understand. Good. She didn't like doing this any more than they did.

When her shovel struck rotted wood, she held up a splinter for both men to see. Not expecting any applause, she kept working, muttering under her breath, "No hermetically sealed metal casket here. This burial dates to the days of the plain pine box."

There wasn't much left of that pine box. It had rotted, then collapsed under the burden of the soil above. Faye had already cleared much of that soil away, so it wasn't long before the angular form of a human jawbone appeared. "Bingo," she whispered, then regretted not saying something more reverent. Or at least something friendlier, like "Hello."

A row of vertebrae, intricately shaped like baroque pearls, lay beneath the jawbone. She crouched there for a minute, studying the bones. Joe and Oka Hofobi looked over her shoulders. When she tentatively reached down a hand and picked up a single vertebra, they both said, "Faye!" in the same outraged voice.

She put the bone back. "Okay. Maybe even I don't want to go that far. But we need some proof to show Sheriff Rutland. Hand me my camera."

Joe scrounged around in her day pack and found it. She took a close-up of the bones, to get enough detail so that no one could argue that they weren't human. Then she tried to think like a lawyer. How would she chip a hole in this case?

The answer was easy. She'd claim that Faye, Joe, and Oka Hofobi had been nowhere near her client's property when the picture was taken. Getting down on her knees and elbows, she shot a series of photos with identifiable landmarks in the background. It was hard. Most trees look pretty much alike. But she found a lightning-struck oak that was as individual as a fingerprint. In another shot, she captured the creek in the background, with a particularly twisty curve and a high red bank. Even better, these photos clearly showed that the grave was on a piece of ground ten feet above the surrounding land. This just might work.

For good measure, she took a picture of the twisted wrought iron fencing at the base of the mound. Pausing for a lawyerly moment to look for holes in her train of evidence, she began to wonder how these people might be identified. It might well be important to know when they were put in the ground, but the odds that Joe and Oka Hofobi would allow her to collect a bone for carbon dating were nil.

She stood over the open grave, looking down at the exposed vertebra. For an illogical moment, she felt that the bones looked bare and cold, and she wanted to cover them up. Instead, she reached down into the hole.

Thoughtful and deliberate, she put her hand into the grave and pulled out a chunk of wood, listening for two disapproving voices to say, "Faye!" again. Joe and Oka Hofobi restrained themselves. She held it up, saying, "I'm just taking a piece of the coffin. If we need to date the burial, this might be important. Then, even if Mrs. Calhoun bulldozes the whole mound, we'll have physical proof that this cemetery existed. That these *people* existed. They deserve that."

The men must have agreed with her, because they let her pocket the wood sample. They looked queasy, but they let her do it.

Chapter Twenty-four

Faye backfilled the excavation neatly, then looked up to see whether her companions had noticed. They were still standing far away from her, as if they were afraid they might catch something. It went without saying that neither of them had helped her with her work.

She cleaned the trowel and stashed it in her day pack. The binoculars at the bottom of the pack caught her eye. The sun was sinking lower than she'd like, but she was too tired to walk all the way back without taking a little breather. It might be interesting to take a look at the countryside from way up here. Raising the glasses to her face, she turned a little pirouette.

Almost nothing manmade was in her field of view. Everything she and her companions had worn or carried to this spot was manmade, of course. The mound beneath her feet was built by humans. She believed more strongly every minute that the rising and falling embankments along the creek were manmade. Or at least some of them were. A patch of light through the trees showed her the location of Mr. Calhoun's pot patch. Everything else—soaring trees, flowing water, broad sky, solid ground—was little changed since the day the Choctaws' ancestors first laid eyes on this country. They had decided to stay, and Faye understood why.

A bright spot of artificiality intruded on the moment. Faye trained her binoculars on its rather prosaic source. Mrs. Calhoun had turned on her garage light. Faye could never have seen it if she'd been standing on the ground, but it stood out like a beacon from this elevated vantage point.

She squinted at that light, and a forty-year-old mystery was solved. Part of it, anyway.

Faye trained the binoculars on a spot slightly nearer to her than the light. The Calhoun mound was obscured by trees and gathering darkness, but she could see its hulking mass. Which meant that somebody standing on top of it could probably see her, too, if they had binoculars. How much better would that view be if the intervening trees were forty years smaller?

Another detail surfaced. Mr. Judd had said he was attacked in the early spring, when the redbuds were blooming. None of the other trees would have leafed out yet, so the view from atop the Calhoun mound would have been even sharper. Mr. Calhoun was known to go out birdwatching every afternoon with a pair of binoculars in hand. What had he seen on the day Lawrence Judd was kidnapped?

Faye thought she had enough information to piece together a coherent story. Mr. Calhoun had gone out for a visit with his birds. He had caught a glimpse of a strange car driving along the rutted paths that networked the woods in this part of the country, built to move agricultural equipment from one field to another. Faye knew now that he hadn't owned this land in those days, but he would have been curious about why this car was where it didn't belong. He might have been especially concerned that the driver would happen upon his marijuana field, which property records said he had owned since he inherited it from his father. Of course, he would have hurried out to investigate. Would he have anticipated what he found? A bound and hooded young black man being beaten to death?

She hadn't known Mr. Calhoun well. Actually, she hadn't known him at all. He had seemed irritable, misguided, defensive, but she couldn't say that she had any indication that he'd been evil. Even if he'd moved four gravestones for his own material gain, that wasn't the same thing as standing by and letting a young man die horribly. On the basis of the evidence, she now believed that he had rushed in to save a man he didn't even know, at a real risk to his own life. And, though it had taken forty years, she believed that this risk had indeed cost him his life. Grief stirred in her.

Mr. Calhoun had prevented Preston Silver from doing murder. Then, for whatever reason, he had kept quiet. Immediately afterward, Mr. Judd had left the state without seeking help from law enforcement which, at that time, might have been no help to a black man at all. There had been an uneasy equilibrium for all these years, until Lawrence Judd had come home and asked for justice.

Victim. Attacker. Rescuer. The three pieces of the puzzle fit. Lawrence Judd was the known victim and somebody had recently tried to kill him, twice. Carroll Calhoun was the rescuer, and someone had succeeded in killing him. It only made sense that the killer in both cases would be Preston Silver, who was finally faced with the possibility of standing trial for his crime. Recent history showed that Mississippi was now willing to deal with these old sins. When faced with killing the two remaining witnesses, or seeing his face plastered all over CNN, Silver had chosen murder.

Technology was letting Faye down. Her cell phone had worked reliably all week since she arrived in Neshoba County. Even rural citizens demanded decent cell phone service, these days. Still, there were limits to what could be expected in a low-population area. Faye guessed she'd strayed too far from the road, putting her out of contact with the nearest tower.

No matter. She needed to walk toward that road, preferably arriving before dark. That meant she'd be walking into cell phone range. She'd be able to call Neely in less than an hour and impress the sheriff with her new insights into Mr. Judd's attack. It was time to stop dawdling and start walking.

Faye wished the sun would slow down, because she'd made time to solve yet another mystery. A series of wet holes that were roughly the size of a man's foot had drawn her eye to a sandbar nestled in a tight bend in the creek. A heavy deposit of gravel in that bend immediately made her think of Chuck.

She knew that there wasn't much stone worth quarrying in Neshoba County. At times, prehistoric inhabitants of the area had traded for good stone, but they had generally gathered local gravel for their tools in places like this. Wading out to the gravel deposit, Faye was rewarded with traces of Chuck's exploration. A few holes where larger chunks of rock were scratched out of the ground, a pile of rock samples stored under an overhang—these things spoke to her of Chuck.

She held up a broken rock for Joe to see. "A checked pebble... somebody's been looking for rock worth flintknapping. And they were willing to trespass to do it."

"Chuck?" Oka Hofobi asked.

"He'd be my guess," Faye said. "Don't you know he'd love to try to replicate the artifacts we've found with local materials? As soon as he looked at the project map and saw this bend in the creek, he would've been itching to find out whether there was enough local gravel of good quality to support the activity level at our site without outside trade."

Faye would bet good money that Chuck had found that question so irresistible that he'd spent much of the last few days checking pebbles. A simple stone-on-stone blow could knock away a quarter of the pebble, exposing its interior so that its suitability for flintknapping could be assessed.

Dr. Mailer could rest easy. Chuck had earned his dirty, torn clothes the old-fashioned way...by being so fascinated with an archaeological possibility that he couldn't bring himself to respect somebody else's property rights.

She had reluctantly passed on the opportunity to poke around and get a better look at Chuck's work. It was time to get back to the car. As they walked, she fished the apples out of the day pack and gave one to Joe. Oka Hofobi opted for a bottle of water, and Faye was glad to get sixteen fluid ounces off her back. She was getting tired.

She jerked her head in the direction of the creek, and they slogged back to its bank. The vegetation was overgrown and rank there, but there was no better landmark than a full, flowing body of water. If she kept close to the creek, at least she could be sure they were heading in the right direction. This was no time to get lost.

A muffled ring from deep in her day pack told Faye that she had walked back into cell phone territory. They were approaching the open field where Calhoun had died. Maybe the lack of trees improved reception, or maybe they'd just gotten close enough to the well-traveled road to pick up a signal.

She checked the phone's display as she answered it. Neely Rutland was on the line. Just the person she'd been trying to reach.

"Faye, have you been trying to call me?" The sheriff's voice was strained. "Every time I tried to answer, you were gone."

"The service out here is poor. I've probably been walking in and out of range."

"Out where? Where are you?"

Faye didn't want to say. "I'm working, but—"

"You're not at your work site. I'm there, and I'm all by myself. There's nobody in the trailer or in the house."

"Chuck must have gone to the hotel. And I guess Mrs. Nail isn't home from work yet. Oka Hofobi—"

"I'm not interested in listening to you call the roll like some kind of demented elementary school teacher. I need to know where you are." Neely had clearly grown tired of asking politely and letting Faye sidestep her questions. "It's a law enforcement matter, and a matter of safety. Your safety, Faye."

Faye looked around her. She saw two men, one of them large and both of them friendly. And she saw a lot of trees, but not much else. She felt plenty safe, but maybe she was wrong. "What's going on?"

"Mr. Judd's feeling better, and his doctors are checking on his medications. You did a good thing telling me about his wife's concerns. The situation seemed under control, so I thought I'd drive home to check on Daddy. We live hardly a mile past the Nails."

Faye knew that, because she'd been snooping into their property records, but she didn't say so. "What happened?"

"Just before I got to the Calhoun house, somebody took a couple of potshots at me—in my marked car. They knew exactly who I was, and they knew I was an officer of the law, and they shot at me anyway. This person is motivated. Considering where the shots came from, I have to assume they're related to Carroll Calhoun's death, until I prove otherwise. Anyway, I called in backup, but I was worried about Mrs. Calhoun and Mrs. Nail, so I came here to check on them while I waited. Neither of them is home. You'd told me that you'd be out here working until dark, so I was worried about you, too. Except you're not here. When I got those missed calls from you, I was afraid you were trying to call for help."

The sheriff didn't sound good, but Faye didn't know how she'd sound after she'd endured what Neely had over the past week. Probably like a frazzled, raving wreck. She tried to sound reassuring. "I'm fine, Neely, truly. I've got Joe and Oka Hofobi with me and we're..." It was time to come clean. "We're on the Calhoun property, near where his body was found. We're trespassing, I know, but I think I found out why Mr. Calhoun was killed. I'm pretty sure he was the man who saved Mr. Judd. I think he was killed because he knew too much."

"You think you're safe out there? Are you crazy? Didn't you hear me say someone just tried to shoot me hardly a quarter-mile up the road? If somebody comes after you, they won't need a gun. You're so close, the shooter'll be able to hit all three of you with one rock."

"*That's* an appealing mental image."

"Are you on the far side of the pot field? On the same side of the creek?"

"Yes. Right on the creek bank."

"That's as safe a spot as any. Sit tight, and tell the men not to do anything stupid. I'm coming out there to get you. Try not to get shot before I get there."

It was getting dark, and Faye couldn't decide if that was a good thing. If there was a bad guy prowling around in the woods—like, maybe Preston Silver—he'd have as much trouble seeing her as she'd have seeing him. The flashlight in the bottom of her day pack gave her a comfortable feeling, but she didn't haul it out and turn it on. Why call attention to herself? If it was so dark that the bad guy required a flashlight to find her, then she'd see him coming. She didn't intend to return the favor by turning on her own flashlight and showing him where she was.

Oka Hofobi and Joe were utterly still. How many times had she seen Joe go inside himself in this way? Was it because he was a hunter? Because he was a seamless part of nature? Was it a gift of his Native American heritage? Maybe. Oka Hofobi certainly exuded the same strong calm.

Faye herself was jittery, inside and out. She needed to fidget. She wanted to talk. She wasn't cut out to be a hunter, nor prey.

She told herself to breathe, but not to make any noise doing it. This was harder than it sounded.

Joe had chosen the spot where they waited, on the edge of Calhoun's open field. Sheltered by a copse of large trees, they could see anyone who might cross the field. The creek was at their right side. It didn't offer absolute protection; it would be no big trick to lurk on the far side and shoot them. Still, no one could walk up and grab them from that direction, so it acted as a buffer in that small way.

Faye pressed her back to a tree that was wider than she was, resting the day pack on the ground between her feet. No one would be sneaking up behind her. Oka Hofobi and Joe did the same, pressing against the same tree so that the three of them faced outward in different directions. They were as prepared for an attack as they were likely to be, considering that none of them was armed. For the first time, she regretted urging Joe to stop carrying his primitive weapons around all the time. The fact that Joe was usually a walking arsenal had proven useful in the past. But not tonight.

Faye had emptied her pack, looking for weapons. They were brandishing the pitiful results. Oka Hofobi was holding her other flashlight like a drawn sword. Faye clutched the trowel in the same position. Joe would have snorted when she offered him the last bottle of water, but he was too much of a woodsman to make that much noise. He had emptied the bottle and set to work fashioning something sharp out of the empty plastic.

They waited, and the light began to fade.

Chapter Twenty-five

The footsteps didn't come from the direction Faye expected. The sighing sound of grass on shoe leather came from straight ahead. Neely's gunman had been on the far side of the Calhoun house, which would have been to her left. Maybe this was the sound of the sheriff coming to their rescue. If so, Neely would call out any minute, so that they'd know a friend was approaching.

Thirty seconds passed. A minute. Still no voice calling, "Faye, it's me. You can come out now." There was no sound but footsteps.

Joe and Oka Hofobi stood so close at her sides that she could feel their forearm muscles tighten as each of them slowly clenched his fists. They were armed with nothing but fists against a gun, and that gun was in the hand of someone who had recently pointed it at a sheriff and pulled the trigger.

When Neely's voice finally sounded, Faye felt Joe's shoulders sag with relief.

"Faye? Are you out here, Faye?"

Joe was leaning forward, ready to step out and call to Neely, when Faye realized that he was seconds from suicide. Taking advantage of the fact that he was off-balance and in mid-stride, she put her shoulder into his rib cage and shoved him over the tall bank and into the creek. Oka Hofobi, showing that he trusted Faye even when he didn't know what was going on, jumped after him.

Faye knew that to look back was to waste time, but curiosity was her defining quality. She went over the bluff backside first, and not just to avoid breaking her neck in the shallow creek. She wanted a look at the sheriff's face. Something inside her would know whether her instincts were true, if she could only see Neely's face.

Sometimes the subconscious has to be jostled into awareness. Faye's subconscious had stubbornly held onto a key piece of information, only letting it go now, at the last minute. Listening to the anonymous footfalls make their slow way through the thick woods, Faye had wondered at their pursuer's ability to maneuver while the darkness only grew thicker. And when the sheriff had finally spoken, Faye had wondered why Neely waited so long to call her name.

The first question was easy to answer. Neely's father had owned much of this land during her lifetime. She would have run free in its woods, and she would have almost lived in its creek. Of course she knew her way.

This answer pointed to the solution to her other question. And it solved a murder and two attempted murders, as well. If her family owned land around the cemetery mound when Lawrence Judd was taken there and beaten, then Preston Silver wasn't the most likely suspect. Neely's father was. He had associated with Silver, a known Klansman, all his life. There was precious little left of his mind, yet he retained enough of his memory to refuse to let his daughter take his business anywhere but to a Klansman. He was as likely as anyone to have attacked a young black man in 1965.

Would Neely Rutland have killed to protect her father's good name? Faye remembered her devoted care of the old man. Yes, Faye thought she might. What was more, she thought Neely might have had more intimate reasons. Shame is an odd emotion, a primitive one. Faye suspected that Neely would do anything to keep people from knowing what her father, her own flesh and blood, had done. She would be desperate to avoid admitting to anyone, even herself, what the man she worshipped really was.

And this gave her the answer to the second question: Why had Neely waited so long to call out to Faye? She had waited because she needed to have a sure shot.

Faye had told her outright that she knew Lawrence Judd's medicine had been tainted, and she'd told her that she thought Carroll Calhoun was killed because he knew too much about Judd's attack. She'd been right on both counts. Her methodical approach to the puzzle of Calhoun's killer had borne fruit, but she'd used the knowledge to settle on the wrong man. Neely knew that Faye would eventually sift through the rest of the evidence and come to the right answer. And now, this minute, she had.

Neely had crept up to them slowly, inexorably, because she couldn't afford to miss.

As Faye tumbled backward, the last light of day glowed red on the muzzle of the sheriff's gun. She could tell by the recoil of Neely's arm that the handgun had been fired. The noise was instantaneous and deafening. A flutter of wind passed her face, and then she was falling. Perhaps that flutter was simply the wind. Or perhaps it was air being shoved aside by the bullet that barely missed Faye's face before smashing into a tree.

In daylight, they would have had no hope. They were not swimming in a mighty river at the base of a yawning canyon. They were staggering through a creek that was chest-deep at best, between banks that were eight feet high, at most. In places, the land's rolling topography brought those banks so low that Neely would be able to step down into the water with them, gun in hand. Though why would she want to do that when she could just stand on a bluff and shoot them, like fish in a barrel?

In daylight, there would have been no place to hide. The creek water was stained with tannins from pine needles and oak leaves. It looked like strong tea, dark brown but clear. If there had been any light at all, the water wouldn't have hidden them. In the dark, they had a fighting chance.

Faye struck the water an arm's-length away from Oka Hofobi and went straight to the bottom. She hit the creek bed so hard that she nearly gasped a couple of lungs full of water, but her survival instincts held. She waited until her face broke the surface and dragged in a full dose of oxygen, but she did it too loudly. A gunshot said that Neely had heard her.

In front of her, Oka Hofobi's back was visible at the surface of the water, like a breaching whale. Joe had assumed the same position, so Faye followed suit. She found that the men were onto something. If she let herself float in shallow water, she could push herself along by scrabbling at the creek bottom with her hands. If she accidentally ventured into deeper water, her knees or feet could serve the same function. Careful motions ensured that no splashing sounds gave away their location. A slight turn of her head brought her face out of the water long enough to take a sip of air.

Joe was leading them toward Neely's side of the creek. It was counter-intuitive, but this was the safest place to be. To see them, she'd have to stand right on the edge of the bank and look down into a ditch that was now black-dark. Faye remembered the spots where the bank was eroded at the base, leaving sizeable over-hangs. She fervently hoped one of them would collapse under Neely's feet. If it did, maybe the gun would drop out of her hand as she fell. That was a pleasant fantasy, and Faye indulged herself in it while she clawed her way through the chilly water.

One of them must have made a noise, or maybe a stray bit of starlight lit a wet body, but another gunshot sounded. Faye wondered whether Neely might run out of bullets, then lost another chunk of her faint hopes. A trained law enforcement officer would not set out to kill someone unless she had adequate ammunition. Even if the creek bank obeyed Faye's wishes and collapsed beneath the sheriff's feet, she would have the training and the survival skills to ride it down and maintain control of her weapon.

This was no ordinary killer stalking them.

In the quiet blackness, Faye understood how a person could believe in a spectre who stalked the woods by starlight. The notion of a Devil who would imprison a lonely girl in a cave seemed real, more real than anything that happened while the sun shone. If an unnaturally white arm were to reach up and drag her into a cold deep pool, Faye would have been terrified, but not surprised. At that moment, she knew why people passed their stories down to their children. People tell tales because they make sense of the unexplainable.

People tell tales because they are true.

Faye shoved herself a few more feet forward, working to keep up with Oka Hofobi and Joe. She let herself harbor another hope, because hope made her arms and legs work better. It was a plausible hope: Maybe someone had heard the shots. There had been three gunshots now. If someone heard them, surely they would investigate.

She mentally searched around for someone to hear those shots and act, but came up short. If Neely could be believed, Mrs. Calhoun wasn't home. She'd also said that the Nail house was empty, and that Chuck had locked up the work trailer. Nobody else was in earshot, except maybe Neely's father, and he wouldn't be riding to their rescue. He couldn't even feed himself any more.

Their only hope was that a car would pass just as Neely squeezed the trigger. Even then, what would a concerned driver do if they heard shots deep in the woods? They would call 911, who would call…the sheriff. If Neely handled her dispatcher well, she'd be sent out to investigate her own crime. Again. Faye imagined that Neely would be very good at feigning regret for the loss of three more lives.

Once, a long time ago, Carroll Calhoun had saved Lawrence Judd's life, not so very far from here. Unless Faye missed her guess, there was no one to do her, Joe, and Oka Hofobi that same favor. They were on their own.

Her hope, and a lot of her strength, seeped out of her body and into the chilly creek water.

Faye should have expected that Joe would know where he was going. She'd been following him blindly because, frankly, she couldn't see. It had been disconcerting to realize that he was leading them away from civilization, deeper into uncharted territory.

There was no moon to light their way. Faye knew that it would rise later, but it would be too late. There may have been stars, but Faye couldn't twist her head enough to look up, not without a significant risk of getting that head shot off. Falling off the bank and hitting the water had been disorienting, but Faye still possessed enough of her mind to recognize which direction the creek was flowing. They were moving away from the road, and away from any hope of being found. Was this because Joe had a plan? Or was it because Joe always felt safer in the wilderness, away from people?

Faye rather liked people, when they behaved themselves and respected her privacy, but she'd love to be rid of one particular person. Neely moved quietly through the vegetation above them, only occasionally giving her position away with the sound of a breaking twig. It made Faye's heart freeze just to know that she was up there.

When Joe took a quick right turn, Oka Hofobi followed, and so did Faye. If she hadn't had her face in the water, she would have laughed out loud. Joe had led them to the old cave where Mr. Judd had hidden from his attacker. From Neely Rutland's very own father. It burrowed deep into the ground under Neely's feet. She'd never see it unless she got down into the creek. Even then, she would miss it in the darkness, unless she got incredibly lucky with her flashlight beam. With any luck, she'd be a hundred yards down the creek before she even realized that they weren't in the water below her.

The opening was partially flooded, since water levels were significantly higher this summer than they'd been in Mr. Judd's youth, but the cave still offered a safe haven. Faye leaned happily against a wall that felt like hard clay, and she let a delayed adrenaline rush leave her trembling and breathless.

She wished she could hear the quiet footsteps and breaking twigs that still marked Neely's passage, but the cave's walls insulated all sound. Oh, surely, she hadn't seen them duck into this refuge. She grabbed at Joe, found his elbow in the dark, and squeezed it in gratitude. This might just work.

Faye had never seen darkness so thick, so opaque. Its only saving grace was the blot of gray—or was it simply a lighter black?—where starshine lit the mouth of their refuge. Her head ached from the effort of listening for their stalker's movements. She heard nothing, but the periodic tensing of Joe's shoulder muscles told her that he still heard Neely's every move.

The darkness and the quiet and the relentless waiting gave Faye a chance to decide that this was all her fault. She had told Neely that something was wrong with Mr. Judd's medications, setting a killer on her trail. And she'd unwittingly dragged Joe and Oka Hofobi along with her.

What was Neely's first response to Faye's revelation? To instruct Faye, in her most intimidating sheriff's voice, to meet her at the hospital. This had been an inspired tactic. She was ensuring that Faye didn't get to the hospital before her, thus controlling any contact Faye had with the doctor. More than that, Faye expected that Neely's plans didn't include letting Faye talk to the doctor at all. She would have found a way for them to have a woman-to-woman conference in her safe-looking cop car, from which Faye would never emerge alive.

When Faye thought of her last conversation with the sheriff, she wanted to groan and sink down into the water lapping at her thighs. What had been the entire text of that conversation?

Where are you, Faye? Quit messing around. I'm the sheriff. Tell me where you are.

And Faye had bought it. The woman was trying to find her and shut her up for good, and she'd calmly told her exactly where to do it.

Faye was still clutching Joe's arm when he lurched backward, knocking her off her feet and into the water. Violating his naturally chivalrous character, he didn't help her to her feet. He just grabbed her under her armpits and scuttled backward. She felt enough jostling knees and swinging hands to be sure that Oka Hofobi was keeping up with them as they all rushed away from the mouth of the cave. A primitive part of her wanted to reach out for the fading spot of charcoal gray that was her only connection to light and fresh air.

Then she heard the hissing sound of sand on sand.

For a moment, the dim light illuminated single grains of sand as they fell. They had the hard, glinting beauty of diamonds. Then the avalanche came, a great sighing rush of sand as it slid over the mouth of the cave. Gravel and rocks came next, punctuating the sand's soft roar with their noisy splashes.

Faye had been so quiet in her hopes that Neely wouldn't hear them...that she'd never find them. At this undeniable evidence that those hopes were dashed, she felt a full-throated scream leave her. Then she realized that she'd never seen true darkness before.

Chapter Twenty-six

Faye leapt to her feet, grabbing for her right back pocket. Long-standing habit had made her slip her trowel in that pocket when she made the decision to go into the creek. It had made its presence known repeatedly—first, when she landed butt-first on the creek bottom, and again during the avalanche, with every bump Joe dragged her across. Now, when she had a pressing need to move some dirt, she was grateful for the huge bruise that the trowel had left on her backside. She was going to dig a hole and get the three of them out of this tomb.

Joe, who seemed to have had a penchant for manhandling her lately, wrapped both arms around her and jerked her back, whispering in her ear. "Don't be stupid. She's still out there. Wait."

Faye didn't wait well, but she couldn't deny the wisdom of Joe's advice. She pocketed the trowel and reached out her arms to take the measure of their prison. It was wide enough to let the three of them crowd shoulder-to-shoulder, and it was just barely tall enough to let Faye stand up straight. This meant that Joe and Oka Hofobi were certainly hunched into an uncomfortable crouch.

She pulled her cell phone from her pocket, hoping to see its face light up when she pushed the power button. Nothing. They made them tough these days, but not tough enough to survive a prolonged dip in the creek—which meant there was little hope that Joe or Oka Hofobi had a phone that had fared better.

Joe put a warning hand on her shoulder that she intuitively knew meant, "Wait here." He moved toward the pile of earth blocking the cave's mouth, but he didn't scrabble at it with his hands the way Faye would. She knew this because she heard absolutely nothing. Oka Hofobi shifted his weight slightly and Faye knew it because she was close enough to feel him move. Once Joe moved out of physical contact, he was simply...gone.

A flicker of panic shook her, but she shook it off. Joe was still there, and she knew what he was doing. He was listening. She knew this as surely as she knew what he looked like and how his voice sounded. Joe could hear a mockingbird land on a dogwood branch.

When the loud crashing sound of gunshots came, again and again, another scream was ripped out of her throat. The roof of the cave opened up over Joe's head, and Faye did what her instincts told her to do. She lunged forward—groping, feeling, slapping at the walls—and she didn't stop until her hands made contact with Joe's body. Oka Hofobi was right beside her, and the two of them yanked Joe away from the falling earth.

There was sand in her eyes and dirt in her mouth, and the pebbles bouncing off her head were getting larger by the second. There was nothing for the three of them to do but to keep backing up and hope the whole roof didn't come down. When Faye found that she was still alive, thirty seconds after the thundering roar commenced, she began to hope that the ceiling would survive. And maybe they would, too.

"I'm okay," Joe said, directly into her ear. "Scream, Faye."

She did as she was told.

The earth continued to empty itself into the water ahead of them, but the roof over their heads held. Joe clamped a hand over her mouth. "Good. You can stop now," he said. "There's no way she can hear you."

How could that possibly be a good thing?

Darkness and quiet left Joe plenty of time for self-blame. He should never have dragged his friends into this hole, but he didn't think well when faced with a gun. He didn't much mind bears or sharks or snakes. Creatures lashed out with the weapons God gave them, and he didn't blame them. God had given him some gifts, too. When faced with nature, Joe always felt like he was on firm footing.

Manmade weapons were different. It could be impossible to defend oneself from an attack with a gun or a tank or a nuclear bomb. Joe liked to have a fighting chance. This cave (or drainage culvert or whatever the heck Faye said it was) had looked like that fighting chance.

If only he'd remembered something else Faye said. She'd told him that Neely's father had owned this land when she was a kid. A single look at the woman's tanned face and weathered hands said that she'd spent her life outdoors, just like Joe. What were the odds that she didn't know about this hiding spot? And what were the odds that a woman with her woods skills wouldn't recognize the overhanging bank as a chance to bury them alive?

If his ears told him true, Neely had stood outside the cave and swung a big branch up at that overhang, knocking down just enough dirt to seal the opening. Even then, Joe had held out hope that he could dig them out of this hole, once he was convinced that Neely and her gun were gone. But she and her gun had confounded him again. She'd stepped back and fired at the shelf, bringing down tons of sand and rock. Though Neely couldn't know it, her shots had been even more successful than she might have hoped, collapsing part of the roof over their heads. The most valiant efforts of Faye and her little trowel weren't going to get them out of here.

Joe sniffed the air. It was still sweet, and the water around his legs was too cool and fresh to be stagnant. There was still hope.

"Why did you tell me to scream, Joe?"

"Talk a little quieter, Faye."

She wondered whether he really thought Neely could still hear them. A skin-crawling thought occurred to her. Maybe he thought the ceiling above them was still unstable.

Faye had spent hermit-like years when she'd had no one to talk to, and she hadn't much cared. Now she found that being buried alive had loosened her tongue. She was willing to talk quietly, but she was going to talk. Joe and Oka Hofobi didn't seem to mind.

Joe explained his thinking in a quiet voice that still managed to warm their dank, cold surroundings. "We want Neely to go away. She probably heard you scream the first time, so she would have been worried that you were still alive. I thought if she heard you scream while the roof was falling in, then you never made another peep, well, maybe she'd think you were dead. Oka Hofobi and I never made any noise at all, so I bet she's out there hoping we're dead, too."

This conversation was creeping Faye out, but it was interesting. "So do you think she gave us up for dead and went home?"

"Nope," was Oka Hofobi's succinct answer. "I wouldn't. Would you?"

"Nope," echoed Joe. "I'd give us time to suffocate."

Faye had been trying not to breathe too much, but now that the word "suffocate" had been spoken, she felt every muscle in her chest spasm.

"You're not smothering, Faye." Joe didn't sound like a man measuring his breaths in shallow sips.

"You're sure?"

"There's a breeze, Faye."

"I don't feel it."

"I do." There was surprise in Oka Hofobi's voice. "I didn't before you mentioned it, but I do now."

Faye decided to take their word for it. Joe's senses had always been far keener than hers. "So there's an opening. We can breathe. Great."

"Probably more than one, since the air's moving."

Faye had to take Joe at his word on that one, too.

"And the water's moving," he said. A slight splash told her that he had dipped a hand in the water. Faye's legs were freezing.

She couldn't imagine voluntarily dipping another body part in water that felt, to her Florida sensibilities, like snow melt.

She had to remind herself that it rarely snowed in Mississippi, and never in July. Cold water in these parts didn't fall frozen from the sky. It welled up from the ground. "Mr. Judd said that there was a spring in here. Can you tell which direction the water's flowing? Is it heading toward the mouth of the cave?"

"Yes."

"Then we should look for the source of the spring. If the water changes direction there, it might be a sign that there's another way out of this hole. We could follow it, and maybe find an opening that's not closed up," she said, hoping she understood the thinking of ancient engineers properly. "This doesn't seem like a natural cave to me. Or maybe it started out as a natural cave, but it was enlarged by humans sometime in the past. I've read that some of the moundbuilding civilizations used culverts and drains to control the flow of water. Notice the word 'flow.' If the water's going out somewhere, then maybe we can, too. It's worth a try."

"No. I mean, yes, it is," Joe stammered. "Let's try it, but not yet. We need to wait."

If Joe told Faye to sit down, be quiet, or wait one more time, she planned to smack him. The dark silence was stealing her sanity. "Why should we wait in this dank pit even one more second?"

"If we wait until daylight, the opening might show itself," he responded in an insufferably reasonable voice. "We might never find a tiny little hole in the dark, but if light were shining through it…"

"…we couldn't miss it!" Now Oka Hofobi was finishing Joe's sentences for him. Faye was charmed to find out that she was buried alive with the Doublemint twins. "Joe's right. We should wait."

So this, Faye thought, was hell. She was trapped underground with two contemplative types, when every fiber in her being was screaming, "Take action! Do something! Even if it's wrong!"

"There's another reason to wait, Faye." Oka Hofobi seemed to feel a need to placate her, because he didn't know her all that well. Joe was well aware that she'd squawk and grouse, but she'd eventually settle down and do the sensible thing. "If we wait until daylight," he continued in his conciliatory tone, "Neely might decide we've suffocated to death and go away. We can't be sure she doesn't know about the other opening."

"If there is one." Faye was enjoying her moment of sulking negativity. Oka Hofobi might be worried about her bad attitude, but Joe knew she'd get over it.

"Let's presume there is one," Oka Hofobi went on. "If Neely ran these woods as a child, she may have found it. She may be sitting there watching it. If we don't show up at sunrise, she'll walk away."

"So why are we talking when she could be sitting out there listening to us?"

"That's why I told you to talk quiet. Also, listen to the way our voices bounce off these walls. There's no opening anywhere near us to carry our voices outside. I think it's way back there." Faye felt Joe's arm move, without seeing it. "And I think we'll have to crawl through some tight spaces to get to it."

"So she thinks maybe we're dead. And she's either sitting out by the creek, or she's sitting by the back door to this culvert. What makes us think we'll know when she's gone?" Faye found that negativity had enduring charms. "When will she feel safe in assuming we're dead?"

"She doesn't care all that much if we're dead when she leaves." Joe's voice echoed oddly off the culvert walls. "If she's sure we can't get out—and she'll be pretty sure if we don't come out pretty soon after the sun comes up—then she can leave us here to die slow. Don't forget that she'll be in charge of the search parties. She'll make good and sure we're never found."

A killer with a badge had an unfair advantage. When the three of them were reported missing, a sheriff could easily sabotage the search. Earlier that day, Faye had unthinkingly told Neely where she was, simply on the basis of a crisply barked order.

Neely had even been in charge of the crime scene investigation when Calhoun was killed. How easy it must have been for her to obliterate any forensic evidence she might have left behind. Even her footprints had told lies. By treading over the entire crime scene in the line of duty, she'd made it impossible to distinguish her new footprints from any she left behind during the killing.

And if Mr. Judd's doctors ever suspected a problem with his drugs, Sheriff Neely was poised to frame Preston Silver for poisoning him. The whole county—and thus the entire jury pool—suspected he was capable of violence to a black man. A trusted sheriff could railroad him in a heartbeat.

Faye pondered the fact that Joe had been willing to step out when Neely called, while she and Oka Hofobi had hung back for that critical millisecond. Faye's great-great-grandmother had been born a slave, and she herself had been the first member of her family born after the Civil Rights Act draped its protection over them. Oka Hofobi had been born to people still digging out from the debris left behind by the Indian removals. Broken treaties and unjust laws had knocked the Choctaws from prosperity to dire poverty with the stroke of a pen. She and Oka Hofobi had been born to suspect the law and its agents.

Joe, despite his Creek heritage, had been born to people who had turned their back on that culture. His father drove a semi, criss-crossing America's interstate system on a weekly basis. His mother had cooked TV dinners and shopped at Wal-Mart. His hunger for the heritage they'd forgotten had made him, in some ways, as Creek as anyone born on the reservation. But he'd had to do it for himself. He'd sought out people that could teach him the religion and handcrafts and philosophy of his ancestors, but the mistrust that rests in the bones of the long-persecuted had been lost in translation.

Somewhere in the night, a woman wearing a badge was hanging her hopes on the likelihood that they were dead. Joe thought they could outwait her. A few hundred years of bad history made Faye desperate to do so.

"How will we know when it should be daylight?" Faye asked, then she remembered who she was talking to. Joe would just know.

Chapter Twenty-seven

Faye was waving her trowel around again. She could tell it made Joe nervous when she did that, so she kept doing it.

"You're not going to get anywhere, digging into that wall."

"Yeah, but I'm using my muscles, so I bet I'm warmer than you." She scooped out some more clay debris and let it fall into the water. "Later on, I'm gonna be a lot warmer than you."

Joe grunted, but Oka Hofobi was willing to humor her. "How you planning to manage that?"

She continued working on the pile of broken clay that she guessed remained from some earlier time when a segment of the wall had collapsed. Using her trowel to clear a flat place to perch, high and dry, she said, "I'm digging myself a ledge to sit on."

The tone of Joe's next grunt signified interest.

"Can I borrow that trowel when you're done?" Oka Hofobi didn't seem to mind humbling himself, not when everyone concerned had to admit that her idea was a good one.

"Yes, you may borrow my trowel. If you ask nicely."

"May I borrow your trowel, ma'am?"

Faye hauled herself out of the water and onto a new-made ledge just wide enough to accommodate her hips. She felt around for Oka Hofobi's hand before giving him the trowel. Otherwise, she might have put his eye out. "Just make sure you dig yourself a ledge right next to mine. We don't want to waste any body heat tonight."

Before long, the three of them had dug out a fairly respectable perch—although "before long" was a relative term. Faye couldn't say that she had any notion how to judge time in this place.

Was she warmer or more comfortable than she'd been while standing in chilly water? "Warmer" and "comfortable," too, were relative terms. The dampness evaporating from her clothes was sucking all the body heat out of her. Joe and Oka Hofobi didn't seem to be generating enough body heat to share, either. Her teeth were chattering like an excited squirrel, but she guessed it might have been worse. They could have all been floating in the creek, riddled with gunshot wounds.

The thought did nothing to warm her.

A vision of Mrs. Nail rose unbidden in front of her, and she knew that rescue was at hand. "There's no way we're going to be here all night," she burbled. "Your mother will have the whole county looking for you." Faye was certain to her core that all Neshoba County was awake and on the move, because Mrs. Nail had made it happen.

Oka Hofobi said only, "Um."

"What?"

"My mother likes you a lot. Also, I'm over thirty, so she's desperate. No offense."

"None taken."

"She knew that I was going to ask you for a ride. My car's gone. Your car's gone. When I didn't come home…let's just say that she's probably leafing through bridal magazines right now."

Faye wrapped her arms around her legs and squeezed tight, hoping to warm either her arms or her legs.

"What about you and Joe? Aren't your roommates missing you by now?"

"Think," Faye said. "Who are our roommates?"

"I don't know. You guys disappear to the hotel every afternoon. I don't know who sleeps with who."

"Oh, I bet you do. Joe's roommate is Bodie. My roommate is Toneisha. Toneisha hasn't slept in her bed in days. How about you, Joe?"

"I've been living high on the hog in my private room. Sometimes I eat crackers in his bed, just to keep myself entertained."

"Face it, guys," Faye said, hugging her legs harder. "No one's gonna miss us until we don't show up for work."

Mrs. Nail crawled quietly under the bedcovers, careful not to wake her husband. It seemed that Oka Hofobi had acted on her not-so-subtle comments that Faye Longchamp seemed like such a lovely girl. Smart. Independent. Caring.

Those were fine qualities to have in a wife. When Mrs. Nail allowed herself a small moment of pride, she claimed those qualities for herself. Smart. Independent. Caring. Her husband had never complained about those parts of her. It made him crazy when she worried obsessively about their kids, or when she poked into their neighbors' business, but he appreciated the fact that she did a good job of looking after all the details in their family life. She knew that she made him happy. He made her crazy with his nostalgia for the good old days, which weren't all that good most of the time, but he was a steadfast and self-sacrificing husband and father. He made her happy.

He'd work out his differences with Oka Hofobi eventually, but she was impatient with his timetable. No one was immortal, particularly not men his age. It would be a great tragedy to die suddenly, unexpectedly, without making peace with a well-loved son. She prayed for that peace every night.

She had nearly given up on seeing Oka Hofobi find the happy family life she wanted for him. Interesting work was all well and good, but books and artifacts gave off no warmth at the end of the day. Maybe Faye would help him find that warmth.

Ross Donnelly returned the clunky hotel room phone to its cradle. Again. He'd poked Faye's room number into it for the last time. The last time tonight, anyway.

He'd skipped the political fundraiser, after all, because Mr. Judd had looked so shrunken and frail in his hospital bed. No one with a heart could have left him there, not even with a sheriff to take care of him. He'd called Faye several times to let her know, hoping she'd stop by the hospital to check on their friend. If he were completely honest with himself, he'd have to admit that he was looking forward to an hour in the hospital cafeteria with Faye, drinking bad coffee and eating stale doughnuts. But she hadn't come, and she hadn't answered his calls.

Women usually made themselves available, just on the chance that Ross might call. They didn't always sit by the phone, though some did, but they certainly didn't turn off their cell phones. Usually, it was a moot point, anyway. Usually, they called him.

Why did he care? The Fair was over tomorrow, and he'd be driving back to Atlanta, where a lot of pretty women snatched up their cell phones when they saw his number on the screen. Were they prettier than Faye? Not really, though they certainly dressed better. Still, Faye's work shirts and poplin pants and heavy boots couldn't cover up a bone structure worthy of an Egyptian queen. Nor a mind that just might be sharper than his own.

Good Lord. Now he was waxing poetic over a woman who was usually wearing a stray spot of dirt somewhere on her shapely body.

Yes, he was going home to Atlanta tomorrow, but he'd already checked the mileage from his house to her improbable island mansion. It was three hundred miles from his doorstep to hers. Well, not her doorstep, actually. It was three hundred miles from his doorstep to a boat ramp where Faye could bring her boat to pick him up. It didn't take long for a car like his to travel three hundred miles.

He picked up the phone again, though not to break his promise to himself. He didn't dial Faye's room number. He dialed the number for her friend, the enigmatic Joe Wolf Mantooth. Ross was pretty sure he would like Mr. Mantooth, despite his grizzly man exterior, if it hadn't been for Faye. The woman claimed that Joe was just a friend, but Ross wasn't sure he believed it.

He listened to Joe's phone ring, wondering what he was listening for. Was he wondering if Faye would answer? Was he planning to listen for the sound of her breathing in the background when Joe picked up the phone and said, "Who do you think you are, calling at this time of night? Don't you know it's almost midnight?"

As it turned out, nobody answered the phone at all. Ross turned out his bedside light, but he didn't sleep.

The Legend of the Snake

As told by Mrs. Frances Nail

We Choctaw set great store by Sinti Hollo, who is said to be an invisible horned serpent dwelling deep in a cave, underwater. Sinti Hollo can bring the heavy tropical rains that make these lands like a garden. His voice is like thunder, but it is not thunder.

It is said that Sinti Hollo revealed himself to Sequoyah, who first wrote down the Cherokee tongue in an alphabet of his own making. Many say that this must be true, for the serpent comes to young men who possess wisdom beyond their years. Only to those lucky few does he show himself, and only those few receive the gift of his ancient wisdom.

Chapter Twenty-eight

Friday
Day 8 of the Neshoba County Fair

Faye couldn't feel her lips. It was cold and she had been silent too long.

"Are y'all awake?"

"I was dreaming of summertime," said Oka Hofobi. "Thanks for waking me up."

"It *is* summertime. Just not here in this cave. Listen, we can't just sit here and get hypothermia. Move your legs around, and listen. I've been thinking."

"Great," Joe said. "Wasn't it you that threw me in the creek? Maybe you shouldn't think."

"I've been figuring out how Neely pulled it off."

"What? Killing Calhoun? Or poisoning Mr. Judd?"

"All of it. The part about killing Calhoun is pretty straight-forward. She probably used a stone knife from her father's collection. Joe said the killer was shorter than Calhoun. Neely's small, and a sheriff would certainly have training in hand-to-hand combat. It wouldn't have been hard for her to break Calhoun's arm and slit his throat. And we know Calhoun knew her and trusted her. You saw how she talked him out of the tractor. She could have just walked up, said hello, fussed at him about growing marijuana, then sliced his throat."

"Do you think it was her driving the tractor chasing us that night? Or Calhoun?"

Faye had never even asked herself that question. "If it was Calhoun, then he must have high-tailed it into the woods just in time to get himself killed. More likely, he was already dead, and it was Neely in the tractor, trying to scare us away from the murder site. I bet she didn't want the body found until the next day. She would have wanted her trail to get cold. Besides, daylight would have given her a chance to make absolutely sure that she didn't leave any evidence behind."

"You and Joe ruined that devious plan. Good going."

Faye didn't hear Oka Hofobi. Her brain was already chewing on another problem. "Dr. Mailer said Chuck was all upset about a tool that was missing from his collection. But I don't think Neely had access to that collection—at least, not before the killing. If anybody had broken into the trailer, I think we'd have heard. Think about it. Chuck would've noticed if anything had been disturbed. He would have had a spasm."

"Why do you say she didn't have access to the collection before the killing?" Oka Hofobi asked. "Could she have gotten her hands on it afterward?"

"Don't you remember? She came to the work site and asked me to show her some examples of tools with sickle sheen. I guess she could have palmed one while I was showing them to her. I think I even left her alone with them. Why wouldn't I?"

"We're wasting our breath." Oka Hofobi's voice sounded tired. "Why would she steal one of Chuck's tools when the deed was already done?"

"Maybe she wanted to swap it with the real murder weapon." Joe's voice sounded strong in the blackness that hid his face. "If she killed Calhoun with something out of her father's collection, she'd always have to worry about someone recognizing it."

Of course. Stone weapons might not have serial numbers like guns, but they were no less unique. If Neely's dad had been showing off his arrowhead collection for decades, there was a very real risk to using one of those pieces to do murder. Neely had stolen one of Chuck's blades so that she could swap it with the one retained for evidence—which a sheriff was easily able to do.

"Nice detective work, Joe. If we ever get out of here, you can bet that Chuck will be able to identify the one being held as evidence as one of his. And you can bet that he'll have it well-documented in his notes."

Random sentences from textbooks and professional journals flitted around Faye's mind, distracting her from her physical misery. She was certain that the cave where she sat was inextricably linked to the mound that loomed over it.

Monumental architecture in the Americas had been shown, time and again, to be linked to geological formations. The Pyramid of the Sun at Teotihuacan in Mexico was built atop a cave. Part of the largest mound at Poverty Point extended over a natural pit that had been twelve feet deep. Siting the mound there must have been a meaningful decision, since it meant that the community would be hauling many tons of dirt just to fill that pit before they could even begin raising the seventy-foot-tall mound.

If the mound's site had been chosen by priests to link it to a cave that, perhaps, had religious significance, Faye found herself wanting to applaud the pragmatic engineers who she believed had found a way to make it useful. Unless she missed her guess, they had enlarged and extended an existing cave to divert surface water and springwater that could, over time, have eroded away the mound they'd worked so hard to build.

If she ever got out of this trap, she would crawl on her hands and knees and beg Mrs. Calhoun for permission to investigate this remnant of a remarkable culture.

A tiny plop sounded somewhere to Faye's left, reminding her that, though the prehistoric engineers' work had survived an astonishingly long time, the ceiling above her was frail. If one more rock fell out of that ceiling and dropped noisily into the water, she planned to scream. Except Faye found screaming unsatisfying when none of the sound reflected off the earthen walls of her prison.

On the plus side, she'd found that the deadened silence focused her mind. She'd figured out how Neely managed to tamper with Mr. Judd's pills, even though she wasn't in possession of a pharmacist's license.

It all fit together so nicely now. She could see the sheriff's hands competently sorting the pills. Nobody could have known the medications of an aging man better than Neely. At a guess, Faye would say that Mr. Rutland weighed twice as much as the congressman, and he was a lot sicker. She was no doctor, but surely the dosage of his blood pressure medicine would have to be at least twice as high as Mr. Judd's, maybe a lot more.

By filling her father's prescription and giving it to Judd, Neely nearly committed the world's easiest, most bloodless murder. Of course, Mr. Judd had suffered a catastrophic drop in blood pressure. He was given a significant overdose of a drug *designed* to lower blood pressure. If he'd died of the overdose, as Neely had planned, his body would have gone undiscovered till morning. He survived because Faye was knocking on his door at the very moment he collapsed. Five minutes later, he'd have been unconscious and unable to answer her.

She'd rushed him to the hospital, where they'd overlooked the discrepancy in the dosage and sent him home...so he could take the same overdose again. And five more overstrong doses waited in his pill case. If Sallie Judd and his doctors couldn't figure out what had happened—and why would his doctors suspect such a thing?—he would take an overdose again as soon as he was released from the hospital. And he'd do it every day, until those high-dosage pills were gone, or until he died. If Faye and Joe and Oka Hofobi died, there would be no one to warn him.

Faye found that the silence wasn't just conducive to thought. It was conducive to prayer. She spent quite a bit of time praying that Sallie Judd had been able to communicate her concerns to her husband's doctors without relying on the sheriff as an intermediary. Otherwise, Neely would be able to keep trying to kill him until she succeeded. It didn't seem so selfish to pray for her own rescue, not when her death might condemn Lawrence Judd, too.

She wondered if Oka Hofobi prayed. She knew Joe did… although, as she thought of it, she realized that the sight of Joe in prayer was little different from the sight of him going about his everyday business.

"What time is it, Joe?" she asked, though time could hardly be less relevant in a world that light couldn't penetrate.

"About midnight."

Midnight. No wonder she felt herself sinking into a dark night of the soul. In the early hours of the night, she'd clung to her confidence that there was an exit to this trap. Now, when the sun was on the other side of the world, as far away from her as it was going to get tonight, she felt the questions creep in. If there had ever been an exit to this culvert where they were trapped, was it still there? She let herself remember the sliding sand noises that had punctuated the night. Was that sand slowly obliterating their escape route?

And what if they found an opening to sunlight and fresh air, but it was too small? What if the opening wasn't a hole, but a simple drain, ringed with rocks to keep it stabilized? What if they couldn't dig themselves out?

Faye had been keeping hypothermia at bay by sheer force of will. Though she was sitting, she was in constant motion, arms swinging, feet tapping, hips squirming. If morning found the three of them standing helpless in front of a tiny hole, one that let in light but not heat, she planned to throw herself into the water and wait for shock to set in. Better that, than waiting to starve.

She kicked Oka Hofobi. "You're not moving enough to keep yourself warm. I'm not about to tell your mother you didn't make it because you gave up."

Oka Hofobi twitched and said something unintelligible, but he did move. Then he laughed.

Long fangs and a voice like thunder.

Oka Hofobi hadn't known until this very moment that he didn't believe in Sinti Hollo. He had been interested in the old stories in an anthropological way, but he'd never considered the physical reality of a snake god. Not until now.

There wasn't room in this little chamber for the snake's muscular coils. How odd that he was aware of the room's extent, when he hadn't been able to see since Sheriff Rutland sealed its mouth. Did Sinti Hollo bring his own light with him? Or did he bring the ability to see in the dark?

Oka Hofobi opened his mouth. Maybe he could see with his tongue, like a snake. The idea made him laugh. Then he froze, because he had the feeling that one didn't laugh in the presence of Sinti Hollo.

He'd always been told that the snake came to young men with wisdom beyond their years. Then why did he feel that all reason had left him?

The light was going, and the snake was going with it. Without speaking, Sinti Hollo had let him know that he had an important task ahead of him. Oka Hofobi didn't know what it was, but his vision of the snake had given him the confidence that, when the time came, he would be able to face the task and do it well.

He felt a moment of giddiness when he realized that he would survive this cold wet tomb. Otherwise, how could he expect to accomplish Sinti Hollo's task?

The giddiness passed when he realized that his task might be short and simple: to die well.

Oka Hofobi exhaled with a loud hiss. Then he flinched so hard that Joe could feel it from where he sat, on the other side of Faye. Joe reached out a hand and grasped his friend's upper arm, partially to keep him from falling into the water, but also to calm him. It seemed that Oka Hofobi had never seen Sinti Hollo before.

"Did you see the snake?" he asked, then he laughed as he felt Faye jerk her arms tighter around her legs. "Not that kind of snake, Faye."

"I've heard of Sinti Hollo all my life…" Oka Hofobi's arm was still trembling so hard that Joe didn't feel safe letting it go. "He was here."

"He's still here," Joe said, slowly letting loose of his friend's arm.

"You can see him?"

"Sometimes. But he's here all the time. He's very big tonight."

Faye wasn't in the mood to listen to people talking over her head, and she wasn't in the mood to be nice about it, so she barked, "Who on earth are you two talking about?"

"Sinti Hollo. He's an invisible horned serpent who lives in a cave, underwater," Oka Hofobi began, in his best "I've-got-a-Ph.D." voice.

"Well, I can see why he'd be down here in this wet cave," Faye said in a decidedly unimpressed tone of voice, "but I don't understand why you two are talking about seeing some invisible snake. Invisible. That means you can't see it."

"The people who can see him are exceptionally wise…" began Oka Hofobi-the-doctor again.

"Wise? And that counts me out, but includes you two?"

"If you'll let me finish. Sinti Hollo appears to exceptionally wise young men."

"Oh. Well, if he tells one of you men something important, be sure and let this little woman know. Okay?"

"Sure thing, Faye," said Joe, who wouldn't know sarcasm if it smacked him in the face.

"Joe?" Oka Hofobi asked. "When you said that Sinti Hollo was big tonight, did you mean that you'd seen him before?"

"Lots of times. You see plenty of things when you slow down and just look at the world. The snake don't say much, but he makes himself understood all the same."

Faye was mortally tired of fidgeting around, just to stay alive. She'd never really figured on spending the night between two attractive men but, if she had, this wouldn't have been the way she pictured the experience.

Something was happening to the light. Well, there wasn't actually any light. Something was happening to the darkness. It was pulling back into her peripheral vision. In the direct center of her field of view was…something that couldn't possibly be there.

She couldn't possibly see without light. Physics told her that. But she saw.

She was hallucinating. Rationality told her that. But every atom in her body told her that what she saw was real.

The snake was truly there. It was solid. It made its presence known without light as she knew it, and it spoke without sound as she understood it. Faye's analytical mind surrendered, and she believed.

She tried to speak but nothing came out but a sigh. Joe's hand clamped down on her shoulder, and that was the only thing that kept her rooted in the here and now.

Horns. Fangs. Sparkling scales. And a message so powerful that it didn't have to be spoken. Within seconds, the snake was gone, and the air was black again

Faye pressed her face into Joe's shoulder. "It's okay, Faye. He didn't come to hurt you."

"I know."

"Faye saw the snake?" Mischief entered Oka Hofobi's voice. "But she's just a *woman.*"

"I figure that means that he has an extra big task for Faye," Joe said.

She rolled her head back until it rested on the wall behind her. "That's what he said."

Chapter Twenty-nine

When the voice sounded, Faye thought for a moment that the snake had returned.

Joe spoke again. "It's time, Faye."

Then it must be daylight outside. Not just dawn, but broad daylight, because Joe had said that they should wait until Neely would be certain they weren't coming out. Faye wanted—no, needed—to be out in the sunshine.

Faye jumped off the ledge that had held her out of the water all night long. The cold shock of water didn't even bother her. She jostled Oka Hofobi until he joined her. Feeling around for Joe, she asked, "Where to?"

There was no break in the blackness, but Faye thought that this might be a good thing. If the opening they sought were obvious, then Neely would surely have found it when she played here as a little girl. They wanted an exit hidden deep in the dark. Joe set out to find it with confidence, which buoyed Faye's hopes.

It was hard to stay oriented in the darkness. Every few steps, Faye lurched when her foot rested on an uneven patch of floor, and her brain readjusted its opinion of which direction was up. She dragged a hand along the wall to give herself a frame of reference, and it helped a little. Regular grooves, probably tool marks, cut into the wall at irregular intervals. They supported Faye's suspicion that someone—a lot of someones—had built this drain. Maybe they'd started from scratch, and maybe they'd simply enlarged the cave to meet their needs. Their work was crumbling, but it had stood for centuries, and maybe for millennia.

Faye was thrilled, and terrified, too. How would people with these skills have constructed an outlet for their drain? She pictured an ancient manhole cover of heavy stone, pierced with intricate carvings and held in place by a millennium's worth of silt. They would have had to trade to get such a significant piece of stone, but their trading networks snaked out far and wide. Such an exquisite artifact would have let the water out, but it might trap Faye and her friends underground as long as they lived. Which wouldn't be a long time, but it would sure seem like it.

Faye had recovered her equilibrium. By paying attention to her feet and hanging onto the wall with the hand that wasn't clutching Joe, she felt pretty sure she knew which way was up. She was also pretty sure that her feet were pointed down.

Her panicking animal brain screamed, *We're moving down! Away from the sun!*, but her rational brain rose to the occasion, reminding her that they wanted to be moving down. If the purpose of this culvert was to drain water from the creek when it got too high, then the exit had to be lower than the entrance. She was pretty sure that she could sense the faint motion in the water that Joe had been feeling all night. It was flowing in the direction they were walking. They were going the right way.

Oka Hofobi, whose hand was on her right shoulder, staggered. Her hand shot out to steady him and, bare inches from her shoulder, struck a wall. The culvert had narrowed suddenly. Poor Oka Hofobi had discovered that fact by planting his face into the wall.

"I'm okay. I don't think my nose is broken. Keep going."

Faye moved her face as close to Joe's back as she could get it. Behind her own back, she felt Oka Hofobi take the same defensive position. Within twenty steps, all three of them were on their knees in the rapidly narrowing drain. Within twenty more steps, it was clear that only Faye was small enough to go on.

"It's lighter down there, Faye," Joe said.

She had to take his word for it, but that was okay. She already knew her eyes were nowhere as good as Joe's. If he thought the exit was within spitting distance, she believed him.

"If it gets really tight," Joe was saying, "you'll have to decide whether to put your arms out in front of you, or whether to hold them by your sides. Kinda like a snake."

Faye was still worried that the opening might be silted up, or sealed by an ancient grate. She wanted the use of her hands. "I'll put my arms in front."

She patted the rapidly narrowing walls. "I can do this. You gentlemen can expect a rescue party as soon as I get to a phone."

Joe'd had the foresight to squeeze aside and let her take the lead, just before the passage grew too narrow for such a complicated maneuver. Oka Hofobi, who still brought up the rear, thrust a hand forward until it rested on her back. "Now we know why Sinti Hollo said you had a great task to do."

Faye wished the snake god had taught her a little more about slithering on her belly.

Joe said nothing. He just slid an arm between her back and the culvert's ceiling and squeezed her tight. She felt secure and cradled in the crook of his arm, but there was no time to linger there. It was time to move forward.

The irregular shape of the drain squeezed Faye's body into one shape after another. Early in her passage, she felt her left side dip down at a point where the widest portion of the passageway was across the diagonal. Within a few feet, her body was level again, but it was recoiling from the pain of dragging her belly over a sharp rock. Then, at the bottom of a short, steep dip, she found herself rounding a curve in a slight backbend. This last discomfort didn't bother her in the least, because the curve hid something precious.

Light.

"I can see it!" she called back to her companions. "It's open, but it's pretty small." She oozed forward, reaching for the little hole with both hands. As she'd feared, a tidy ring of stones had held it open all these years. If her hips were wider than that circle…

She wished she could bend back and take a good look at those hips, but what would have been the point? Either she fit through the hole or she didn't.

Not having experienced childbirth personally, Faye could only go by what she'd heard. Still, she'd found the Lamaze classes she'd attended with her friend Magda to be enormously helpful in her current situation.

Her head went through the opening easily. This was a good thing, since she didn't have a newborn's ability to let her head be molded into whatever shape its mother's pelvis requires.

Her shoulders were too wide to go straight through, which wasn't a good sign. Faye's shoulders were almost too narrow to be fully functional. Her bra straps were forever sliding off one side or the other. Fortunately, the Lamaze lady had demonstrated how a baby exits the birth canal one shoulder at a time, twisting its body behind it. (She'd also said that, on occasion, a baby's shoulder is broken by the birth process, but Faye chose not to dwell on that little detail.)

With both shoulders through the opening, Faye paused to rest, and to glory in the sight of the wide world. She was resting at the bottom of a grassy slope. Velvety green plants lined the damp track where water left the drain that had been her prison. If Joe and Oka Hofobi hadn't been still trapped in the dark cold, she would have paused for a nap right there.

Grabbing at some handy saplings, Faye tugged herself forward until the rim of her pelvis caught on the drain's opening. This was the moment. Either her hips could be dragged through, or they couldn't. And if they couldn't, then she, Oka Hofobi, and Joe would die.

No, they wouldn't. Not yet. Not when Faye could scream and hope to be heard. Not when she could claw at the stones holding her in this spot. And not when she could dig in the dirt for worms that she and her friends could eat. Faye was not known for giving up.

She pulled hard again, tilting her hips in every direction she could reach, looking for a place where the opening was out-of-round. She gained an inch, then found herself stuck again. Completely stuck. She couldn't move forward or backward. She couldn't even swivel.

The Lamaze teacher had been big on good posture. She had taught that too many women went through life swaybacked, which was particularly damaging when they were carrying a heavy load in their uterus. At a guess, Faye would say that a swayed back took up more room than a straight one. Following the Lamaze teacher's instructions, she tilted her pelvis in the only direction left to her—tucked under.

And she slid out onto the fresh grass, landing in a curled-up heap at the base of a mound that had once lifted up a grave-yard.

"Can you guys hear me?" Faye bellowed into the drain opening. "I'm out. I'm okay. I'm going for help."

Their responses were joyful, but unintelligible, soaked up by soil and rock and water. "Hang on," she called to them. "You won't believe how fast I'll be back."

It took Faye only seconds to get her bearings, locating the creek on the far side of the cemetery mound and wading upstream to locate the tree where Neely had found them. She shouldn't have been surprised to find that her day pack was gone. A sheriff knew all there was to know about eliminating evidence. Was it at the bottom of a lake far from here? Or would it be carefully planted someplace where Neely wanted the search parties to waste a few days?

The day pack mattered for just one reason. Faye's car keys were in it. This narrowed her options, but it wasn't a tragedy. Her first goal wasn't to reach her car. She just needed to get to a phone, which could be had at the Nail house. Then she'd need a car, but Mrs. Nail would surely lend her one.

Faye pointed her face in the general direction of the road and ran. If she kept the creek on her right, she'd come out of the woods just a few steps from Oka Hofobi's home.

Oka Hofobi wished he could crowd down into the passage that Faye had just traversed. His body would have still been soaking in springwater, but at least he could have stretched his face toward the warm sun. It was a ridiculous wish, because he could never fit through the narrow opening. And it was a selfish wish, because he would have been putting himself between his new friend Joe and the same warm sunshine that he craved.

So he couldn't go forward. And he didn't dare go back to the ledge where they had spent the long night. It wouldn't do to be out of earshot when Faye brought their rescuers.

He and Joe hadn't discussed the issue of where they should wait, because the answer was so obvious. Standing in this exact spot, they had heard Faye call back to them that she had freed herself. So the two of them were just going to stand in that spot until she came back with help.

The frenzied flight from Neely's gun had sapped most of his strength. A night spent soaked with springwater had taken the rest. His trembling legs would fail him soon, but he knew he wouldn't live until Faye came back if he collapsed into the cold water. He vowed to stand another minute. Then another. The faint light showed him that Joe's legs were quivering just like his, so he vowed to hold him up, too, if need be.

He couldn't do it for an hour, but he thought he could do it for sixty minutes, if he took those minutes one at a time.

Faye checked the sun. It must be higher in the sky than it looked, because Mrs. Nail had already gone to work. It couldn't be too late, though, because her archaeological colleagues weren't here yet.

She looked around for a rock. If anyone ever had an excuse for breaking a window, Faye knew she did, but she hesitated. It was going to be hard to call in a search-and-rescue team without alerting the sheriff to the situation, but Faye was developing a plan. She was sure she could get Joe and Oka Hofobi saved, and she was pretty sure she could corner the sheriff at the same time, but a simple phone wouldn't be enough. Faye needed a car.

She looked across the road at the Calhoun house. Mrs. Calhoun's ill temper had been gossiped over all week, but she'd never been ugly to Faye personally. There weren't many people who would close their door on a life-or-death request. Not when they had recently lost a loved one to violent death.

It was time to face the formidable Mrs. Calhoun.

Chapter Thirty

A closed screen door separated Faye from Mrs. Calhoun. The widow stood impassively inside the door. She was a big woman, just as her husband had been a big man. Her dress was worn. Her apron was worn. Her face was worn. This was not a woman who had led an easy life.

Faye knew that her own bedraggled appearance was the only trump card that she held. Her tale of being trapped underground all night would ring true for anyone who got a good look at her. Her final escape had left abrasions on every bit of exposed skin. The mud smeared on her clothes was starting to stiffen and dry, and her body seemed shriveled from the night-long chill. Mrs. Calhoun had been called a racist by people who knew her, but Faye didn't know it for a fact. Besides, compared to the blood and bruises and mud that covered her, her dark skin was fairly unobtrusive.

"People are in danger. I need help."

Mrs. Calhoun opened the door without speaking a word.

"There are people trapped in a...a cave on your property," Faye began, gesturing vaguely toward the back of the house. "We need to—"

"I'll call Neely Rutland. She'll have someone out here to—"

"No!"

Mrs. Calhoun blinked. Even Faye was surprised at the huge sound that came out of her own mouth at the sound of Neely's name.

"My friends are in danger, and Neely Rutland put them there."

"Why, I was Neely's Girl Scout leader. A smarter, nicer girl I never hope to see." Mrs. Calhoun's hand was on the phone. Faye prepared herself to rip it out of the wall, rather than let this woman warn Neely.

"Neely killed your husband."

Now the old woman's hand was off the phone, and she was using her body to crowd Faye toward the door. "That's crazy. How dare you even suggest—"

Faye gambled that Carroll Calhoun had been one of those men who told their wives everything. "She found out what her father did to Mr. Judd. And she was afraid your husband would tell his secret."

The gamble paid off. Mrs. Calhoun took a step back, though she was nearer to the phone than Faye would have liked.

"Neely always did think her daddy hung the moon, but she never saw his mean streak. Carroll told me he thought Kenneth Rutland would have killed that young man, just for the sheer fun of it. And he knew he could get away with it, because the young man was black." Mrs. Calhoun's voice was uncertain, almost feeble. "What are we going to do? You and I can't dig those people out of that cave with our bare hands."

Faye'd had a long night to muse over the relationships between people and their lawgivers. Mrs. Calhoun would never have believed her, if she hadn't offered the telling detail of Kenneth Rutland's guilt. This county had elected Neely sheriff. Most people obviously liked her and trusted her. Who could be trusted to help Oka Hofobi and Joe without calling in their beloved sheriff for assistance?

Faye knew from her own family history that African-Americans could well believe that a person's government might betray her. But she needed government-level help. She needed a search-and-rescue team with lots of training and equipment. Black people didn't ordinarily keep that stuff lying around the house, no more than anybody else did.

How fortunate that there was a sovereign nation just a few miles away, one with a long memory that stretched back to a time when it had been betrayed by the United States of America. If anyone could be persuaded that an official of the government might lie and kill, it would be the Choctaws.

Chief Matt Hinnant of the Choctaw Fire Department felt his bad-news meter rise when his assistant Pete handed him the phone, saying only, "I think you'd better handle this one, Chief."

At first, he'd thought the young woman wasn't making any sense. She sounded like she might even be slipping into shock. "Are you warm enough, ma'am? Do you want to put down the phone and get a sweater? I'll wait for you."

Her outburst was so vociferous that he felt reasonably assured that she wasn't in immediate danger. He just wished her story wasn't so far-fetched.

"You're not on the reservation, but you want our rescue team, not the county's...because why? Because Neely Rutland tried to kill you?"

Chief Davis had dated Neely's best friend, when they'd all been in high school. He had rarely met a straighter arrow. Neely never smoked a cigarette. She never sneaked an underage beer. She never even missed her father's ridiculously early curfew. Not once. "Let me call Neely," he said, "and we can get this straightened out."

The word "No!" blasted out of the phone, darn near blowing out his eardrum. "I told you that Sheriff Rutland left us to die in a flooded cave. My friends, Joe Wolf Mantooth and Dr. Oka Hofobi Nail, are still there."

The Chief straightened in his chair. Two of the firefighters on duty today were related to Oka Hofobi Nail. One of them was his brother, Davis. If Oka Hofobi was truly in trouble, Chief Hinnant knew he'd have some personnel who wouldn't be at their most objective. Personal feelings got people killed. "I hear you, but we have a jurisdictional problem here. We can't just go rushing willy-nilly onto non-reservation property. Other departments call us in for help all the time—our dive team was just out last week—but they have to ask us to come. If we go barging into Sheriff Rutland's territory—"

"Why is it so hard for you to believe that an agent of the government might commit a crime? Haven't you ever heard of broken treaties? Why are the rest of the Choctaws in Oklahoma today?"

This woman, whoever she was, knew how to deliver a sucker punch straight to the gut. Did Chief Hinnant believe that Neely Rutland was a cold-blooded killer? Not hardly. But could anybody raised by Choctaws believe that the government always had their best interests at heart? Hell, no.

"I hear you, ma'am. Tell me where you are, and everything you know about the condition of the victims. We'll be right out."

Chief Hinnant stood before a group of men and women who had been enjoying a hearty firehouse breakfast. He was hardly thirty seconds into his description of Faye Longchamp and her plight, but they were already gung-ho to violate the jurisdiction of the Neshoba County Sheriff's Department. No, "violate" wasn't the right word. "Annihilate" fit the situation much better.

"Now this isn't an official action for us, not as I understand it," he told them. "I can't order you to go, but you can go as private citizens. Matter of fact, maybe you shouldn't be in uniform."

"Should we take our private vehicles?" asked Pete, a whip-smart 25-year-old.

"Good idea." Chief Hinnant watched Davis Nail hit speed-dial on his cell phone. The family had been alerted. Now he *really* needed to put a crew on-site, before the Nails got out there with their shovels and brought a few tons of dirt down on those two boys.

"What about our equipment?"

The clock was ticking, and two people were in danger. They couldn't go out there empty-handed. Their official vehicles were ready to go, and they were chock-full of the best equipment money could buy, thanks to all that casino money. It would be idiotic to leave their equipment behind. Taking the time to guess what they might need and throw it in the back of a convoy of pickup trucks would be silly. People could die while they were doing it. And what if they guessed wrong, and somebody died because a critical piece of equipment hadn't made the trip?

This was nuts. He was the chief. He would make this decision and live with the consequences. "Tell you what. Why don't we just keep wearing our uniforms? And why don't we just get in the department's trucks and get out there and save some people. We can let the Tribal Council deal with the politics of this thing."

And so, on a sunny morning in late July at the very dawn of the twenty-first century, uniformed representatives of a sovereign nation invaded the United States of America.

Chapter Thirty-one

Faye wished she'd insisted on driving. Mrs. Calhoun, showing surprising mental flexibility for a woman of her age, had seen the wisdom in Faye's plan to corner her husband's killer. Faye had hardly finished explaining what she needed to do, when she found herself bundled in a blanket and sitting on the passenger seat of Mrs. Calhoun's car. It was just too bad that Mrs. Calhoun drove like a woman of her age.

Faye mashed an imaginary accelerator to the floor. She knew precisely where Neely Rutland was, right this minute. There was no time to waste.

She comforted herself with the knowledge that the most important task was getting done. She'd told Chief Hinnant exactly where to find Joe and Oka Hofobi. As extra assurance, she'd left a detailed map for him, taped to Mrs. Calhoun's front door. Perhaps he would find the ancient drain even before Faye reached the fairgrounds. And perhaps he would have pulled her friends into the sunshine before Faye passed her final challenge.

With a little prodding, Mrs. Calhoun nudged her car up to a speed that Faye felt was appropriate to the situation.

Oka Hofobi had held himself up, minute by minute. After a time, he'd leaned on Joe, and Joe had leaned on him, and they'd held each other up. Now, they were leaning together against a clay wall, slowly sliding down into the water. The water was too cold, and their body heat had been seeping into it all night long. They'd had no food to replace the energy they'd burned in their frantic escape. There was simply nothing left inside them to keep them warm, nothing to keep them alive.

There was hardly a splash as their two shivering bodies slid down into the waiting water.

The fairgrounds were crowded, as would be expected on the last day of the Neshoba County Fair. The drinking folk were surely already partying in the cabins surrounding Founders Square, just as there were certainly people still sleeping off last night's party. The churchgoing family folk were flipping pancakes for their kids. Everybody else who was up and walking had gathered at the Pavilion to see why CNN was there.

Lurking outside the Pavilion and peeking in, Faye could see that Neely was at the podium, but she wasn't presenting the speech she'd been planning to give. Lawrence Judd's health was yesterday's news. Faye and Joe and Oka Hofobi were the stars of the moment, and their stars shone more brightly because, by coincidence, the media folks who came to cover Mr. Judd's situation were already in place. Neely stood in front of a stand-ing-room-only crowd, giving a status report on the evolving missing-persons crisis. Television cameras and radio crews were broadcasting her every word. It was life-and-death situations like this one that got incumbent sheriffs re-elected.

Neely's amplified voice echoed over the fairgrounds. "The situation is still developing. We know of three people who are missing. One is a local man, Dr. Oka Hofobi Nail, who has been working at an archaeological site on his family's property. The other two missing persons are visiting our area as part of the same archaeological project. Their names are Joe Wolf Mantooth and Faye Longchamp. Dr. Nail is a Choctaw man of average stature. Mr. Mantooth is over six feet tall with long black hair. Ms. Longchamp is a small, slender woman with dark skin and short black hair. All three were last seen wearing work clothes and heavy boots. The project supervisor, Dr. Sid Mailer, just notified us that they're all more than three hours late for work, unusual behavior for any of them. Some might think that Dr. Mailer was premature to call law enforcement so quickly, but when three people are missing in close proximity to a recent murder site...well, we commend him for his responsible behavior."

Yeah, right, thought Faye. *You probably wish he'd waited all day to call in the law. It would have given us more time to die.*

"All three missing persons were last seen at five p.m. yesterday by their colleague, Dr. Chuck Horowitz. Shortly before that, they were seen by Don Atkins, when they dropped off Mr. Nail's car for repair at his shop. Mr. Mantooth is not known to own a car. Ms. Longchamp's car has not been located."

Bet you'd like to know where it is. During her long night, Faye had hung onto her car as the only piece of evidence that might point toward their underground prison. Neely could take Faye's day pack clear across the county and leave it as a red herring for a search team, but she couldn't move that car unless she found it before anyone else did.

"An eyewitness saw three people fitting the description of our missing persons in Winston County, near Nanih Waiya Mound. An employee at the Golden Moon, where two of the missing persons are staying, stated that she overheard them talking about looking for archaeological sites on private land in that area. We have a team on our way there right now."

And there was Neely's red herring. She was telling the truth about what she, Joe, and Oka Hofobi had planned to do that evening. She'd simply moved their jaunt over one county, ensuring that her search team would never find them in time. Faye wondered if there was anything more dangerous than a criminal in a position of power.

A tall latecomer hurried toward the Pavilion. As he neared Faye, his eyes locked on her and he dropped the briefcase in his hand. She put a hand to her mouth, silently begging him not to speak. Ross nodded. For the moment, he silently agreed to just stand there and look at her.

"I'll take some questions now," Neely said, nodding at the media folk and their microphones.

Faye stepped into the Pavilion and made her way toward the podium. In a voice loud enough to carry to all four corners of the Pavilion, she called out, "Good. I have a few questions I'd like to ask."

Heads turned at the sight of her muddy, battered body. She was quickly recognized, based on the description of her that Neely had just read. How many petite, thin, short-haired, brown-skinned women wearing filthy clothes and heavy boots could there possibly be in Neshoba County?

Faye was aware that she was exposing herself to a murderer wearing a sidearm, but confronting her in public was the only way to make certain that Neely was convicted of her crime. Neely might think that if she shot Faye where she stood, then Joe and Oka Hofobi would never be found. She might or might not be able to explain shooting Faye, but she'd be eliminating the only person who knew for sure who killed Carroll Calhoun, then tried to kill three more people.

And there might be a way the sheriff could get away with shooting Faye in front of this crowd. If Neely could make an opportunity to plant a gun on Faye's dead body, she might be able to craft a story about how she'd known that Faye posed an immediate danger. Even better, what if Neely could make people believe that Faye had walked onto the crowded fairgrounds with a bomb strapped to her chest? She could consider herself elected sheriff for life.

But Faye didn't think Neely would do any of those things. If she'd killed Calhoun out of shame, so that no one would ever know what her father had done, then killing Faye in full view of the entire Neshoba County Fair made no sense. All those watching, judging eyes would stay her hand. Faye felt safe. Pretty safe.

The sheriff's first words said that Neely would not be shooting Faye quite yet. "Get my father out of here!"

Someone took hold of the handles of Kenneth Rutland's wheelchair and someone else cleared a path through the crowd, which melted aside to let the infirm man pass.

Faye advanced on the podium. "You buried me alive, and both my friends. You tried to kill Lawrence Judd. You did kill Carroll Calhoun. Am I going to tell these people why? Or are you?"

"I never knew…nobody ever told me…" A sob interrupted the sheriff, but she stifled it and went on. The microphone in front of her broadcast every word. "I was as shocked as anybody when Mr. Judd stood here and told us about the day he was attacked. The words were hardly out of his mouth when Mr. Calhoun pulled me aside and explained how things were going to be. He said that my daddy was the one that tried to kill Mr. Judd, and I had to do what he said or he'd tell…he'd tell everyone." Her voice drifted to a whisper, then died.

"Maybe he was lying, Neely," said an old man in the front row. He stood to face her. "Why would you believe something like that about your own father?"

She leaned against the podium but, like a trained law enforcement officer, she remained alert and she kept her hand within striking distance of her firearm. "Because I knew it was true. I'd spent the last night on top of his mound. You can see forever up there. When Calhoun told me he'd stood up there and saw my father's car way out there where it had no business being…it made sense. Besides, I'd heard Mr. Judd talk, and I ran those woods when I was a kid. I knew where his cave was, and I knew where that cemetery used to be. The things Calhoun said were…awful…but they explained something I never understood. All those years, my father sold our land, one chunk at a time, and I never knew why. We didn't need the money. Now I know it was because Calhoun was blackmailing him into practically giving it away. Daddy's past blackmailing now, so Calhoun figured it was time to start with me. Only this time, he didn't want land."

Faye was suddenly glad she'd asked Mrs. Calhoun to wait in the car. She'd wanted to keep the old woman safe from any danger that might erupt when Neely was exposed, but Neely was about to say some things that Calhoun's widow would rather not hear.

"He wanted to take advantage of the fact that I was the sheriff. He wanted me to look the other way when he and his friends dealt their drugs, and he was going to sell that protection to every two-bit crook in the county. Calhoun wanted my guarantee that I'd look the other way for the criminals who bought him off. How could I live with that?"

How can you live with murder on your soul? Faye wondered. But she hadn't heard an unequivocal confession yet, and she had to have one. She advanced another step toward the sheriff. "So he asked you to meet him that night to talk about this perverted business deal."

"I went out to tell him no. I couldn't let myself be used that way. I didn't go out there to kill him—"

"But you took a deadly weapon out of your father's arrowhead collection with you." Faye's voice was calm and pleasant, but she was determined to make this woman admit what she did in front of all these people. Neely had known everyone here all her life, and this was her jury pool. The only way Neely Rutland would be convicted in this county was if she admitted everything in this most public of places. "Why did you meet Carroll Calhoun with a stone blade in your pocket? Why did you kill him?"

Neely almost bowed her head but, at the last minute, she yanked her chin up again. "I killed him because he bulldozed my family's graveyard. Because he stole our land. Because he was trying to force me to do wrong. And because he hurt my father."

She broke and ran, one arm wrapped defensively around her chest. Her other hand was raised up to shield her face. Whether Neely hoped to escape, Faye couldn't tell, but her bolt to freedom was short-lived. While she'd been speaking to Faye, word of the drama in the Pavilion had gotten out into the cabins, and the crowd was swelling by the second.

Neely ran like a woman hoping to escape judgment, but she didn't run far. There were fifty thousand people to block her way.

Chapter Thirty-two

Ross liked his car. He was proud of his car. But he had never been so proud to own a car that was blindingly fast until this moment.

He'd also never been so proud and happy to be a big man, capable of wading into a nervous crowd to fetch out a small woman on the verge of collapse. Faye was safe at his side right now. Neely was a small woman, too, but the crowd surrounding her had seemed peaceful enough. He trusted that someone had dialed 911, and that one of her deputies would arrest her and set the wheels of justice to turning. So he'd left her in custody of the crowd.

When he'd opened the car door for Faye, she'd sunk down into the passenger seat's buttery black leather, and then she'd kept sinking. Arms clutched across her chest, she'd hunched over, leaning further and further forward until her head rested on her knees. Then the shivering had started.

He'd tried to rush her to the emergency room, but she wouldn't hear of it. At her insistence, his precision-made German engine was taking them out in the country just as fast as it could. Faye remained as she'd been, huddled face-down, but he'd thrown his sport coat over her back to hold in what little body heat she had left. Then he'd put the car's top up and cranked the heat as high is it would go. It gets very cold in Germany, so his car's heating system was precision- engineered, too.

He wished Faye would say something, so he'd know for sure that she was conscious.

"Nobody lives forever."

Joe's disembodied voice hung in the dark air. His voice was quiet, as always, but it penetrated the stillness of their prison and the gathering fog in Oka Hofobi's head. Wondering why the man was stating the obvious, Oka Hofobi said, "I'd hoped to make it past forty."

"I wasn't talking about you. I was talking about your old man. You're going to be sorry if he dies before you two work out your problems."

"It wasn't me that stopped talking to him."

Joe didn't seem to want to talk about the wrongs Oka Hofobi's father had done him. He just kept on with his philosophical musings. "People our age…we've got it all. We're strong. Our eyes still work good. All the rest of us still works good, too. And the world makes sense to us, because it's the world we grew up in. I bet your dad struggles to live in our world."

Oka Hofobi smiled, though he knew Joe probably couldn't see him in the dim sunlight that seeped out of the hole where Faye had escaped. "Ma has to work the DVD player for him. It's funny. He could play videotapes, no problem—you just plug them in—but navigating the DVD menu is one step too far for him."

"You could help him with the DVDs. You could help him with all of it."

Dammit. This conversation was making him feel like a rebellious teenager, and Oka Hofobi knew he wasn't. He'd tried, time and again, to reason with his father, one grown man to another. Their broken relationship was not his fault.

"What are you trying to say? If you know some magic solution to the fact that my father can't treat me like an adult—"

"You've got it backward. Your father's all balled up inside because *he* don't feel like an adult any more."

"You think I should treat my father like a child?"

"Nope. You talk to him like somebody you love and respect, but you have consideration for his weaknesses. He knows he has 'em. And he's gonna have more. You're the one with the power now, but you need to be careful with it. Your brother—you can work things out with him man-to-man. You can have a fistfight, if you want to. To make things right with your father, you're just gonna have to overlook some things. That's what grown-ups do."

Light dawned, just as surely as Sinti Hollo had filled their dark prison with light.

"How do you know so much? Do you and your father get along?"

"Well, actually, I spent most of the night figuring all this out. When we get out of here, I'm gonna call my father. I hate to say it, but I think he'll be surprised to hear from me."

"Okay," Oka Hofobi said. "Here's the deal. I'm going to talk to Pa. And you're going to call your father. Where's he at?"

"Oklahoma."

"I'll make peace with Pa, and you'll call Oklahoma, by sundown today. Presuming Faye's able to bring somebody to dig us out." The cold took a firmer grip on his bones when he thought about what it would mean if Faye failed…if Neely Rutland had been still waiting outside, ready to kill her before she saved them.

"You can count on Faye."

Oka Hofobi had known Faye exactly one week, but he knew that this was true. "So how long you planning to keep pretending that Faye's just a friend to you?"

"Faye ain't figured out what she's looking for yet, but I don't think it's me."

Oka Hofobi decided to let that one lie. He changed the subject. "So when are you going to stop wearing white man's clothes?"

"You got a lot of room to talk. You and your khaki pants. Maybe I'll get me some polo shirts like yours."

"My clothes suit me. Yours don't. But they did. When I first saw you, I thought, 'There goes a man who's comfortable in his skin.'"

"I'm not full-blood like you and your folks. Not just your family, but all your people. You've got thousands of people right here to teach you about being Choctaw. Both my folks were mostly Creek, but the only things I know about being Indian, I taught myself."

"I've seen you knap flint. Did you make those clothes you were wearing when we met? Moccasins and all?"

"Yeah."

"Then wear them. Be who you are, Brother."

"Okay. I'll wear them. As soon as we get out."

When Oka Hofobi thought of escaping the cave, he thought of being warm, but that thought was a trap. It only reminded him of the clammy cold, and of the fact that he and Joe were one step from shock and death. He fought that fear by reminding them both that there was hope—only one hope, but it was real. "We're getting out soon. Faye's coming."

"I know."

The car's delicately engineered suspension was not made for rutted farm roads, but Ross pushed it hard anyway. Faye had raised herself into an upright position and was giving directions. She peered into the dense undergrowth with life-or-death intensity. Every so often, she raised a hand and pointed.

"There. Turn there."

Branches dragged along both sides of the car, from bumper to bumper, but Ross figured he could get a new paint job. When he realized that he was further from a paved road than he'd ever been in his entire life, he knew for certain that he was a city boy.

Shortly after that, the shiny red of a fire rescue vehicle leapt out of the dense green woods. Ross pulled off the road and parked next to it, and Faye was gone.

He followed her as she staggered to the flanks of something huge, something that could be nothing other than an Indian mound. A rescue team was clustered around one victim, while another set of rescuers was gathered around a dark and tiny hole in the base of the mound. While Ross followed Faye on her single-minded trek, the rescuers hauled a second victim right out of the ground. The bright warm sunshine beat down on the two wet bodies, and Ross had a timeless sick moment while he searched them both for signs of life.

Faye tottered on her feet, and Ross wasn't sure she'd get where she was going. She pressed on.

The firefighters were checking pulses and opening airways. Ross rushed on, close behind Faye, ready to be there if the news was bad. He could see Joe and a young Choctaw man who must be Faye's friend Oka Hofobi. He silently urged them to move.

A rawboned paramedic was checking Oka Hofobi's pulse. He looked just like an equally rawboned older man who stood nearby as if hoping someone would tell him what to do. A stout woman crouched on the other side of Oka Hofobi's motionless form. Then the young archaeologist's body broke out into a head-to-toe shiver, and he curled into a fetal position. He looked miserable, but he was alive. The paramedic covered him with blankets, and the woman re-arranged them, like a young mother tucking a child into bed.

The older man barked, "Quit fussing with those things, woman," then sat down and tenderly lifted Oka Hofobi's head onto his lap.

Joe still lay motionless, his big hands limp at his side. Ross took a step in that direction, ready to be there for Faye if…if he was needed.

Faye dropped to her knees at Joe's side and collapsed with her head resting on his chest. Slowly, both of Joe's arms reached up and encircled her. Only then did she start to weep. Ross could see her chest heave with each sob.

Ross was drawn to Faye. He liked her a lot, and he admired her. With time, he was pretty sure she could mean more to him than that, a lot more. But she was taken.

And she didn't even know it.

Ross, however, was not known as a man who gave up easily.

Chapter Thirty-three

Friday evening
Three weeks after the close of the Neshoba County Fair

August had passed quickly for Faye, as time does for a person who is doing good work. After their job in Mississippi was done, Dr. Mailer and the others had gone home for a week of rest before beginning the fall semester, but she and Joe were lingering until the last possible moment. They had worked seven days a week all month and they were tired, but it was a good kind of tired. Soon enough, they'd be home again, just in time to be named godparents to Magda's and Mike's little Rachel. Until then, Faye was willing to do all it took to get the work done.

The highway department project had ended well for everyone. Dr. Mailer's team had cataloged some interesting artifacts, but nothing that would prevent the traffic engineers from straightening the dangerous curve that had triggered the entire project. So the client was happy and Dr. Mailer was happy.

The Nails were still a little sad to sell even a portion of the land they'd held since the Treaty of Dancing Rabbit Creek, but it was a slender slice of land and the price was very good. Besides, Oka Hofobi had earned a salary funded by the government, as well as accumulating data for future publication credits, all for doing work he wanted to do anyway. Faye considered that to be partial payment of a very old debt.

But the project had only kept Faye busy from Monday through Friday, leaving her weekends free for fun things like…more field work. She and Mrs. Calhoun had become fast friends from the moment the old woman understood that Faye had solved her husband's murder.

"Honey, if those two old mounds and that cave mean so much to you, why don't you spend some time looking them over? Or bulldoze them. I don't care. Never did. Carroll was the one that was so protective of his precious property. Look at where that got him."

So Faye and Joe had dug test pits. They had surveyed the surface contours of key sites along the creek, looking for proof of Faye's suspicions that much of the land had been re-formed in antiquity. They had conquered a few lingering fears and gone back into their underground prison, looking for clues as to who built it. And those clues pointed to…a lot of people. Her research told her that the people who built Poverty Point were thought to have constructed water control devices within their elaborate earthworks—not to mention the fact that they had dammed up the bayou that ran beside their settlement to create a haven for fish. But Poverty Point was built three thousand years ago. Could the drain have survived that long?

Or maybe the people who had knapped flint on the Nails' property had built it. She'd read everything she could find on the water control structures at Fort Ancient, which were built about that time…only *two* thousand years ago. Did they enlarge a cave to build the drain to protect the cemetery mound during floods? Did they repair and maintain a thousand-year-old drain left behind by the Poverty Point people? Or maybe someone even later had built it. Faye didn't know if she'd ever find these answers, but she loved the questions.

She and Joe had spent evenings with Mrs. Calhoun, eating her zucchini bread and pawing through her husband's arrowhead collection. There were real treasures among the things he'd uncovered during a lifetime of farming, but nothing that might prove Faye's fondest hope—that a vast complex of monumental earthworks had once graced the Calhoun property. And, Faye realized as she thought of Neely with an odd pang, those ancient monuments had once graced the Rutland property, too.

Later on those same evenings, Faye and Joe and Mrs. Calhoun had stayed up half the night, playing with Faye's new telescope. It was a fine instrument with precision optics, because Ross valued well-engineered products. When it arrived, shortly after Ross returned to Georgia, Faye considered sending it back. How could she accept something so expensive from a man she'd just met? Then she read the card, which said only, "A woman who knows the stars as well as you do should have the opportunity to see them clearly."

Ross had included his phone number and his e-mail address, but not his home address, cleverly ensuring that she couldn't send it back without talking to him first. After some thought, she'd called to thank him and to invite him to visit her at Joyeuse, where he could see her island's spectacular skies for himself. After all, her mapping software told her that it was only three hundred miles from his doorstep to hers.

As the fall semester approached, Faye had begun reconciling herself to the prospect of going home without proof. On this, their last day in Mississippi, she and Joe were digging test pits around the big mound where all the summer's problems had begun. They were probing into the eagle's wings. Or, rather, they were digging where Faye thought its wings might be.

As she worked, Faye heard that blessed "click," the heart-racing sound of a metal tool striking stone. She felt for the source of the noise and was rewarded with something hard and cool, something more angular and knobby than the natural stones in these parts. This rock was no longer wearing the shape that God had given it.

Faye forced herself to wait, to do things right. She took the object's photo *in situ*, right where it lay. She made copious notes in her field book. Then, finally, when the time was right, she pulled it out of the ground, brushed it clean, and laughed out loud. Perched on her palm was an effigy bead, a tiny carving of an eagle with its wings outspread. And, unless she missed her guess, she could see the beak of another eagle poking out of the soil at the bottom of her test pit. Somebody had carved these birds and buried them here, where the tip of the eagle mound's wing faded into the ground.

Faye knew academics, and she knew that many journals would expend many pages of scholarly discussion over whether the Calhoun mound could be definitively called an eagle effigy, but Faye knew it in her heart, that very minute.

On the far side of the mound, someone was digging his own test pit, someone who would understand more than anyone else in the world what this little eagle meant to her. She hopped to her feet and hurried in his direction, calling out for Joe.

Guide for Teachers, Students, and the Incurably Curious

Because Faye's archaeological adventures are being read in schools, I began posting interesting historical and scientific information on my website. Teachers and parents and students responded so well to this kind of background that it only makes sense that I include it right in this book.

Then I found that the same questions were being asked when I spoke to readers' groups. Thanks to the wonders of the Internet, I get questions at all hours of the night and day from people wanting to know things like, "Did Andrew Jackson *really* say that Native Americans didn't have 'the intelligence, the industry, the moral habits, nor the desire of improvements' that would make it possible for them to live side-by-side with white American citizens?"

Well, yes, he did say that, during his fifth annual address to Congress. I've compiled that reference, along with a long list of other books that I used to write *Effigies*, especially for the compulsive learners among us—people like me.

Hollywood has done an excellent job of engraving the western Native American tribes on the American psyche, but the southeastern tribes are far less well-known. I've enjoyed the opportunity to acquaint readers with the Mississippi Band of the Choctaw Indians, who valiantly refused to be relocated to the West, then suffered through a century and a half of poverty before rising to prosperity. As a native Mississippian, I'm proud to portray the state at the beginning of the 21st century as it leaves a troubled past behind. I've anticipated a few of your historical questions here, and I've thrown out a few discussion questions of the literary sort for book groups and English teachers. Please e-mail me at maryannaevans@yahoo.com with any other questions, or just to chat.

Questions for readers:

1. **What was your impression of the portrayal of the Deep South in *Effigies*?**

   I'm a seventh-generation Mississippian, and I've seen my home state portrayed in many ways in the media. Often, those portrayals appear factual. But there are those times...

   I recently read a novel set in Mississippi which featured a small town where many of the streets were not paved. Within the first chapter, I realized that the author believed that this was still commonplace in that part of the world. After reading a few pages further, I realized that the author had probably never even visited the state.

   In *Effigies*, I have tried to portray a modern Mississippi. The past is receding, though it is not yet dead. Many people are educated, and a lack of education does not necessarily mean that a person is stupid or ignorant. All conflicts, political and personal, are not based on race, and any crime investigator who assumes otherwise is taking a tremendous risk. Do you think this portrayal feels realistic?

2. **Compare the narrative voice for the main part of this book with the voice of Mrs. Nail telling her tales. Did you enjoy the contrast? Did the tales enhance the story?**

   I enjoyed "being" Mrs. Nail, and letting her tell the old stories in her own way. I wanted readers to feel an intimate closeness with modern-day and ancient Choctaws, and the folk tales seemed to build a wonderful bridge. Paging through a whole book of tales, I chose stories that related to Faye's experiences, hoping they would help my readers feel the cool water on their feet and the dank cave over their heads. In a way, they take you on a vacation to an unspoiled part of a beautiful state.

3. **Faye treads on a few ethical boundaries here, notably trespassing. How did you feel about that?**

    Faye hasn't always trod the legal straight-and-narrow, though in my mind she has her own set of ethics. They might not be *my* ethics, but she's consistent in applying them. (Or she's as consistent as most of us are in applying our ethics.) She trod close to some ethical boundaries in *Artifacts* and *Relics*, too, but most people were willing to cut her some slack. From an author's point-of-view, pushing ethical boundaries gives me some conflict—inner and outer—with which to work. How did you feel when Faye was more interested in pursuing the truth than in respecting Mrs. Calhoun's property rights? And did the need to prevent further crimes justify disturbing a grave?

4. **Oh, heck, let's forget this literary stuff. Should Faye allow herself to fall in love with Joe?**

    Joe was created to be completely unsuitable as a lover for Faye. I wanted them to have a platonic and absolutely true friendship.

    He's nine years younger than she is. When she met him, he was unemployed, barely literate due to serious learning disabilities, and homeless—but he looked good and he cooked good, so she let him stay with her.

    Joe grew into much more of a fully rounded human being than I expected, and he is a completely likeable person, worthy of Faye's love, but I'm not sure she's ever going to let herself recognize that. Ross is the kind of person she always pictured herself loving. We'll have to see what she decides.

Historical and scientific questions:

1. Are Mrs. Nail's folk tales real?

Yes. With some exceptions, I modeled them on actual stories collected by folklorist Tom Mould and presented in his book *Choctaw Tales*. The original storytellers who helped ensure that these tales were recorded for posterity should be recognized, I think, and this is as good a place as any:

The Choctaw Creation Legend—Isaac Pistonatubbee, 1901

The Cornfinding Myth—Ilaishtubbee, 1899

Wild Geese and the Origin of Corn—Baxter York, 1975

The Girl and the Devil—Unknown, collected in 1909

The Spectre and the Hunter—J. D. McDonald and Peter P. Pitchlynn, 1850

Kashehotapalo—Ahojeobe (Emil John), 1909

Okwa Nahollo, or White People of the Water—Heleema (Louise Celestine), 1909

Kowi Anukasha—Ahojeobe (Emil John), 1909

2. So which folk tales are the exceptions?

The quotes attributed to real people—Andrew Jackson, Pushmataha, and Army Major Armstrong—are real, though not strictly folk tales. In Dr. Mould's book, there are recorded stories that tell of actual historical events, so I took those as a model. I incorporated several historical quotes that I thought were significant to *Effigies* into stories that I wrote myself for Mrs. Nail to tell. Similarly, the tale of the donation of seven hundred dollars from Oklahoma Choctaws to the starving Irish during the potato famine is a true story that I put into Mrs. Nail's mouth.

I found two references to the Pied-Piper-like tale of the Devil luring Choctaw children into Nanih Waiya Cave, then walling them up to die. Unfortunately, neither of those sources was a scholarly folklore text. One was a long out-of-print book, *Caves of Mississippi*, published in 1974, that mentioned this story in passing while describing the cave. Another was a personal communication from a non-Choctaw who had heard the tale sometime prior to 1961. I asked Dr. Mould, an expert on Choctaw folklore, whether he knew of the story. He said that it was common for tales about unusual places like caves to "travel." People hear a scary story about a cave, then turn around and tell it as though it happened at their own local cave, in a process called "localization." This is how urban legends develop. In his opinion, this is a story that has been attached to the cave in relatively recent times. I decided to consider it a modern folk tale, because it was too good not to use.

Another tale that lacked an iron-clad scholarly basis was the legend of Sinti Hollo. A full confession is necessary here. I found the story of the snake god on the Internet. (Do a web search on Sint Holo, an alternate spelling. You'll get a flood of hits.) Unfortunately, that was the only place I found it. Dr. Mould told me that the prehistoric ancestors of the southeastern tribes left behind references to a snake god, predating the existence of the Choctaws as a separate group. Snakes figure into their folklore, but not quite in the way presented in the Sinti Hollo story. Again, this was too good a story to keep to myself, so I used it, but I'm confessing its questionable heritage here. (And let that be a lesson to you—always double-check anything you learn on the Internet!)

3. **I've never heard of any caves in Mississippi...**

Mississippi is not known for huge caverns festooned with stalagmites and stalactites, though there are a few medium-sized caves with some interesting formations. By the standards of a place like Mammoth Cave or Carlsbad Caverns, many Mississippi caves look, well, a little bit like mudholes. Some of them are interesting, though. There's one cave in Mississippi that was formed by cows licking at a rock outcropping with a high salt content. I know, you're picturing a shallow depression in the ground, but no. This cave is the size of my bedroom, and it was dug with cow tongues. Let's all think about that for a moment...no, wait. Let's not.

Nanih Waiya Cave is also unusual, in that it is located in a clay formation, instead of the usual limestone. I've been there, though I was alone and not brave enough to shinny into the tiny opening. We'll leave that kind of foolhardy activity to Faye. First-person accounts of the cave tell us that it is quite extensive, with multiple chambers. It is said that some of them once held Choctaw artifacts, but very little archaeology has been done there.

With a novelist's boldness, I supposed that if there was one cave in clay in the area, then there could be two, and Faye's underground prison came into existence. Some people say that the Choctaws enlarged the real cave in antiquity. Some people say that they dug the whole thing. As you have seen, I left open the question of whether Faye's cave was completely or partially manmade.

4. **Are the Nanih Waiya mounds real?**

Absolutely. I've been there. And they are so evocative that I was compelled to set the first scene of my book there. One of them was built about two thousand years ago, and it was originally part of a complex that included several smaller mounds and an encircling set of protective earthworks. Sadly, almost all traces of the other mounds and the earthworks have been plowed until they no longer exist.

The other mound looks very like the manmade one, massive and flat-topped, but it is a natural geological feature—just a big hump in a flat country, if you will. It is honeycombed by Nanih Waiya Cave, and it's in an incredibly scenic location on the bank of Nanih Waiya

Creek. The state park where it's located is closed these days, but I was able to visit it by borrowing the key from the owner of a nearby store—no, I don't know why he had it—driving as close to the site as I could without driving my car into a crumbling culvert, then walking a half-mile into the woods. Writers generally sit alone at their desks all day, but this was an adventure I wouldn't trade for anything.

5. **What about Faye's effigy mound? Is it real?**

   Not that I know of. As I did with the cave, I presumed that many interesting things could lurk on private property where archaeologists have never trod. There are no undisputed effigy mounds in the Southeast, though many people say the great mound at Poverty Point is a bird. (I've heard that someone showed a picture of it to a group of school kids. They thought it looked like a mushroom. So there you go. Perhaps effigies exist mainly in the eye of the beholder.) At the end of *Effigies*, we are left with a mound that *might* look like an eagle. Faye doesn't yet know its age, but she hopes that it is very old. And she believes that it might be part of a collection of mounds and earthworks—which we know existed nearby at Nanih Waiya. Is someone likely to find a site like that lurking in backwoods Mississippi? Who knows? But it'd sure be fun to try...

References and Recommended Reading

Armstrong, Army Major F.W., 1832. Correspondence from Army Major Armstrong on the Choctaw Removal. *A Century of Lawmaking for a New Nation.* United States Congressional Documents and Debates, 1774-1875. United States Serial Set Number 244. Senate Document #512. Correspondence on the Emigration of Indians 1831-1833. 1:412.

Atkinson, Jim. Personal correspondence to Gregg Keyes. 1997.

Blitz, John Howard. *An Archaeological Study of the Mississippi Choctaw Indians.* Jackson, Mississippi. Mississippi Department of Archives and History, 1985. Archaeological Report No. 16.

Brown, V., and Owens, L. *The World of the Southern Indians: Tribes, Leaders, and Customs, from Prehistoric Times to the Present.* Leeds, Alabama: Beechwood Books, 1983.

Carleton, Kenneth H., 1999. "Nanih Waiya (22W1500): An Historical and Archaeological Overview." *Mississippi Archaeology.* 34:2:125-155.

Choctaw History, Culture and Current Events Staff of the Mississippi Band of Choctaw Indians. *A Choctaw Anthology.* Philadelphia, Mississippi: Choctaw Heritage Press, 1983.

Connolly, R., and Lepper, B. *The Fort Ancient Earthworks: Prehistoric Lifeways of the Hopewell Culture in Southwestern Ohio.* Columbus, Ohio. Ohio Historical Society, 2004.

Connolly, Robert, 1998. "The 1980-1982 Excavations on the Northwest Ridge 1 at the Poverty Point Site." *Louisiana Archaeology.* 25:1-92.

Fitzpatrick, Marie-Louise. *Long March: The Choctaws' Gift to Famine Relief.* Tricycle Press, 1999.

Jackson, A. President Andrew Jackson's Fifth Annual Message to Congress, December 3, 1833. *Journal of the House of Representatives of the United States of America.* 27:22.

Jahoda, Gloria. *The Trail of Tears: The Story of the American Indian Removals 1813-1855.* New York: Wings Books, 1975.

Kappler, Charles, ed. 1904. *Indian Affairs: Laws and Treaties.* Washington: Government Printing Office. 2:310-319.

Knight, E. Leslie. *Caves of Mississippi.* Hattiesburg: University of Southern Mississippi, in cooperation with Southern Mississippi Grotto of the National Speleological Society, 1974.

Lauro, J., and Lehmann, G. *The Slate Site: A Poverty Point Lapidary Industry in the Southern Yazoo Basin, Mississippi.* Jackson, Mississippi. Mississippi Department of Archives and History, 1982. Archaeological Report No. 7.

Mann, Charles C. *1491.* New York: Knopf, 2005.

Mars, Florence, with Lynn Eden. *Witness in Philadelphia.* Baton Rouge: Louisiana State University Press, 1977.

Morgan, William N. *Precolumbian Architecture in Eastern North America.* Gainesville: University Press of Florida, 1999.

Mould, Tom, 2003. *Choctaw Prophecy: A Legacy for the Future.* Tuscaloosa: University of Alabama Press, 2003.

Mould, Tom, collected and annotated. *Choctaw Tales.* Jackson: University Press of Mississippi, 2004.

Peacock, Evan. *Mississippi Archaeology Q&A.* Jackson: University Press of Mississippi, 2005.

Purdy, Barbara A. *How to Do Archaeology the Right Way.* Gainesville: University Press of Florida, 1996.

Swanton, John R. *Source Material for the Social and Ceremonial Life of the Choctaw Indians.* Choctaw, Mississippi: Choctaw Museum of the Southern Indian, 1995.

Swidler, N., Dongoske, K., Anyon R., and Downer, A., eds. *Native Americans and Archaeologists: Stepping Stones to Common Ground.* Walnut Creek: Alta Mira, 1997.

To receive a free catalog of Poisoned Pen Press titles, please contact us in one of the following ways:

Phone: 1-800-421-3976
Facsimile: 1-480-949-1707
Email: info@poisonedpenpress.com
Website: www.poisonedpenpress.com

Poisoned Pen Press
6962 E. First Ave. Ste. 103
Scottsdale, AZ 85251